ACCIDENTAL
DESPERADOS

Praise for Lee Lynch

"Lee Lynch has been writing lesbian fiction since the 1960s, and is an important influence in modern lesbian literature."—*RVA Magazine*

Sweet Creek

"Like Chaucer's pilgrims, Lynch's characters tell stories throughout the novel. The novel wanders through stories of the characters' past lives and present events at a leisurely pace. Chick, Donny, Jeep, and the women who comprise their closest circle of friends are compelling characters, and readers will want to know more about their motivations, fears, and dreams. Lynch has to be commended for tackling a novel of such grand scope. From characters who lived their early years deeply closeted to characters who have benefited from the pioneering work of those women who were brave enough to break away and blaze the trail to places like Waterfall Falls. These women—warts and all—show the reader that this pilgrimage is still underway."—*Story Circle Book Review*

Beggar of Love

"Lynch is the master of creating the 'everydyke,' championing the underdog and providing a protagonist with whom garden variety lesbians can relate."—*Lambda Literary Review*

"The highest recommendation I can give Lee Lynch's writing is that you will not mistake it for anyone else's. Her voice and imagination are uniquely her own. Lynch has been out and proudly writing about it for longer than many of us have been alive. In her new novel, *Beggar of Love*, she creates a protagonist, Jefferson (known by her surname), so fully realised that the story seems to distill the last several decades of lesbian life. Lee Lynch finds the words."
—*Lesbians of North London Reviews*

Lambda Literary Award Finalist
An American Queer: The Amazon Trail

"Thirty years ago, Lynch moved from the East Coast to the West Coast and started her amazing journey depicted throughout almost 400 'Amazon Trail' columns. Editor Ruth Sternglantz has distilled these through the selection of 73 Trails, providing the author's half-century perspective of lesbian life as lesbians have moved from invisibility to public life and even marriage—for most LGBT people in the United States...*An American Queer* follows the tradition of 'the personal is political' in an accessible quick read, both heartfelt and gentle, that stays in the reader's thoughts. It is recommended for all public and academic libraries."—*GLBT Reviews: ALA's Gay Lesbian Bisexual Transgender Round Table*

"This very fine collection of columns by Lee Lynch, spanning the period from the 1980s to 2010, is required reading for those who want to remember and for those who are hazy or inadequately informed about LGBT history. *An American Queer: The Amazon Trail* is not a stiff academic text. Lynch is a passionate advocate with a quiet humor, and her columns are an entertaining yet informative read."—*Carol Rosenfeld*

"Lynch, whose novels, such as *Old Dyke Tales* and *Sweet Creek*, have won numerous awards, deserves to be in the pantheon of legendary lesbian journalists since her columns straddle the literary and the journalistic, always contemporary in their look at queer women's culture and beyond."—*The Advocate*

"Some stories crawl under your skin, diving deeper until you can't separate yourself from them. Reading that kind of book is like throwing down a time marker, because who you were before is not who you are when you've finished it. And even when you try to explain to someone why it's so important to you, you may not be able to access the right words because you're trying to describe an experience, which is so much more than a plot or set of characters. And yet, try you must because all you want is for someone else to love the book as much as you do."—*Curve Magazine*

Rainbow Gap

"Sometimes it is hard to write a review because you can't find the words, in this case it's hard to find words big enough to describe such an epic tale…This is both a coming out and growing up story, but also a timeless work of literary fiction, with classic writing that draws you into its world. *Rainbow Gap* will win awards across the board, and deservedly so. It is simple in plot, but complex in emotion. It is a genuine classic telling of nothing more or less than real life. More than anything it's a story of the birth of our community and the fight to be openly who we are."—*Windy City Times*

"*Rainbow Gap* by Lee Lynch is a book so exquisite that I just want everyone to go read it. Like, seriously, stop reading this review, buy it and read it right now…*Rainbow Gap* is not only a wonderful, moving book, it's also an important book that should be required reading…it reminds us that we've been here before and we can do this again. I cannot recommend it highly enough."—*The Lesbian Review*

"[T]his book covers a broad period of lesbian history, seen through the eyes of two relatively ordinary women…A real feel-good novel: I can see I need to catch up with this author's back catalogue."—*The Good, the Bad, and the Unread*

Visit us at www.boldstrokesbooks.com

Previous Books by the Author

Bold Strokes Books

Rainbow Gap

An American Queer: The Amazon Trail

The Raid

Beggar of Love

Sweet Creek

Naiad Press

Cactus Love

Morton River Valley

That Old Studebaker

Sue Slate, Private Eye

The Amazon Trail

Dusty's Queen of Hearts Diner

Home in Your Hands

The Swashbuckler

Old Dyke Tales

Toothpick House

Flashpoint Publications

Our Happy Hours, LGBT Voices from the Gay Bars,
Curated With S. Renee Bess

TRB Books

The Butch Cook Book, Edited with Sue Hardesty and Nel Ward

New Victoria Publishers

Rafferty Street

Off the Rag: Women Write About Menopause,
Edited with Akia Woods

ACCIDENTAL DESPERADOS

by
Lee Lynch

2021

This Trade Paperback Original Is Published By
Bold Strokes Books, Inc.
P.O. Box 249
Valley Falls, NY 12185

First Edition: April 2021

CREDITS
Editor: Ruth Sternglantz
Production Design: Stacia Seaman
Cover Design by Ann McMan

Acknowledgments

My deep thanks to:

Radclyffe for keeping my stories in print and Bold Strokes Books alive.

Ruth Sternglantz for shepherding *Rainbow Gap*, *Accidental Desperados*, and *An American Queer*.

Sandy Lowe, Cindy Cresap, Carsen Taite, Stacia Seaman, the proofreaders, and everyone who keeps the wheels turning at Bold Strokes Books.

Jenny Fielder and KG MacGregor for their support of the Golden Crown Literary Society and KG for your lesbian writing.

Karin Kallmaker for being a lesbian writer.

Renee Bess for opening my eyes wider.

Ellen Hart for the inspiration of your long career and your stories.

Ann McMan for being writerly together and your eloquent covers.

The greatly missed Cate Culpepper for letting me use her name, her dog, and her words to help bring this story alive.

Sue Hardesty for having the guts to tell her stories. Nel Ward for her incisive mind. And both, for my exposure to the vacation rental and construction industries.

The Golden Crown Literary Society for making a place for us.

Saints and Sinners for its extraordinary work.

Connie Ward for Kajen, MJ's Connie-isms, and your lasting friendship.

Fran and Marcia from the New Mexico book group.

Sandy Thornton and the Jewel Book Club.

Jane Cothron for letting me dip into your vast knowledge.

Heather McMaster for Boston slang.

Mary Davison for Southernisms.

Becky Arbogast from Naiad to Bella, and that's a long time.

Mark McNeese for your years of positive energy.

NOTE: There was no hurricane in Florida in 1984.

NOTE: Both Sinclair Brass and Rich Slumkey are lawyers in Charles Dickens's books.

This book is dedicated to Lainie Lynch
with gratitude for your devotion to quality lesbian literature,
and, in my life, your unwavering patience, presence, love, humor,
acceptance, and extraordinary competence in everything you do.
I love you beyond measure.

And to my friend, writer Lori Lake, for the staunchly dedicated work
you do on behalf of lesbian writers and readers—including me.

CHAPTER ONE

October 1975

MJ Beaudry readied herself each time the driver's eyes slid her way. She stayed awake the first two hours by anticipating the marvels of the tropics: palm trees, crocodiles, maybe flamingos. Tired to the bone, she plunged into a brief sleep.

"I like my chicken tender," the driver said in a gravelly voice, waking her, brushing her cheek with the bristles on his red-veined white face.

She saw that he'd pulled into the empty lot of a closed strawberry stand. The cab sat so far up, no one could see in.

Aw, shoot, she thought as his damp hands touched her. Just before she napped, he'd exited onto this secondary road, and she wondered if he'd lied about driving to Key West.

"What's the matter with you? You said I remind you of your daughter."

He snorted a laugh in her ear. "What daughter?"

Crossing the country by bus, she'd developed the habit of keeping her hand in her pocket, around her only weapon. With her thumb, she unsnapped the leather sheath, eased the short buck knife out, and with the strength of her fear, jabbed at his exposed ear. He yelped and drew back. She hit the door handle and reached for her pack, but he grabbed her wrist and yanked her toward him. She saw then that the wound was shallow, a disappointment after what he'd tried. He touched the ear, saw blood on his hand, and scrunched his face in anger as he roughly put the truck in gear.

He eyed her again and again, obviously debating with himself.

She prepared to jump from the moving truck, but he pulled to the curb and said, "Get out."

"No problem," she snapped at him. Her father told her the same thing last week. *Get out.* She was proud of defending herself this time but wanted to slash the trucker's tires.

Shaken, backpack in hand, she jumped from the air-conditioned cab into a shock of moist heat, sounds of construction, and boom box reggae. All manner of traffic rumbled, cruised, hurtled, and crept by on this divided highway, leaving the scent of hot tar. Her legs were unsteady, and the majestic Columbia River was far behind her now, but the river's vigor, she knew, flowed in her blood, a driving force. She straightened her spine; MJ Beaudry, age fifteen, was now in Florida, impatient to start her real life.

She held a hand at the top of her glasses to shade her eyes and squinted into a sun of the truest yellow she'd ever seen. The truck driver came around the cab toward her, holding to his ear a white paper towel stained with a bit more blood.

Two guys sat in the shadow of a paler yellow block-and-brick building against a chain-link fence tangled with weeds. A handwritten sign read *Car Wash.* An arrow pointed to an uneven asphalt lot behind the fence where several buckets sat in a line and clean rags hung. A hose ran from the building.

One of the men sat in a wheelchair. He was white with a gray beard, downward mustache, and granny-style sunglasses. The other man was younger and dark skinned. In their grimy pants and loose short-sleeved shirts, she thought *bums*, her mother's word. She fingered her ribs where her mother's curtain rod had left bruised stripes and concluded she didn't have a mother anymore, so who cared?

She, the driver, and the bearded man were the only white people on the street, both porcelain pale. Dear Old Dad often pointed a finger and called her a squaw because of her dark eyes and obsidian-black hair and declared she wasn't from his side. She knew how she must appear to the men watching her. She let no one but herself razor-cut her ragged-edged hair. Her hips were narrow and her rear end small-scale; except for her nuisance breasts, she might be a boy. Sweat slid her patched, black-framed plastic glasses low on her narrow nose.

The well-muscled dark-skinned man came toward her. She smelled marijuana on him.

"This man hurt you, sugar?" he asked, positioning himself between her and the driver. *Shug* was how he pronounced sugar.

"The sleaze tried." She showed him her knife.

The truck driver claimed, "That's my little girl. Get away."

"Sugar, is this your daddy?" asked the car wash man.

"No way, nohow. He wanted a reward because he gave me a lift. I poked him in the ear to back him off me."

The car wash man advanced on the driver.

"I got this," said the guy in the wheelchair. Briefly, he flashed a gun. MJ backed into a doorway.

As the driver retreated, cursing, the car washer said, "Toss me that touch-up spray." The seated man reached into a bag hanging from the arm of his chair and threw the paint underhand.

The driver was above them in his cab, taking a few seconds to shake a shotgun at them. He shifted, and the truck started to roll.

The young guy ran in a crouch after the truck. He covered the rear license plate with black paint.

The old guy held up both middle fingers. "With any luck, he'll have that shotgun on his seat when he's pulled over."

The driver went to the next gear, his load threatening to tip as he rounded a curve.

Earlier that day, in Tallahassee, she'd calculated that she didn't have enough money to both eat and pay for a ticket to take her to her dream destination, Key West. She wanted to find a nice woman driving that way, because she'd not long ago read a new library book called *Against Our Will: Men, Women and Rape*.

She'd walked along Tennessee Street, stopping at gas stations to ask the service guys where to catch a ride. One station was getting a fuel delivery. The truck driver overheard her question and chided her for hitching, adding that she reminded him of his daughter. She thought of the considerate logger who'd driven her away from Depot Landing, Washington, her hometown.

"I'm headed south," he'd said with a shrug, and she admired the imposing shiny tractor trailer with a bit of awe. She couldn't turn down a once-in-a-lifetime chance to see the world from one of those elevated seats.

That was the last ride she'd accept from a stranger, she pledged. She could still hear the driver's eight-track tape of Merle Haggard's "Movin' On." Wherever the hell this was, she was home.

Not a word was exchanged after the car washer returned with his spray paint, but the three of them bent over laughing.

The car washer caught his breath first. "Come away from that doorsill where we can see you. Make sure you're not Patty Hearst running from the law again."

Still laughing, unsure what to do, she knew she couldn't stay put. On the bus, she'd read that the United States service academies had begun to admit women. She visualized herself in a Coast Guard uniform, MJ Beaudry on her name pin. *Bow-dree!* the sergeant would yell, and she'd salute. She pushed off the door, prepared to hightail it if need be.

"I'd lay odds you're hungry," said the older man.

"That's Professor Shady talking, and I'm plain old Tad."

She wasn't rattled enough to give her name—the police couldn't send her back to her parents without a name. That Coast Guard name fit. "I'm MJ."

"What's that stand for—maryjane?" plain old Tad asked.

He horse-laughed; the graybeard joined in, sounding like a hoot owl. In the South, would everyone remind her of the animals back in Depot Landing?

"Seriously?" She held back her last name. "It's Emma Jean," she said, lifting her pack and shrugging it on.

"Em-jay?" Tad spelled out.

Weary, sweaty, uprooted, she replied to them with her noiseless laugh. "I wish they'd called me a name that fit me, Sam or Pat or…"

Professor Shady grinned, his teeth bright white behind the whiskers. "My father gave me a woefully inappropriate name too. Please call me Shady."

Bums didn't speak like him. He reached out to her. In the spirit of their shared amusement, she shook his hand, showing her strength.

She offered her hand to the young guy also. Handsome, eyes smiling, his manner respectful despite her youth, he spoke with a distinctly Southern accent. "Be careful. He's called Shady for good reasons, not only about his shades."

"Don't listen to him. He's full of envy because his mother decreed him Tad, meaning teensy-weensy."

"Leave it be, Shady, or I'll knock your teeth out."

"And he's capable," Shady confirmed. "Doesn't believe in violence, but don't provoke the man. Let me introduce myself more formally: Morton Sokol, PhD, as I'm known to my parents." He waved a hand over his legs. "As capable as I can be after the bike accident."

Tad spread his arms wide. "Bike accident, my foot. A speeding dump truck full of gravel mowed him down."

"I'm sorry," she said. "It's no wonder you were quick to point a gun at that truck driver."

Shady wrinkled his forehead. "From the mouths of babes," he said. "I thought I was protecting you. Apparently, I persist in coming unglued at the sight of innocent vehicles."

She filed his words away, sensing a lesson in them.

Shady went on, "I don't want trouble for any of us, and that depraved trucker is going to get stopped sooner rather than later. I recommend we get off this corner in case he comes back."

Tad went behind the fence and collected their materials, dumping hoses and spray cans, window cleaners, and dry cloths into a shopping cart. She shouldered her pack. He glanced at her when her stomach loudly, embarrassingly, growled.

"Don't you have folks?" he asked.

"Not anymore."

"Your choice or theirs?"

She thought about it and said, "A lot of both."

A palm tree grew at the corner of the fence. She walked over and, with the pads of two fingers, explored first the trunk, then a frond. She grinned. She'd made it to the magical land of palms and sunshine.

"You never saw a palm tree before?" Shady asked.

"Not close-up. Don't they grow coconuts?"

"They bear a resemblance, but there are actual coconut trees. Not many around here. A few hours of freezing temps, and they're kaput."

"It freezes here?"

"Once in a blue moon."

Tad said, "Shady, we need to move your geography lesson off the street. MJ, you're dog-tired, hungry, and you had a scare. Take yourself that way." He pointed to a door she hadn't noticed. She stood back and saw, stenciled on the front window, in the same lettering as the car wash sign, *Pansy's Home Cooking*. "That's my mother who has the storefront café. Money or not, tell her Tad sent you and to fatten you up."

She thanked him. All at once her pack weighed a ton. She headed for the café, wobbly on her feet from the adrenaline rush of her encounters. Tad's prank had her smiling the smile that was never more than a tug of the left side of her mouth and a deep dimple. She'd never smiled much.

CHAPTER TWO

On that same day, two miles north of Pansy's Home Cooking, Berry Garland and her longtime partner Jaudon Vicker left their home in Rainbow Gap for a honeymoon, six busy years after they became lovers.

"*Jaw-dun*, honey, slow down," Berry cried at each picturesque sight, camera at the ready.

In those six years, Berry had earned her Bachelor of Science in nursing with scholarships and money Gran put by for that purpose. Jaudon skipped the degree but took a load of business courses and earned a CPA license.

When they returned after the honeymoon, Jaudon would step into her ailing mother's shoes to take over the family business, seven drive-through liquor and sundries stores called Beverage Bays. Berry was using piled-up vacation time from the medical practice where she worked as a registered nurse.

Florida was a sultry state. Once travelers left the highways and the coasts, it offered a taste of the old South overlaid with faded and rusted midcentury tourist facilities that drew Northerners ravenous for sunshine. The honeymooners roamed Route 301 North through Thonotosassa, Zephyr Hills, Dade City, and Lacoochee, before bearing east on 50 through a hitch in the road called Mabel.

"*May-belle*!" Jaudon shouted. They sang Chuck Berry's song "Maybellene" out the wide-open windows.

Twenty-four-year-old Jaudon, her large hands on the wheel, arms gnarled with muscle, drove north. She was sturdily built, often taken for a man with her barely tamable facial hair, short, straw-straight straw-blond hair, and a semipermanent cowlick. Jaudon couldn't countenance beauty shops. The one time she tried going to a barber, he asked if she wanted a shave. Berry had cut her hair ever since.

Also twenty-four, Berry wore ladies' shorts, a cardinal print yellow blouse, and plain white tennis shoes with white anklet socks. She was freckle faced, with short, bouncy naturally wavy and curly hair. Her earring collection kept growing. The night before, Gran, who lived with them, gave her the Seminole medicine wheel earrings she fingered now: black, red, yellow, and white beads, in a quartered circle. Gran Binyon, her mother's mom, brought her up, and Gran was part Florida Seminole.

Berry flattened Jaudon's main cowlick. "Let's stop for lunch at that restaurant we passed a minute ago. Its parking lot was full."

They were in a shadeless four-block farm town they'd never heard of. The white waitress was pretty far along in years and half watching *Somerset*, the TV soap opera. The cook stared at them, shifting a toothpick from one side of his mouth to the other. Berry ordered a few side dishes to make a vegetarian meal. Jaudon spent the time comparing this deep-fried catfish to Mudfoot's Fish Camp back home.

The waitress asked where home was. "*Law*," she said when they told her, "I have a cousin over there. I asked her how Rainbow Gap got its name. She said no one knows."

Berry swallowed the last of her tea. "My gran told me a party of white settlers followed a rainbow into the gap left by early centuries of flooding waters. They farmed the fertile land successfully and credited the rainbow with their good fortune. But a friend at work says the name goes further back. The whites stole the name—and the story—from the indigenous people they drove away."

"Well, you know what they say. May the best man win."

Berry started to object, but the waitress stacked their plates on her arm and, with the enthusiasm of an evangelist, told them how lucky they were to come by on a Monday because the flea market across the road was open.

"Watch for that patch of purple thistle," Berry called from the driveway, but Jaudon, always partial to a shortcut, was disentangling herself from the sharp spines. "I'd like to toss that waitress into these thistles."

In the long, poorly lit former barn there were more vendors than customers.

As Jaudon passed by, a tall white man selling guns said, "Hey, is that a St. Pete jersey?"

In her rumbly voice Jaudon asked, "Were you a fan?"

He came around his table and fingered the sleeve, nodding. "I played for them when I was young. Haven't seen one of these in—"

"Did you watch the Sox beat Cincinnati last night?"

"Game six? Now that was baseball." He stepped back, examined her, and folded his arms. She was pretty used to some people getting mean as spit when they saw her unwomanly gait and stance, her cargo shorts over unshaven legs, though who set the standards for womanly she didn't know. To bridge the gap with men, she often used sports. Once they got talking, they mostly let her be—to them, mercifully, she was a white oddball.

He continued telling her about the game she'd watched until Berry caught her eye, holding a jadeite glass pitcher.

Jaudon excused herself and hurried over. "It's the same as Gran's jug that was buried in the sinkhole. We need to buy it for her."

Across the railroad tracks from the Vickers, Gran's former small homestead—a single-wide manufactured home, a shed, and a small travel trailer—lay in a forested, swampy wetland on a dirt road called Stinky Lane after the smelly mushrooms that, a couple of times a year, thrust through the soil by the hundreds. One day, a sinkhole opened up, swallowing the manufactured home, Gran's mother's jadeite pitcher, and everything else except her car, the clothes she wore, and the travel trailer. Ever since, Gran and Berry lived in what was, since Momma bought her upscale residence, Jaudon's house.

It was getting toward dusk when they landed in Astor, named for the robber baron's family. They sat on a screened-in veranda overlooking the St. Johns River, licking Popsicles from the gas station store.

"Peaceful," said Berry.

"It sure is. I'd as soon sit here for two weeks, between visits to the bed. Nobody around here trying to assassinate President Ford, no families having to go to court to take a kid off life support, and who cares if New York City goes broke?"

"You've never traveled farther from Rainbow Gap than Tampa. We're not wasting this opportunity, my darling workhorse."

They unpacked their nightclothes in the tiny 1940s vacation cabin and, after making love long and slowly, fell asleep on their backs, holding hands.

In the morning, they headed west. Both of them wanted to see

Alachua County where Marjorie Kinnan Rawlings wrote *The Yearling*, right off South County Road 325.

"Jiminy. Her house reminds me of home."

"It should—it started out a cracker house too."

"So many windows for catching a breeze. They knew how to build for the climate in those days. Now they cobble together any flimsy structure because they have air-conditioning."

Jaudon chose dated motor courts or motels each night, the kind with half-burned-out neon signs, ceiling fans, washed-thin bed linens, and old Florida pastel colors. They only stayed if there were TVs. Jaudon couldn't do without *Starsky & Hutch* or *M*A*S*H*. Berry loved *Welcome Back, Kotter* and *Hawaii Five-O*.

Sleepy and sexy, they took their good time leaving each mostly empty motel.

"I'm crazy about honeymooning," said Berry one morning, dabbing at her light lipstick.

Jaudon came behind and wrapped sinewy arms around her shoulders, nuzzling Berry's neck. "We'll take a honeymoon yearly. And if I win my lawsuit against the county, I'll take you right to the top of the Grand Canyon."

A few years back, their best friends Cullie Culpepper and Allison Millar, both Southern white girls, sought refuge at the Vicker home on Pineapple Trail. At the time, Allison was a radical feminist on the run from US Marshals and the sheriff over a false bombing charge. During the melee, a deputy sheriff hurled Jaudon headfirst into the corner of her barbecue where her ear connected with the pointed end of a brick. Jaudon lost most of the hearing in that ear. She hated taking anyone to court but was finally convinced the county should be held responsible.

"My poor angel, they're going to pay for hearing aids the rest of your life if I have my say." She touched the gold studs Jaudon gave her on their fifth anniversary.

Jaudon stepped away. "Hearing aids cost an arm and a leg. Customers know to honk their horns if I don't hear them drive in. If we get that money, I'll buy you a diamond ring and update all of our Beverage Bay stores."

Berry held her tongue. In the mirror she saw, from Jaudon's open-mouthed smile and eyes filled with light, that her mind raced with plans for the stores. She was well aware of Jaudon's tendency to neglect herself for the family business.

CHAPTER THREE

MJ's stomach no longer growled—it hurt. There was nothing in it but her jumpy nerves. To conserve money on her trip, she primarily ate peanut butter crackers and soup. She read on this café window, *Pansy Lanamore, Proprietor.*

A wind came up, tousling the leaves of the few trees behind the old yellow building. Goose bumps rose on her sun-heated skin. She could get used to all this warmth.

The little restaurant's interior was painted apple green and rusty red. Fans blew around smells of coffee, chicken, and sweet corn. A group on the radio sang about fighting the power. One of the customers sang along between bites of pie, pumping his fist in the air. A table of four gray-haired women played cards. Toward the back several men in business suits sat at three pulled-together tables, laughter punctuating serious talk.

She drank icy water until Mrs. Lanamore left the pitcher on the counter for her.

Though she did have fifty-two dollars left, when she finished stuffing herself with a generous plate of open meatloaf sandwich, mashed potatoes, and succotash, Mrs. Lanamore refused her money.

She sounded mad, but her eyes were kind. "I can see a white person calling the police on you, child." She wiped her long face, shiny with moisture, and added, "But I know what they do with lost children."

"I'm not lost," she said, believing it. "Honestly."

Mrs. Lanamore pressed a strawberry milkshake into her hands. "If you come across a child of a different color than yours in trouble, you remember this day, little miss." She frowned. "Tell me your name."

"MJ." She hesitated but wanted to hear it aloud. "MJ Beaudry."

"Now, where are you headed, MJ Bo-dree?"

She was so tired. She prodded an index finger against the counter. "Right here."

Mrs. Lanamore walked away from her, head shaking. Her bottom was big compared to the rest of her and seemed to maneuver after her in the narrow space behind the counter. When she returned with what remained of the shake to pour it into MJ's glass she said, "How does anyone land where we do? You say you're not lost. Do you know where *here* is at?"

"'Course I do: Florida."

Mrs. Lanamore raised her eyes to the ceiling. "Oh, for pity's sake, I know a lost child when I see one. You're at the southern tail end of Rainbow Gap, Florida, which is less than a town. That's called Laudre Flats Boulevard out there, once a two-lane. Now it's four lanes, and it'll take you directly to Tampa in twenty minutes and the Gulf of Mexico in an hour."

MJ sucked in a slug of frozen strawberry and nodded. Her so-called parents were never going to find her in a non-town that was nothing but a spot to pass through. If they bothered to come after her. From the radio Barry White's sonorous voice sang out, "You're the First, the Last, My Everything," her song with Christine. She scowled to hide her pain.

Mrs. Lanamore met her eyes. "We had a wild man living in the Green Swamp north of here a few months ago. They sent him back to his family in China when they caught him."

Wild man. Swamp. The words fanned her enthusiasm until Mrs. Lanamore added, "I bet your family misses you. I know I'd miss my sons if they ever ran off."

She almost set the shake on the counter with her cash, swiveled toward the door, and left, but she owed it to this lady to fill her in. She lifted her shirt high enough to expose the lines of bruises left by her mother's curtain rod. Mrs. Lanamore also regarded her cockeyed glasses and the deep cut over her eyebrow where the curtain rod broke. "My mother," she said, her voice husky with all her unshed tears.

"That's going to scar you for life in the shape of a *J*. You say your own mother did this?"

It didn't matter anymore who knew. "She was upset because I was caught with a girl."

Mrs. Lanamore made a hmm-ing sound. "I can see she'd be upset, but you can't beat out what you don't favor in a person." She called, "Duval Lanamore."

One of the customers raised his head from pie, coffee, and a newspaper. He resembled Tad except for his slighter build and an immaculate lime-green uniform shirt and shorts. She pushed her glasses tighter on her face to read the embroidered label.

"Duval, take this lost child to the university with you. She can use the same jobs bulletin board you did. A white girl will get work quick enough." Mrs. Lanamore gestured to her restaurant. "You do what it takes to get by."

Duval was as quiet as his brother Tad was mouthy. The step van Duval drove to collect and deliver linens had the smell of her ex-mother's detergent. He delivered her to the university.

At the bookstore she lingered in the classics section, but she'd read most of them. Instead, to impersonate a Floridian, she bought a polo shirt embroidered with the university's logo.

On Duval's advice, she walked into the gymnasium and used a shower. The jobs list was in yet another hall. By day's end, after a few nervous phone calls—she'd never had to search for a job before—and an interview in which she lied that she was a student, she moved into a room about a half mile from Mrs. Lanamore's restaurant. For food, a room, and thirty dollars a week, her job entailed cooking dinners, doing laundry, and cleaning a two-bedroom apartment that smelled like movie theater air-conditioning without the popcorn or the chill. Mrs. Belda's two air-conditioning units were in the living room window and by Mrs. Belda's bed.

She turned on the small night table fan, unloaded Hop, her stuffed animal, from her bag, and sat on her new narrow bed holding tight to his worn bunny body. Mrs. Belda, a cranky eighty-two-year-old widow, gave her a shopping list to take to the nearby Publix.

Cranky she was used to. Sometimes her ex-mother ignored MJ altogether, and other times she turned on her, lashing out with words and slaps, hurling a potholder, an ashtray, a hairbrush at her before breaking into tears and diving to clasp her little Emma Jean, pet her, use loving words. At such times MJ grappled to get away—fear and love entangled within her. She'd been a well-behaved kid, good at entertaining herself, but most of the time her mother was cranky with her, or glum.

She'd never forget the winter morning when, miserable with the mumps, she'd gone into the kitchen to ask her mother for a glass of something cool to soothe her sore jaw. Her mother stood at the kitchen sink, staring out the window, and gave not a flicker of response. She'd half sat, half fallen to the floor, afraid her mother had transformed into the pillar of salt the pastor talked about.

She once asked if she was praying at those times. Her mother answered, "What times?"

CHAPTER FOUR

November 1975

Their elderly dog Zefer did her best to jump all over Jaudon and Berry when they arrived home. Jaudon led the way into the Vicker homestead, converted over three of generations of her forebears from basic cracker house to a white four-bedroom home with a wraparound porch deep enough to keep the worst of the heat out. Gran had the color TV on and a talk show guest was having conniption fits over rumors George Wallace might run for president.

Jaudon sniffed Gran's apricot preserves in the air. "Is that roast pork I smell?"

"Your welcome home dinner, with slow-cook grits and butter, and brussels sprouts."

Gran hugged the girls hard a few times each, and Berry presented her with the jadeite vase.

"Oh, my word. It's the very same piece, pet." Gran held it out and squinted at it. "To think, both my mother and my granddaughter gave me this vase." Her eyes were wet. "It's precious to me. But I'm forgetting. Jaudon, your pops wants you to call him the minute you get home."

Jaudon and Berry exchanged alarmed glances.

Pops answered his phone on the first ring. "I'm fine. Your momma's her usual. Your brother's fine. I'll be right over. Don't go to the stores until after I talk to you."

She stared at the phone. "He hung up without letting me ask diddly-squat, and that's not the Pops I know."

"Did all your stores burn to the ground?" Gran joked.

Jaudon gave her an evil squinty look.

They took their suitcases to their rooms, Zefer herding. Although Jaudon and Berry each had a room to herself, Berry learned years ago that Jaudon was immune to the sweaty sock and wet dog blend issuing from hers. They slept together in Berry's bed.

Soon after, Jaudon stood in Berry's doorway. "Hey, my Georgia gal. For all the fun of our honeymoon, coming home may be my favorite part."

Berry deposited a jumble of laundry into Jaudon's arms and pointed her to the washing machine.

Pops came in the kitchen door, his habit before Momma bought the big house nearer town. This kitchen was an original room with copper fixtures his father added. Pops sported a good head of hair, gray going white, and stayed clean-shaven because of the heat. His short-sleeved shirt hung over a round belly Jaudon sometimes poked to tease him.

She didn't tease today. Pops's chiefly smiling mouth drooped, and his eyes were grim behind rectangular wire-rimmed glasses as he removed his trucker's cap and stowed a number eight grocery sack at his feet. He neglected to remark on the cooking smells. The quick swishing sound of the neighbor's sprinkler became oddly distinct and irritating. They were bound and determined to grow a lawn back there, lowering the water table with each sweep of—

"Sit, Daughter. Please."

She stood. "This doesn't sound good."

Gran switched the TV off.

"Momma got hornswoggled by that Reverend Skunkweed or whatever his name is."

"Reverend Scully, Pops. Momma dotes on the man."

"Skunkweed has taken advantage of her since before we knew about her little strokes. The way I see it, your momma has worked so hard all her life she's burned away chunks of her mind. He charmed the whole nine yards, with the exception of our operating revenue, from her. I can't pay most of my vendors, can't pay what I owe the store crews. I'm able to pay the mortgage on the new house because I put aside the you-know-what money for many years and grew it with loans to good prospects. Momma never knew about that."

Jaudon finally sat. "His church? Is that where the money went?"

"Went is right. We'll never see that money again. He'll always be Skunkweed to me."

"But Momma is famously close with a dollar. We left her in charge too long."

Pops fidgeted with the top button of his shirt. Momma became fed up with the habit years ago and taught him to sew on his own buttons.

"We did. She hid her losses well. All the while she hung on Skunkweed's lying words. A Yankee carpetbagger if I ever saw one. Talked as if he was a Kennedy. At church she was the queen bee. You met him at one of Momma's get-togethers: clerical collar, a wolfish white-tooth smile."

She remembered the man in preacher's clothing who once declined to shake her extended hand.

"I didn't take to the guy except he gave your momma an interest aside from business. I considered a church might mellow her out."

Overhead, the ceiling fan spun round at its highest setting, yet sweat soaked the back of her shirt. She averted her eyes from Pops and hung her head, sick to her stomach.

"The church did keep her perkier, but I was unsettled with all the time she spent with Skunkweed. From the git-go I thought he was as much use as a cat flap in a submarine, going on about wanting a better house of worship for his flock. Momma introduced him to Christian businessmen, and I knew she chipped in some."

She outlined the blue and white squares of the tablecloth with the tip of a finger. "How much, Pops?"

Berry put a light hand on Jaudon's shoulder.

Pops took Jaudon's hands in his. "I swear, I didn't know how bad when I told you we were in high cotton. Skunkweed must have noticed Momma was...not quite herself. Then Rouie discovered that Momma took out loans to pay the bills."

Jaudon had interned with Rouie Waver, their accountant, while studying for her CPA.

"Rouie laid it on the line. Momma told him she was using the cash for expansion and improvements, but the stores showed no such changes. When Rouie put a stop to that, she snuck around us, took out a second mortgage on the new house, then a third, when the interest rates were close to ten percent. She skimmed cash from the stores. When Rouie noticed the declining receipts, he said Momma took over the books herself and fired him, the most trustworthy guy in the business. I hired him back when I saw these overdue statements."

He reached into his sack and gripped a bundle of mail in one sizeable hand. With the other he dealt envelopes, many with green registered mail stickers attached, onto the kitchen table. "The bread companies, the beverage distributors, the electric bill, the dairy." He slammed the rest on the tabletop piecemeal. "Who don't we owe? Rouie is busy with our numbers, trying to save the stores."

She took a bill and realized her hand was shaking. "Save them? It's that bad, Pops?"

He pressed the pads of his fingers to his eyes, as if massaging the tiredness out.

Jaudon raised her chin. "I don't care what Momma said, the competition advertises, and it's time we do too. We'll find the money to put in gas pumps and go one better—deliver orders to the customers' cars at the pumps. I've wanted to make these changes for a while."

"Oh, Daughter." Pops put an arm around her and pulled her in close. She smelled his familiar barbershop hair tonic and talc. "It's too late for that. Momma also took out a second commercial mortgage on the business itself."

In school, she studied enough business to know this spelled disaster. Her heart raced.

Berry laid a steadying hand on her shoulder again, saying, "We can work out a payment schedule."

"Lawyer says we'll be fighting foreclosure."

"Are the police searching for this Reverend Scully?"

"Lawyer says all was done on the up-and-up until the darned minister cut and ran. Thing is, there is no new church. The lawyer checked records at the county, and no one's bought property for a church. To top it off, the lawyer checked Skunkweed's divinity degree—it's hokum. Momma was chewed up and spit out."

"I'll kill him," she said. "I'll kill him with my bare hands."

CHAPTER FIVE

December 1975

MJ missed home, such as it was. Instead of discovering critter trails along the brown cliffs and rock outcrops, she explored the half mile of humidly luxuriant green passageways of Lecoats County between Mrs. Lanamore's café and Mrs. Belda's condo. Weeds and cultivated bushes smelled of rampant growth, even in winter. She heard no silence here like the silence in Depot Landing where she listened to the swish of bald eagle wings. Here in Central Florida, tree toads made a ruckus at twilight, competing with traffic, riding mowers, her footsteps. They put her to sleep trying to delineate their calls.

She sometimes took a shortcut through a worn trailer park. A row of dirty aluminum mailboxes on wood posts lined the entryway. The trees were deciduous and plentiful, the unpaved sand roads carpeted with decaying brown leaves and pothole puddles. But the sun shone, and she could count on one or two residents to lift a bottle of beer in greeting from wobbly wooden steps, gracing her with big gap-toothed smiles that mirrored deteriorating fences. The trailers were aluminum skirted and plain white with occasional colorful shutters. Some owners had built small decks, askew with age, with weeds ambitious for light crowding through gaps. Others had narrow gardens that boasted blooming bright blue lobelia, many-colored pansies, yellow, white, and pink snapdragons.

Unused to winter heat, she summoned memories of cold winds in the heights over the Washington side of the wide Columbia River. She absorbed Florida's warmth, enjoyed the hot bath of it as it seeped into her muscle history of tensing in the cold. She was eager to adjust to the discomfort of overheating, of pouring down stinging-the-eyes sweat which drew mosquitoes. She scratched bites bloody on her skinny arms and legs. But she was learning: during the day she wore shorts, and in the evenings she protected her legs with a pair of full-length pants from the Lanamores' church's thrift store. There she bought rainbows of polo shirts, triumphant when she came across those embroidered with Florida alligators. She wore them daily, buttoned to the neck.

She went to dollar movie matinees more for the air-conditioning than the films. She regretted seeing *Jaws* and read an Anita Desai library book in an attempt to erase the horrors of the film, only to discover the disarray of Calcutta, a chaotic city beyond her comprehension, and as sweltering as Florida could be.

Most of the time, between chores and errands, she sat in her stuffy room with Hop, fan at top speed, steamed she was too young to get a real job or a rental and too illegal to go to any school. Her anger made her fretful beyond bearing. In the background, Mrs. Belda's endless game shows played at high volume to compensate for a growing deafness. MJ speculated about ways to move on as a free person and imagined a whole lot of nothing.

From the window of her room in this Depression-era three-story resort hotel that had been converted to cheesy condominiums, she looked across a narrow alleyway. In her view was a freshly painted light blue wall and the near ends of balconies on a swank modern motel, sumptuously restored to draw nostalgic upscale buyers. A full complement of idle residents drank by a large swimming pool most of the day. Many of the apartment owners in Mrs. Belda's building got around on canes and walkers. Ambulances were common.

Afternoons at two thirty, a man Mrs. Belda called Ike Keister sat on his elegantly furnished second-floor balcony tying the laces of his shiny black shoes. He'd made his money in sugar, according to Mrs. Belda, retired in his fifties, and did nothing from that point on but laze on his keister counting the cash. MJ never learned if Keister was his real name.

She'd read about the horrific effect of the sugar industry on Florida's ecosystem. Easy to see how the man afforded a condo with all the trimmings. She stood at her window and watched him, wringing her hands. She sat, paced her room, lay on the narrow bed, went back to the window.

What a waste of resources people like Ike Keister were. One day she'd had enough. She peeled her forearms off the sticky windowsill and stood. *Wheel of Fortune* was on the living room TV, and the audience applauded as if they were winners, not dupes providing the network with free marketing.

In her first week she'd plotted both covert and run-like-hell routes to Mrs. Lanamore's restaurant, on the remote chance her family reported her missing and the even more remote possibility she could be traced here. She'd had a nightmare that Dear Old Dad came to drag her home. Or maybe some small part of her wished he wanted to. It was a lamebrain thought, but she was prepared. Trash went out a side door with a bar opener and set off an alarm if residents used it. The back door led to a walled parking lot. Her heart quickened as she pictured the drop from Ike's balcony to the ground.

A sob hiccuped from her. She twisted her hands together until they hurt, as if twisting off a faucet of tears.

The meadow atop a basalt cliff in Depot Landing had been, to her, sacred land, a high prairie sanctuary. Last spring, she'd led Christina to the wide, shallow cavity that collected rainwater and attracted the most amazing singing, honking, cheeping, cawing birds in migration. Yellow buttercups, pink prairie stars, and plum-colored shooting stars sparkled. In the distance, blue camas lilies encircled the plowed land as if to shelter new crops of seedlings. On a still day, the sun teased aromas from the wildflowers and grasses, richer than perfumes.

If only Mrs. Obrenger, Christina's mother, hadn't come searching for them, shrieking that MJ had attacked Christina. If only she hadn't seen them, blouses unbuttoned, touching in that thrilling way. Mrs. Obrenger shepherded them down the hillside, swatting at Christina.

If only, two months ago, Mrs. Obrenger hadn't come across the new poem to Christina and called Emma Jean's parents.

MJ's father bellowed and frothed curses. Her mother cringed and wept on a kitchen chair. MJ said nothing.

Dear Old Dad asked, "Is it true, what the Obrenger woman said about that sick foolishness with her kid?"

She folded her arms and spoke, embarrassed by her tremulous voice. "You taught me to be honest, so here's the truth: my kind of love is not foolishness."

His upper lip curled into a sneer. He was an uncomplicated man, a soldier and a well digger, with no tolerance for the unconventional, but why did he call her sick? For loving someone?

"I can call what you were up to a lot of things, but love isn't one of them." He told her mother, "Straighten her out." As he grabbed his cowboy hat and opened the back door, both little brothers ran through the room, one shooting a water pistol, the other slashing air with a toy whip. Her father smiled at the boys, then met MJ's eyes. "Or get out. Before you spread it."

He left, and she heard his diesel engine. Pea gravel splattered against their rental house from the outsize tires on the family vehicle, an extended cab pickup with *Bo Beaudry Pump Services* stenciled on the sides.

"See what you did," said her mother, as if Dear Old Dad never before washed his hands of MJ. "He'll go to the tavern now." She leaped at MJ, pounding with her fists, strong from a lifetime of house and yard chores.

Her mother's eyes were slits, her face shone with blotches of high color, her nostrils flared, and she smelled of the fish and Spanish rice she'd prepared for dinner. She seemed intent on either killing MJ or driving her away, as usual growling at her for an ungrateful, grumpy, godless child.

MJ barged into the bedroom she shared with her little sisters, who gaped the way they did at *The Jetsons* on the TV. Her mother followed, became entangled with the curtain that served as a door, and in her wild frustration, ripped it and extracted the rod. The little girls cowered.

MJ fell to her narrow bed and covered her head for protection. Her glasses dug into her face, and she feared they'd warp. She held Hop tightly as she waited for blows from the curtain rod. Her mother hit her ribs until MJ almost broke her silence with the scream reverberating in her head: *Stop blaming me, stop blaming me, stop blaming me.* She would never forget the sound of the rod striking flesh, her mother's grunts, and the deep, radiating sting. She was certain her mother was punishing herself as she cried and cursed her child, her husband, her hopelessness.

"You won't lend a hand with the babies," her mother screeched, "so I can get away once in a while."

MJ moved to safeguard her ribs. It struck over her left eyebrow, breaking the rod, gouging and drawing blood.

For crying out loud, she did lend a hand to maintain the fall-apart rental Dear Old Dad's erratic earnings afforded. Laundry, cleaning, dishwashing, maintenance—she undertook any chore she could stomach. It became her job to walk the wild pack of four siblings to and from the school bus at the end of their road, but she refused to take over mothering the irritating curs.

A wheezing cough, smoker's voice hoarse, her mother menaced

her with the jagged end of the rod. "I married him to give you a name—you were born tainted."

She raised her eyes to her mother's. "What do you mean?" She'd read plenty of books about unwed mothers and tangled messes of families. She was fond of *Madame Bovary* and *Tess of the d'Urbervilles*.

Her mother cursed and prayed to end her misery and wailed a chant as she teetered from the room. "Evil, evil, twisted child."

In the middle of that night, she packed Hop, her paperback dictionary, a few necessaries, and tried to straighten her glasses. She had held back half of the money from her summer, weekend, and after-school job at the aggregate company west of town. Work was scarce for high school students in Depot Landing, but her teacher's husband owned the business. He'd asked his wife for her smartest student. MJ worked there close to three years, saving for college.

Dear Old Dad wanted her to get out? Well, she wasn't about to be there when he came home stewed and stewing and beer breathed. Her doting mother took a rod to her to beat the evil out? Bullshit—she filled her backpack and left through a window.

She hiked down and down a bluff along a dry creek bed—they only got about fourteen inches of rain a year—slipping where last week's hail had formed ice patches, toward the Columbia River, picked her painful way between boulders, scraped knuckles and knees, and stayed off the road almost to Route 14 where a locomotive groaned in the night, warning people and cars away from the tracks. She wore a straw farmer's hat, won at the county fair, pulled low over the bloody bandage that covered the welt her mother left on her forehead.

Finally, she saw the bright lights of the train depot next to the river. Her father was unquestionably at the down-at-the-heels Tracks Tavern and Grocery across Railroad Avenue from the depot, drinking with his Vietnam era buddies and bashing President Gerald Ford.

No pedestrians or bicycles were allowed on the bridge she needed to cross. She was counting on getting a ride from someone at the quarry, but a ponytailed man stopped in a wheezing, disorderly sedan that smelled of pine sap and babies. She knew he was a local because he pronounced Depot Landing with the accent on the *po*. He wore the suspenders of a logger and was on his way to Hood River to meet the crummy that took lumber crews out to logging sites. At his friendly urging, she told him her plans.

"You're sixteen?"

"My birthday's at the end of this month."

"The bank will never let you withdraw money. They have to call your parents and get one of them to sign off."

She puffed out her cheeks in dismay. Her so-called family banked in White Salmon, but the bank had a branch across the river. Not a kid to fritter away money from her relatives' gifts, she'd squirreled most of it in a savings account from an early age. Today, she had only what lay deep in her pants pockets—half her last paycheck and bonuses her boss, the quarry owner's wife, gave her in cash with promises not to tell her family. She'd send in her resignation and thanks from an outlying post office.

"But why? It's my darned money."

"The government won't stay away from our lives, that's why. Those crooked politicians have no business telling us what we can and can't do."

The Greyhound station was across the river, buses cheaper than trains. Parked at a twenty-four-hour café, the logger left her thinking about the one lesson she without a doubt learned last night: honesty got you nowhere. Not if you were an evil, evil, twisted child.

The logger returned from the café, gave her a hot chocolate, a sack with an egg sandwich, and three ten-dollar bills before catching his ride. That gesture alone gave her the boost she needed.

A workhorse of a freight train without end, covered in graffiti, rolled beside the river. And here she was, Emma Jean Beaudry, striding through the breaking dawn to buy a ticket for as far away as the bus would take her.

CHAPTER SIX

Early spring 1976

The library allowed MJ to borrow a paltry number of books on Mrs. Belda's card, so she haunted thrift shops for more. At Mrs. Lanamore's café, where, with care, one tea bag lasted for several infusions of hot water, MJ was working her way through all of Upton Sinclair's books. Her paperback dictionary already showed wear. The customers routinely distracted her, especially the regulars, a few of whom sort of adopted this respectful white girl, which they thought gave them carte blanche to sit, chat, and—she eventually discerned—pry.

Inside Mrs. Belda's humble condo apartment, MJ read, schemed her future, and routinely paced the big braided rug in her room, her existence out of whack, her mind filled with the fires of impatient, directionless yearnings and her constant anger. She needed more to do.

The guy with the black shoes, Ike Keister, sat on his cushioned wicker balcony chair again. The air was laden with moisture and a faint smell of decaying vegetation. The game shows went on and on, Mrs. Belda calling encouragement and insults at the contestants. From the top of a lamppost, a gull laughed without ceasing. She plugged her ears with her fingers; too much noise filled her head.

Christina, Christina, I need you. Christina knew how to smooth MJ's feathers with silliness or a tease or a playful game of Chinese checkers.

She marked Ike Keister's fixed routine: retying his shoelaces, standing, and tightening his belt as he left the balcony preparatory to walking his daily route. With a *Wall Street Journal* under his arm, he'd return to his balcony in exactly an hour.

She decided to rock and roll, and did not for one second question her compulsion.

The TV was showing riots in China, and Mrs. Belda was asleep on her gray couch with its faded yellow starbursts. The wallpaper in the bathroom was bubbled, and the tub and toilet showed permanent rings. MJ flushed, washed her hands and wiped them on a thin towel, and crept from the apartment.

Her knife was always in the pocket of her cutoff jeans. She was filled with boiling apprehension and bile, exactly as she'd been that moment when she bought her bus ticket to Florida.

A window in the hallway lay right above Keister's balcony. The distance she needed to jump across the alley was short. Checking left and right, she stretched yellow rubber gloves from Mrs. Belda's kitchen over her hands, lifted the window, and swung her legs over the ledge.

Don't look down, she told herself, but did. Her stomach rolled over the way she remembered from the roller coaster at the Klickitat County Fair.

She sprang, caught hold of the black metal railing, and vaulted onto the balcony, her hands seared by the heated metal, smeared with seagull droppings. She wiped them on her shorts, fast. She crouched and tried the sliding glass door.

Keister hadn't locked it. She slid it open, slowly, without sound, teeth gritted, thinking who made the stupid rule against loving a girl? Because of it, she had to stay invisible and was forced to help herself to someone's extra stuff.

The condo was saturated with the damp cardboard odor of seeped-in cigar smoke. She sailed through as if she owned this elegant space.

Faced with an ornate mirror, she admired what she saw: a lean, daring prowler, wayward and watchful. She'd locate a pawn shop to sell what she took. She swore to shave her hair Marine short and break into houses for a living. Mrs. Belda, who pinched pennies, groused about her high taxes, unaware that she wasn't the only deserving person in the world. She seemed to relish telling MJ how a hurricane filled in the fountain and uprooted the royal palms next door. Trees, she said, crashed into windows and tore off balconies. After an extensive restoration and updating, moneyed new residents bought the condo apartments. MJ wanted to see one of those hurricanes lash a mansion or two someday.

Why should affluent people have more than they need while

others fought to fish in their native waters or jeopardized their lives in dangerous railroad jobs?

She'd seen Ike Keister drive the glossy light blue Jaguar parked in his condo lot, but his bathrooms smelled mildewed. His furniture was dark heavy stuff that must have cost a fortune new. Someone carved that mahogany and sewed that needlework by hand a long, long time ago—and for pennies.

Keister's brocade living room drapes were the sort of pomp and tassels she imagined in a castle.

A castle. That's what she'd wanted, a castle for Christina, filled with antiques. MJ's ex-mother loved antiques. Christina visited the Beaudry's rental frequently, touching the few relics with those slight, pretty fingers, asking what this was and that was. MJ's mother sent Christina to the library for books on antiques. The two of them sat side by side at the Beaudry kitchen table, picking photographs of favorites, Christina reading the text aloud. At the time, MJ absolutely believed her mother appreciated having Christina around enough to accept her as something like a daughter-in-law.

The objects on Mr. Keister's marble-topped telephone table blurred. The castle she wanted for her and Christina was not going to materialize. They'd never let this evil, evil, twisted child see Christina again. She deserved nothing more, having abandoned Christina to face alone the consequences of falling for another girl. But, *Evil, evil, twisted child*, her mother called her. *Get out*, her father said. *Get out*, the truck driver said. She'd go back someday for her Maid Marion, she'd be lionhearted, wayward, wrathful—the MJ in the mirror.

She yanked open the telephone table drawer.

Bingo. Dear Old Dad kept twenties and fifties there, and so did Mr. Keister, who'd also stashed a sheaf of two-dollar bills, newly minted for the bicentennial. She left the two-dollar bills, swiped the thinnest watch she'd seen in her life—gold—and shoved them deep into her pockets. What other easy pickings did the man have? She pocketed a pair of aviator sunglasses in their case and a miniature camera. She left the Nixon/Agnew campaign button. Ruthless, she stalked into the huge bedroom and stuffed her pockets with a coin collection and what might prove to be diamond-studded cufflinks.

Shady and Tad hung around with men in the market for these goods and would help her sell them if a pawnshop wouldn't.

MJ's sideways smile crept along her cheek. So what, if she was too young to register for school. So what, if she was too young to apply for a library card. So what, if circumstances forced her to prepare for her GED at a library, with no teachers. So what, if she lay low until age eighteen to order her birth certificate, apply for a Social Security card. All over were countless roomy snowbird dwellings, empty for months at a time. The stupidly affluent were going to pay for her college education.

Why the heck not—Dear Old Dad claimed she was already damned. She'd come away from the Pacific Northwest, bearing its raw power, righting wrongs. She opened another drawer.

Without warning, she was falling, jerked back by her collar. The fabric tightened against her neck and choked her to the floor.

"Hey, punk," said Ike Keister. "What the hell are you doing in here?"

She jumped from the floor, hit his arms, kicked with her heels. An unbathed stink came from him. His hands were on her back, grunting from the effort of pinning her.

She tried to reach her knife and stopped herself. Evil, evil, twisted child. Her goose was cooked.

"What are you doing in my house, boy?"

She kept her head down to hide her face. *Get out*, she told herself, quoting Dear Old Dad.

She clenched her jaw. If she moved fast enough, she'd be in Mrs. Belda's apartment before anyone saw her.

He wasn't a brawny guy, and his strength soon gave out. She rolled, squirmed, twisted away, and rose, light and quick.

He blocked the front entrance; she thrust open the balcony door. Once over the far rail, she let herself plummet. With one hand, she caught a twisted spindle, wrenching herself to a painful stop before letting go again. The ground floor came fast. She caught a concrete ledge, almost losing her gloves, but it slowed her fall. She collected scratches and cuts from a good-sized shrub full of bright orange blooms.

The branches trapped her. She heard Ike Keister bellowing for the police as she struggled to stay free any way she could.

CHAPTER SEVEN

She tore out of the hibiscus shrub, orangey blossoms falling from her hair, loot in her pockets. Her heart raced like the teeth on a chainsaw. She was the only pedestrian on the street and slowed to avoid attention, following the route she'd mapped in her head if Dear Old Dad reported her missing, which she doubted. When she got there, Pansy's Home Cooking was closed for the day, but Mrs. Lanamore lived upstairs. Tad opened the door to her frantic knocking.

She plunged in, pushed the door shut, and put her back against it, arms and legs spread-eagled. She was short of breath from taking the steep wood stairs two at a time and could get no words out.

The arched living room windows filled the space with light. She dared to peer at the empty street. The distant view caught her eye. The Lanamores were able to see clear over houses, roads and businesses, dozens of bodies of water and marshland to blue, blue Hillsborough Bay.

"What is the matter with you, child?" asked Tad, gawping at her.

She examined herself and saw the bloody scratches from her fall. Her shoulders burned so badly she suspected she'd ripped them from their sockets swinging off the balconies. Her polo shirt now sported air vents.

"Mam, come see. Your number one white girl flipped out for real."

Mrs. Lanamore stretched to see her from her recliner in front of a TV news show. The glint of amusement in her eye said, *I told you so, wayward child.* "Did someone come to drag you home?"

She gulped air as fast as she could and turned her head away, chastened, yet she learned something important today—she was strong and could take care of herself.

Her voice came out ragged. "I need to hide. I need to hide these things. And I'm totally serious." MJ reached into her cargo shorts and pulled out the gold watch, cufflinks, and camera. She offered them to Mrs. Lanamore. "I can pay you." She showed them the cash.

Mrs. Lanamore scowled.

"Let me see them," said Tad. He dangled the watch. "You can keep yourself in style for a while, you sell this baby."

"Did you steal that?" Mrs. Lanamore asked.

"Not on purpose."

"It fell into your pockets?"

"Not exactly."

"Is the owner trying to find you?" Mrs. Lanamore made a shooing gesture with her hands. "You better get a ticket for one of those new Concorde jet planes to take you far away. TV says they're fast."

"Oh, Muma, they only go to Rio." Tad checked the window. "You didn't lead the cops here, did you?"

She reversed toward the door, waving her hands back and forth in denial. "The rich guy didn't come after me, and I dodged from sight before any police showed up—if he called them."

"Why?" asked Mrs. Lanamore.

"Why? Shoot. Because they didn't want me around anymore at home. Because I liked a girl, not a boy. Because of all the wealthy white people around here who do nothing and have plenty while you work day and night to get by. Because I have no way to get what I need. Because, at my age, I can't be treated as a legitimate person. And because Robin Hood was my childhood hero."

Mrs. Lanamore shook her head. "I don't condone stealing, Robin Hood or not. You're welcome in my home, but take your business outside, and don't get my boys in trouble." She muted the ad on her TV. "If I was you, I'd stop acting put-upon. That's what's going to get you in trouble."

"I'll never stop being mad."

"You children believe everything is forever. Go take your mad elsewhere—we have enough of our own."

Tad led her to the door. "Let's you and me find Shady."

"Oh yes," said Mrs. Lanamore, leaving her chair. "Let the police see a grown Black man and this white baby girl together."

"I'm no baby."

"I don't know as I believe you, the way you're thinking today. I want you to open your eyes and see the dangerous waters you're wading into. I want you to think about who'll be in hot water if the police catch you when my son is with you. I'll tell you what's forever—your white skin is forever."

She twisted her hands around themselves. "You're right, Mrs. Lanamore, and I apologize. I was careless and selfish to come to your home. Tad, can you tell me where to find Shady?"

Tad insisted on going with her. "There's cash in it for me," he told his mother.

Mrs. Lanamore made a beak shape with her lips. "Let me get back to my news. They've stretched it to a whole hour." She narrowed her eyes at them one more time. "Don't neither of you come back here with any illegal goods."

Tad let loose with his owl laugh. "Not even your favorite bathtub gin?"

Mrs. Lanamore swatted at Tad. "Shut your mouth, son."

Aha, she thought. Mrs. Lanamore wasn't straight as an arrow about every trifling thing. She tried to suppress her crooked smile. A siren sounded nearby.

❖

As MJ and Tad hurried down the stairs from Mrs. Lanamore's apartment, Tad said, "Shady's not far. Put on my Dolphins cap, hide your face." He eyed her and hooted again. "It covers half your ears— you're Charlie Brown on the pitcher's mound."

Checking over her shoulders, MJ followed Tad through an unpaved alley behind the restaurant, along a street of down-at-the-heels houses, and around a corner. Shady sat in his wheelchair by one of a row of doors in a two-story low-income housing project. The roof overhang shielded him from the sun. A girl of about three played on the ground, dressing or undressing a doll.

"Hey, Professor Shady, you want to see what our MJ's holding."

Shady reached in his shirt pocket and peeled the cellophane off a Saf-T-Pop. The child heard the wrapper and reached to him. He withheld the pop. "What do you say to Uncle Shady, Michelle?"

She teetered over to hug Shady's leg. He surrendered it to the child.

MJ gave him her spoils. He held the watch. "You're lucky you didn't get rolled if you came cross-country with this."

She kept her mouth closed, surprised he thought she brought it from home.

"This camera? Do you know what these are worth? It's the classic Leica M3, small, but the best camera ever made. You can't buy one now for less than, what a thousand dollars, fifteen hundred?"

Her arms were folded, chin tucked in, as if she knew all that and plenty more. The camera had weighed heavily in her pocket but was only about five inches in length.

"Tell her how we work, Tad, while I go to my pad and make calls."

Tad watched over the little girl as he spoke to MJ. "The truth is, you're not going to make a mint off this breaking and entering."

"I don't need a mint, Tad. The senior lady I'm taking care of pays me room, board, and thirty dollars a week."

"First off, don't be telling people personal details. Let them assume you want top money or they'll rip you off."

"Thanks. I won't tell the pawnshop a thing."

"Pawnshop? You'd be a fool to take hot goods to a pawnshop. The police keep watch on them."

"Where do I sell it, wise guy?"

"Cool it. Don't let on to the welfare that Shady lives here with his sister and her grandkid—Michelle's mother chose drugs over mothering her child. He's in the same situation as you. Selling is what he lives on. He'll be fair to you, but he's the one taking chances now—he needs his cut, and he'll give a portion of that to me for connecting you."

"Fair enough."

"I want you to understand. Say a score brings a hundred dollars retail—you'll get five percent, sometimes more, if you're lucky. See, because it's not an aboveboard sale, the guy who's going to buy these things from Shady can't sell at full price on the street. He has to watch for undercover cops and police informants. He may be paying protection money. He also has to hire someone with the tools to take the engraving off a piece of jewelry. That takes skills and equipment—you can't be using steel wool."

"Good to know. A lot of risk for peanuts."

Tad spoke kindly, as if trying to ease her disappointment. "Not exactly peanuts, but you might want to consider babysitting, or walking dogs, over burgling."

"I'd be bored stiff." What she didn't want to reveal was the lifting of her anger as she violated Ike Keister's private space, as she helped herself to his cash and fancy gear, and her elation as she extricated herself from the bush, running, running, running free, a trail of orange blossoms behind her.

"Here's another thing," said Tad. "I don't steal from the lean. They have less than us and collections of this and that—nothing worth chancing jail for a limited market."

"What kinds of collections?" she asked.

"Bar coasters, maybe, or bottles, matchbooks. Junk it's hard for us to get rid of and means a lot to them."

"I get that. I left my toy cars behind. The boys have wrecked them by now."

He scoffed at her. "You need to make a living, not collect shit."

"How about these snowbirds who leave their houses empty half the year. I mean, two homes? Come on. They don't need half the things they own."

Tad rubbed his fingers back and forth on his jaw. "From the age of twelve, I thought lifting cigarettes from behind a store counter or getting my fingers on somebody's wallet was fun. Did it one too many times, went to juvenile detention, and broke Mam's heart. You try to get a job after that, and if you don't see the no on their faces because of your color, it'll be there if they find out you did time in juvie. Your record may be expunged, but once word is on the street, it stays there. None of that stopped me—I just learned to do it better."

"I'm meticulous and quick and aim for cash."

Tad looked at her cockeyed but said, "You're pretty grown-up for a kid, you know that?"

"Maybe more nimble witted than some."

"No maybes about it. I'll tell you, though, big cash is usually harder to find, but people leave it in dumbass hiding places. Check drawers first."

Shady pushed out the screen door, letting Michelle inside. He pressed tightly rolled cash into MJ's hand. "Here's the scratch for the watch. I need to go see somebody for the other items."

"One fifty? Thank you."

"You're such an innocent," said Tad. "Don't count it in the open."

Her face heated up. She shoved the money deep in her pocket.

"Gullible child, you have a lot to learn," Shady said.

"Someday I'll write *Stealing for Dummies*."

"Then put this in your book. I actually owe you another two fifty before the camera, but I need to pass your trinkets on before I can give you the rest."

"Oh, one fifty is enough."

"Child, Shady means two hundred and fifty."

"I wish."

Shady and Tad exchanged glances and shook their heads in unison.

"Come by tomorrow, and I'll have it for you, Emma Jean."

"Don't call me that. It's their name, not mine."

"Okay, okay," said Shady, arms crossed in front of his face to deflect attack, but grinning. "Don't be a lamebrain—learn the business like your life depends on it. There is no midterm exam."

"Can I ask you a question?"

"May I," said Shady. "You can, but you use may when asking permission."

She knew that. Who exactly was this Shady? "Why are you in sunglasses day and night?"

Shady pulled a roll-up cigarette from his shirt pocket.

"He's stoned most of the time," said Tad, nodding to the cigarette. "The pain."

"Oh," she said. Had she put her foot in her mouth? "I'd better go cook dinner."

"You sure you want to go back?" asked Shady as he lit the joint. "Cops might be there."

Tad took the Dolphins cap from her and tightened the strap. "Wear this and buy different clothes on your way. You don't want to be recognized."

She displayed the rubber gloves she'd worn at Ike Keister's. "I was with you all afternoon, right, Tad?"

He crooked his head. "First I give you my mother's cooking, then my hat, now I'm your alibi? And what's with the bright yellow gloves?"

"Fingerprints, right? I'll share my pay with you." She reached for the money.

"Don't flash it."

"Right," she said, a finger at the temple of her glasses, adjusting them. "Hide the cash."

Tad had a great wide smile. He positioned the cap on her head. "Just funning you, partner. You get on home. And toss the gloves. Never use the same pair twice. The police can read glove prints too."

Shady said, "Don't buy all the gloves in one store, or someone will notice. You need to keep your eyes and ears alert to everything, everyone. You get caught—Tad and I get caught."

Partner, she thought as she walked toward Mrs. Belda's, smiling. She could get used to that idea. Tomorrow she'd get sunglasses and hats, and definitely buy rubber kitchen gloves, black if they made them. She checked out each dwelling she passed with an eye to her next break-in and a focus on unearthing hard cash.

CHAPTER EIGHT

Berry's fingers massaged her shoulders, but Jaudon didn't want to be touched or distracted in any way from the unimaginable news about the Beverage Bays.

Pops's eyes, studying her, looked wounded with concern. "We never had troubles like this when your momma had her full mind, Daughter. Some days, I'll catch her in the driveway saying she's doing her rounds of the stores, but she's likely to show up for dinner at some stranger's house two counties away or else crash the car. I can't leave her alone."

"No wonder she didn't let me near the company books. You didn't notice, Pops?"

"I'm just an old phosphate hauler, laid off from the mines. I don't know enough to catch sight of tricky business."

"And she took advantage of that, but Rouie Waver's an accountant. He should have known."

"I'm real sorry. I only learned since all this. She fired Rouie."

"She wouldn't. Not our good, loyal Rouie." She rubbed her eyes, leaking tears of anger and betrayal. "He didn't tell you?"

"He wouldn't. I stole Momma from him a long time ago. He probably blames all this on me."

"Momma said she'd never let her children be in want the way she was."

Pops patted the air the way he always did to calm her. "She thought she was buying us all a spot in heaven through Skunkweed."

Berry said, "We'll find a way through this."

Jaudon rested her head on her father's shoulder, which over the years had become soft with fat. "Berry's right, Pops. We'll save the stores."

He patted her back. "I made you an appointment to talk to the lawyer and Rouie." He pecked each of them on the cheek. "I better get back. I have a neighbor sitting with Momma."

He donned his trucker's cap and slumped out the kitchen door.

Jaudon rifled through Pops's sack of overdue bills. She couldn't return to her store—she was ashamed to face her employees, especially her first hire and good friend Olive Ponder, and Olive's son. Emmett went missing during the Vietnam War, but he slipped his squad through enemy lines and now was a law student. Then there was Cousin Cal Vicker who worked with Pops, doing the heavy lifting of restocking and resetting the stores. Her best bet was to decrease staff by attrition since turnover was high in this business. The government claimed the recession was over, but small enterprises faced an uphill slog.

"Pops and Momma can have their former room if they lose their place. I'll take over Bat's." Her older brother Bat's name was short for Momma's maiden name Batson, just as Jaudon was her maternal grandmother's surname.

"If it'll save your bacon, we can sell our land across the road," said Gran.

Berry said. "No, Gran. If the stores are everything to Jaudon, your wooded wetlands are equally important to you and me."

"Maybe grilled tomato and pimento cheese sandwiches with hot sauce will cheer us."

It was her favorite lunch, but Jaudon's craw proved too full of sorrow and worry to choke down food. Berry led her away by the hand.

They lay together on Berry's bed, Jaudon nestled in the cushion of Berry's breasts.

If anyone could put her Jaudon together again, it was Berry. She'd done it before. As she rocked her heartsick lover, Berry sought the comfort and wisdom of the Great Spirit. She moved in with Gran Binyon at age eight and soaked up tales of their Native ancestors' beliefs. They made sense to her.

"This will take a long spell of patience," she told Jaudon, "and we need to start with forgiveness, if we can."

❖

The next week, Jaudon was in a sweat about meeting with the lawyer and accountant by herself. She welcomed Allison Millar's offer to go along. Feminist Allison was the county supervising public health nurse and sat on a nearby city council. Her lover, Cullie Culpepper, earned her living as a pool cleaner but wanted to be a cop. The two couples were close. Allison knew how to talk to lawyer types despite her youth of marches and protests.

Jaudon, in her customary cargo shorts, stained Beverage Bay vest, wrinkled Hawaiian shirt, and sneakers, gallantly opened the door for Allison. At the sight of the classy office, though, she instantly reverted to Momma's mannish, surly, grubby daughter. Allison had to nudge her to a tufted and tacked leather couch.

"Leave it to Momma," said Jaudon.

"The furnishings?" Allison asked.

"Showy. Ritzy."

"Brass, Brass, and Lightwood is the oldest, most prestigious law firm in town. They wouldn't hire a female or non-white attorney if she'd served on the Supreme Court."

"Momma doesn't believe in women ambulance chasers."

"I remember waiting in an almost identical room while my parents met with their attorney. A radio was playing, and I danced on the thick carpet."

"Your family went to offices like these?"

Allison waved a hand around the room. "Don't let this cow you, cutie-pie."

A buzz emitted from the receptionist's desk, and he led them along a hall hung with golf course photographs. Balding Rouie Waver, with his drinker's nose and smoker's cough, was already there.

The elder Mr. Brass introduced himself with the civility of a wide well-groomed antique and spoke to a spot over Jaudon's head. "I represented your mother for many years, Ms. Vicker. Let me express my sympathy for the demise of her modest empire."

Seven stores that grew from a roadside stand over twenty years was nothing to sneeze at. "Demise?" she said aloud.

"I'm afraid so. Rouie has spent the past hour showing me your documents and police reports from other states where the pseudo-Reverend Scully operated."

Allison might come across as petite and delicate, but injustice provoked her. "That nasty piece of work was never caught? Why isn't the FBI involved?"

"That's a law enforcement matter, Miss Millar. It's not our main concern here."

"Not our main concern?" said Jaudon with a distressed wave of her arms.

Allison, her professional self again, put a hand on Jaudon's arm.

Brass placed the palms of his runty hands together. "If this Scully is caught, we may be able to recover a portion."

Rouie sighed and huffed. "He means you'll never see that money."

Brass said, "The initial step, Ms. Vicker, is to pay creditors. Do you have means to do that?"

"Would I be here if I did? Losing my business is no run-of-the-mill event."

"It is, kid," said Rouie. "It's as common as Tuesdays."

"Not for the Vickers, it's not."

Allison intervened again. "The second option?"

"We file for bankruptcy."

"When pigs fly." Jaudon didn't know whether to cry or throw up. She wanted to go hide under the porch for the rest of her living days. "Listen, I didn't hire you to get told my outfit's not worth a plugged nickel. Now, can you get us out of this mess, or not?"

"Hear me out," said Brass. He handed her a preprinted list of documents to read and forms to fill out, including details of her assets.

"What assets? Zefer's dog tags?" Zefer, about seventeen, recently died. The memory of him in his big basket made her weepy. "I have to prove that we're failures? Isn't humiliation enough?"

Brass warned, "No hiding assets, or the outcome of your petition is jeopardized. If we can use Chapter Thirteen, we may save your homes. Understand, no one is taking away from you. They're making it easier for you to reorganize and pay the debts incurred by your mother."

Rouie said, "We'll set up a long-term repayment plan. And if you sell one or two stores, you'll be decreasing the debt faster than a hot knife through butter."

Her voice squeaked. "Sell my stores?"

"My goal," said Brass, "will be to persuade the court to let you pay about perhaps ten cents on the dollar, keep your and your mother's homes, and get the stores back on track in three to five years' time. That's if our plan is approved, which I presume it will be, based on your mother's medical issues."

"Five years? How do I pay my crews in the meantime?"

"Oh," said Brass, "you won't be doing any of that."

"I have to have staff."

"Naturally. The cash goes straight to the trustee. He will pay your staff, the creditors, and you."

Jaudon half stood. "Pay me my family's own money?"

Allison scowled at her until she sat again.

Rouie said, "There might be one other way, Sin."

The attorney sat back in his chair and steepled his fingers. "Jaudon has a good case pending against the county."

"Oh?" said Brass.

Rouie reminded Brass about a deputy's attack on Jaudon, resulting is deafness in one ear.

Brass rubbed his fingertips together. "You say it's my firm's case?" He swung his chair to face the window. When he swiveled back, he made a note and without raising his eyes said, "I'll research the delay. Someone in my office will call you."

"What good will all that do?" Jaudon asked.

Rouie cleared his throat. "Sin can't say this, but he'll by the by mention he's handling that case as well as this. See if it gets their attention. That way they suggest the arrangement, not us."

"What arrangement?"

"They make the foreclosures go away—we don't file the suit."

Was this the way the law worked? Was justice nothing but a backroom deal?

Allison said, "Jaudon needs time to study the options, Mr. Brass."

Rouie promised to call when he finished disentangling the books.

Jaudon floundered out through the hallway, steadying herself with the walls.

In the evening, Berry and Jaudon sat on the porch swing. A ruby-throated hummingbird poked its beak into pink flowers.

"Pops stopped by the office this morning. He said last Sunday, Momma remembered about going to church. She wouldn't listen to Pops when he said it was gone, so he showed her the old storefront church is now a Caribbean restaurant. He drove her to the building Skunkweed claimed to have bought and renovated. It was vacant, with boarded windows, and a haggard condemned notice."

"Did she understand?"

Jaudon smacked at a mosquito. "She's past connecting acts with consequences. I had a duck fit. Remember Momma was treasurer for the chamber of commerce? Well, she wrote nine thousand dollars in chamber checks to Skunkweed."

"They could have had her arrested."

"Pops paid them back today." Jaudon took a long breath. "I'm going to have to close two of the stores. Rouie Waver is figuring out the lowest earners."

"I'm sorry, my angel. It's the smart thing to do."

"Aw, heck, Berr, I wanted to grow, not shrink."

"Do you want to keep all seven stores?"

"Yes. Yes, I do."

Life wasn't going to be much fun until the company was in the black. And Berry's plans? Back on the shelf.

Berry's gran came to the porch door, asking for help with a vacuum cleaner belt.

Jaudon propelled herself off the swing.

Berry caught her hand. "Before you go, do you want a little good news?"

Jaudon lost her woebegone manner at once.

"The clinic approved making me Dr. Garza's nurse exclusively."

Jaudon leaned over and kissed her on the cheek. "You've always wanted this. Congratulations—I'm so proud for you."

"She's as concerned as I am about accessible health care for women, plus she's working with Allison's committee on contaminates from the old phosphate mines. I'll be part of that."

"You're going to make a difference in this world, aren't you?"

CHAPTER NINE

Fall 1976

It was the strangest thing. Back in the spring, when MJ snuck home to Mrs. Belda's condo with one hundred and fifty dollars in her pocket and groceries for dinner, she found no police in the vicinity. Hop gazed at her from their pillow as usual. She'd dreaded meeting Ike Keister, but a month later they passed on the street. He didn't look twice at her. Another gold watch was prominently wrapped around his wrist. From that triumphant moment, she gave up any hesitation she'd had about relieving the well-to-do of their extravagances.

Reconnoitering for prospects was a heady game she looked forward to every day. Two blocks from Mrs. Belda's, she noticed a covered sailboat was gone from its usual spot next to a driveway.

Tad had advised her to zero in on residences where she wouldn't be visible from the curb: high hedges, sloping land, bunches of trees, stone walls. A curved street didn't hurt either.

These hedges towered, all right. A cut-through from the neighbor's backyard shielded her more.

She'd seen the well-dressed thirty-something joker who lived in the fancy house. Not a snowbird, but he drove a BMW, employed a maid service and landscaper, owned the big boat, carried a spiffy briefcase, and moved with the haughty confidence of a god. He was rich enough, she thought, to buy a new boat when he got this one wet. Each weekend he brought a different throwaway girl home. She yearned to rob him of the privileges he enjoyed. He used women, while she'd lost her Christina.

She was always angry prepping for a job. She cursed at her targets as she studied them, was short with Mrs. Belda, became distraught over news stories—most recently one on South Africa's racist politics and another about the three and a quarter million dollars spent on a Rembrandt. She thought of all the good that could be done in the world with those millions.

That morning she mimicked the playboy's slick walk, breached the cut-through. She smelled the newly cut grass and knew the landscaper wouldn't return for three or four weeks. The screen door to the lanai and chlorine-heavy pool was unlocked. Tad had taught her how to pop a sliding glass door—easy with nothing blocking the track. This bozo hadn't bothered to use a broomstick or a piece of PVC pipe.

She was as happy as she'd been in her life.

She assaulted the house, by the same token damaging an unnamed element in herself, but she cared nothing about that as she laid siege to the playboy's belongings. She'd stop stockpiling revenge once she completed college and secured her future.

Within her chilly focus, her blood might have stopped running and her heart gone into hibernation. He'd left the sterile-smelling air-conditioning with its endless drone on high, as to be expected, wasting energy, filling the outdoors with poisonous gases. A veteran of numerous burglaries now, she no longer took her time—she moved swift as a bird, primal smart, a creature who hailed from the Northwest woods. She darted to the easy spots: countertops, canisters, freezers, kitchen cabinets, dirty laundry, under and inside mattresses.

What she discovered were expensive cameras—five of them. Revolting excess. In the playboy's swing-out bar, she unearthed his cash—just as Tad predicted—this time in a silver shaker stuffed with it. She rolled his soft cashmere sweaters around two unopened whiskey bottles from an impressive collection and laid them flat in the innocent-seeming beach bag she'd brought along.

She ambled home from the playboy's house with the cameras, whiskey, and cash and used Mrs. Belda's phone to arrange a meet with Shady for the next day.

CHAPTER TEN

To Jaudon's sorrow and discouragement, Rouie's calculations showed that the Beverage Bay on Mobley Road produced the least income.

Packing the store about tore Jaudon's heart out, especially doing it by herself. She made price changes as she worked to raise the cost of each item in stock, one to two cents. Every little bit helped. She did take immeasurable pleasure in the expensive, easy-load price gun she ordered when she took over. Momma hadn't been keen on expensive anything.

At the edge of a freeze-annihilated orange grove, not far from the Vicker homestead, stood that very first Beverage Bay, a rust-stained, corrugated steel Quonset hut, its front eave propped with a twenty-four-foot piece of lumber. Before acquiring the hut and its land, Momma sold cold drinks, strawberries by the box, homemade strawberry shortcake, and penny candy off a table, under the scrub oaks, itchy weeds, and saw palmettos that screened their house from Eulalia Road.

That was so long ago, before Jaudon learned she was different, before she and Berry met at age eight, before they acknowledged their love.

Old Mr. Mobley sold the hut and its patch of land to Momma for the price of the storage space he'd lose, which wasn't much at all. Since they weren't connected to electricity at that point, Pops hauled in discarded iceboxes people had replaced with refrigerators. The hangar-like structure was ample enough for Pops and two of Momma's brothers to fashion drive-through doors, which allowed Momma to continue delivering orders to car windows. Pops built the shelving on his days off and brought blocks of ice every morning. After school and summers, Jaudon and her brother Bat worked there.

Mobley wasn't a main road, and the people who lived at that end of the county lost their wages when the phosphate mines closed. Many of them claimed injuries and never did go back to work.

What kept the Vicker family solvent at first was their special product. Twice a week, out the back of the metal store, Pops sold moonshine his brother cooked. Their father and before him their grandfather and great-grandfather guarded a secret recipe, smooth and strong enough to make legal distilleries go broke. They called it Dinkey Dew because they hid the forty-gallon copper still in a stretch of woods between a creek and a railroad spur line where miniature locomotives called dinkies pulled freight cars.

Pops shared the recipe with Jaudon, who put it away with family photos, birth and death certificates, and similar keepsakes. Unlike most moonshiners who were in a rush to make a buck, the Vickers took care to make a quality brew. Dinkey Dew was triple filtered and aged a bit more than most. Pops swore by the practice of tossing out the first quart of a batch to keep the liquor pure. They flavored it with the juice of ripe persimmons, an arduous process in itself, but the fruit grew wild and was free for the picking. When they built the second store, next to the one-room post office on Church Pond Road, Pops installed a narrow storage area behind the walk-in cooler and freezer. Momma hired her family to run the legitimate and illegal businesses.

Jaudon lifted equipment and stacked cans in cartons. She raised the radio volume when she heard "Still Crazy After All These Years." Her memory brought back the smell of straw on the floor of the early Mobley Store. Her skin remembered the cold of metal buckets filled with ice. She tasted and smelled the licorice pipes, soft caramels, and peppermints they sold. In the summer rains they didn't get much traffic. The three of them—Momma, brother Bat, and herself—sat on wood-slatted foldout chairs dry as plain toast. Momma talked about soon paying off the hut and its patch of nutrient-deficient land, her plans to scout sites for a third store. When the thunder and lightning came near enough to scare them, Momma let them share one icy, sugary, nose-stinging Coke.

Jaudon's eyes misted when she boxed the strawberry milkshake machine. She'd expected to open, not close, stores.

CHAPTER ELEVEN

"Nobody wants to be in Florida in summer," Tad told MJ. "It's the best time to hit snowbird homes."

She'd used the summer to polish her skills in the strange, irresistible hodgepodges that passed for neighborhoods in flat Florida. Generations had lived in these spread-out white clapboard, brick, or shingled houses. Jaudon Vicker's family went back to the days of Florida cowpunchers and cracker homesteaders. She supposed it was what you were used to, what you learned early on was good, whether you grew up in twenty-four-seven air-conditioning or awakened to a cold woodstove that had to be fed all day.

From the fancier homes, she'd made enough money to start her college stash. Tad and Shady convinced her that she had too good a mind to waste on crime forever. Tad worked nights cleaning businesses. Licensed and bonded, he did his own marketing, cold-calling, sales, and labor in order to be his own boss. He'd left what he called his stolen years behind, but he was willing to share the ins and outs of that former livelihood.

He directed her to Shady's office, a storefront bar close to their car wash, to do her transactions. She hesitated at the mouth of the graffitied, sour-smelling alleyway lined with open dumpsters but found the heavy back door and put her shoulder to it. Shady wasn't at the booth Tad said he habitually commandeered.

As her eyes adjusted to the darkness, she saw him wheeling her way with a bottle of beer, a can of Coke, and a glass. They bumped fists, his protected by cutoff batting gloves for operating his wheelchair. The smell of pot on him overwhelmed the bar's reek of beer and cigarettes.

"What's going down?" asked Shady. "Any trouble?"

She poured the soda slowly, listening to the snap of tiny bubbles. "Getting nabbed that first time by Mr. Keister was one too many times for me." The more break-ins she did, the more confident she became, and the fewer mistakes she made. The anger that fired inside her also made her senses keen and kept her focused.

"See, that's one thing that's cool about you. A white girl can access neighborhoods someone with darker skin, for example my confrere Tad, cannot."

She'd learned over the months that Shady published poetry in literary magazines and was formerly a professor of English literature.

"Some office you've got here." She examined it more closely. "If we were in Philadelphia, I'd be afraid of Legionnaire's disease."

He answered, "If a Florida gin mill was good enough for Kerouac, it's good enough for me."

In ninth grade, she'd read all the Kerouac books the librarian ordered for her. *On the Road* was her favorite.

She quoted her favorite lines, about the ease of leaving, from memory.

Shady closed his eyes and quoted back a different line. "I'm glad to meet another Kerouac freak." He reached to shake her hand before getting to business.

Surreptitiously, Shady examined her latest haul and made a call from the pay phone by the toilets. She scanned the bar. The walls held faded tin signs for beers, dated license plates, and early postcards hung on a clothesline. Shady returned from the phone and passed her, under the ratty bar table, her advance. She eased it low in her pocket.

"Sweet haul," he said. "Easy to move. You have the knack."

A prickle of conscience attacked her, but no, that playboy asked for a comeuppance by the way he lived.

No one was paying attention to her or Shady, but she was skittish. She thanked him and stood to leave.

He'd patted the table. "You haven't finished your drink."

"Shouldn't I get out?"

"The fuzz won't be checking IDs on a Tuesday afternoon, but I'm pleased at your caution. You're a good kid, resourceful, smart. I don't want to see you busted and locked in with deadbeats. May I give you a little advice?"

What was wrong with the way she was doing things? "If you must," she said.

Shady scratched his cheek through the beard. "Leave your neighborhood."

She cocked an eyebrow at him.

"I know, I know. You're familiar with the territory and think you're safe there, but your face is getting too much exposure. Take a bus. Find new hunting grounds."

She began to object but didn't want to seem mouthy or ungrateful.

"Try neighborhoods on the lakes, the bayous, the canals," he said. "Waterfront houses are hotspots."

"I don't know. I'd have to visit the neighborhood and watch the house over a matter of weeks. A bus driver might remember me." Her mother called her a know-it-all because she challenged everything.

"Buy a used bike."

She remembered hours-long bike rides past the high prairie farms and accelerating downhill till she thought she'd fly over the railroad tracks into the river. She could use her money to buy a bike, but she was loath to dip into her college savings. The playboy stored a fancy bike in his garage, too conspicuous to steal. And she wasn't about to steal another kid's transportation. At times, she experienced a deluge of regret and silent arguments with herself about ethics. Other than stealing, she was very deliberately honest and fair.

She'd told him she would branch out somehow.

Today, she asked, "Do you have qualms about what we do?"

"Why? I'm a recycler of goods, an equalizer in a world of income disparity."

She wasn't sure whether to laugh or agree. He was rationalizing. She pushed her glasses to the top of her nose and said, "You and the late Chairman Mao."

Shady switched gears, educating her more. "Can you recognize an alarm system?"

"Besides barking dogs? I've seen pictures."

"You watch. They'll become common when prices fall, and they'll make your work harder. Go to a library and study alarm schematics."

"I will, Shady."

He peppered her with questions. "The best way to get into a house?"

"The hidden key. People are dumb. Under the mat, in the flowerpot tray, hanging behind the porch steps. It takes about thirty seconds to find them."

"And if you can't get in after sixty seconds?"

"Honestly? I'm gone."

"When you see premises that appear to be easy pickings—"

"I don't go near without a plan and surveillance."

Shady's mustache twitched as he thought. "You need to develop a sixth sense that's aware of every single sound and shadow."

"I'm from the country. You better believe I hear spiders crawling on walls."

"That's a good skill to have in Florida. Don't forget that pills are fast cash."

"Uh-uh. Too many kids at my school were a mess from drugs."

"Then the good news is you won't get caught for possession of coke or 'ludes with intent. Do you go in nights at all?"

"That gets spooky. Why wait till night when cops and rent-a-cops get serious about patrolling?"

"Do you watch for trash pickup days?"

She nodded.

"Where did you acquire this vast knowledge of the criminal arts?" he asked. "Did your school have classes on theft?"

"I've learned more with each job. And I read."

"Interesting. Obviously, I read the wrong books in my youth." Shady lowered his sunglasses. His eyes were brown and pouchy. "Do you find cash money?"

"Once in a while."

"Aw, you crafty fibber. It's okay, I want you to stash it away, go to college, and get out of this life."

Get out. There it was again. Get out. Shady meant it kindly, but her hackles rose.

"The older you get, the tougher it is out there. And you're not cut out to live a life of crime."

"Why? I revel in this freedom."

"You're too smart. Did they tell you your IQ in school?"

She gave her half smile. "A kid in my class pilfered the test results and read our IQs aloud."

"And?" asked Shady, sunglasses now hanging from his mouth.

"Let's say it shut up my classmates. They never teased me again for wearing glasses or having no spending money. They called me the Brain."

"I knew it," he said, slapping the table. "You'll go to college, make a success of yourself."

She almost tipped the table over getting up. She regretted letting Shady into her personal life. "You don't have a say in my life, and I don't need another parent."

Shady righted the table and grabbed for her sleeve. She yanked her arm back. Didn't he see she needed her freedom as much as he did his?

"MJ, MJ. I'm trying to gift you, not take away your autonomy."

She remained standing on the sticky floor, but she didn't leave. Shady, in fact, did seem to care. She'd have to consult the dictionary for the meaning of the word *autonomy*.

"Let me lay one good deed on you. I can boost your preparation for college. Academia and I weren't meant for each other, but I miss teaching fresh minds, and that's what I trained to do."

"You'd do that?"

"I got Tad to the point where Florida Southern accepted him, but he's a man who can't be inactive. He claims to have classroom claustrophobia, which nails the academic vibe exactly."

"That's why he cleans offices?"

"He's establishing a solid work history."

She reflected on the GED preparation book she'd bought at a yard sale. About the questions she couldn't find answers to and couldn't ask a librarian without drawing attention to herself. Shady had an abundance of answers.

His glasses were back on. "I do miss the classroom. It would be my honor to teach your outstanding mind."

The next day Shady took her, in the balky car Tad's backstreet mechanic friend retrofitted for driving by hand, to a dusty used bookstore where, from swarms of disorganized books, she bought a sack of texts.

CHAPTER TWELVE

May 1977

MJ plied her trade with the eagerness of an avenger. On her hardware store calendar, she marked the days until her eighteenth birthday in late December. Until she was no longer a minor, and probably beyond, she wanted no record of herself, no chance for family or social workers to interfere in her life. With ever-increasing caution, she expected to amass a consequential bankroll by the time she graduated. She'd accelerate her education—a degree in three years should be a cinch. Anyone could take courses without matriculating, and she planned to matriculate for a degree at the last possible moment.

She met with Shady three days a week. Usually in the bar, usually while Shady drank. She didn't know how he stayed this brainy with liquor and dope constantly in him, but his puns and wordplay kept her on her toes. She took pride in matching his cleverness. She and Tad punned on puns until Shady surrendered.

Shady had no experience with the new math, but Duval Lanamore was a whiz. Shady talked him into tutoring her.

Science put her to sleep. Shady woke her interest with a visit to the Clearwater Marine Aquarium, and on field trips to beaches and cypress swamps that were accessible to the balloon-wheeled, battery-run go-cart he and Tad rigged up. They went to Cape Canaveral for a day. The trips led her to the library for more learning.

Tad taught her how to pick locks and worked with her on cracking safes. He knew the secrets. She was an avid scholar in this subject.

"The fools put burglar alarm stickers on their windows when there's no alarm," Tad said. "Like we can't tell? They hang fake alarm boxes. They make sure nobody's getting their shit, but they pay big bucks to a security company."

"It's alarming," said Shady, completely straight-faced. He'd thrown out the challenge.

"Be careful you don't al-arm the bomb."

"Or strongarm it."

"Underarm it?"

"You'd need strong armature."

She ventured, "Arm and Hammer deodorant?"

Tad and Shady grimaced.

She rucked up one cheek and said, "Sorry."

They shared a laugh. Shady told her to go study. She lowered the books she needed into her backpack.

Home was changing. Mrs. Belda's grandson was getting married, leaving a room for Mrs. Belda in her daughter's apartment in New Jersey. The Beldas wanted MJ to babysit the condo until it sold. MJ celebrated by dancing Hop around her room. Mrs. Belda kindly left her library card.

MJ hadn't made friends her age in Depot Landing, except for Christina, and had not one thing in common with boy-crazy high school girls. Boys barely existed for her, except to get in her way. The bookmobile librarian had become a friend, a cheery round-cheeked Native Alaskan woman with skin as tan as a lot of Floridians. They talked about writers, the librarian recommended books, and she made MJ promise to go to college.

She caught the bus that traveled to the college library in Four Lakes. The route passed a pond with an ibis rookery. Most of them were off fishing, but a few glimpses of white feathers in the trees made her smile at the magic of their existence.

As she thought of the ibises' homes, she fumed at extravagant, land-hogging residences and the pandemic of shabby strip malls. The air-conditioning wasn't operating, and the open windows let in pesky love bugs. She carried a bandana to sop sweat from her face and glasses; today she used it to bat the bugs away. Right then, she couldn't imagine the freak local January snowstorm Shady told her about.

The bus made a stop at a half-built-out development of homes. She'd seen the new movie *Star Wars* the weekend before, and the music returned, full volume, in her head. On impulse, against her sworn resolve not to be impulsive, she pulled the buzzer and swung off the bus. Hadn't Shady recommended that she work farther from home?

Cars entered the development by a front coded gate, but pedestrians walked right in.

How pedestrian, she thought with a grin. She needed to share that one with Tad, though guaranteed to set off a cascade of puns involving crosswalks, happy walks, winking walk signs, pedometers, and who knew what else.

The Mediterranean-style homes were one story with no children or toys in sight, which signaled mature, established owners. A brown-skinned man drove a riding mower along the lawns, throwing a seductive scent, but she knew the appalling amount of water grass demanded and how little such workers earned. She ambled, covertly studying the houses, silently humming the *Star Wars* theme. The development boasted a pond, a clubhouse, swimming pools in most of the lanais, and, according to a sign, a nine-hole golf course.

She thought of the comical wild turkeys she was thrilled to see return each year in Depot Landing, poking at the ground with their harems following. A pair of wood storks paraded this private street, a strange long-legged mix of unappealing and lovely, especially in flight, when they spread their black underwings. This development was once their home. What right did humans have to destroy it? To come in and raze the land for a profit, to live in comfort and luxury, while animals fended in tighter and tighter territories?

These absent thieves of nature enraged her—they didn't use the land half the year. These were the streets paved with gold. Was the American dream solely about greed?

She'd put no gear in her book bag today. Tad was forever on her for recklessness, but shoot, why not hack away at their comfort as they hacked away the trees that held nests?

One of the houses was set off to the side a bit. No security signs were on view. She peered in the garage window and saw a golf cart under a storage cover, unplugged from its charger, and raised above the ground to keep the weight off its tires. So they favored golf courses over trees and birds, did they? This household deserved it; she was going in. These people weren't returning anytime soon.

The garage side door faced a blank garage wall next door. Its simple contractor's lock took seconds to spring, but damn, the door into the house itself was deadbolted. From a seam in her denim shorts she dug out the paper clip lockpick Tad made for her.

Stinging sweat ran into her eyes, and her glasses slid down her nose. She tied her bandanna around her head. Foolishly unprepared, she hurried, fumbled, repeated the whole process with clammy fingers. She saw the wire that ran under a braided entry carpet. A pressure pad? She skirted it with large steps. The smell of a flowery deodorizer permeated the air. She sneezed. Her K-Mart watch showed almost five minutes had elapsed. Quick, quick, quick, she told herself. The hutch drawer held nothing but a telephone book.

The living room boasted a wall of books. She remembered Tad telling her how often he'd found stashes behind heavy art and reference books. She pulled out a few and, new as the home was, didn't find a thing except mouse droppings. No wonder they used a deodorizer— mouse pee stink wasn't far off from ammonia.

Bag in hand, she sped through the closets, the mattresses, behind the dressers in the master bedroom. They'd left nothing behind. The residents used that new horrendously potent Irish Spring soap in their bathrooms. She sneezed again and, by rote, tugged at a tissue from a decorative box holder. The whole unit rose with the tissue and made a clunking sound.

Shoot, she thought, she almost missed this trick. A couple of baby blocks had been glued inside the plastic holder, propping up a flat box of tissues and creating a hiding place. Hello, green stuff.

Nine minutes now. She stuffed the envelope of cash into the back of her underwear, securing it with a weensy binder clip she carried in a pocket for that purpose. Get out, get out, get out. She shouldered her bag to sweep through the kitchen. From a cabinet she knocked to the counter a box of crackers.

"Freeze," a commanding female voice said.

She swung around and threw the crackers at a head over a blue uniform.

In the second it took the cop to catch the crackers, MJ whirled away and dashed across the smooth tile floors, book bag thudding on her back, toward the front door. Which was triple locked.

One lock was keyed from indoors. Trapped, she sneezed again.

CHAPTER THIRTEEN

"Hands against the door," ordered the cop. "Legs spread."

MJ hesitated, glancing left and right for a window, a clear route, and holding her hands where she could strip her gloves on the sly.

"*Now.*"

She sucked in her stomach and stood straight in hopes the clip in the small of her back would go unnoticed. Her eyes watered from whatever was making her sneeze.

The cop didn't search hard but politely patted her down enough to find her knife.

The *Star Wars* theme returned and she said, "Hey, that's my father's."

The officer kept an eye on her and slid the knife from its sheath. The tip had broken off during another job, when she pried open a stuck-solid window.

"Doesn't your father know you're supposed to sharpen these things? Turn toward me with your hands on top of your head."

Her head had become a helmet of sweated hair. She sneezed. Her glasses were at the tip of her nose. She rotated slowly, a child again, the officer her mother.

"Why, you're a baby," said the cop, sympathy softening her authoritative voice. Regardless, she slid the knife into a pocket on the side of her uniform pants.

Why did people say that? The officer was white, her name tag read *Culpepper*, and her badge labeled her Four Lakes Auxiliary Police. She wasn't wearing a gun.

"You want to tell me what you're doing in here, kid? Let's start with your name."

"Don't send me home. Put me in jail before you send me back there," she pleaded, nose running and helpless to wipe it.

"That bad?"

She thought she saw, in the officer's eyes, another flash of sympathy.

"Name, kid."

Her brain scrambled for any name other than her own.

"Oh, come on. How long can it take the simplest person to conjure a name?"

"I'm not the simplest person, and you're not a real cop." She pointed at the Auxiliary patch.

Officer Culpepper put her hands on her hips. "When we get the rules changed, I'll be the first woman on the force and, hands-down, the greatest patrol person who walks this earth." She winked at MJ.

"The female Kojak?"

"Without the Tootsie Pops. Until then, I marshal munchkins across streets. I watched you leave the bus."

"Aren't you going to arrest me? To show them you can?"

The officer folded her arms. "I'm thinking about it, but President Carter pardoned the Vietnam War draft evaders. Who am I to show less mercy?" She was studying MJ. "Depending on your story."

"I'm MJ Beaudry," she said and idly kicked at the box of crackers on the floor. "I'm hungry."

"No beating around the bush—how'd you get in?"

"The door was unlocked."

"Tell me another one. Did you know your face turns pink when you lie? Where is home?"

"Houston."

"Yeah, right, and my name is Ben Franklin. You may know how to pick a lock, but I can suss out a lie before someone finishes telling it. You sound about as Texas as my dog Kirby."

"If you send me back, I don't know what will happen to me. And I'm not trying to kid you." The house's scent hadn't stopped tickling her nose. Worried about the envelope coming loose, she stifled a sneeze.

The officer searched her bag and handed it back. "Come on, let's slip away from this smelly house"—the cop had sneezed too—"and find you a burger and a shake while we talk about your situation."

She thought of running for it, but at that moment, she wanted nothing more than to follow Officer Culpepper wherever she led. She had the impression this woman—with her tanned, strong arms, big smudged glasses like her own, sun-bleached hair cut in a mullet, and a laugh so deep it had to start in her heart—might understand about Christina.

At the A&W they ate in the cab of the officer's pickup truck, which she suspected had been manufactured before air-conditioning was invented. Pool cleaning equipment lay in the bed. The fries were overly salted, and the smell of the charred meat revolted her. The radio played the mournfully exciting "Hotel California." On the floor of the cab Cheetos bags, both empty and full, lay scattered.

Although Officer Culpepper asked too many questions, MJ became more and more convinced the woman was an ally. Despite that, no way was she leaving herself open.

"What will you do now?" asked Officer Culpepper.

"Isn't this my last meal? I thought you were taking me to jail."

She recognized the expression on the cop's face, which reminded her of Christine's when MJ had spun wild dreams for her.

"I was pretty squirrelly as a teen. Maybe I made mistakes too. I don't think you can look after yourself properly any more than I could."

She wiped her mouth with a napkin, folded it, and put it in her pocket. "I'm fine. Thanks for the meal."

"Sheesh. You don't give me much of a choice. How can I let you go when I'll only catch you stealing food again? No way."

"You won't."

"Because you won't break into another house or because you'll be more careful?"

Lying came too naturally to her. "I told you—I was hungry."

"What's plan B?"

She was getting tired of this do-gooder charade. Was she nuts, giving herself over to a police officer who needed to make approximately one lousy call to discover she was a runaway? She knew better than to trust a cop.

"May I be excused to use the restaurant bathroom?"

"I want you to leave your bag with me. I'll drive you to wherever you lay your weary head."

That's what I'm afraid of, she thought as she entered the A&W, hoping the officer would return the books in her bag to the library. A counterperson gave her a key and directed her to the toilet. As she exited, she held the key up for the cop before walking around the side. With the open door briefly hiding her, she took off running.

She crested a hill into someone's backyard, hurtled past a rope hammock, sprinted the length of a long, unpaved, sandy driveway and into a dead-end street. The only way out was through the jungle across the street. At any rate, her sneezing stopped in the fresh air. Though not actually jungle, the shrill calls, squawks, and chatter within the bushy thickets and trees made it sound as jungley as the movies.

Dodging low, stiff fronds and thorns that sliced at her legs, she stormed straight through wild feathery plants, vast spiderwebs, and giant sword ferns. Mosquitos fizzed past her ears. Flies circled the top of her head. At a glimpse of a black snake, her legs pumped harder. Despite the pursuer and her discomfort with all this glorious strangeness, she wanted to shout at the sheer adventure of running through it.

Who knew if Officer Culpepper was sincere? MJ didn't flee family captivity to be cooped up in a more restricted situation. She was as wild as Florida. No, wilder, like the river she left.

Ahead, the low scrub she charged though opened up. Tall, branchless tree trunks provided no cover. She tromped on weeds and trash that raised a noxious stew of smells, then lurched to a faltering stop at the bare edge of a sandy drop, gulping air. Below the steep slope, a trail led left and right, several yards above a river. What choice did she have? On her bottom, she slithered in near free-fall to the path. This reminded her of the night she left Depot Landing, descending to her real life. She ran left, the quickest route to cover.

In spots the trail had collapsed. She didn't want to take a tumble and clawed across each gap using roots and stunted plants. She'd be lucky not to grab poison oak or ivy or the sumac Mrs. Lanamore warned her about.

The cop was not in sight—she slowed. The trail was barely visible here—it wasn't safe to run, but the woman was in all likelihood calling for real police. An alligator sunned itself on the sand below. She hurried to pass it, thinking she'd rather meet Ted Bundy, who'd escaped yet again and could be anywhere.

She cried out when the packed sand crumbled under her step, and she dipped to her knees. The alligator stirred directly below her. She scrambled for traction on the cliff itself, caught one thick half-buried vine, and stretched a leg toward the next solid ground. The root drooped under her weight.

A stout knotted rope bounced in front of her.

"Grab it."

In a fraction of a second, she recognized the officer's voice, noted a second alligator waddling from the water, knew she didn't have time to make a decision between the alligators and the law, and thought of the saying, *up to my neck in alligators*.

She grabbed the rope.

"Hang on," called the cop.

Try as she might, she could not gain a foothold. She wished for those rubber gloves between her hands and the bristly rope. She caught sight of a second figure pulling as the strength ebbed from her hands and arms. The rope wore away the edge on the cliff above, its sand falling into her mouth, her ears, her eyes. How fast did alligators move? Maybe Florida wasn't as fantastic as she'd thought.

If she made it to the top, she'd run fast enough to evade the cop again. But was that fair, after this rescue?

The cop and her backup dragged her over the edge by her wet armpits. The cop put her rope-burned hands in cold steel handcuffs.

"Why did you run?" asked the cop, panting and sweating as hard as MJ. "I wasn't arresting you."

"No way you're shipping me back where I came from." Her voice shook from anger and draining adrenaline. "I'm serious about that."

She flashed to her last morning in Depot Landing, standing on the side of Route 14 in the biting wind. That week she would catch her breath riding the bus, alternately lamenting the dumb sadness of the disappearing act she'd pulled on her so-called family, and wildly excited about the life she anticipated in Key West.

The cop sat her up. "You sorry, desperate kid."

Through glasses streaked with sand and sweat, she made out the other rescuer, a guy with short light hair also plastered with sweat and a jacket with a name embroidered across the chest pocket.

Officer Culpepper said, "Meet my best buddy, Jaudon. I called her on the A&W phone when I saw you go toward the sand cliff. Jaudon brought the rope. Sheesh, munchkin, can't you see I'm trying to keep this a civilian matter? You're not making it easy."

Jaudon walked with the slight forward slant of someone climbing a hill at top speed. Wrapping the rope as she approached, Jaudon grinned and said, "I'd offer to shake with you, but I see you're tied up."

What kind of joker was this raspy-voiced woman?

She supposed the cold metal handcuffs meant she was undeniably arrested. She'd never get away with these two teamed up.

The cop reached to steady her as MJ struggled to stand with her hands behind her back. She shook the make-believe cop off but followed her. To her surprise, they were close to a road. If she'd known to take a right before her plunge, she could have caught a bus.

CHAPTER FOURTEEN

June 1977

Jaudon moved on from Mobley Road to disassemble the store on Church Pond Road. Customers continued to drum on the roller door, pleading that they were short of milk or beer. It got her wishing Pops had continued to sell his backwoods liquor. This lonely road with nothing but an orange farm across the street and the white shack of a rural post office next door would be an ideal outlet.

She heard someone at the side door. She flexed her broad toughened hands, always dry and sore from handling cardboard boxes and stacking product in the cooler. She yelled, "We're closed."

"It's Cullie. Open up."

She went over and cracked the door. "You gave me a shock, Cullie Culpepper."

Cullie brushed past her, smelling of pool chemicals. Behind her, she hauled the same black-haired teen they rescued from the alligators about a month ago. Her hands were again shackled behind her. Cullie was in uniform.

"What in tarnation? Can't you keep this ragamuffin clear of trouble?"

Cullie jangled her substantial key ring until she isolated the right one and unlocked the handcuffs.

"She's a lost puppy." Jaudon imagined Berry calling her an appealing lost puppy, because MJ was going to be handsome one of these days.

"Or a jumpy squirrel," said Cullie. "I cuffed her to keep her with me this time."

The kid stood like she was waiting for the starter gun, peeved eyes cast downward, mad as all get-out if Jaudon read her right.

"Glad to see you again."

MJ dipped her head once, saying nothing.

"You look beat."

"She's had a hard day. Haven't you, MJ?"

"Don't patronize me," the girl said.

Cullie, playful, shook MJ by the shoulders from behind. "I caught her wandering a neighborhood. Gosh knows if she was casing houses for her dinner again. She needs a job and safe digs, or she'll be in real trouble and sent home, wherever that is, to a bad situation."

"I'll tell you right now," MJ said, "it's no home."

Not what Jaudon needed today, a cantankerous adolescent. "A job, Cullie? You know I laid off this crew at the beginning of the week, and they were all related to my mother. How can I offer a stranger a job?"

"Sheesh. You have a job under a table somewhere, mi amiga. Say she's your sister."

"I can't pay her legally without working papers. I won't pay her under the table. This is an honest business."

MJ jammed her glasses higher on her nose. "Honest? Where does honest get you?" She sidled toward the door.

Jaudon opened her mouth, but had no words.

"You're not doing me any good here, grouchy," Cullie said, pulling her back. "Don't be so paranoid. No one's snooping in the Social Security files to see if you're earning wages. Go sign up. If your folks haven't located you by now, they're not trying."

"There you have it. I'm not hiring Miss Underage if she has to hide. And if I paid her off the books, you'd have to arrest me for hiring her," said Jaudon, offering her hands for cuffing.

"Come on. Don't make me deliver her to Child Welfare. Picture yourself there."

Cullie bored into her with her eyes. "What—" Jaudon started to say. She remembered Cullie had a notion MJ was family. She had her doubts; this little girl would call an alligator a lizard to get what she wanted.

"MJ?" She watched the girl's threatening eyes. "Are you a thief?"

MJ raised the left end of her mouth, dimpling her cheek, not saying a word.

"She was hungry," Cullie said.

"You keep saying that till you believe it, Cullie. And you want me to hire a thieving squirrel to work for me? I sell food, and she's mad enough at the world to bite the hand that feeds her. Dollars to doughnuts she'll give me squirrel rabies."

MJ started toward the door. "Give it up, Officer. She doesn't want me either."

Cullie caught her wrist. "Hold your horses, amiga. I'm jeopardizing my future career for you."

"I never asked you to."

"Did the chief put you on the payroll yet, Cullie?"

"Fingers crossed. The city councillors vote on hiring women patrol cops Monday night. It'd be great if you and Berry showed up at the courthouse in support. You too, Squirrel."

MJ performed a backward hop, her voice a squawk. "The courthouse? Are you crazy?"

"Maybe so, maybe so," Cullie said. "As a matter of fact, I'll deliver you to the lockup where I'll have you on site."

The child dropped into a fighting crouch, her nose squinched to keep her glasses from toppling off her face. "If James Earl Ray pulled off that Tennessee prison escape yesterday, don't you think I can too?"

Jaudon feared for this scared girl, foolishly brave, who sounded at the end of her tether. If they sent her back where she came from, she'd run again, get herself in worse trouble. What if she gave her a job, let her know she was not alone? They might make a good citizen of her yet. Jiminy, MJ was their next generation.

She heaved her chest in surrender. "I suspect this will come back to plague me, but why don't we go talk to Berry and Gran."

MJ moved minutely away from Cullie. "I have a job and a roof over my head and friends of my own."

Cullie looked confused. "Didn't you tell me your job ends in a few days, and your friends are crooks?"

MJ got right in Cullie's face. "I didn't call Tad and Shady crooks. They treat me better than my former family, never harmed me, and they take me seriously. Shady's preparing me for college."

"Sure," Cullie said. "Locksmith college."

Jaudon tried to figure out who they were talking about. Someone a tad shady?

Cullie held out her arms in appeal. "After you left for your store that day, MJ and I got serious. I warned her to stay away from her friends. One is a petty thief and the other a fence."

She wasn't surprised. "Lie down with dogs and you'll get up with fleas."

"I'm afraid they'll use her and drop her in hot water she can't escape. Meanwhile, she's a live-in caregiver for someone who's leaving Florida in a few days. There goes her living space. She's family, Jaud. She needs us."

"No, I don't. My employer asked me to stay on until her apartment sells."

She now doubted every word that left this kid's mouth. "Bridle your tongue before you tell another lie."

MJ made a reproving face, but asked Cullie, "What did you mean about family? That I'm family?"

Cullie and Jaudon exchanged glances.

"I'll tell you what," said Cullie.

Jaudon put a knuckle between her teeth. She held her breath, but nodded an okay to Cullie.

"We like women."

The side of MJ's mouth rose into an unexpected dimple. "There's a family of us?"

Jaudon laughed her tension out, reminded of her innocent self. She and Berry were in college when they met Rigo, their starter gay friend. He basically filled them in on the life, dragged them to a bar, and, over the years, ate Gran's home cooking until she threatened to open a restaurant.

Cullie checked her watch. "I need to move along, lickety-split. I have a pool job that needs doing north of here. If it doesn't get too late, I'll stop by your house."

Cullie used the store bathroom to change into her pool cleaning shorts, company shirt, and the straw safari hat that had been on its last legs for years. Jaudon kept packing and lugging heavy boxes onto a platform cart to roll to her car. She heard the nasal honk of a peahen on the post office stoop threatening a patron.

Jaudon snuck peeks as MJ traced her upper lip with the stem of her glasses. The little squirrel was completely free to take off.

On the contrary, MJ straightened her shoulders, returned to the store, and, in a resolute voice, asked, "Can I give you a hand? You don't have to pay me—so you don't get into trouble."

Moments later, Cullie came rushing to her pickup, a bag of Cheetos in hand. "I left cash for these on the counter," she called. She stopped dead and gaped at MJ, who now wore a Beverage Bay vest.

Jaudon winked from the back of the company van as she took hold of the cash register MJ hoisted to her.

CHAPTER FIFTEEN

July 1977

Berry was fixing dinner with Gran when Jaudon brought MJ home two weeks later.

Berry moved toward MJ. "Who have we here?" She held the rumpled, fiery-eyed girl at arm's length.

"MJ's been helping me out at Mobley Road."

"You look like you might need a hug as much as you do food." Berry opened her arms and wrapped them around the girl, who shifted away once released.

"I smell my pan burning up," said Gran, hurrying back to the stove. "I've never been this scatterbrained before."

"What are you cooking?" Jaudon grabbed a few croutons from a bowl and dipped them in grated American cheese. She made a show of sniffing the air. "Jiminy, that's sweet pea, ham, and noodle casserole. You're in for a treat, MJ Beaudry."

"Shoo, shoo," said Gran. "That's the topping. No stealing."

"Hear that?" Jaudon was looking at MJ. "No stealing."

MJ looked away.

Gran *tsk*ed. "Not Reverend Skunkweed again."

"That's yesterday's news."

The screen door off the front porch slammed. Berry asked, "Who else did you invite, Jaudon?"

"No one, to my recollection."

"Yoo-hoo. I smell my supper cooking."

Rigo Patate appeared in the doorway, cherubic and husky, in his middle twenties, with a head full of long loose coppery curls, and skin the tone called olive. Berry saw his convertible Valiant, the car that replaced the fancy Camaro he sold when his father cut off his sissy son's funds. Rigo's wardrobe took a hit too and now consisted almost entirely of well-laundered light-colored chinos and 1960s T-shirts. Proudest of his Rosa Parks *Nah* and *God Bless Tiny Tim* models, today he wore his flirty sailor muscle shirt.

"How are you, my darlings? It's been forever. Jimmy Neal sends his regrets." Rigo narrowed his eyes at Jaudon. "He's beyond busy running your store and finishing his degree."

"Let's hope there's a store to keep running."

When Rigo was disinherited, his strapping lover Jimmy Neal Skaggs insisted on picking up the slack and applied for work at the Beverage Bay. Momma, who knew nothing about him, especially that he was gay, hired him. Jaudon made sure she gave him a stable schedule to complete his nursing practicum nights in the ER.

"Oh, hun, are your save-the-store efforts too late?"

"The lawyer and the city are duking it out. I'm shutting two stores. I'm opposed to bankruptcy on principle."

Jaudon went to the kitchen for some Cokes, and Berry followed to help Gran.

Berry hiked her eyebrows at Jaudon. "You took on someone new when you're cutting back?"

Jaudon was balancing three bottles on her way out. "I'll explain later."

Gran whispered, "If that child's working age, I'm two years older than dirt."

"She only comes off as young—MJ says she's almost eighteen. And I'm hoping to help her dodge trouble."

"She's prettier than a glob of butter melting on a stack of wheat cakes," Gran said. "I'd watch that devilish flare in her eyes, if I were you."

"Like a little boy about to pull a prank." Once alone with Gran, Berry confided, "I'm pleased Rigo showed up. I'll be interested to see his take on this MJ. We don't need another Lari."

Gran asked, "Was that the one who went crazy on you? Living in a tree trunk across the street on our land? Just her appearance gave me nighthorses."

Berry smiled and untwisted a waist tie on Gran's starched and ironed apron. She knew Gran wasn't going to change her ways. "She didn't go crazy. She stopped taking her medications. Allison keeps in touch. Lari's doing well back in Minnesota."

"Whatever you want to call it, she acted crazy as a bullbat. You know this one's trouble too. It's like she fell from the sky. Now come over here and pay attention. I want you to remember how to make this casserole. I won't be here forever."

"Okay, but you need to write your recipes for us someday."

"These egg noodles? A pound of them goes quite a ways. You'll end with eight to ten cups. You don't want to overwhelm the other ingredients."

Berry heard new voices and poked her head around the kitchen door. Cullie and Allison were with the rest in the living room. Cullie, orange-lipped, offered around her Cheetos.

Berry reported back, and Gran said, "Oh, my Lord, we're stretched to feed Rigo, never mind two more. Rigo and Cullie could eat a Popeyes empty on their own."

"Rigo's only dropping off psych materials. I'll go see if the others are staying, Gran." She pecked her on her soft, sun-wrinkled cheek. "And don't worry, we can make do. Your concoction smells wonderful. I may steal it away to eat by my lonesome."

"Raise that window down before you go, pet. I'm about to bake into a casserole myself."

Berry met Allison leaving the kitchen. "Tonight's the important meeting about sworn female police. We can't stay, but keep me up to date on your problem child. I can put you in touch with resources. We need to support our next generation."

"Is ten years a generation?"

Allison replied in a thoughtful manner. "It may be a generation for gays."

Berry took in MJ's feisty brown eyes, the easy, almost Elvis, pout of her lips, the troublesome glasses. Arms folded, chin up, MJ now adopted the insolent stance of a teen boy about to take on the world. Her gaze was direct and serious and sensual. Yet the tips of her ears, poking out from her rebellious hair, were bright pink.

"Don't get worked up over nothing," MJ said. "I'm not a child, and I'm not a problem unless you make me one."

"Are you an emancipated minor?" asked Allison.

The side of MJ's mouth rose into an oddly charming smile. "I'm emancipated. I'll tell you that right now."

"In your mind," Cullie said.

Berry caught Allison watching her. Allison mouthed the words *cute kid*.

She went to the kitchen to tell Gran to relax, the others weren't staying to eat. Gran followed her back out, fanning herself with her apron and settling in the wing chair.

When Momma moved, she left behind both living room chairs. The cushions were of faded green bark cloth with a yellow pineapple pattern, worn, but good enough. The thick nubby curtains—patterned with jumbo bubblegum-pink hibiscus, hulking green leaves, and mango-colored parrots—were closed to keep out the heat. Nevertheless, the squeaky ceiling fan was on high, and the room was bright and, just then, noisy with guests. White swan end-table lamps sat at either end of the long Monkey Ward sofa. The cushions on both rattan chairs matched the curtains. Berry had switched the spindle-legged coffee table of her childhood with a cushioned storage unit where they kept the cat and dog toys.

"You'd know if you were an emancipated minor," Allison was telling MJ. As a city councillor and health department employee, Allison intended to drag the town into the second half of the twentieth century. Through her efforts on the council, Cullie would become a full cop.

"What's made you this resentful, MJ?" asked Rigo. "Why resist? We want to make life easier for gay people. We can get you counseling for anger management, housing, the means to finish school."

MJ said, "Are you kidding me? Why manage my anger? It serves me well."

MJ struck Berry as dog-tired.

Rigo said, "If anger's your engine, you're running on empty, hun."

MJ held out her wrist, too thin for its heavy-duty black field watch. "I need to catch a bus across town. I'll get fired if I miss making her dinner."

Cullie said, "I didn't fall off the turnip truck. Don't deny it—you'll go back to stealing, and you'll be homeless once your job ends."

Jaudon told Berry and Gran the story.

"If you find a bus to catch out here," said Gran, "let me know. With my little red Corvair gaining in years I'll need it."

MJ was lifting her bag. "There are buses on 60."

"That's two miles from here." Berry appealed to Rigo with her eyes.

He said, "My valiant Valiant will get you there in no time. You're not arresting this baby dyke, are you, Officer Culpepper?"

Cullie scratched her furrowed forehead.

"She's not," said Allison, a hand staying Cullie. "Let the child choose the life she wants to lead."

Jaudon stabbed a finger toward Allison. "You rabid feminist types, you won't admit women need protection, laws or no laws. Gran stood up for Berry, and Pops championed me, but who's looking out for MJ, except a couple of guys who might be using her?"

It was common knowledge that Jaudon disagreed with Allison on most issues, but Berry spoke up. "Allison's right. If you commit MJ to the authorities, she'll be in jail or in foster care or sent back where she didn't belong. Some families are as hurtful as any jail. Or more."

Berry and Allison spoke about the conditions at juvenile detention. Berry had seen several pregnant teens from that facility at work.

"You can see I can't close one store alone plus run the open ones," Jaudon said in a quiet voice. "We can work out payment. If I give you bus fare, will you come see me tomorrow?" From a pocket, she offered MJ a crumpled and damp ten. "That okay with you, Cullie?"

Leave it to Jaudon, thought Berry, to find a way.

Cullie made a skeptical face but nodded assent.

MJ said, "Shady's taking me to a book reading at the Tampa library tomorrow after I give my employer lunch and do her laundry. I can come by the next day," said MJ, accepting the bill. "Seriously, I promise I'll be there, if I can make it back to fix her dinner." She eyed Cullie again. "You won't bust me if I hang out with Jaudon, will you?"

Cullie grinned. "Don't bet on it."

After Cullie and Allison left, Jaudon and Berry walked MJ and Rigo into the dusty July heat. Two peacocks wandered in the front yard on full display, screeching in competition with each other. MJ watched their antics.

"Your first peacocks?"

MJ nodded, eyes fixed on the birds, an open-mouthed smile on her face.

"They don't make them better than Cullie Culpepper," Jaudon told MJ. "She's as easygoing as a baby's cradle and can make you laugh when you want to shoot yourself over your woes. There isn't a better friend."

Berry was nodding in agreement.

"Pardonnez-moi?" said Rigo over the roof of his car.

"Present company excluded, natch."

MJ turned away from the peacocks, face all innocence, and asked, "Seriously, can cops be fine people?"

Berry wondered: Can burglars—uncertain if that's what this sharp squirrel was—be fine people?

CHAPTER SIXTEEN

Autumn 1977

MJ continued helping at the old-fashioned Beverage Bays. She'd seen pictures of these drive-through stores, made possible once the automobile became popular. She enjoyed the physical labor and learning about business. It helped that Jaudon seemed to think she was parenting her—paying her under the table, slipping her extra cash, and promising, despite the Beverage Bay's financial state, to cover any dentist or doctor bills that came up.

Nurturers or not, she let neither Jaudon's store nor her studies with Shady interfere with her illegal activities.

Berry invited her to stay in a trailer out back of their house on Pineapple Trail, perfect except for transportation and her privacy. Also, she'd watched the swooping swallows patrol pretty Rainbow Lake; so many mosquitos, not nearly enough swallows.

Mrs. Belda's condo hadn't sold yet. For now, it belonged to MJ and Hop, empty of furniture except for her small bedroom. She ventured out to use the kitchen and bathroom and to keep things dusted. She'd stick with the place she knew and keep her freedom. She saved money like a Scrooge and schemed further independence. Maybe she'd one day take a crack at another neighbor in the ritzy condos next door.

While she boxed up goods, Jaudon made runs of equipment and products from the Church Pond Road location to the five stores Jaudon wrestled to keep open. Jaudon's red eyes and enduring air of bewildered distress told her that each visit to the lawyer brought more bad news.

Jaudon's mother was universally known as Momma. She'd built the Church Pond store to give jobs to her Batson family. The store was busy enough, though the relations didn't keep it any too clean, and an undeniable portion of the inventory walked off, never to be seen again. Jaudon said she advised closing it years ago, but her opinions never held water with Momma. MJ knew that scenario all too well.

Despite the closed sign, men came by after their shifts and trod around the store, hunting for a way to buy their tax-free whiskey. Jaudon explained this store used to offer home brew out the side window.

She rolled a dolly full of canned lunch meats to the truck when a wrinkle-faced man with a full gray beard, a stained neckerchief, and a tall, wide-brimmed hat spat tobacco juice on the driveway and walked into the open bay.

"Hey, we're closed," she told him, thinking here was another typical Florida character. She stopped to mop her face with a dust cloth and saw the man wave for Jaudon to follow him.

He lifted a tarp that lay over the bed of his pickup, packed full of gallon bottles. Jaudon was saying no repeatedly but took the scrap of paper the man passed to her.

MJ usually worked in silence, reviewing in her mind what she was studying with Shady. After what she'd seen, she took a chance and said, "I know people who might move that guy's bottles for him."

Jaudon continued to pack canned foods. "You didn't see that ol' cracker, buckaroo," she told MJ over her shoulder. "And, by the way, Berry said to invite you to come over to the house for dinner and watch that new show, *Love Boat*, with us. Rigo says he and Jimmy Neal adore it. They'll be there too. Want to come?"

MJ was sliding parts of a shelving unit into her cart.

"Excuse me, Boss. You can change the subject and ignore me, but I can't ignore what I saw. I'm not saying it's the best solution, but you could use a new source of income." Without waiting for an answer, she trundled away.

When she wheeled the empty dolly back. Jaudon was seated on a sealed box, back hunched, hands hanging between her knees. MJ knew she'd hit a nerve because the boss never idled. At the backroom sink, she rinsed out a wet dust rag. The water was tepid, but cooler than the air. She dunked under the spigot, not bothering to dry off, a useful trick for acclimating to her new home state.

She dripped in front of Jaudon, who burbled with laughter when she saw her. "Tell me more, please, Squirrel. Nothing I try to save the Bays is possible without capital. I need some right-minded options."

MJ was fond of the nickname. She continued to squirrel away

money and live hidden in her squirrel den. The name was always used with teasing affection.

She said, "Tad and Shady are pretty savvy. You know what I'm saying."

"Those two? Cullie says they're trouble."

"They're good to me, Boss." She lifted her chin, looking at Jaudon with narrowed eyes. "And they're my friends." She turned her back to jam soup cans into a carton.

"Home must have been pretty bad if you think you're safer with outlaws."

"Shoot, they're my breed of outlaws."

Jaudon said nothing as she stacked the dolly and wheeled it to the door. "Okay, Squirrel," she said. "Let's set a time to meet your kindly men."

CHAPTER SEVENTEEN

March 1978

The March evening was cool, Berry noted, only sixty-two degrees. Sunset was in full swing, gold spiking through the trees. The red tubes of coral honeysuckle flowered, drawing hummingbirds and bees. Jaudon pulled on a sweatshirt while she grilled barbecued ribs. The smoke pretty much kept the mosquitos away. On the plank table, Berry placed a casserole of fresh-picked green beans, cheese, and Tater Tots, then lit a citronella candle.

Gran did most of the talking over dinner. She thought the prices were lower at the Winn Dixie, but sometimes she'd go to Publix for the air-conditioning and to weigh herself on the free Toledo scale at the front entrance. She encouraged the girls to let her tidy the kitchen and take their evening walk before daylight disappeared.

Berry said, "We'll be home in time for *Laverne & Shirley*."

"Never doubted it. I'll have the TV warmed up."

They waited at the Eulalia Road railroad crossing while a maddeningly lengthy freight train took its time going west, its whistle howling. They'd both slept beside train racket since birth and waited for its passage with accustomed patience, voices raised to exchange the details of their day.

The crossing gates flipped open and they moseyed to Buttonbush Drive, which featured the only sidewalk in the neighborhood. Berry told Jaudon a funny story involving her boss Dr. Garza, a precocious child, and its mother, but Jaudon's gloom was almost visible, a weighty laundry sack of examination gowns on her hunched shoulders. With Jaudon's hands deep in the pockets of her cargo shorts, Berry whipped the mosquitos away with her hand.

Red, purple, and yellow azalea bloomed around set-back houses on large lots of grass. Camellias were bare of their red winter flowers, but patches of blue periwinkles bloomed on, and the leaves had returned to the buttonbushes, their green pods on the verge of popping into white spikey blossoms. This time of year was Berry's favorite, with spring a pod itself, waiting.

Jaudon sneezed at the early spring pollens.

"Angel." Berry heard the weariness in her own voice. "I can't live this way much longer. Your worries are eating you up. I need my angel back."

"I know, I know." Jaudon flicked a bug off her arm. She seemed to be trying to part an imaginary veil between her troubles and the self she had been before they beset her. "You're my forever romance—don't be riled at me, okay? I'm stuck in this no-win situation."

"I'm not judging you."

"Remember taking ethics in school? The theories seemed night-and-day easy to figure out."

"I remember medical ethics. Not the slightest bit simple."

"So, here I am, trying to live a normal life despite"—she swept a hand up—"this body and being born gay. Throw in a mentally ill mother, lose half your hearing, face bankruptcy, find yourself empty of resources, take chances with lost strangers—then, jiminy, a person has more problems than a math book. I said no to this idea when MJ suggested it, a couple of months ago."

"What idea? A seventeen-year-old comes to the rescue?"

"As of last December, MJ's a wily eighteen-year-old with business smarts. She has friends who have contacts." Jaudon peered at her through the twilight, perhaps gauging her reaction. "And we have Pops's connections."

She stumbled on a tree root between the cracks of the sidewalk and reached to steady herself against Jaudon.

"You're not talking about taking on your Pops's Dinkey Dew business, are you?"

"Pops bowed out from under-the-counter liquor sales a while back, Berr. Don't you remember Momma's relatives were running it at the Church Pond Road store and how incensed they were when I rousted them?"

"What a pile of trouble they are."

"Their legitimate inventory was evaporating, but Cousin Roy Jack and his hangers-on compensated with back door white lightning sales. Momma paid it no mind."

They were at the aged store catty-corner to a plant nursery. Jaudon held the door open, and they entered a den saturated with cigarette smoke. Berry asked for two Cokes. The proprietor, a mopey chain-smoker who'd known them since their childhoods, said, "What kind you want?"

"Grape, please."

"RC Cola."

The owner uncapped their bottles, wheezing, using the same behind-the-counter opener that Berry remembered from nearly twenty years ago. Jaudon brought a newspaper to the counter and paid.

The dusk had deepened. She heard the man lock the store behind them and saw him flip the open sign to closed.

Jaudon coughed. "I try to hold my breath in there."

They tapped the bottles together, as was their habit, and started home. Sporadic traffic passed. Jaudon opened the newspaper so Berry could see the headline under the date: March 21, 1978. "San Francisco Passes Extensive Homosexual Rights Bill." They locked eyes. Berry mouthed the word *wow*. Jaudon hid the page.

They crossed a street. She said, "But here and now, I have to tell you, this home brew business is making me uneasy."

"Believe me, Berr, I'm not about to go into it half-cocked."

"I can see that. You must have stewed on it a good while. Didn't we agree we'd never lie to each other?"

"I wasn't lying." She hung her head. "I was pondering. But what do you think? The county voted to stay damp way back when, meaning I can't legally sell anything over the 6.243 percent beer we stock at the Bays. I can't see another way out from under. It's worked for my family before."

"Why do you think this scheme will make money? What makes men buy illegal liquor?"

Jaudon shrugged. "Because it's a bit dangerous? And a lot cheaper."

Dangerous for who? Berry wondered.

Did she trust her lover's judgment or not? Was she capable of stepping away and letting her soul mate make business decisions? She had to, no matter she wanted to say, *Don't do this, Jaudon.* Fail or succeed, as Allison said about morally immature MJ, Jaudon deserved to take her lumps under her own steam, whatever the consequences. Jaudon never once intervened in Berry's path and encouraged whatever Berry proposed.

This, though, was criminal activity. Jaudon might suppose MJ and her pals were exposed, not her, but Jaudon was the conduit. When Pops had his Dinkey Dew sideline for years, he sold it neighbor to neighbor. For Jaudon to amass enough money to clear her—Momma's—debts, the operation Beverage Bay Inc. had to grow leaner. And more lucrative, but within the law. She wished their lawsuit had resolved. Elections since Jaudon was injured meant their lawyer basically started over with each county attorney appointed by the new Board of Commissioners.

One last mosquito whined in her ear, and she swatted it dead when it attacked her face. Where were Jaudon's highly prized principles?

Berry surprised herself with irritation at Jaudon's beseeching eyes.

She walked faster. "What I think is you better sleep in your room for a while."

"What?"

She quickened her steps. Sometimes she thought Jaudon didn't hear her on purpose.

Jaudon caught Berry's elbow.

Berry tugged on her left earring, a habit she used to center herself and silence sharper words. "We have such a good life. Why put it in jeopardy? What will I do if you're jailed?"

"Do you mean," Jaudon asked in the most pitiful, tiny voice Berry remembered hearing from her, "do you mean that you don't want to be with me anymore?"

"I don't want to be with someone who hates herself."

Jaudon jutted out her jaw. "I don't."

"You will."

Again, Jaudon asked what she'd said.

She wanted Jaudon to see an audiologist. Not hearing well wasn't good for business or for them, but Berry didn't want to nag. Nor did she want this conflict between them, but how to condone such a wrongheaded plan? How to shield her unsullied angel from herself? What about her own personal passion? She wasn't in the master's psych program for the money. She wanted people to have a chance, especially people like themselves. Jaudon among them.

Jaudon kept pace with her. The frogs were singing their raucous torch songs. "If I can pay off these debts, I can avoid bankruptcy. If I don't have to declare bankruptcy, I can honorably keep all the company's assets and get back on my feet. People depend on me. Employees, Pops and Momma."

"But who will back us? Your parents are responsible for the fallout from Momma's blunders. Not you personally."

"That's what I thought, but Pops took Bat off the Beverage Bay paperwork and substituted me. Don't forget, Pops is a truck driver and warehouseman by trade—he didn't know he needed to protect me. If we go into bankruptcy, I'm accountable. I lose my credit, and I'll be shamed in front of the whole county."

"Like they say on TV, you're left holding the bag, Jaudon. I've watched you drowning in this sea of troubles for months now. No wonder you're unreachable. I blamed it on your hearing loss."

"I'm trying to find a way out."

Thunder rumbled in the distance, but they were almost home.

"If not, the people you owe and the lawyers will take all we have? The house we live in?"

"I don't know if they can take our home or not," Jaudon said, giving in to her tears. Never good at stanching them, she didn't want Berry to see her cry yet again.

Passing another buttonbush, Berry wished for a button to push and right her world. "The creditors are out to steal your soul while they're at it."

"I know."

At times, the Great Spirit seemed to talk through her. "I love you all the way to your soul. I want you to fight for it. I can drop my master's degree plan and support you, Gran, and me with nursing, but I'm not bailing your parents out."

Jaudon balled her fists and struck her thighs with them. "I wouldn't hear of you paying my way, and you know it, Berr."

Berry walked to the porch steps. More thunder rolled overhead. This time they saw the lightning, but the temperature had risen, and after walking the drizzle fell cool and pleasant on her bare arms. They sat. She put one arm around Jaudon's waist and lay her head on her shoulder.

She closed her eyes, breathed in the fecund plant smells, and thought about the Great Spirit. She didn't know if she was tightening her hold on Jaudon to cushion her or to anchor herself. She visualized the Great Spirit embracing them both with a love beyond what she was able to summon or fathom. That's the love she needed here, above her narrow view of worldly concerns. *I can't live any life except my own. It's my job to leave her to her dream.*

"I don't want to know about the liquor."

"I won't tell you."

"I won't hazard my career in nursing, doing what I'm born to do."

"There's no way you're legally associated with any of this. Leave it to me. I'll be your safety," said Jaudon.

How, thought Berry, can someone look vulnerable one minute and powerful the next? The combination ignited her every time, and after telling Gran they were too tired to watch TV, she pulled Jaudon toward her darkened bedroom.

CHAPTER EIGHTEEN

"Make sure you lock your car, Boss," MJ instructed with the assurance of a Rainbow Gap native. "Car thefts are the order of the day on Laudre Flats Boulevard."

She got together with Jaudon at Pansy's Home Cooking on an early Saturday afternoon. A couple of great egrets, bright in the sunlight, hunted in the high weeds and rushes that grew in brackish water behind an outbuilding at the back of the car wash lot. The birds in Florida took her breath away each time she saw them, a letdown too, as they shouldn't have to hunt behind the concrete that covered what once had been their homes. She thought herself privileged to live among these masterpieces of nature.

"I never stopped at this restaurant before," said Jaudon. "And I've lived by the railroad tracks on Eulalia all my life, not two miles from here."

They leaned on the car and, over the noise of traffic, trying to make her arrival sound like a grand adventure, she told Jaudon about the truck driver becoming mean and abandoning her on Laudre Flats Boulevard and how Tad and Shady defended her. How Tad's mother fed her, and Duval took her to find work. Her story, even without the light-fingered parts, brought to mind myths she'd read. Telling it gave her a sense of wholeness, affirmed who MJ Beaudry was.

"Tad's mother, Mrs. Lanamore, owns the restaurant. The best food in town. Come on, I'll treat you to the best old-fashioned shake in Lecoats County."

"I'm about to close," Mrs. Lanamore called as they entered. "My word, it's our lost child. Go ahead and lock the door and pull the shades." She looked at Jaudon. "Who's this?"

"My boss at the Beverage Bays, Jaudon Vicker."

"You're too much of a cub for such a responsible job, Jaudon. I'm pleased to make your acquaintance."

Jaudon grinned. "I'm glad to meet you too. Your restaurant does smell of home cooking. Now I know about you, I'll be bringing Berry and Gran. We usually go to Mudfoot's Fish Camp Restaurant."

"Word is, Mudfoot's is good, but I prefer somewhere more comfortable for my people."

Jaudon patted her cowlicks into place. "Jiminy. You're right. There's no one but white people in there. I'm sure sorry, Mrs. Lanamore, and I will say something about it to Mudfoot."

Mrs. Lanamore briefly closed her eyes and sighed. Presumably, she heard the same words from every third white person and was too gracious, or too weary of it all, to say more. "What can I get you girls?"

"A couple of your shakes," MJ told her. "If it's not too much trouble."

Mrs. Lanamore called over her shoulder. "*Tay-ud?* Have you cleaned the milkshake machine yet?"

"I'll get to it, Muma."

They followed Mrs. Lanamore to the counter and took stools.

Jaudon's voice, quieter than usual, sounded humbled. "I hear you're feeding this orphan squirrel."

"Squirrel. Yes, she is that." Mrs. Lanamore scrutinized MJ, now a robust five seven, her fuzzy midlength crew cut giving her yet another inch. "At home, how the squirrels raided our ackee trees."

MJ pointed to the ackee and salt fish on the café's menu, and Jaudon made a face.

"Never heard of it, business lady? It's the national fruit of Jamaicans." Mrs. Lanamore addressed MJ. "I know you want a vanilla shake, rascal. How about you, Miss Jaudon Vicker?"

"I grew up in Rainbow Gap. You might guess I want strawberry."

"I use berries from a friend's quarter-acre plot in Plant City. Luscious despite freezing."

Jaudon said, "Good to know there's one independent farmer left. There aren't as many fields as there used to be. Dig, dig, dig, build, build, build."

Over the roar of the milkshake machine, Mrs. Lanamore said, "You must be sitting pretty, all the new homes coming in. I'm getting more regulars."

Jaudon grimaced. "I wish. MJ's been backing me while I dismantled two of our stores. My momma has dementia, and we didn't catch what she was doing with the money from the business soon enough."

Mrs. Lanamore's eyes lost their usual sternness. "That's hard. Will you recover? Will she?"

"The doctors can't predict about Momma. I've worked in the business since I was a toddler, my brother is an Army lifer, and Pops is home taking care of Momma. I'm in charge. The accountant and lawyer are doing what they can about the stores. I don't know what I'll do if I lose them."

Jaudon tipped back her head. For a grown woman, she cried more than all four of MJ's sisters and brothers combined.

Mrs. Lanamore delivered the shakes, handing Jaudon extra napkins. MJ paid her and left the two businesswomen to talk while she went to visit with Tad, sucking creamy vanilla through her straw.

She watched Tad clean the griddle with a pumice stone. He asked, "What do you think about Leon Spinks beating Ali?"

"That was a month ago."

"I can't get over it. Ali was my man."

"Ali couldn't be world champ forever. How much did you lose?"

"I was too broke to bet. Wish I was as good as you at finding cash."

"I have an idea that might make us all money." Jaudon had waited until after the holidays to prepare her side door business, so MJ bided her time until today.

"You going to tell me your idea or stand there congratulating yourself?"

"Do you know anyone who buys homemade liquor?"

"Why? You got some?"

"I know where to get it."

Tad shook his head. "You are a resourceful kid. I have to give you that."

"There'd be money in it, but mostly it's a way for the boss to save her stores."

"What's wrong with them?"

She told him the story.

"I hear you."

"The way I see it, I know Jaudon has contacts, or her family does, with people who make the stuff. We're emptying one of the shut-down stores. Men come to the side door trying to buy homemade liquor.

I glimpsed unlabeled gallon jugs one local tried to sell Jaudon. The boss's relatives used to run the operation. Her father has a secret recipe they call Dinkey Dew."

"I know that Dinkey stuff. You can't get it anymore. It slid down your throat without burning and smacked of a fruit I cannot, to this day, name."

"The boss keeps saying no to these people, but what if we ran the operation for her? She'd keep her hands clean, and we'd move the product."

"She may lose her legitimate operation."

"She's about to lose it anyway. Jaudon's such a square shooter—I don't know if she'll go through with a dishonest venture."

"What's dishonest about giving people what they want?"

"Exactly. It's illegal because the liquor industry has the clout to get laws passed in its favor. The government says it's protecting the public, but seriously, do taxes need to cost as much as the product itself?" She untangled her hands and shoved them into the pockets of her shorts.

"Whoa, doggy. You don't need to convince me. I'm interested. We can get trade going for the whites and the unwhites. Both have green money."

"If we made enough, we could all benefit. Even the customers, though why they drink it, I don't know. Tastes worse than kerosene."

Tad laughed. "In your vast experience of guzzling?"

She hung her head. She knew she was sometimes a pretentious know-it-all.

"Better if you don't sample what you sell," said Tad. "Can you get that Dinkey Dew recipe off your boss? We could manufacture, distribute on our own."

"It's a family thing, Tad. It's definitely not available."

"Too bad. I'll talk to Shady tonight. He's at Busch Gardens with his grandniece right now."

"The boss is on the fence about it. Come and meet her."

Jaudon was filling napkin dispensers alongside Mrs. Lanamore. Tad and Jaudon shook hands.

Mrs. Lanamore looked like she'd pop if she didn't get a word in. "We're going to help each other out, me and Jaudon," she said to her son.

Tad stopped still.

Jaudon kept a wide smile on her face as she announced, "Pansy's Pastries."

"Say what?" Tad asked.

"Two new projects at once?" asked MJ, before she remembered the liquor sales were hush-hush. "I mean, closing stores and changing them."

"You heard the woman," said Mrs. Lanamore. "We're going to supply her stores with home-baked pastries, pies, muffins, whatever she can sell. I'm contemplating a scratch recipe for Pansy's World Class Breakfast Cookies to go with Jaudon's new coffee makers."

Jaudon jumped in. "They can get their coffee to-go with a Pansy's Pastry. It'll be the best coffee in the county if we have to go to South America to buy the beans. Ice coffee too, cold as we can make it, and sweet tea."

"You'll include a sample cookie free with each coffee order to give the people a taste of what we do. It'll bring more business to both of us," said Mrs. Lanamore. "Duval can do the deliveries on his way to work. And, Thaddeus, you're baking beside me. Early hours and production baking ought to get you off the streets."

Tad opened his mouth, apparently to object, but Mrs. Lanamore gave him the my-way-or-the-highway look that with no exception scared the daylights out of MJ.

She was a bit puffed that she was the one who connected Pansy's Home Cooking and the Beverage Bays, but she couldn't linger—studying for her heavy load of classes awaited her. She left Jaudon talking bakery details with the Lanamores. She wove her mazelike path home to Mrs. Belda's, planning how to make certain Jaudon got the bulk of any liquor profits.

Business was fun.

CHAPTER NINETEEN

A week later, Jaudon's cousin Cal drove off with the giant dismantled Beverage Bay sign just as Shady, MJ, and Tad arrived at the concrete block store on Church Pond Road.

Jaudon wiped her sweaty hands before she shook with Shady. He came off as disreputable as MJ described him, with that untamed gray beard and hair, shades, and a fug of weed about him. Tad's eyes, though, were clear and direct, with a touch of humor as she took his hand.

"You're wearing cobwebs in your hair, Boss," MJ told Jaudon.

"This store is plain dirty. I'm happy I closed it if for no reason but to chase out Momma's bone-lazy relatives."

"Will they give you trouble, taking over their backdoor business?" asked Tad.

"It's Pop's father's bailiwick, not Momma's relatives."

"You said there's hidden storage?" asked Shady.

"Pops and his brothers added it when they built the store. Come on, I'll show you. Don't mind the sour milk and mildew smells. MJ's taking on that job."

MJ pranced ahead to the walk-in cooler, light-footed as a forest creature. She showed a purposefulness Jaudon had come to count on. And she was sharper than a bee sting.

Jaudon said, "Before I cleared this space and took most of it to a food pantry, the crew kept the heaviest inventory stacked right against that wall."

"And one of the metal sheets moves," Tad said.

"It's a James Bond thing," said MJ. She inserted her fingertips behind the farthest sheet and lifted it aside. Jaudon switched the lights on.

Shady eyed the entrance and spun his chair to enter the narrow corridor backward. The room stretched the width of the premises. To one side was shelving all the way to the ceiling. A straight ladder was propped against the wall.

"Ace setup," said Shady. "Way out here in the boonies."

Tad scratched his jaw. "And right next to the post office. Practically foot traffic."

"So how did this work?" asked Shady. "Customers ordered when they drove through?"

"Yes, then they came around the side of the store." Jaudon led them away from the cooler. "There was a window here." MJ unshuttered the opening. Sunlight spilled in and revealed a neglected wooden window box hidden in plain sight. "By the time the customer takes his purchase, the panel's closed."

Shady rolled back to the hidden cooler. "But you're not going to have an operational store."

"Don't need one. We'll set hours, and word will get out about our part-time operation. There's enough cussedness about government taxes and hanging on to country ways that we'll have to slap them off with a stick."

As MJ replaced the secret panel, Tad reached to assist her. "Stand back, big guy," MJ said. "I need to do this when I'm alone here." She joggled and pushed until it aligned perfectly.

Jaudon saw her own pride and determination in MJ. "I hope we're not delivering her to the sheriff's station."

Shady said, "MJ's hip to the consequences of her actions. You can't stop her once her mind is made up."

"It's a first offense for me—I won't go to prison. Shady researched it."

Jaudon said, "I thought you were afraid you'd be sent home."

MJ put her hands on her hips. "I'm not a minor anymore."

"Don't get worked up," said Shady. "I'd be here. They can arrest me."

MJ folded her sturdy arms. "Don't you trust me on my own?"

"You'll need wheels."

"The bus stop isn't that far."

Shady countered, "I'll be your chauffeur. We'll study. Bring Tad along, sometimes, to manage storage. You two will fill Mason jars from the gallon jugs."

I need to chance this, thought Jaudon, though she imagined herself and MJ teetering on a tightrope.

"Cash only," Jaudon said.

"For a fact," Tad said.

"No names."

"Swear to God."

"Seventy percent to the Beverage Bays. I'm supplying utilities, storage, a sales outlet, original contacts, and taking the prime risks."

Tad said, "Fifty–fifty. We'll bring the Four Lakes customers."

Jaudon folded her arms. "Seventy, I may be able to bring back my family brew."

"Sixty–forty, Jaudon, and you pay MJ's wage," Shady countered.

"No wage. MJ gets twenty percent of my seventy."

"Forget it. We won't take fifteen percent each," Tad said.

"Stop it." MJ stamped a foot. "What are you two putting into this? Shady will supply transportation for me what, an hour three times a week? And presumably sample the goods while you, Tad, will work with me bottling and stocking."

"I hereby accept the job of taster," Shady said.

Tad replied, "You don't like whiskey, Whitebread."

"All the better. Chill, Tad," said Shady. "Fifteen percent, if we rally the customers, is better than what's coming in now."

Tad sucked his teeth, the sound both contemplative and annoyed. "You have us over a barrel, Boss."

MJ's hands were in fists. "The whole point is for Jaudon to save her company."

"How about this," said Jaudon. "Once I pay off Momma's debts, I'll leave the business. No percentage, no involvement. You find a new distribution point, and I'll sell you my part of the operation."

"How long are you willing to wait for full payment?" asked Shady.

"That depends on business. The more liquor we sell, the faster I get out. Believe me, it can't be soon enough."

"But you figure—"

"Three to five years? Sooner if we can."

MJ put her fists on her hips. "Honestly, it's an investment in your future, Tad."

"If we don't get busted before then, Squirrel."

Shady shook his head, frowning. "The gendarmes are a hassle.

You want to spread around protection money or free whiskey. Am I correct?"

"Pops will know how to take care of that," said Jaudon.

The men seemed to consult each other with their eyes. Both nodded.

"Deal," said Tad.

CHAPTER TWENTY

Summer 1978

Someone spray-painted in red the misspelled words QUEER BOOS across the front of the Church Pond Road store. MJ had to smile. Was the sprayer trying to expose the boss as queer or warning the liquor was tainted?

Under Shady's direction, she gathered a pint tin of acetone, steel wool, a bucket, and rags. "Jaudon's suspicious the Batsons did it—her momma's family. They made plenty on their moonshine profits. They didn't have Dinkey Dew to sell—that's a Vicker recipe and her father wasn't about to share it with the shiftless Batsons—but plenty of other off and on home distilleries supplied them. Pops's uncle is making the family 'shine now."

Shady was chuckling. "You sound like an old pro, throwing around the lingo."

She flicked her rag at him. "Seriously, who else graffities way out here? Underage kids try to buy, but they expect to be told no, so it's not them." The post office was the only near neighbor, and the lone postmistress sent her husband over for a couple of quart jars a month, *To have on hand for company*, the postmistress whispered whenever MJ saw her.

This area had a real old Florida quality to it, and she was going miss it, away from the incomers and the hectic main thoroughfares. There was an old peahen who was fond of whatever insect populated the post office stoop. The storybook Spanish moss that grew on trees like it was nothing special never lost its romantic appeal and she half expected Janie Crawford and Tea Cake, Zora Neale Hurston's characters, to appear walking along the railroad tracks hand in hand.

"I'm sure it's those Batsons," she said. "Not, from what I hear, that you can tell much difference between Jaudon's mother with dementia and her relatives without."

"Don't give them another thought," said Shady. "What's it taken them, months to launch an attack? Far out." He pointed skyward through the side door. "A bald eagle. You don't see many of them in town."

She followed the bird's flight, entranced; she hadn't seen an eagle since she left Depot Landing. She forced herself back to business. "That family's not going to boot us out. Not while I'm here."

Tad was testing liquor with an alcoholmeter to make sure the proof was acceptable. He poured from a jug of homemade sour mash into the large funnel Shady held steady over a quart mason jar. This batch did a good imitation of boiled cabbage, and MJ backed away from the smell.

Shady sampled the mash before MJ paid the moonshiners. Somehow, despite his excesses, he retained his acute senses of smell and taste and sounded the alarm if he sniffed a hint of an off odor, chiefly methanol, which was bad news. One shifty would-be supplier tried to pass off swill he made using a car radiator for a condenser. Shady spat the stuff out. "Tastes of lead and antifreeze."

Hopping mad, the man shouted in Tad's face. "I'm going to town to sell it to your kind."

Tad tore the bottles from the trunk of the poison-maker's car, smashing them on the tar-and-chip driveway. He rushed the schemer and stuffed him in his driver's seat.

Watching him, Shady said, "That's not a bad idea."

"Smashing bottles?" asked MJ.

Tad said, "Have you ever heard of nutcrackers? Not the kind in your mother's kitchen. They're a fruit juice slushy. A certain mix of liquors go into them. Started up in Harlem maybe the beginning of the century. Now nutcracker hustlers sell them in New York in sealed plastic bottles, at beaches, parks, on the street, barber shops, bodegas, five bucks a pop. Completely illegal, but you can see the potential for our beaches, Ybor City, hot nights in my neighborhood. With rotgut, not pricey store-bought, it'd be even more profitable."

The man stared from his car. He made a pistol of his hand, threatened Tad with it, and drove off.

She cheered Tad, who walked around the broken glass and handed her a push broom and dustpan while he unrolled the hose. As they worked together to clean the mess, she saw that Tad wasn't mopping sweat from his face, but tears. She was surprised.

"I don't care for that part of myself," he muttered.

Shady wheeled out to them. "Defending who you are?"

"Letting loose at him."

"You did the righteous thing," said Shady.

The hand that held tight to her broom handle shook. She'd been initiated into the rough side of their business. "Thank you, Tad."

She lifted her bucket and started to work on the graffiti.

After MJ told her what happened, Jaudon installed a Dutch door with a peephole. Customers reached directly from their car windows to knock. If the driver passed muster with her, based on her limited experience and instinct, MJ opened the top of the door and conducted business.

After a few weeks, a routine set in. She minded the enterprise Tuesday, Friday, and Saturday. Most of the home brewers brought their goods early on Tuesday. Usually, they resembled the man Jaudon had called a leftover cracker.

Customers, predominantly white and male, stopped later in the day, a couple of them riding their farm tractors, or on their way home from work in Tampa.

At the picnic table, she studied with Shady. They talked and talked—from philosophy to car repair. They called the store the Schoolhouse and were, as Shady said, stoked about how well the business was doing.

"Consider the property tax initiative in California—people can't afford all this taxation," said Shady. "We're getting a spillover benefit all the way in Florida because we sell tax-free."

She acknowledged his thoughts with a nod. "The antitax mood this part of the country is in, pretty soon there'll be another Tea Party."

The combination of no taxes on their product and fair prices had them raking in money. Her college fund grew to the point she was banking it because Shady advised her that interest was the way to make money grow. She'd needed to get an ID to use a bank, drive a car, and, in due course, make investments.

Before she left the West Coast, she'd been a shadowy nonperson, insubstantial; a stranger could practically walk through her and never notice. Here under the tonic of a bright sun, she was becoming solid, sturdy, casting a shadow of her own. She wrote Klickitat County for her birth certificate and hoped some new clerk handled the request, someone who didn't know the Beaudry family.

CHAPTER TWENTY-ONE

Early June 1979

"*Sick and sad*?" Jaudon yelped. "Some has-been singer called us sick and sad?"

Berry hadn't missed Jaudon and Allison's political tiffs, or refereeing with Cullie. In the past, the four of them came together monthly, but with the press of Berry's master's degree and Jaudon's struggle to keep the stores, it had been a while.

Allison, Berry, and Cullie were founding members of their feminist women's group. All three eventually stopped attending meetings. Like them, non-gay women were interested in abortion rights, child care issues, and domestic abuse. Unlike them, the rest of the group refused to involve itself when the Dade County ordinance that prohibited discrimination on the basis of sexual orientation came under attack. Nor did the women take seriously the resultant orange juice buycott.

Eternally pregnant Samantha O'Connor, an activist for breast-feeding in public, had complained, "I can't raise my children without orange juice."

Gran wasn't home. Berry had spurred on Gran's idea to join the Senior Center jaunts. Jaudon was tight as a drum, so getting away would do Gran good. She was on a bus to Mobile to see the *USS Alabama* Battleship Memorial Park.

Good thing, she thought. Allison was stirring Jaudon up about politics again.

"You didn't follow the whole Anita Bryant versus gay people battle a couple of years ago?" asked Allison. "We have her to thank for Florida Gay Pride and the march we're going to in Miami."

"Jaudon eats, sleeps, and breathes the Beverage Bay crisis," Cullie said, straightening from her accustomed slump.

"The woman's a loudmouth singer." Jaudon's fists slammed the tabletop. "What's she get from coming down on us? What does she know about us?"

Cullie walked her fingers along the table's surface. "Her and her churches mistakenly believe they have to defend their munchkins against us creepy-crawly cannibalistic varmints." Her active hand pounced on one of Berry's hands and tried to drag it away.

"I don't understand why anyone votes about our lives at all," said Jaudon. "We're as American as the next joe."

Berry stroked their dog's floppy ears, concerned at Jaudon's intensity, but for the moment relieved she wasn't fretting about the store. She batted at Cullie's hand and trapped it.

"Ugh. Splat," Cullie said. "Now look what you did. You squashed my creepy-crawly homosexual hand and made a mess of your clean table."

Allison's Buckhead accent hadn't disappeared since she went renegade on her upper-crust Atlanta family. "Anita Bryant's power to ruin lives was frightening. Churches weaponized her to get more members. Larger flocks bring in more money and greater power to their ministers."

Jaudon shook a fist. "If she shows her face in Tampa, remind me to punch her lying mouth. Recruiting children, my foot. She's the recruiter. It's drummed into their heads that they don't have choices about who to love."

Cullie lifted her bottle of cola to drain the dregs. She wore the chlorine-faded shorts and T-shirts she worked in as a pool boy. "Once I'm a sworn officer of the law, don't expect me to arrest somebody for throwing a pie in her face. Why assume I want to molest anyone, much less a kid?"

"She's one big publicity stunt," Allison said. "Her voice won't last forever, but the churches will keep booking her anyway."

"I'd rather listen to Lana Cantrell any day," said Cullie with a sigh, her eyes momentarily unfocused.

Berry ran a finger along Jaudon's arm. "Cullie may need another cola from the icebox."

Jaudon was on her feet in an instant. "Can I get anyone else a drink?"

Allison said, "An itty bit more ice, if you don't mind."

Berry said, "Are you any closer to joining the Four Lakes police force, Cullie?"

Cullie said, "Soon, mi amiga, soon. The city ordinances were updated, thanks to Allison. I swear she'll be mayor of Four Lakes before you know it."

Allison grimaced. "The chief isn't hiring anyone in hopes the female applicants will give up."

"I predict," said Berry, "fighting back on this anti-gay campaign has our politicians all bent out of shape. They're rabid about a woman staying home to serve her man and raise his offspring."

"Especially Anita the Oklahoma girl, in her twenty-seven-room waterfront home," added Cullie. "Too bad she wasn't crossing the Sunshine Skyway Bridge last month when it collapsed."

Berry put a finger to her lips. "Shh, don't wish such a thing on anyone. Thirty-eight people dead in a minute."

Cullie muttered, "The wrong thirty-eight."

"Here's what else she said." Allison read from a flyer advertising the Miami march. "*If gays are granted rights, next we'll have to give rights to prostitutes and to people who sleep with St. Bernards and to nail biters.*"

Jaudon rubbed her lips with a knuckle. "What's she talking about, granting rights? They've always been our rights."

The phone rang. Jaudon went to answer, and they heard her bark instructions into the receiver.

Cullie and Allison had questions in their eyes for Berry.

"Lots of pressure at the stores."

"Sheesh, Jaud needs to mellow out," Cullie said. "I heard she lost a clerk because she was so harsh. Is she making any headway in paying back Momma's losses?"

"I don't exactly know." Berry gazed through a window at the dangling wisteria blossoms and played with an amethyst earring that replicated the vine. "I can't talk to her about it. I expect she may be trying to buffer me from bad news, or...I don't know, Cullie, she's conniving something desperate. Why don't you try to loosen her tongue?"

The phone slammed into its cradle. Jaudon loosened her shorts as she rejoined them.

"You put on weight, cutie-pie," said Allison.

Jaudon patted herself on the bottom. "Pops used to say he was getting so porky, if he needed to haul ass, he'd have to make two trips." She sat with Allison. "Tell me, what rights don't they want us to have?"

"The right to live," said Allison with a look of disgust. "They've concocted a sham issue to agitate people looking for scapegoats. It's not as if rights run out, or someone can use them up. In 1977, Dade County passed an ordinance that said no one can discriminate against gays and lesbians. Anita Bryant, a supposedly good Christian woman, said homosexuals are begging to teach her precious children. You know what that means."

"Ooh, ooh, I know," said Cullie. "The gay teachers will make her brood sick, sad, sinning homosexuals." She dangled Berry and Jaudon's new cat in the air and directed her rescue Westie, Kirby the Second, to sit. An aged Kirby the First died a while back. The kitten fawned on Cullie, as most animals did.

When their dog Zefer died, Berry and Jaudon eased their grief by going to the shelter and giving another animal a home. Gran lost no time naming their funny beagle-corgi mix Puddin. While there, they asked to take home the cat in residence longest. They'd expected a grown cat, but the attendant delivered an adolescent black female who'd been in the shelter since birth—people, incredibly, believed black cats were bad luck.

"I was thinking of my grandmothers this morning," said Gran as she dangled a ribbon for the cat. "Kagee and Jenny, they were. Why not use one of their names? Keep their memory alive."

Berry hadn't hesitated, "How about both? Kajen?"

"Sounds like Cajun," Jaudon said. "Aren't you part Cajun, Gran?"

"Sure am."

"There you go. Kajen it is."

Cullie lectured the lineup—Kajen, Puddin, and Kirby II—about the Anita Bryants of the world. "Obviously, homosexuals endure years of higher education for the sole purpose of recruiting children. Step right up, homos. Here we have the pick of the litter, the pride of the South, anxious to get plucked from the safety of their families and recruited into sin and evil."

"Wait," said Allison, as they laughed. "I want a picture of my pool boy preacher." Allison tried to include the animals, but Kajen fled the room and Kirby II shambled to the front door.

"I'd better take my cherished companion back to nature," said Cullie.

Jaudon teased her. "You're talking about the dog, not Allison, right?"

Cullie threw a nearby catnip toy at Jaudon.

Dinner over, they settled in the living room and Allison continued. "Bryant and her husband spread the word. They campaigned against the law protecting us and got it repealed. Local gay people marched through Coconut Grove waving signs, shaking fists, yelling. It's worse this year since the legislature outlawed adoption by gay people. We're marching because Bryant and the churches did, in effect, take away our rights."

Jaudon, stewing over store schedules, chewed on a pen. "As far as I'm concerned, we need to use our evil influence to get our rights back. If there's one march I want to join, this is it."

When Berry first went to a women's political rally, Jaudon was frantic, predicting rioting and arrests. That worked out better than anyone expected—Allison ran for the city council and won.

Skepticism and ardent hope warred within Berry. "Really, Jaudon?" Berry asked. "You'll really leave the stores for a day and go?"

CHAPTER TWENTY-TWO

MJ badly wanted to march for gay rights with the kids from New York Pizza. She would have yelled her head off, given the chance, livid that gays needed to march at all. Seeing the east side of the state and the Atlantic Ocean would have been a big bonus.

Partly out of loyalty to Jaudon, mostly because she had classes before and after work, she stayed in town to mind the Schoolhouse. Her scholarships covered enough of her school costs that she had to have good attendance to keep them. Shady dropped her off before his medical appointments. It was slow today, so she closed her books, hung a be-right-back sign, and went on her own march. The customers knew to try again.

A working orange grove stretched farther than she could see. Last month she'd stood and watched a man lean a straight ladder against branches and green leaves and proceed to quickly pull off the ripe orbs, then drop them into a sack hanging from his shoulder. He carried the full sack to a giant bowl. Later, a piece of farm equipment with three arms lifted the bowl and spilled the oranges into a container to be processed elsewhere. It didn't matter if they bruised—this was the Valencia harvest season and the juicing plants would be in full swing, bruises or not.

She came to know the horse farm across Church Pond Road with its scents both good and bad, a dark road to a small trailer park filled with well-used small residences converted from vacation cottages, trees and plants she'd never before run across. The flame-red and orange shrubs which Berry called Marmalade Bushes. The clusters of white, pink, blue enchanted flowers in countless delicate shapes whose names she slowly learned. Florida couldn't be more different than her part of Washington, but each was magnificent in its singular way.

In what Northerners transplanted to Florida called the country, thieves weren't expected. She didn't steal from genuine country people. Berry said newcomers who had more than enough of everything came in and tore out the very attributes that made Florida appealing. She'd seen plenty of that in Washington State when the timber companies acted as if the trees were theirs to kill.

In southern Washington, for the most part, if you owned a home, you lived in it. In Florida, mammoth homes stood empty.

It didn't make sense to her that a few people owned two homes or a house with five bathrooms, and the strawberry pickers crowded together in grubby shacks and trailer parks. If some terrible contagious plague were ever to break out again, like polio, or smallpox, the world would be left only with rich people.

That know-nothing troublemaker Anita Bryant and her sizeable family occupied too much space. She kicked fiercely at dried-up horse pucky and hoped some of Bryant's sons and daughters came out gay.

An absentee land-grabber along the road from the Schoolhouse had razed a half acre of rare sand pine scrub to build an unconscionably large house with a circular driveway and a garage in which she'd seen, at various times, a massive pickup truck, a new Lincoln Continental, a white Datsun 280Z, a classy boat, and a moose of a motor home. The whole parcel was landscaped like Mother Nature hadn't done a good enough job. People like these claimed to believe in the Garden of Eden, then tore it down and put up a troll-decorated pseudo-Versailles. Jerks.

She was angry enough when she decided on a walk to cram her pockets with her lock picks, gloves, a 7.5-inch crowbar, and a foldable nylon sack, in case.

She stalked through the remains of the forest, mourning each tree stump robbed of its tall trunk and leafy branches. She'd heard on the news that a tropical storm might glance the area, and overhead the few trees stirred, an infrequent flutter and rustle. At the back of the land-grabber's house perched an enclosed pool, covered. The house had an emptiness to it she'd come to recognize. She sought unlocked windows and doors, though she wanted to steamroll her way in.

She started at the screech of a blue jay and reminded herself to breathe slowly and deeply. Someone left a frosted window slightly open. She positioned herself on the porch rail and, with the force of her inner turbulence, grabbed the sill with one hand, then used the crowbar to raise the window enough that she was able to scrabble her way through.

There, she came face to face with a roof rat. She half jumped, half fell into the house, landing on a hip hard enough that she anticipated a colorful bruise. She'd frightened the rat too; it fled. The bathroom stank of rat nest.

Her heart beat double time. She waited for a response to her noisy entry, but none came. She tiptoed to the closed bathroom door, stepped out, saw the doors to the rooms were shut. She went on extreme alert.

Walking at the edge of walls to eliminate creaks in the flooring, one by one she opened the doors. Sheeting covered the furniture. In the master bedroom, she unveiled a tall dresser, tacky with furniture polish. The man of the family had left absolutely nothing.

The lady's vanity held dried makeup in the drawers. She stopped, listened, heard nothing, and went to the closet, eased the sliding door open. Lots of nice clothes. In a beribboned box on the back of the shelf were love letters. She left them.

Her anger at these selfish people grew. They might not live in Dade County, but she bet they voted against gays. Did they know how fortunate they were to possess two homes? If she owned just this one and sold it right now, Berry's health center was as good as operational. She'd amass enough money someday to make that happen, to give back.

She almost missed it. She scrutinized the master bath from the doorway, and there it hung. A trifold jewelry travel case of pink leather had slipped off and stuck right behind the toilet tank. She worked it free, untied its satin ribbon, and found—nothing. She shook the case and checked under the lining. Shoot.

She wanted to take something from these presumptuous owners. Sporadically, she heard cars pass by. Her hands, in their gloves, were sweaty.

She checked her watch—time to go. Not about to exit through the window, she went downstairs, gave the rooms a quick second look, checked the silent refrigerator, and gave herself a shock as she touched the metal doorknob to the garage.

In the middle of the garage floor lay one wooden box, as if it fell off their car when they hurried to leave. The box held two pristine pearl handled revolvers that gave off the mildly saccharine petroleum scent of the gun oil her father used. Next to them was a box of ammunition. She didn't think; she jammed the boxes into her sack.

Anger appeased for the moment, she ran through the woods well back from the houses. The wind picked up, arguing with grousing trees as she argued with herself. Should she let the guys sell the guns? Better to throw the things off a bridge into deep water. The pounding of her feet on the spongy, sandy soil gave rise to the idea of burying the guns.

She nearly dove for cover behind a tree when a woodpecker rata-tat-tatted on a nearby tree. The guns were jangling her nerves.

Deep in the trees behind the store she dropped to the ground to scoop out handfuls of sandy dirt. Without a shovel, she settled for a shallow hole. Pointless anger had made her take these guns.

CHAPTER TWENTY-THREE

In the passenger seat, Berry closed her eyes. Jaudon had insisted on driving the three hours to the march, leaving competent Olive Ponder in charge of the stores.

A sleepy Cullie, Allison, and the dog Kirby were in the back seat. Air conditioning blew through the vents. They left Rainbow Gap in the dark and drove into a pink and gold sunrise. Berry pointed to a pond off Laudre Flats Boulevard, its mist reflecting the colors.

She peered into the back seat to see who was snoring.

Cullie whispered, "Kirby doesn't snore, but listen to her soft motorboat purr."

"You call that a soft purr?" Jaudon made motor sounds with her lips.

Kirby lifted her shaggy head, snorted, and made herself more comfortable.

Halfway over to the Atlantic side of the state, they stopped for breakfast at Yeehaw Junction, an historic, if not celebrated, crossroads. The Desert Inn had, a fairly short while ago, connected to full-service water and electricity, and smelled of frying bacon grease and batter. A morning TV show was discussing John Wayne's career and death.

Over eggs, home fries, and pecan sticky buns, they watched trucks heaped high with the last of the season's Valencia oranges on their way to processors.

"Not many orchards left in our neck of the woods," Jaudon said, licking a sugary finger.

Berry gave her curly head a gentle shake. "It's a shame."

"You sound like Gran."

"Good—Gran's right about most things."

Cullie chugged a Desert Inn specialty, sweet sun tea. "Do you still plan to carry more convenience store items? I have the perfect slogan for you. *More convenient than a convenience store—shop from your car at the Beverage Bay.*"

Jaudon covered her ears. "That doesn't rhyme."

"Okey dokey, you asked for it. *More convenient than a convenience store and oh, so gay! Shop from your car at the Beverage Bay!*"

When Allison stopped laughing, she said, "You see why I love this woman? She brings fun into my life."

"Aw, heck, Cullie, I'm barely keeping my head above water as it is. I can just about afford the advertising I do in the freebie papers. The chains have the advanced equipment, the computerized cash registers, and MSI ordering devices. The good news is that Pansy's Pastries are bringing more people into the store. Word is getting out about that and about the inventory I added to appeal to moms."

Cullie crooned, "Dang, my little jujube, you should see the baby stuff Jaudon's stockpiled: disposable diapers, formula, wipes, those ring things babies stick in their mouths. You'd deduce she knew a thing or two about children, and you'd be dead wrong. You don't need more stores, Jaud, you need more space right where you're at."

"The chief change I want to make right now is to get on top of this debt."

Allison laid a light hand on Jaudon's forearm. "I wish you weren't too proud to declare bankruptcy. You'd be in better shape if you did."

Berry quickly said, "There's nothing wrong with proud, is there?"

"There's pride and then there's hubris," said Allison. "There's no shame in bankruptcy these days."

Cullie added, "It's one more arrow in a businesswoman's quiver."

"Who can afford a bow to shoot it? Without Berry and Gran, I'd be so poor I couldn't afford to pay attention. We're living on Berry's salary plus Gran's Social Security. Every cent from the stores goes for inventory or to pay what I owe."

Cullie speared a fried tomato from a shared side dish. "Bless Momma's thieving heart."

"You know it's not her fault, Cul—it's her illness. And I may be proud, Allison, but I'm also making certain I'm fair to my suppliers. If I declare bankruptcy, I pay a very low percentage of my debt, and that's not right. They have to pay their bills too. It'll take me more time this way, but Momma, Pops, and I have worked with these vendors for years, and most are offering to forgive a heaping third of what I owe, given the circumstances."

Allison said, "That's exceedingly generous and old-school. It comes of avoiding direct contact with the conglomerates. How are your parents?"

"Pops is Mr. Reliable, as always, doesn't let much ruffle his feathers. He stops by when one of her sisters is available to sit with Momma. He knows I'm working flat out and, I suspect, wants to guard me from what Momma's become. She forgets his name sometimes." She pointed to herself with a thumb. "I may be in trouble, but I'm in charge now, and the situation will only improve."

Berry smiled to hear Jaudon's confidence at a higher level.

Jaudon noticed and gestured with her hand. "I couldn't do any of it without this woman beside me."

Berry scooted closer.

"Aren't they cute?" Allison said.

Cullie whispered to Allison, loud enough for Berry and Jaudon to hear, "Not as cute as my darlin' jujube."

"Jujube," said Jaudon, with her eyes raised to the heavens. "Let's get back on the road."

They drove another hour and, despite every passenger giving directions at once, arrived. Jaudon groused at Yankee parallel parkers. "On the Gulf side we don't spend our lives squeezing into tiny spaces like New York tourists." They hiked several blocks to reach the assembled marchers, scouring around for Rigo and Jimmy Neal.

"I've never seen such a crowd in all my born days," said Berry. "What do you think, Allison, a thousand?"

Allison's eyes were starry with unshed tears. "That we're here at all is phenomenal."

A man with a bullhorn shouted instruction to the crowd.

Jaudon stared, her mouth open. "Are they all gay?"

People of color, whites, preschoolers with moms or dads, diesel to queen to straight, arranged themselves into a stupendously lengthy line. Many chanted, others sang.

Berry took Jaudon's hand. "So much energy in the air."

"Hot diggity," Cullie said, tossing her lavender bowler hat high and catching it before it landed several feet away.

Allison, the veteran marcher, said, "I'm certain most of them are gay. It's good to see straight supporters too. Today is a revolutionary showing for Dade County."

Jaudon pulled the brim of her Tampa Bay Buccaneers cap low. "What if they're spotted? They could lose their jobs, their families."

Someone called, "Berry. Jaudon."

"Oh no, tell me it's not a customer." Jaudon yanked her hand away from Berry.

"It's Rigo," cried Berry.

Rigo and Jimmy Neal locked them both in a hug. Quiet, often morose, Jimmy Neal, in aviator sunglasses, cuffed shorts, and a tight shirt, was uncharacteristically gleeful. He'd grown a brushy new mustache.

"Jaud," said Rigo, "your eyes are as wide as a scared rabbit. You going to run back to Rainbow Gap or walk with us?"

"Ready and rarin' to go. We've tolerated too much for too long."

With the temperature in the nineties, many of the men were flagrantly underdressed, as Jimmy Neal said with an appreciative grin.

Berry watched her relax around the boys. Rigo introduced them to a gay male couple he called their other best friends.

Berry raised both hands to her mouth. "Dr. Riyanto?" she said between her fingers.

"Berry? What are you doing here?" asked a fetching South Asian man in wire-rimmed glasses.

"It never occurred to me."

"Nor I," said the doctor, eyes smiling.

"He's in our practice," she told Jaudon. "Dr. Riyanto, this is Jaudon Vicker, my life partner."

He offered his hand to Jaudon and they shook.

"Jiminy. Is this okay? You two won't be in trouble?"

The doctor, formal and clearly amused, said, "Please call me Larry. At least until the end of the march."

"Rest easy," Berry said. "It will be Dr. Riyanto at the office."

"And this," Jimmy Neal said, "is Gregory Kumar. He practices in the orthopedic department at the hospital. I sometimes assist in his surgeries."

Larry told her, "We met our junior year of college."

Jaudon stared at them. "Gay doctors? I never imagined such a person and here's two of you."

Jimmy Neal ushered them into the sweep of the march, including additional male friends. "Come on, Bub," he called to Rigo.

Rigo hopped onto a palm stump, waving his arms like a conductor, leading a chant.

Jaudon joined in, her voice loud and strident. "We are your

children." Berry surmised she was taunting Momma as well as every intolerant parent.

A man appeared beside Rigo and started a new incantation. "Anita, you liar, we'll set your hair on fire."

"She did us a favor," said Allison. "She organized us."

"By accusing us of molesting children?" Jaudon retorted.

Berry rubbed Jaudon's back as they walked. She feared her dear steam kettle was about to blow her top once again, the way she had so many times in the schoolyard years ago.

A new rallying cry began. "Out of the bars—into the streets."

At work, she'd seen what alcohol did to people. She wanted to shout, *Don't let the churches keep us behind bars—any kind.*

She whispered it to Allison who said, "That's an insightful point."

"It's been forever since I last raised my voice in protest."

"I agree. I'm inside the machine now, getting paid to do good, but they don't make it easy."

"That makes two of us. I want to capture this energy and save it for the women's clinic."

The marchers shook fists and shouted grievances, but the crowd was also playful. A nearby man carried a large tape player on his shoulder.

"Disco," cried Cullie with a leap in the air. She danced as she marched, drawing Allison to her, Kirby at her other side. A block of women and men moved to the beat, dancing in groups, changing partners, partying within this illusion of freedom. Berry, giddy now, partnered with a drag queen drenched in coconut sunscreen. The men flirted and made fun of Anita Bryant's husband.

The dancers returned to marching. Jaudon took her hand and advanced in her heavy-footed manner, eyes ahead, fired up to attack the enemy or defend herself and her people. Noble Jaudon was a soldier willing to fight for civil rights or her stores, her unusual self, or her Berry.

She plain loved Jaudon to distraction.

Heckling increased the closer they moved to the rallying point. The pied piper ratcheted up his boom box. From the back of a pickup, several men shouted, "Mariposo, mariposo," gyrating their hips and fluttering their arms. The male marchers took it in good stride, inviting the farm workers to join them or to meet them later at a popular gay bar.

Then came the Christian Fundamentalists.

"It's sad," Berry said in her softest voice. "They believe they're do-gooders."

The column slowed and stopped. Cullie kneeled and gave Kirby water. "I'm happy our juvenile squirrel isn't here. She'd be mad enough to stir up a fuss."

"MJ?" said Rigo. "She'd taunt right back at them."

Berry heard yelling just ahead. A few lesbians traded insults with the Fundies, the march jammed behind them. Cullie read the bigoted signs aloud: "*Love the sinner, not the sin. Save Our Children. Leviticus: if a man has sexual relations with a man both of them are to be put to death.* Now, isn't that Christian of them? I'm going to get Kirby baptized at the next fountain we pass."

A balding man with a large paunch held a sign that read, *Hands off our kids.* A younger man next to him yelled, *Die, filthy child molesters.*

Jimmy Neal waved and called, "Hi, Uncle Buddy."

"Oh no, not Uncle Buddy," said Rigo.

"They're related?" asked Allison.

Rigo said, "Jimmy Neal's uncle. A work accident damaged his brain, and he can't live on his own. We stop to see him at a church home in North Miami whenever we visit my mom. That sign? He can't write or read anymore."

Jimmy Neal hugged the man. When Rigo did the same, Uncle Buddy reached around and goosed him. Rigo squealed. With small, urgent gestures, Uncle Buddy motioned his friends over until a group formed around them, shaking their hands.

The lesbians had moved on. Cullie and the guys stepped back in line. Jimmy Neal explained, "The church home bused in a dozen people from the facility, handed them signs, and told them what to holler."

"Does he understand any of this?"

"No," said Jimmy Neal, pulling a face. "He goes on trips when they're offered, loves getting out and meeting people. He's bi, which is one reason they institutionalized him."

Allison said, "He should have joined us."

Jimmy Neal shook his head. "No, they'd come after him and make him sit in the bus. Strap him to a seat if he didn't stay put. He's having a good time."

Allison's lips were nearly white from compression. "That's beyond wrong. I'll investigate this practice when I get back to work. They're taking advantage of their residents, including your uncle."

Jimmy Neal put a finger to his lips. "You might not want to use Uncle Buddy as an example. Decades before the brain injury, he connected with boys in the early grades. I don't know of specific incidents, but if any history came up, I don't want him evicted—for everyone's sake."

"Understood," said Allison. "I know a couple of people in Miami-Dade. Resident names will not be mentioned."

They reached the edge of the rally crowd, with more marchers crowding behind them. Berry had developed a blister where her sandal strap rubbed her Achilles tendon. She stabilized herself on Jaudon's arm to take the sandals off.

"Not a good idea," Allison said. "It never fails—you need shoes to run if something bad goes down."

Jaudon took Berry's hand again. "Let them try. I wanted to go pop him one for that sign. I'm glad I didn't. His problems put ours in perspective."

"Like paying debts?"

"And people calling me mister."

"And my grad school exams."

The crowd stopped at a scant stage.

Jimmy Neal put a hand on Rigo's shoulder and pointed to the man at the microphone. "Bub, there's your hero, Bob Kunst."

Rigo rose on his toes to see him. "I think I'm going to swoon."

More people pressed behind them. Jaudon cupped her hands behind her ears to catch his words.

Berry touched Jaudon's arm. "I can't see or hear him either."

Cullie put her arms around both of them. "Come on, mi amigos. We have a three-hour drive ahead of us, and Kirby wants to get to the food in the car."

Rigo insisted on driving them to their parking space. "It's not safe for you to walk through the homophobes," he explained. "And notice the sky."

The sky had rapidly darkened. Bulky raindrops burst on the sandy sidewalk.

"My trusted Westie warrior will defend us if Jaudon's willing to stop and stockpile Cheetos for the drive home."

Rigo said, "Your hairy mutt is about as much use against gay bashers as I'd be. By the way, we're staying over at my mom's, but I'll be back for my shift tomorrow, Jaud."

Jaudon folded her arms. "I'm not worried about the stores right now. Being surrounded by people like us, mean insults or not—jumping Jehoshaphat, I can tackle anything."

Thunder sounded directly overhead. "God's wrath," shouted one of the anti-gay women.

Allison, Rigo, and the others put fingers in their ears. Kirby strained at her leash, as if she wanted it clear she didn't know these humans. Then lightning flashed and the dog was first to follow as Rigo herded them to his nearby car. Rain hammered its roof and lightning flared once more, then utterly disappeared. The rally resumed behind them.

CHAPTER TWENTY-FOUR

June 1980

A year later, at the start of the summer term, MJ raced into her junior year at Bone Valley College. She'd skipped the GED exams, aced the SAT, and financed much of her tuition, fees, and books with scholarships Shady turned her on to, the rest from her break-ins. She distrusted loans of any kind.

She usually worked at the Schoolhouse alone now. Several months back, Tad and Shady opened an outlet in their neighborhood but came for stock and to do the taste tests. She did the buying. Jaudon came by Thursdays to empty the floor safe.

"Who hires economics majors?" Jaudon's rough voice sounded as if she spent her life shouting instructions.

"What can't I do, other than cure cancer?" MJ didn't want to reveal too much for fear of jinxing her dreams. "I want to go into investing, but inflation is stupid high. I think we're about to see a recession."

The way Jaudon tried to hide a smile, MJ understood what she wasn't saying: investment was ambitious talk for a nineteen-year-old. She positioned a completed order in the window box and hooked the hatchway shut. Before Jaudon took care of the cash, she sat at the cedar picnic table they'd brought inside and asked, "How come you're so keen to be rolling in money? Were you raised poor?"

"Not dirt poor, but Dear Old Dad didn't know how to stop making children. They could stretch his earnings over five little Beaudrys."

"When you earn your millions, will you give your family some?"

She supposed she owed them for giving her food and shelter for fifteen years. When Mt. St. Helens blew last month, she pictured the survivalist compound, about seventy miles distant, buried in ash, but that was wishful thinking. The truth was, she wanted to make good money to spite them, though it might be satisfying to send a couple thousand with a thank-you note someday.

"Shoot, their heaviest burden lifted when I left. Money won't make them better people. In any case, I won't be the type of investor who makes millions. If I did, I'd give bunches to gay pride groups."

"What type will you be?"

"Any kind where I'm my own boss. Potentially a small business, your size, but with a better profit margin than retail food."

"For someone with no funds, you sure have sky-high plans."

She hesitated. She wanted to trust Jaudon about where her money came from but scoffed at herself—anyone but Jaudon the straight shooter. "I'm a good saver. If this enterprise makes it until I finish college, I'll have enough to get my own business off the ground in a modest way. I'm comfortable living under the radar. And I'm learning more than you'd think, listening to you talk about running a company."

"I should come to you for advice about keeping the stores afloat. You'd be a good advisor, knowing the rules."

"I may have accelerated my classes to graduate early, Boss, but I'm not qualified to advise anyone."

"Come on. You have a lot better understanding of these things than I do."

"Seriously? There's perpetually a lot at stake. A bad decision in your lawful business can put you in jail and ruin you as fast as selling this moonshine."

"Not hardly likely with the palm greasing I do and my grandfather's recipe. I thank the heavens above my cousin Cal took over the Dinkey Dew still."

"For you, an investor might morph into one more creditor if the business doesn't get stronger."

"That's one of my dilemmas. Plus, I'm obliged to keep it in the family—that's in the terms."

They migrated to the storage area, where MJ affixed labels to jars. The whole operation was sterile—no snoop would smell spilled whiskey or the new item they carried, homemade beer.

"Shoot," MJ said, "making money is not all that different from gambling. The secret to a successful aboveboard business is to keep it modest and simple, don't try to grab more than your share, and stay away from greedy competitors who'll entice you with expansion only to take what they can use and trash the rest. By staying humble and sharp, losses you're naturally going to have are not such a big deal. You can't lose what you don't have." A grin took over MJ's face. "I relish learning this stuff."

"You're way smart, aren't you?"

"I'm good with tests."

"I wish I was. You should thank your good fortune."

"In middle school they gave us a bunch of tests. They saw my scores and—surprise—the teachers wanted to put me in the next higher grade. My parents got a letter about it, and my mother wrote a big fat no. She was too dumb to understand they'd be rid of me sooner."

"What did you do? Put up a fight?"

"I had no say in it. Anyway, I wasn't looking forward to science and calculus."

"That's exactly why I switched to a business college."

They shook hands, MJ's sticky with glue. "We're both smart, Boss."

"I don't know how smart I am, but you'd be living on the street if you weren't brainier than most kids."

"I'm okay for now. My employer's condo was way overpriced, but she has a solid buyer, and he asked me to stay on until he and his wife retire in a couple of years."

She wasn't going to tell Jaudon about the nights in Mrs. Belda's stuffy apartment, a pedestal fan to cool her, waking on a damp sheet and pillow from heat nightmares of her father and Ike Keister, not knowing if a footstep in the corridor meant her belongings were about to be pitched into a dumpster, leaving her and Hop with nowhere to lay their heads.

She prompted Jaudon again to talk about the march and rally, but her mind was distracted. She wanted to smack herself for automatically lying to Jaudon.

In reality, she invented the retiring couple, and Mrs. Belda's buyer, a foreign investor, didn't know MJ never moved out. The apartment was bought sight unseen to leave empty until housing prices rose, when it would be sold without improvements.

She stayed because it was free and kept her off the grid. The maintenance workers saw a familiar face and joked with her. She paid for college with certified checks and used a rent-a-box for her mail, a safe-deposit box for her plunder. No one knew exactly where she lived. She walked over to Pansy's Home Cooking if she needed a lift somewhere.

She had one regret—Mrs. Belda took her air conditioners with her.

❖

On Christmas Day of that lonesome year, MJ rode a bus to Ballast Point on Hillsborough Bay in South Tampa and read the historical marker signs on statues. As she rambled along the trails and out onto the pier, she thought about Confederate soldiers repelling Union forces this far south and how loathsome Florida would be if the South had won the war, that the North was defeated the way some Floridians still thought. That battle might never be over.

She also spent time worrying about a country that could elect a movie star as president, and a country where a mentally ill man was able to procure a gun and shoot peace-loving John Lennon.

At the end of the pier, she breathed in the salt air. The wind was gusty, maybe fifteen miles an hour, and whipping the bay water into choppy whitecaps. Gulls rode the eddies laughing. Brown pelicans perched on pilings. The air smelled almost as pristine as her Columbia River air but lacked the wildness. She wasn't used to cool temperatures anymore—today was in the low fifties—and she didn't last long out there in shorts. She loped back to the park.

Loping right beside her was a panting puppy.

The dog was friendly and wore no collar. Its coat had not yet grown out, and it mightily scratched through its fuzz. No one was calling for the trusting little thing. It shouldn't be roaming free.

She said, "Anika." The puppy took the sound as an invitation and hustled to accompany her, tail upthrust. At a water fountain, she filled her hands, and the puppy drank. Where had that name come from? She remembered—Annika was Pippi Longstocking's friend in the children's books. She'd doted on Annika more than Pippi when she read them, though she'd always misspelled her name.

Oh, Anika, she thought, tugging on her fingers one by one. The dog watched her. *How can I take you in?* The puppy barked once and stood upright, front paws on MJ's knee. She scooped Anika into her arms and let her lick her face, succumbing to the rapture of it.

She rummaged behind a restaurant for the perfect box to conceal the dog on the bus. A woman who'd also seen Anika volunteered to run into an open convenience store for kibble.

"People abandon dogs at this park for some odd reason," the woman told her. "But on Christmas Day?"

"Merry Christmas to me, then. And to you."

Full, and thanks to a dog-loving bus driver, Anika slept silently in her box the whole way back to Mrs. Belda's. One flea bath and a rabies shot later, she started Anika's harness, barking, and potty training. At the Schoolhouse, Anika slept on her folded-up thrift store comforter, with a water bowl large enough for a mastiff, and a squeaky toy in range.

She'd wanted a dog her whole life.

CHAPTER TWENTY-FIVE

December 1980

MJ heard keys in the lock and looked up to see Jaudon.

"Gran boiled an oxtail bone for your new pup."

"Oh, boy, Anika, look what your Auntie Boss brought you." She took the bone, let Anika get a whiff of it, then zigged and zagged the length of the store, hooting and whooping, the puppy right behind her. She tossed it to Jaudon, who held it up until Anika jumped and grabbed it.

"Puppies are more fun than a pogo stick on a trampoline," said Jaudon.

"I love her to pieces, especially when she lets me bury my nose in her fur if I'm feeling bad."

"What's got you down?"

"Nothing now, but honestly, Boss? It's tough having Anika in the apartment. I didn't know what to do about it. The solution came to me yesterday. I'm going to buy a cheap falling-down cottage to live in. After I revamp it, I'll rent it out. Vacation rentals can be lucrative from what I read."

"What do you know about construction?"

"Dear Old Dad had no money for an assistant when he started his well-servicing business after the army. Later, he built houses with his buddies. I was his gofer and learned from watching him and the others."

What if her father never went to Vietnam? Had war ruined him? It must have changed her mother, left alone with spirited Emma Jean for eight years, planning her abundant family, happier times. MJ hadn't been enough to make her mother happy.

When he returned to Depot Landing permanently, Bo Beaudry

established his pump business, and the new babies kept coming: one, then two, three, four. Harrowing battles ensued when MJ refused to be her mother's right arm, outright refused, after two infants, to change diapers, to warm bottles, to mind the toddlers when her mother went out. Well, her now ex-mother realized her big-family wish, but took hand-me-downs and food from the church. The school left MJ in the general classes and didn't challenge her, but she stayed late to read in the school library, missing the bus, trudging that protracted hill when the librarian locked up. Though she wasn't in the smart class, the teachers knew her scores and paid particular attention to her. The other pupils backed off. From then on, she bypassed her parents and made decisions in her best interests, even when that meant forging signatures and lying.

That same year, her father unearthed his gold mine, such as it was.

One day he was drunk with failure and cursing the fates, and the next, through a new customer, he happened on a survivalist community. They needed wells and pumps. He needed an antidote to his war nightmares, a purpose beyond home and family. Many of the survivalists were veterans who'd gone to ground in the far reaches of the country, waiting for the grid to fail and arming themselves against imagined hordes breaking away from the cities to ransack rural strongholds. He worked for the group; before she realized it, he was working with them and buying into their ideas. He and his new pals were pouring a foundation at the compound for the Beaudry family's cinder block home. She hadn't stayed to live in it.

How to reconcile her first fourteen years with this new way of life? It didn't make sense to her. You don't hide from the world to survive—you go out and improve it. If nothing else, from an early age she knew who she wasn't.

One principle for these survivalists involved educating children at home, away from the menace of other cultures and diverse ways of thinking. Her father abruptly pulled Emma Jean from school and told her to teach her siblings to read, write, and do arithmetic daily from eight a.m. to noon. A month or so later, he met the bookmobile lady at the rental house and raged at her for peddling government lies and filth. She never returned.

Afternoons and weekends, in heavy rain, snow, summer heat, she learned to anticipate what her father needed as he dug wells or built houses with his prepper friends.

"I thought your father ignored you," said Jaudon.

"I came in handy until I was offered a money-earning afternoon and summer job at the quarry. Before that, he took me out to his well projects, and I'd hand him wrenches and clamps or sit my bony little girl bottom on pipes to hold them in place. He had the patience of a hungry coyote and a brutish yap when I made mistakes—I learned the hard way to check my work, no matter how insignificant the detail. Believe me, I only needed to hear something once. He dragged me way far from town to the site where he and his nutty prepper buddies were building. One of them brought his son. The father let me listen in while he taught him how to read blueprints, do some construction math, and work out problems for himself."

"It's how my brother Bat and I learned, following Pops around."

"Then you know how handy books and hardware store clerks can be."

"That takes care of your manual skills. You'll need to learn codes, deal with the city, apply for a mortgage."

"No bank will lend to a single woman my age. I'm going to the county seats in Brandon and Four Lakes to bid on abandoned, foreclosed, seized properties or tax deeds they want to get off their books."

Jaudon wrinkled her forehead. "Jiminy, don't torpedo your future working for me here, Squirrel. The next opening at my legit stores is yours if you want it."

"Why? I'm meeting old-timey businessmen, county officials. They go on and on about their grandpas and great-grandpas buying bootleg for holidays and weddings. I know from where I grew up, these contacts may come in handy eventually to get me through closed doors." *And*, she thought, *spare me from government forms and taxes awhile more.*

"You're different from anyone around here. You know a heck of a lot more about almost anything than I ever will."

"Hardly. I'm country too, but the last two years before I left, when I wasn't force-feeding my siblings the multiplication tables and spelling or helping at the site, I worked for a big fish in that small pond. I was in the office, watching and listening."

A car idled, chugging, out front. The engine quickened before it shut off with a rattling shimmy. Anika growled. Jaudon's eyes had gone wide.

"Cops?"

Jaudon craned her neck through the side Dutch window. "Whew, no, it's only Roy Jack, my eldest cousin on Momma's side, in his tired Ranchero. He's a real pill. I wonder what he wants."

MJ smelled overheated metals and took in the cousin's dented, dusty car with a host of offensive bumper stickers, including a rebel flag. Strange that police allowed it on the road. He'd propped open the hood. Steam rose. He hauled a gallon jug of water from the Ranchero's bed and set it by a front tire.

He was trouble, but then, so was she.

On guard, MJ watched Jaudon open the door. Roy Jack was a red-complexioned, wide-nosed man in his forties, with Jaudon's sandy hair, about five foot ten. He wore dirty tan overalls that sagged below his cantaloupe of a belly.

"I don't want to start any family trouble here, cousin, but I saw your car and wanted a word with you." He eyed MJ. "Alone."

MJ wrinkled her nose. Roy Jack smelled the same as organic fertilizer. This must be the cousin with a marijuana crop.

"I'll go check the dairy codes." Anika sniffed Roy Jack's well-broken-in work shoes. MJ hooked leash to harness and kept her close. "Call if you need me, Boss."

"I need you right here. You stay put."

Roy Jack lifted his chin and drew back his head, like a turtle exposing its wrinkly neck. "It's your funeral," he said.

The guy nettled her. Anika folded her ears flat. She thought of the two revolvers she'd dug from their sandy hole. Alone in the Schoolhouse, she'd oiled and cleaned them the way Dear Old Dad taught her when he returned from the war. She'd taken them to the woods out back and practiced on targets, cleaned them again, and hid them in the store. If she needed to wave a gun around to get rid of this guy, so be it.

"You closed here quite a while ago."

Jaudon didn't respond.

"Some folks are wondering if you're planning to hire your family to work in this new operation. Our women are taking cashier jobs at the Winn-Dixie and such. Can't stretch our earnings as far as we used to. I work construction when I can."

Jaudon's hands were in fists, her face reddening like her cousin's. She could see Jaudon wanted to spill it all—about Momma, his aunt, giving the profits to the preacher—but her Pops had decided at the outset to keep it simple and say Momma fell too sick to work anymore.

"Reopening was on my mind originally. I suspect I'm going to upgrade the other stores first. Truth to tell, I'm bound to sell Church Pond to finance the upgrades."

"Think about us, baby cousin. You're making money hand over fist selling mash."

"What mash?" said MJ, the too familiar rush of anger infusing her bloodstream. "Who's selling mash? I'm getting private tutoring courtesy Ms. Vicker. She's lending me this space, and I keep the building clean and safe."

That silenced Roy Jack for a moment. Scratching his head, he said, "But the whole county knows to come here—"

Jaudon opened her mouth, but MJ held a hand aloft. "You must be mistaken. That or someone's pulling your leg."

"Can't you talk for yourself, cousin? Who is this character?"

"I'm MJ Beaudry," she said, straightening her shoulders, lifting her chin.

Roy Jack snuffled noisily, like she was the one who stank. "Huh."

"Hand over fist? Not hardly. Any money I make from the Beverage Bays goes back into the stores."

"I don't know what you did that you closed stores, baby cousin, but you must be a damn fool. We kept the business better than you."

At the sound of footsteps, Jaudon whipped her head around to the open side door. "That's Junior," she told MJ. "Roy Jack's eldest."

Anika whimpered and tried to wriggle from her harness. She didn't know her dog well enough yet to decide if Anika wanted to greet or attack Junior. At the moment she didn't know about herself either. Did she love or hate this gorgeous overdeveloped state and its contrasting mix of Roy Jacks and Jaudons?

"I happened to notice your rig, Poppa. Didn't want to miss out on the come-to-Jesus meeting."

A rumbling diesel pickup parked behind Roy Jack's, and another beside it. She didn't recognize either of them, but Jaudon seemed to.

"Is this a planned meeting, Roy Jack?"

"Don't be ugly. They pass this way going home and saw my ride, right, Junior?"

MJ said, "BS. You must think we're as gullible as you."

Jaudon jutted an approving thumb in the air. "She's right, cousin.

Why don't you go on home and leave us alone? You're a sorrowful overgrown bully."

A clean-cut young Black man fidgeted behind the five white guys. Where did he fit in the family? She held tight to Anika, stooping to run her fingers through her soft coat and coaxing her to sit.

"She give it over to us yet, Poppa?" asked Roy Jack's son, rubbing his hands.

"Hush up, back there." Roy Jack's fists were on his hips. "The gist of it is, we don't understand you hiring outside the family when we have the experience and the customers." He conspicuously sized up MJ, from her eyes to her toes, and said in a brusque, clearly fork-tongued tone, "No offense to you."

She readied herself to reveal the unloaded guns, but she was averse to crossing that line. She knew her whole face was suffused with pink. "I do find that offensive. As if you're such an expert, you can judge Jaudon's hiring practices." She worried she'd be alone if these louts returned.

"And we noticed how you have a colored fellow and a bum in a wheelchair filling out your crew. Now, why can't our boys do that for you?"

Colored fellow? Did the quiet young man with Roy Jack put up with that description? And bum? She admired Jaudon for refusing the bait and answering in the calmest way, "That's MJ's teacher and his other student."

"That is a pure-T lie," came a grumble from a third cousin, followed by nods and a shouted *A-men*.

"Bull pucky," said Roy Jack. "Your momma herself came for her cut monthly, sometimes twice."

Jaudon gaped. MJ advanced on him, summoning Mrs. Lanamore's menacing eye. Jaudon used both arms to restrain her. "Don't be such a hothead."

Roy Jack went on. "Where do you 'spose she contrived to raise the money to knock together new stores on property she bought outright? Not from quarts of milk and bottles of Jax. Jars of white lightning bought that swanky house she lives in, jars her family sold, not some he-she off the street." He sneered at MJ. She sneered right back.

Jaudon seemed to recover herself, though she kept hold of MJ. "Sorry, I'm not dancing to your fiddle to support the Batson clan. You loafers may as well get out there and find real employment. Shame on you, making babies you can't maintain and sending your wives out to earn your keep. Come on, get out."

"Not so fast," said Roy Jack. "Fellas, stay put. This conversation isn't over."

MJ flicked Anika's leash and sidled with her toward the guns.

CHAPTER TWENTY-SIX

"Oh, Uncle Roy Jack, let it lie. Jaudon's a businesswoman and the owner. She gets to decide."

MJ halted and sought out the voice. It belonged to another teenager. Her face was heart-shaped, her skin a freckled brown, she had a broad-bridged nose, and, under closely cropped natural curls, dark eyes glittering with reflected light. She must have edged in after the men.

She immediately admired this defiant reedy girl, a girl as sassy to adults as herself.

The conversation continued, but she wasn't listening.

The girl's forthrightness wasn't all she admired. This girl, she thought, would be reason enough to love Florida. Where Christina had been fleshy and blond, languor permeating every motion, this sprightly girl moved through the men with a reckless grace that spoke of prodigious energy. She'd cut the arms off a denim jacket and wore it over a faded red Tampa Bay Bucs T-shirt, a vee cut into the neck, and white shorts that bragged the luster of her skin color. Her eyes on her uncle were frolicsome, yet her chin was thrust willfully upward.

"Vonnie, come here baby girl," said Roy Jack.

Vonnie. Was there a finer name in the galaxy?

Vonnie stepped away from Roy Jack's pale, red-furred arm.

"Do you want your family to lose our home?" he asked.

Vonnie said, "You're as likely to lose your scrap of piney woods as you are to do an honest day's work, Uncle Roy Jack." Vonnie crossed over to stand with Jaudon and MJ.

That side of MJ's body grew hot. Was she generating the heat, or did it come from Jaudon's girl cousin?

While the men muttered among themselves, Jaudon looked Vonnie over. "You've changed a lot since I last saw you, Vonnie Lowe."

Vonnie opened her arms and hugged Jaudon. "I wish we saw each other more than at Thanksgiving. I dread the family Thanksgiving dinner, and what it does to my father. I may be Black too, but they tolerate my brother and me because we're blood. Shameful half-bloods, but Batsons all the same."

"I'm sorry for that, Vonnie, truly I am."

"My bigot aunts. I'm surprised Aunt Lessie lets my father in her white lady house. As if she's a lady."

"She has no choice—they're sisters."

What a lousy family these Batsons were, she thought, to harbor intolerance toward a relation who outshone them by a mile. Just like her own disappointed, unkind parents.

Roy Jack raised his voice and said, "Whose side are you on anyway, Vonnie?"

Anika sat at attention and stared at Roy Jack. She shushed the puppy's growl.

"I'm not on anyone's side, but I don't go along with bullies, family or not."

Roy Jack said, "I'm not bullying anyone. We're owed, that's all. Jaudon's momma used to do us a service when things were rough."

"You mean by letting you drive our store into the ground?"

Vonnie said, "I've overheard my mother talking. Some weeks you pleaded dire poverty so Jaudon's momma didn't take her percentage."

"Percentage of diddly-squat," Jaudon pronounced. "I never understood why Momma wasn't ashamed to claim Church Pond as a Beverage Bay, the way you neglected it, Roy Jack."

"The store was a tax write-off for her. That's what she told us anyways."

Vonnie, hands on hips, spoke again. "We're talking a free ride for the Batsons, and you know it, Uncle Roy Jack. Find a job if you need money. That's why I work as a server at that big senior living facility near our house—although my parents are both employed."

She was entranced by this young woman. Perhaps trying to impress her, she said, "Shoot, you boys aren't tough enough to stand up to a woman."

The men behind Roy Jack shuffled their feet and studied the floor.

Vonnie nudged her with an elbow. "And that isn't exactly today's headline news."

Jaudon left the group and sat at the picnic table with her paperwork, signaling dismissal.

"I'll be back," said Roy Jack. "I've got high hopes that President Reagan's money will trickle down to us. In the meantime, we gave years to this business, and now we're poor as church mice."

Vonnie said, "You want to lay blame? Go on home and look in your mirrors."

Roy Jack faced the other men. "She wants to do this the hard way. Come on with me to friendly territory, boys. We'll talk. Junior, get us some cold beer at the Winn-Dixie."

The Black teen held back while the other men talked by their trucks. "Want a ride home, Vonnie?" He was freckled like Vonnie, though lighter skinned and a few inches taller, which must, she thought, put him near six feet.

Vonnie told MJ, "My brother Vaughn. Yvonne and Vaughn. Cute, right? Mom is way too clever for a Batson. She gets a kick from our names to this day."

She watched Vonnie with wonder.

Vaughn kneeled, hand out to Anika. MJ let her approach. Why did Vaughn hang around with those rougher men?

"I have my bike. You catch a ride with one of them and find out what they have up their sleeves."

"Exactly what I'm doing, your highness." Anika nuzzled his hand. "You know what Uncle Roy Jack wants with this shop?"

"I knew more was at stake for him than he admitted to," said Jaudon.

"His freaky pal Milo? He has a connection with a Tampa guy who owns a thirty-foot powerboat and smuggles stuff from Cuba. Uncle Roy Jack said cigars and rum, but with news stories about drugs and immigrant smuggling, I don't know. The pal needs space to store and distribute...whatever once he ferries the goods from a mother ship off Cuba to Florida. This Tampa guy is supposed to be rolling in dough."

Jaudon put her hands on her hips. "That explains what lit a fire under him. Acting all family man when he's trying for more easy money."

When Vaughn left, MJ went to the door and double locked both top and bottom. "If you ask me, Boss, that Roy Jack individual is dangerous."

"You're not wrong, Squirrel. Vaughn is asking for trouble hanging out with him."

Vonnie answered, her voice not quite outgrown girlhood. "That's what I worry about. Vaughn's anxious for acceptance. His uncle tries to use him in his schemes."

"He's not the kind to willingly browbeat me into letting the Batsons take over, is he?"

"That's not going to happen. He's been a good person his whole life. Once we graduate, he'll find a job and stay away from our cousins. He decided against college, wants to work with his hands."

As cautious as she wanted to be—the girl was underage and might be straight—MJ was in free fall and wanted to know everything about her. "Is he your twin?"

"He is. Hard to believe I'm related—he's so radically serious and uncool, but I love him to pieces."

"And you are? Ms. Super Cool? By the way, let me introduce you to MJ, aka Squirrel. MJ's my right-hand woman. And that little ball of fur is Anika, MJ's guard dog."

Vonnie held out her hand. The tips of MJ's ears were on fire as she shook it, touching those soft fingers, but Anika was the bigger draw. Vonnie snuggled her.

"She is adorable. What is she?"

"The breed of dog you find abandoned in a park."

"You're my new champion, MJ."

She didn't respond. That was exactly what she feared—and straightway wanted.

"Thank you for rescuing her. She has German shepherd in her, doesn't she?"

She gave Vonnie her Anika story. "When I took her to the vet, the staff crowded around and decided on Belgian shepherd, or a mix of two kinds of Belgians, with that swirl of brown and black coloring and the dark ruff around her neck."

"What happy eyes."

Jaudon gathered her paperwork and stuffed the cash in a number six paper sack. "I'm off to the bank. I know it's a mite warmish in here, but keep these doors shut tight in case they return. Use that peephole."

Vonnie watched Jaudon with the slightly openmouthed expression of hero worship.

She held back a laugh—Vonnie harbored bits of her younger self.

"And thanks for standing up for me, both of you," Jaudon said as she left.

CHAPTER TWENTY-SEVEN

Alone with Vonnie, MJ's bravado took a nosedive. She tried not to stare at this beautiful woman. Rigo would call what she sensed *gaydar*. Anika abandoned them both for a doggy nap.

"Are these yours?" asked Vonnie, examining the textbooks on the card table.

"Required courses at Bone Valley." She pushed her glasses up.

"Bone Valley College? That's a decent school. Why do you work here? Aren't you scared?"

"I'm making good enough money, and the hours fit my schedule." Vonnie wrinkled her nose. "What if you get busted?"

"I'll bet there are good lawyers I can hire."

"You don't talk the way we do. Where are you from?"

"Out west."

"San Francisco?"

Sweat pooled at the small of her back. She raised the power on the standing fan to high and aimed it toward where they stood. "No, not the city. Not any city. I'm from nowhere, farther in the boonies than any map shows."

"Does your hometown have a name?"

She folded her arms and stuck to her rule—erase her past by telling no one about it.

"Florida's my hometown now."

Vonnie touched her lower lip. "Will you show me the setup here?"

She averted her eyes from Vonnie's finger and lips. "Shoot, you're looking at it, except for storage and the cooler."

"I can stand a minute or two of frosty air. Summertime, I might come over to cool off. If you stick around."

"You don't see me leaving, do you?"

"That's half the reason I came over. I heard Roy Jack's trying to persuade the others to blow the whistle on Cousin Jaudon."

She suspected Vonnie's next answer and let her sidelong smile creep along her cheek. "What's the other half?"

"I was curious."

"Curious about the operation?"

"Partly." Vonnie smiled through her eyes.

Neither of them broke eye contact.

"And partly to see MJ Beaudry for myself after hearing the men talk about you."

She backed away, loose fists at chest level. "What in hell do they suppose they know about me?"

Vonnie's smile transformed to an expression of alarm, and her upper body swayed wide of MJ's. In a fraction of a second, MJ wanted to recant her words.

"I'm sorry," she said, stepping in front of the fan again. "I'm having a conniption fit over nothing, except seriously, I'm rattled by the men mobbing us."

Vonnie laughed, quick to forgive, and crooked her finger, leading MJ to the cooler. "Then you better hope none of their women come to call."

"Why?" She opened the door and bowed Vonnie into the walk-in cooler. "Aren't they against the men drinking and breaking the law?"

"They might be on Sundays, but they'll defend their men to the death against a person who tries to take away what they see as theirs by right."

"What about you? Do you agree with your clan?"

Vonnie walked around the narrow space. "Jaudon's my part of the clan. I'm on her side, whatever it is."

"Tell me why your uncle Roy Jack, out of the blue, is hectoring Jaudon for the business."

"He's depending on the new county commissioner to show law and order muscle. You need to understand, it's not always 1980 here— sometimes it's 1880, especially with that cowboy in DC. Moonshining goes way back in their families. It's as much part of their identity as NRA bumper stickers and mud truck races. It's common knowledge things will go back to the way they were after the new guy orders a police raid or two. Uncle Roy Jack is taking advantage of Jaudon's vulnerability right now."

She saw Vonnie notice her hands twisting into a tangle and shoved them into her pockets. "Hey. It's not like we're dealing drugs."

"That will never happen. Jaudon's dead set against them, and she lectures Vaughn and me to stay away from anyone who uses or sells." Vonnie examined the back wall and explored it with her hands. "It was a while ago, but I know one of my cousins taught me how to open this secret compartment. Don't show me—I'll find it."

"You're close to Jaudon?"

"I wish I was. The rest of the Batsons, well, they never recovered when my mother eloped with my father. We see them Thanksgivings."

Someone knocked at the Dutch door. She left Vonnie to her poking around and checked the peephole. She drew back on sight of the patrol car, but it was only the deputy Jaudon called Officer Friendly. Cullie claimed he was gay.

He was reaching from his car window to knock again when she opened the top door. "Listen," he said, keeping tabs on his rearview mirror. "You know a fella named Roy Jack Batson?"

"As a matter of fact, I met him today."

"You might want to weigh moving your operation. He came to the station this morning acting ornery about y'all. It's not the best time to be in the sheriff's sights, if you know what I mean." He checked his mirror again.

"I do. Thanks for the heads-up. I mean it."

He winked. "But don't go too far, you hear?" He double slapped his car door and drove off.

Vonnie had remained in the hidden storage space.

MJ beckoned her out. "Jaudon needs to disown your uncle."

Vonnie rubbed her hands along her arms, shivering. "Not that easy. Uncle Roy Jack is lazy as a snail on a slug. He has it in his head that the Vickers owe him a living since his sister, Jaudon's momma, married one of them. According to him, his other sister ruined the family by marrying Dad and having two non-white kids. He calls us double jeopardy."

"But going to the sheriff when the sheriff himself buys from us?"

"Batson brains are sparse. The sheriff may have finished high school."

"You're thousands of times smarter than them."

"My mother had the mettle to marry a Lowe—my grandmother on Dad's side is a Brandon—though as a colored Brandon, he didn't inherit much more than brains and miserly respect. Our ancestors settled the City of Brandon. My dad's a high school teacher. Mom was a legal secretary but went back to school and became a paralegal. She barely took time off when we came along, in 1963."

Vonnie brought out a protective instinct she hadn't known about. "You better clear out in case your uncle gets us raided. You have solid parents who're giving you a head start in life."

"What about your parents? Are they dead or something?"

"I was born years before my two brothers and two sisters. You can tell when you become extraneous. And they didn't like me much."

"How can parents not appreciate their child? Especially a plucky child like you."

It dawned on her that there wasn't much of that child left. Nearly twenty-one, she'd morphed into a plucky and focused woman.

"I'm as different from them as you are from the Batsons."

Vonnie's eyebrows tilted upward and the smile returned to her eyes. "The way Jaudon's different?"

That she wasn't going to answer without knowing more about Vonnie. "You're like a toddler asking for another bedtime story, Vonnie. I'm serious now—vamoose."

"Are you always this flinty? Do you ever smile?"

She had no answer.

Vonnie went out the door and darted back, quick as a deer spotting danger.

Her heartbeat accelerated. Was it the sight of Vonnie again or fear that the cops were out there?

"Hey, you want to go roller-skating sometime?"

She tried to convince herself she needed to stay away from this girl, this relative of Jaudon's, cousin to the men who'd invaded the Schoolhouse—in other words, trouble. But she'd seen the Sweetheart Roller Rink from the bus, past its heyday, but good-sized and popular. It reminded her of the rink where she and the little ones were sometimes dropped off while her parents shopped. Babysitting on wheels, she called it. She thought she might like skating again for the fun of it, Vonnie or not.

"Okay," she said, subduing her excitement at the guarantee of seeing Vonnie again. "On one condition."

Vonnie's smile faltered again.

"That you don't come back here till you're legal to drink."

"Then we'll have to find more ways to get together, MJ."

Her heart kicked—Vonnie said her name for the first time. Anika stared at Vonnie, tongue hanging, tail wagging. Flinty? MJ feared she came across more like Anika. "Remember, I'll toss you out."

Vonnie stuck her tongue in a cheek, worked it around, and showed her dimples. "Sounds fun." She slipped out the door but returned to poke her head in again. "I'll meet you at the rink this Saturday about seven?"

The Schoolhouse closed at six p.m. The rink wasn't more than an hour walk. She'd walk to the moon for this girl, walk as far as it took to claim her.

CHAPTER TWENTY-EIGHT

That Saturday evening, Berry greeted a teeth-chattering Rigo and propelled him indoors.

"Silly boy," she said. "It's not that cold."

"You're not as delicate as I am. The farmers will be spraying the strawberries tonight to keep them from freezing."

Gran called out, "There goes the water table. I wish they'd go back to smudge pans. All that spraying leads to sinkholes."

"Lucky you," Rigo said. "You're all warm and snug."

"True enough, but I'm babysitting such a batch of critters in here you could stir them with a stick."

Cullie and MJ were at the house, dropping off Anika and Kirby. Puddin and Anika wrestled, Kirby watching from a distance. Kajen sat on a windowsill and flicked her tail in annoyance.

Jaudon had volunteered Berry for the outing, explaining, "MJ's near twenty-one. She's sweating about dating a seventeen-year-old who sets her heart on fire."

"I'd be leery too," Berry had answered, capturing Puddin and lifting her into her lap for a brushing.

"I'm covering for Emmett Saturday night. You can go, can't you?"

Leave it to Jaudon to ask her after the fact, thought Berry. "Sure, I'll go. You won't be there to catch me if I fall, though."

Jaudon nuzzled Puddin's too-soft upright belly. "Make it a party. Ask Cullie and Allison, Rigo and Jimmy Neal."

Jaudon and Berry had watched Vonnie grow up. Until age twelve she was Jaudon's Thanksgiving shadow and a raging tomboy. She shied away from them in her early teens. Berry said at the time that they were the cause of Vonnie's anxiety. She'd heard the way the Batson side of her family talked about their queer cousin and her Georgia trash girlfriend.

Cullie blew an air kiss to Gran and called out, "Smooch." MJ settled beside her in the back seat of Rigo's car.

Berry asked if Rigo knew Vonnie Lowe.

Rigo switched the heater on full force. "Vonnie, Vonnie, Vonnie. I've tried to picture someone by that name since you invited me."

Rigo was finishing his PhD and often babbled about the obscure points of his dissertation on evolutionary psychology as it pertained to homophobia. He considered himself the pioneer in the field.

Berry prodded him again. "How about at the bar? She wouldn't be the first underage child to show a fake ID."

"Oh, babe, bars are so sixties." His laugh was abrupt, a mix, he once told her, of his mother's unfettered mirth and his father's humorless grunt. "Thinking," he said, tapping a foot. "There's New York Pizza, near the bar. The owner is known for feeding runaway gay teens, and I trip over the multitude of twinks and baby dykes sipping Cokes."

He put a finger to his temple, raised it, saying, "Aha. Vonnie's a girl. That's why I had a hard time picturing her. She's that gorgeously wild schoolkid, rides her bike like the god Mercury, doesn't seem to care who knows she's gay. We've all fallen for her. She's queer sunshine."

"That's her," said MJ from the back seat, her voice breathy. "A ray of light."

MJ had a growth spurt since arriving in Florida. She came off natty in her now customary outfit—black polo, no longer buttoned to her neck, sleeves rolled tight on her biceps, and black jeans. She'd put goop on her hair to slick it into submission, and it transformed her into an innocent-looking, tall, ten-year-old boy. From working at the stores, her muscles developed to the point that the shirts no longer drooped on her arms.

Cullie said, "Ah, how well I remember seventeen. My exes were piling up."

Rigo gave a dramatic sigh. "The next queer generation is falling in love already. We're aging fast, girls."

"I'm not in love," said MJ.

Berry laughed in the soft way taught her by Grandma Garland, who'd tried to teach her Southern church lady manners.

Rigo entered the parking lot. Vonnie stood with a group of

teenagers under the large neon roller skate. She was silhouetted against the sunset, her tall frame curved slightly over her bicycle, her dark curly hair gloriously backlit.

MJ breathed out the word, "Wow."

Vonnie was locking her bike to the sign. "What is this?" she asked, pointing with her chin to MJ's escorts. "You're afraid to be alone with me?" She gestured toward the rink, the smokers in the parking lot, the guard at the front door. "In this crowd?"

MJ didn't answer. It was obvious she was watching Vonnie's eyes glimmer with reflections of the sign's colors.

Rigo stepped forward. "We wanted in on the party, but you can ignore us if you'd rather."

"Where have I seen you before?"

"New York Pizza."

"That's it. But I've never seen you without Mr. Muscles."

"Jimmy Neal? He's my manatee man."

"There isn't a boy there who doesn't want to follow him home."

"To his husband's waiting arms," Rigo said.

Cullie said, "You'd better be talking anatomical arms, not the kind you shoot."

"Excuse me, Ossifer. This is Florida—I have a right to defend my private property."

Berry laughed lightly. "Rigo's private property is on night shift at the hospital."

"Isn't Cousin Jaudon coming?" Vonnie asked.

Berry said, "She's covering for Emmett Ponder. He has exams."

"Where's your dog?" Vonnie asked MJ.

MJ was enjoying the pleasure of the winter night's soft warmth and of hearing Vonnie speak. "With Gran."

"I notice you haven't asked the whereabouts of my little coconut," Cullie said with a sniff of indignation.

Rigo groaned as he faithfully did at the sight or mention of Kirby the Second. "That dog."

"What?" said Cullie. "My revered Kirby is cuter than any ten puppies." She pulled out her wallet and showed Vonnie a photo of Kirby. "I will say MJ's Anika is the next most lovable dog in existence."

Vonnie's face relaxed. "I adore Anika."

Rigo teased Cullie. "Is it the muddy feet that drew you to Kirby? The teensy eyes behind her swarm of dusty fur?"

"Don't talk about your husband that way." Cullie turned from him.

"Can my wife and I adopt you, Vonnie? Purty, purty please? I want to make sure the world treats you right."

Vonnie angled her head as if unsure whether Cullie meant to tease her too, but Berry saw the excitement in her flushed face and wide, excited eyes at all the attention from this older, worldly-wise group.

Vonnie asked, "Are you seriously married to a woman?"

"Oh," said Cullie, casting her eyes this way and that, two fingers held to her lips. "Wasn't I supposed to say that?"

Vonnie crowed. "You're gay, right? Every one of you? This will be a great party. Come on, it's disco night." She grabbed MJ's hand and pulled her toward the entrance.

Berry scanned the lot. No one watched. Were all the fledgling lesbians this open?

Rigo whispered to her and Cullie, "They are inevitable."

Cullie hunched her back and pretended to use a cane. "We may as well go home and knit booties for the grandchildren, or whatever fogies like us do when we see young love."

"Old?" Berry pulled at Cullie's sleeve. "Speak for yourself, Deputy Culpepper."

"Deputy?" Rigo asked.

"Sworn and badged," Cullie said. "The city council put off their decision to hire women once too often—the county sheriff snapped us up and sent us to finish our training at the Academy."

Rigo ran at Cullie and hugged her, pounding her back. "Hot damn. You did it. Congratulations."

The blast of music when Berry, Cullie, and Rigo opened the door silenced them. Berry inhaled buttery popcorn fumes. They joined MJ and Vonnie at the skate rental counter.

Cullie reached past her to a rack of snacks. "Thank the Goddess, they have my Cheetos. I got hooked on Cheetos here when I had to wear double socks to fit infant skates."

"Silly," Berry scoffed. "There's no such size as infant roller skates."

"Your chaperones are here," said Vonnie, stabbing MJ in the ribs with an index finger.

MJ flinched and went pink. She gained control, though, paying for both pairs of skates. Vonnie seemed to take the chivalry for granted. She led MJ to a bench. As they laced their skates, Vonnie chattered like a tree full of nervous house sparrows.

The chaperones gained their sea legs by circling the wooden

flooring of the rink a few times. Rigo glided ahead, made a half turn, and skated backward through the crowd, swiveling his head to avoid other skaters. His thick red curls sparkled with reflections from the revolving ball on the ceiling.

Cullie shouted over upbeat dance music and the hum of dozens of wheels on wood. "Presenting Olympic skating star Rockin' Rigo."

"Shh," Berry joked. "We don't want make a spectacle of ourselves." All the skaters watched Rigo. Jaudon should be here; she'd always exhibited a feral agility, but on skates, as in the stores, Jaudon was grace itself.

With a quick twirl, Rigo stopped ahead of them. They rolled to the wood railing, its red paint peeling to reveal layers of other colors beneath.

"Rigoberto," said Cullie, "you have my undying admiration."

"You never said how good you were," Berry said.

"I try to stay humble about my many talents."

From the corner of her eye, she saw Vonnie and MJ speed past them on the inside of the track. In midglide, they rotated to skate backward, then forward, alternating around the rink.

"Well," said Rigo with a huff. He took off, caught up, and circled them. They gained the upper hand and circled him. Rigo grabbed Vonnie's hands, and they whirled together to a stop and separated. The onlookers applauded.

Vonnie took MJ's arm.

"She's not a bad skater, MJ's pal," said Rigo, as he caught his breath against the rail.

"Not bad?" said Cullie. "You two should try for the Olympics."

"Is roller-skating a category?" Berry asked.

"You're asking the wrong person," said Cullie. "But it should be."

Rigo rolled back and forth on one foot. "I'd be bored to death if I spent hours practicing now. I learned one summer in Cuba from a guy who worked for my father. Carlos was crazy for skating at his advanced age. Or plain crazy, according to my father, who'd rather I spent my time hacking tobacco leaves from their stems." He struck an effeminate pose. "I am deathly afraid of machetes."

The high-pitched outcry of a child sounded, and the three of them spun toward it. Berry skated that way full speed.

Right in front of Vonnie, a sprig of a white girl lay on the flooring. Vonnie used an instant toe stop and bent to the girl, who appeared to be about seven. A slightly taller boy who resembled the girl grabbed her by the hand to stand her up, but she screeched again. Vonnie sat cross-legged on the floor and put her arms out. "Don't move her," she said as Berry arrived.

Cullie and Rigo directed skaters around them.

The boy accused Vonnie of hurting his sister on purpose, claiming, in rude words, the rink should have stayed segregated.

Berry said, "Back off and shut your vicious mouth, boy." The floor attendant blared a whistle and observed her. "I'm a nurse," she told him. The music stopped.

As the girl wailed, Berry examined her legs and ankles, which were fine. The child offered her wrist. "You landed on your hand?" The girl nodded. "It's painful, isn't it, hon?" She examined it and saw it had started to swell. Someone handed her the plastic bag of ice she'd asked for and she laid the girl's wrist on it. "Go with the attendant and call home," she told the brother. "Can you handle that?" she said.

But the mother was in the parking lot, just back from the hairdresser's, and someone fetched her. One look at her hair and Berry had to wonder how many hours the children had been here. No wonder the girl fell—she must have been tired.

"My baby." The mother, a hefty person, shouted and pushed through a clutch of the curious. Berry feared a collision and held a cautionary hand. "Careful, she hurts."

The mother slapped her son on the head. "I told you to watch out for her."

"I did," the boy whined. "That colored girl must have tripped her." He pointed at Vonnie where she still sat with the girl. MJ was hunched chivalrously over Vonnie.

"I'll see to that one in a minute," said the mother.

Berry told her, "You'd best have an X-ray at the ER to make sure it's no more than a sprain."

"We'll go directly to our doctor, thank you anyway." The mother stood and approached Vonnie, one accusatory finger raised.

MJ moved in front of Vonnie. "Your daughter fell on her own. It's a miracle we stopped as fast as we did. She hit the floor with her fingers splayed." She imitated the little girl. "Just so. Didn't you teach her to land on her fists, big brother?"

The attendant was cross. "Lucky she wasn't hurt worse. I can't keep an eye on every skater every minute of the day. Weren't you watching her, boy?"

"He skated right next to her," Vonnie said in the thin voice Berry remembered from Vonnie's childhood. "He didn't do anything wrong except insult me."

"No harm done other than the wrist, then," the attendant said, lifting the girl.

Berry tasted bile. "That's a disgusting thing to say."

The attendant raised puzzled eyebrows and carried the child to a bench where he kneeled to unlace her skates. The penned crowd surged ahead, and after a shrill whistle, the music blared again.

MJ's face was red and her eyes narrow as she helped Cullie off the floor. "I have never seen such ignorance. You know the son learned it from that parent."

"Welcome to my life," Vonnie said.

"Hey, Squirrel," Cullie said. "What are you going to do, spank the junior racist?"

"No. The jerk who said *no harm done*. And Vonnie's supposed to take that abuse? Like you have no emotions, Vonnie."

Cullie said, "You know you can't raise the consciousness of ignorance."

"Or," said Vonnie, "change the reality of living as a Black person in America by attacking one ignorant white man."

"But you're half white." Cullie hit her forehead with the heel of her hand. "Stupid comment. I don't suppose that makes a difference."

"It doesn't. They see the color of my skin, not my blood. Wherever I go, whatever I do, I am permanently Black. Thanks for being concerned, though I hear a lot worse than this."

"He belongs where I come from. It's thoroughly homogeneous," said MJ, eyes glowering at the attendant's back.

Berry slipped an arm through MJ's to keep her from acting rashly.

Vonnie said, "Americans can speak by voting. That's what my parents believe. Won't make white people respect us more, but besides education, it's our most effective defense, representation in government. At the school where he teaches, my dad's a target. Parents blame our race for their children's behavior, grades, and truancy."

Berry rubbed Vonnie's shoulders.

"Well, that was certainly unpleasant," said Rigo. "You're a class act, Vonnie, speaking for that odious white boy."

"You deserve to have fun now." MJ danced Vonnie away.

Berry dropped onto a wooden fold-down seat. "I'm wrung out." The three chaperones removed their skates.

Out on the wood, "Rock the Boat" played. MJ, rolling backward, pulled a laughing, protesting Vonnie.

"They've practiced," asked Rigo.

Cullie said, "It's the second time they've met. Ms. Cupid is engineering this."

"That's Mr. Cupid to you," Rigo said, peering down his nose at her.

"I don't guess," said Berry, "people will be calling Vonnie more names tonight. I believe she can outskate anyone in the crowd."

The couple came off the floor triumphant and winded. Vonnie took MJ's skates. "I want to go thank the attendant for keeping the arena under control."

"Isn't she amazing?" said MJ.

Cullie gave MJ a light punch. "And mucho pretty too."

Berry thought Vonnie might have suggested a skating date in order to show off.

MJ sighed. "But she leaves for college in September."

"Are you going to escort her through her seventeenth summer, Romeo?" asked Cullie.

"Like skating and to the movies?" MJ adjusted her glasses. "If she wants. I'm not going to touch her, though."

Berry said, "You can find a job near her college."

"No, I'd be a weight around her neck. She's excited about the whole living on campus thing."

"What if she meets someone else?"

"Oh, she will. She will."

Berry was impressed by this bit of wisdom and doubted MJ's ability to be as laid back when the time came.

Cullie asked, "What if it's a man and she marries him?"

"I'd buy a cheap plane ticket and hike around France, see where my ancestors lived."

"So harsh on her—and yourself?" asked Berry. "You'd leave the country?"

Cullie answered that question. "I'd like to see you watch Jaudon do that."

The idea was beyond imagining. "What a horrifying thought."

MJ said, "Vonnie wouldn't put up with a man. She has better things to do with all her energy, her self-confidence."

They were quiet, watching the skaters, hardly a dark face among them. It unsettled her that she'd never paid enough attention to the preponderance of whiteness around her. She'd talk to Dr. Garza and Dr. Riyanto about serving a wider range of patients and hiring people of color. And what about the migrants' children, where were they?

MJ said, "Vonnie will not stay away from the Schoolhouse like I told her to. Honest to goodness, I don't want to get her in trouble."

Berry said, "Never mind Vonnie—I wish you didn't hang around the Schoolhouse."

"It's only till Jaudon is debt free. I have plans to earn legitimate money myself."

She met MJ's eyes and took her hand. "I worry."

"Okay. I'll remember that." MJ gripped her hand tightly.

Vonnie and Rigo returned.

"We're going for ice cream sodas," said Rigo. "Can you believe it? On a Saturday night? In days of yore…" He indicated the rink with a hand. "Never mind, I am a married man after all."

CHAPTER TWENTY-NINE

February 1981

Berry's adolescent psych class was taxing after a full day at work, and the treat was tempting, but she waited to present Jaudon with the hand-packed quart of strawberry ice cream from their favorite dairy stand.

"Oh, heck, Georgia gal. How'd you know exactly what I needed? You make everything better."

"I can't make it better, but I can help make it bearable."

With a flourish, Jaudon scooped the treat into two bowls. She tempted Kajen from the table and onto her lap with a finger dipped in ice cream. As the little cat licked, she said, "Now, tell me about your day."

Berry did, the ice cream cold enough to make their teeth smart. She ended by saying, "My class brought Vonnie to mind. She'll be eighteen in April, but she won't be any less an adolescent. I assumed she had a schoolgirl crush on MJ. As for MJ, she's infatuated with all things Florida. It makes sense she'd go for the first eligible Florida woman she met. Now I'd say it's more serious. Your aunt Lollie called me today to ask what we know about MJ, and I told her, truly, not much. I reassured her, though. MJ is completely taken by that child and acts as though Vonnie's a princess."

"Vonnie's not made of porcelain."

"To her mother she is."

"True, and you were right to reassure Aunt Lollie. You know how love takes you and spins you together with the right person. I'm certain that's what's happening with Vonnie and MJ. I know it in my bones, as surely as I did with you." She closed her eyes as she bit into a frozen piece of strawberry. "Tastier than any candy bar." Berry's ice cream was melting in its bowl. "What's the matter? You got a burr in your saddle?"

"Cullie said our new county commissioner is pushing law and order. Can you close before then?"

"Oh, I don't know that the sheriff will bother us on a new commissioner's say-so. If I have to, I can get money for the property, but that might take a while. Next time I talk to Rouie, we'll have a ballpark. I need to start paying myself again soon."

"I worry about you and MJ being saddled with criminal records."

"You think I'm pushing my luck?"

"The more time you're at it, the more exposed you are, and I know Gran will go back to work rather than see you in worse trouble."

Abruptly, Jaudon's eyes dampened and she wiped her nose with her wrist. Kajen was on her shoulder, sniffing her hair and ear. "I wish I had a mother like Gran, Berr. She has no malice in her."

"My sad angel." She went around the table and pulled Jaudon's head to her breast. "Your momma's sick. I'd venture she has been for a long, long time. You have us now."

"Gran's not getting a job on my behalf, and you're not going to quit school. I've improved my business skills. If we can keep going another year, we may be out from under."

"You're usually the most law-abiding person I know." She ran her hands through Jaudon's short hair.

"You know I despise this illegal stuff." Jaudon took a napkin and honked into it. "I'm keeping things lean as I can. I'm putting in ample hours to avoid hiring more staff. I ditched Momma's fancy office for the back room at the Buffalo Street store. This debt on my back weighs a thousand pounds. And there's the women's clinic we need to save money for. Your dream is as important as mine."

"You're terribly spent, practically dead on your feet. How did I not notice?"

Jaudon's eyes were closed again, but tears slipped from under the lids. "Because you're Super Nurse at the clinic and finishing your psych degree and keeping the house running and taking a runaway child on her first date."

"Don't be silly. That was fun."

The front door opened. Berry let go of Jaudon and craned her neck to see.

Gran shuffled in and hefted the heavy tote bag she used as a purse onto the kitchen table. She lifted the bottom and slid vegetables and melons into a heap. "These were going in the trash. These too," she said, producing dried beans. "Put the beet greens and cabbage in the crisper, but leave the strawberries out. They're overripe, so we'll have them for dessert unless you want to freeze them. Boil half those dried red beans for two minutes. Let them set an hour, and put the unused beans in the cupboard, please. I didn't pay a cent for any of it. But oh, my aching feet."

Berry raised her voice. "Where have you been?" Gran's hearing was starting to get as bad as Jaudon's.

"I started a job today, children." Gran filled the kettle and set it to heat on the stove. "One of my senior center friends works at Padgett's Produce Stand and they needed a new lady. The owner hired me on the spot. Showed me what they wanted pulled from the bins and what stayed and how to tend the boiled peanuts. What a treat to work with the smell of those salty nuts. We can take our pick of the spoils."

Jaudon exclaimed over the strawberries, located a huller in the utensil drawer, and prepped them for later.

Gran pulled a basin out from under the sink. She filled it with Epsom salts and the heated water, sat at the table, and gradually lowered her feet into the steaming basin. "Ahhh," she said.

"You must be outside your mind, Gran," said Jaudon. "You've worked enough in your lifetime."

"We can use the extra money, and I enjoy seeing people."

"But your sore feet."

"I need to toughen these little piggies, that's all. I used to stand on them eight hours a day sorting berries at the packing plant."

Kajen jumped on Gran's lap, wound herself into a compact ball, and commenced purring.

"Jaudon's right, Gran. You're not eighteen anymore. Or forty."

"You know what I'm going to do?"

"What fool scheme are you going to propose this time, Jaudon Vicker?" asked Gran. "Don't you be telling me you're selling dope from Church Pond Road."

"You know I'd never do that. No, I'm going to keep the liquor flowing till the job's done. Berry and I were discussing shutting it, but if I can get more profit sooner, that'll shorten its run naturally."

"How in the world?" asked Berry, who had assembled the ironing table and was painstakingly pressing her white uniform, her first with slacks.

Gran said, "You can't exactly get more business by putting a circular in the paper for your bootleg."

"No, but I can put a cousin or two to work in commission sales and send them into other areas. I may not like them, but I'm a Batson, and I pity the younger ones."

"Child, you bulldoze your way into the competition's territory, and they'll come back at you. Believe me—I've lived in this world a lot longer than you."

"If there's competition, Gran, and they want to get rid of us, it'll be my lazy cousins running, not me. It might get the rest of the family off my back."

Berry and Gran glanced at each other.

Gran said, "I went to school with the Batsons. Not a one of them is worth his or her salt except for your dour mother who had smarts, but good Lord, she'd start an argument in an empty house."

"Oh, for pity's sake," said Berry. "I'm putting my foot down." She carried a small bottle of water from the deep farmhouse sink to the ironing board and plugged a cork sprinkler top into the bottle. "You know your momma's relatives will mess you up. They'll blab to the wrong folks. They'll hold out money from you the way they did from her. The authorities will come down on you, their employer, and your efforts will be for nothing, absolutely nothing."

Gran had that wise loving-yet-vexed expression again. "Think who else you'd bring trouble to."

"I do," she said.

Berry shook water along the back of her uniform blouse. "Think about Vonnie."

Gran asked, "Vonnie Lowe? She and her twin come to Thanksgiving at your aunt Lessie's. How does she fit into this?"

Berry said, "MJ thinks the sun rises and sets with Vonnie."

"Then she won't want Vonnie involved in any of your jiggery-pokery."

"She doesn't." Kajen vaulted at Jaudon from Gran's lap. Jaudon disentangled her claws from her shoulder and held the cat to her chest. "Vonnie has a mind of her own. She all but claimed MJ for herself the day they met."

"Sounds like a real firecracker, that one, and MJ's her flame in more ways than one. I see what you're worried about." Gran dried her feet with a towel. "Lordy, lordy. I about have one generation settled when the next gets in a heap of trouble."

Berry spooned out the remainder of the ice cream for Gran.

Jaudon took the carton and scraped at the dregs. "And I'm not free from trouble yet. I want to generate dollars before this hole Momma dug buries me, but jiminy, you two are right. I've dragged too many people into this. I'll think of something—I promise."

CHAPTER THIRTY

June 1981

MJ, Tad, and Shady met with Jaudon for a final time at Church Pond Road. The small U-Haul was loaded by twilight with the last of the liquor and equipment.

MJ watched Jaudon's fast fingers count the week's take and thought about challenging her to a bill counting race. Between the talk of raids and Berry's insistence over the past few months, there would be no more income from the moonshine business. A Tampa real estate broker Jaudon met at the Miami march had pounded in a For Sale sign.

Maybe the breaking point for Jaudon was Gran's refusal to quit the produce stand job when Jaudon admitted she was desperate enough to need tainted money, which gave Berry grounds to convince Jaudon the liquor business had to go. Jaudon and MJ worked out a deal for Tad and Shady to buy the business and stock with monthly payments.

Jaudon gave MJ her cash and an envelope.

"What's this, Boss?" she asked, pulling out a graduation card and a hundred-dollar bill.

"Berry and I want you to buy yourself a treat or have fun. Never mind squirreling it away for the future."

"I—I don't know what to say." She really didn't. Innocent Jaudon had no idea she had another source of income or of the possible profits from one lucky visit to an unoccupied house. Ever since the wealthiest Northerners left in early spring, she'd busily helped herself. Florida was made for burglars.

"Your BA degree in three years," said Shady. "You're a damned dogged squirrel, as well as the smartest student in my memory."

"You run an outstanding prep school, Shady."

"You hardly needed me. I'm going to have to find a new prodigy."

"A negligible part of me wants to let my parents know I'm not worthless," she said. "That's one reason it means a lot to have Mrs. Lanamore and you and Tad at the ceremony. Cullie and Allison are giving me a graduation party at the skate rink—before the rink opens that day."

"Send your parents a Xerox copy of your diploma."

She saw red but stifled it and told Jaudon, "Honestly? They couldn't care less."

Nothing was left in the warehouse to buffer sound. Nothing to hear but Jaudon zipping shut her bank bag before she jammed it under the band of her shorts at the small of her back.

She thought about what an easy mark Jaudon was. Several times in the last few days, ominous shudders brought goose bumps to her arms. She dismissed her apprehension as a reaction to the end of this part of her life and nerves about starting her career as a real estate investor.

She'd received her birth certificate from Washington State, which enabled her to apply for a Social Security number, register to vote, carry a credit card, and, ironically, sell liquor.

Florida proved to be her promised land. With her savings, she'd won her bid on a tax deed sale at a county property auction. A week later, she chanced an insultingly lowball offer on a FSBO—For Sale by Owner—a one-bedroom house within walking distance from Clearwater Beach. The roof was new, the foundation showed no cracks, the area was zoned for short-term rentals, and the owner was in a hurry.

She stopped congratulating herself in time to watch Jaudon shake hands with Tad and Shady and thank them for rescuing her from her cousin's vendetta. They'd finished emptying the cooler.

Shady said, "Methinks it's time for Tad to get in the U-Haul and deliver the last of the bottles and jugs to their new home."

Tad was examining the walls, ceiling, and flooring. "This could be a nice mini warehouse. What are you asking for it?" Tad asked.

"Not much. I want to sell it as quick as I can."

"I have another use for it," Shady said.

She grinned at Jaudon. Shady's interest in repurposing was exactly what they'd predicted.

Jaudon told Shady, "I need the cash."

"You won't rent it out for income so you can keep the building and reopen in due course?"

"Nope."

MJ folded her arms and in her firmest voice explained, "She doesn't want to have to monitor what goes on in here, and I don't blame her. You know what I mean, especially with the special storage space?"

Shady teased her. "What were you in your last life, a guard along the watchtower?"

She gave it right back to him. "You going to sing us some Bob Dylan songs now?"

Someone knocked at the Dutch door. Recently, Jaudon seemed to have difficulty identifying where sounds originated. She was still fighting off hearing aids.

"Oh, man," MJ said, on her way to the peephole. "We're not open."

"What a gas if it's Publishers Clearing House." Shady began his hoot owl laugh, but after a sharp glance from Jaudon he stifled it.

"Let's hope it's not my shifty relations again."

"Hi, Officer Friendly," MJ said loudly as she opened the top of the door. The workspace was sweltering, the outside air barely cooler, though the frogs had started their night songs.

"Hey," he said. "One of the boys got wind that you're selling out."

She didn't answer.

"And that you're reopening in a Rainbow Gap neighborhood the boys try to avoid, if you get my drift."

"They don't run this business."

"Hey, I'm trying to do you a good turn. They're gearing up now to come over and kiss your shop good-bye. Orders from on high."

From a distance, the first siren sounded.

The cop said, "I'm supposed to watch the perimeter."

"Wait a sec." She ran for a jar of Dinkey Dew, shoved it in a paper bag, and presented it through the window. "Thanks for letting us know."

He smiled, said, "I'm sorry to see you go," and rolled away.

She locked the door and wheeled around to give orders to abandon ship.

No one was there.

❖

MJ kept the presence of mind to extract the box of revolvers from their hiding place and run through the darkness to toss them on the back seat floor of Jaudon's car as she hurried Anika in. Behind the

Schoolhouse, Jaudon loaded Shady's wheelchair into the truck, pulled the rear door closed, and slapped it twice. Tad took off. Sirens sounded from south of them.

Jaudon headed to the store.

"Boss. No. What are you, crazy?"

"I'm going to shoo the cops off my property."

She latched onto Jaudon's elbow. "No, you're not. From what Berry told me, the last time you challenged the police, you lost half your hearing. She'd kill me if I let you stay."

"There's nothing for them to find."

"Damn it, this isn't about your pride. It's about not getting more entangled in the legal system."

Jaudon put a hand to her head.

"Run now, Boss. Think later."

"Run where?"

"I know a bolt-hole." She hurried Jaudon along to the car. By the time she pulled her door closed, Jaudon was rolling. "Turn left onto Church Pond."

"That's where they're coming from. Listen."

It wasn't—yet. She hid her exasperation but determined to urge hearing aids on Jaudon. "Trust me, Boss, and hurry."

Jaudon sped north. MJ directed her into a driveway. She jumped from the car while Jaudon coasted to a stop. She leaped to the roof rat's window, relieved to meet no rats, squeezed her way in, and plunged through the house for the garage door button. She signaled Jaudon to drive forward and manually closed the door to hide the overhead light.

Out on the road, the sirens were close.

"I need to go outside for a minute," she said. She poked her head through Jaudon's open window, "Don't budge, Boss. And I'm serious about that."

She knew Jaudon was a woman of action, like herself. She backed away slowly, motioning with a raised hand for Jaudon—and Anika— to stay. The box of revolvers she held below Jaudon's sightline. Reassuring as they were to have on hand, they scared her. People were shooting at everyone, most recently, Queen Elizabeth and the Pope. She remembered her father and his survivalist friends target shooting at paper cutouts of authority figures, nearly foaming at the mouth when they compared new gun purchases.

She crouched, wiped the box with her shirt, and set it back on the garage floor. Hastening along the garage exterior, she was alert for signs of occupation. She commended herself for making black her signature color. If the owners were in town, though, nothing was dark enough to hide her.

There. The kitchen's café curtains were slightly parted. She heard a humming sound—the refrigerator was running. A windbreaker lay on a chair. What were they doing here in June? And how soon before they returned to open the garage with a remote control? What to do, what to do?

She joined Jaudon, closing the car door as silently as possible. They waited. She tried to still her hands. More sirens wailed by. Jaudon held knuckles to her mouth, scraping them with her teeth.

Cherry season was starting back in Depot Landing. Roadside stands would be setting up. What she wouldn't do for a basket of round red Washington freshness. She whispered, "Don't ask. Just do not ask."

Jaudon was watching her. "I don't get you. You always have a trick up your sleeve, like you're a pixie or something."

She didn't plan to tell anyone about her outlaw life as a thief, a squatter, a former runaway. Especially now, diploma in hand, beginning her career.

"We'll sit tight as long as possible before we check to see if the coast is clear."

"Do you know the people who live here?"

She tapped Jaudon's knee, scabbed, as usual. "Honest, Boss, you don't want to know."

She listened for sounds over Anika's panting. What if the owner returned? Or, with no windows in the garage, were they safer staying put? If they were caught, she planned to offer Roy Jack's smuggler buddy Milo in exchange for freedom for herself and Jaudon.

Jaudon spoke, startling her. "You should have gone with Tad or Shady. And we need to get to Buffalo Street where Olive Ponder is manager. She'll swear we were with her this whole time. If I hadn't panicked, we'd be home free."

She shared with Jaudon the instinct to run, not sit, and she itched to go. She hated to be hemmed in, a sitting duck. Her glasses steamed up. Getting caught was not an option; the police would take Anika to a shelter.

Jaudon played a tattoo on her knees with her fists. "How did I let this happen? We're hiding out like a couple of desperados."

"To be perfectly honest? We are a couple of desperados at the moment."

"Not on purpose."

"We'll be okay, Boss. The Schoolhouse is a closed, barebones structure now."

"It's humiliating. Over a century ago, a Baptist preacher established the Church Pond Missionary. His name was T. H. Jaudon. And his great, great grandniece is a criminal."

"Let it go. I'll bet your reverend fancied a toot of firewater now and then."

"He didn't sell it."

They waited a long nervous while for the police cars to leave. She interlaced her fingers, twisted her hands palms out. Jaudon tapped a foot, stopped herself, started again. Cullie or Berry would take in Anika.

Engines revved along the road and car doors slammed. She heard a police radio nearby.

"Damn."

"They're searching house to house," Jaudon said.

"In pursuit. Or talking to people about what they've noticed going on at the Schoolhouse."

"And they'll talk." A line of sweat dripped off Jaudon's jaw. "They'll be pouting because I took away their handy source of cheap liquor."

A car braked, idling. She swiveled to clamp a hand around Anika's snout before the dog growled. Had the owners forgotten the door's remote? A moment later, a fist banged at the front door, and a yell, "Open up. Sheriff's Department." It was all she could do to keep Anika silent, but she was relieved it was a cop. They listened to him walk, equipment jangling, to the door at the side of the garage. He jiggled the knob.

Jaudon's eyes were wild.

What in hell had the boss thought? That no dangers were involved? She slid to the floor of the full-size Buick.

"Just in case," she whispered, but to Jaudon's bad ear again, so she yanked her by the sleeve of her Hawaiian shirt.

The door of the police cruiser slammed, and the cop drove around the circular driveway to the road.

When she heard nothing but cicadas, she crept out the side door and checked. No red and blue lights flashed at the Schoolhouse. She pushed the lighted button to raise the garage door, motioning Jaudon to back out. Jaudon drove cautiously through the soft, dark night to the Buffalo Road Beverage Bay. Olive Ponder was on nights that week. She asked no questions when Jaudon told her they'd been at this store working for the last three hours.

CHAPTER THIRTY-ONE

July 1981

"They informed on you, MJ."

"Hold your horses, Vonnie. Who informed on who?"

Jaudon and Berry had invited them over, and they were on their way. MJ had been looking forward to showing off the car she bought, but Vonnie barely commented as she dropped into her seat, her eyes on MJ.

"The Batsons. It's no surprise, but I finally confirmed that's who ratted her out to the cops."

"They told the police Jaudon did more than rent out the store?"

"Oh, the whole county knows that," said Vonnie. "Once the backwoods blabbermouths officially complained, the new county commissioner set the police on you all."

"They're shooting themselves in the feet."

"Roy Jack is livid that Blacks are earning the money he thinks should be his."

"That's his problem, not yours."

Vonnie tightened her lips.

"What?"

"I can't believe you said that. It is my problem. It's everyone's problem. I thought you understood."

"You're going to have to spell this one out for me." The car wasn't air-conditioned, and Vonnie was fanning herself with her pretty but ineffectual hand. MJ worried that her ego chose this classic car, not her common sense.

"Racial hatred is a universal thing. Not that it's a shocker to see it blatant in my relatives. Because Roy Jack isn't the only one. Oh no, they sling hateful words in front of Vaughn and me without a second thought."

"That I get. People put you down constantly because you're you. And nobody tells you why."

"I try to explain what their prejudice does to us, but I might as well be rapping them on the knuckles with dandelions. They go right on thinking what they think, never mind facts."

"I run into plenty of Roy Jack types. I walk away. Not the most enlightening response."

"Silence is no antidote for institutionalized racism. We can't walk away from what's in ourselves."

"I am dead serious now. You mean to tell me I bought the same lies about Black people as that boy at the roller rink?"

"Beyond a doubt you have. And so have I. So have I."

The monstrous thought that she was prejudiced shook her up. She parked in the Vickers' rutted front yard, immobile, appalled. "What? How...There must be a way to undo how I think."

"When you figure that out, let me know. It'll save lives."

All too soon Jaudon paraded over to the car, smiling and wagging a finger at them. "Take it inside, you two. You don't want me accused of running a house of ill repute, do you? Gran and Berry are in there being mushy over reruns of Prince Charles and Princess Diana's wedding."

They followed, their moods restrained. Vonnie repeated her news.

"Which one talked?" asked Jaudon. Kajen leaped to drape herself around Jaudon's neck.

Vonnie said, "Who else would they get to do it? Snitching spoils a man's reputation. They told lies to Aunt Floxie until she was raring to spill the beans. Aunt Floxie's the one who wears dangling cross earrings."

"Pantywaists," said Berry. "You and Vonnie inherited the last bits of gumption left on both sides of the Batson family."

Anger at the Batsons and anger at herself silenced her. She sat with her chin scrunched up, burning a hole in the carpet with her eyes, holding a handful of Anika's fur. She pictured a house she'd passed that had all the signs of being ripe for the picking.

Jaudon pulled the chain for the living room ceiling fan. "I tell you what. Vonnie's more Lowe and Brandon than Batson. I thank my lucky stars I'm more Vicker. Momma's mother's people, the Jaudons, they're an industrious bunch who mostly moved away for decent jobs."

"The good news," Vonnie said, "is that nothing can be proven.

Nobody knows who Tad and Shady are, and Jaudon made sure MJ works at a Beverage Bay out of Batson territory."

"I get bona fide paychecks," said MJ, poking fun at herself and lightening the bitter atmosphere.

Jaudon poured them tea and Berry served them homemade skillet cookies. They made sport of Roy Jack and toasted Officer Friendly. Anika marched in front of them, head high, with one of Puddin's sock toys in her mouth. Puddin followed, trying to tussle it back. MJ snagged Anika for a hug, tossing the toy. Puddin went stumping toward it, oblivious to their laughter.

"Doesn't take much to amuse us plain folk," admitted Jaudon.

Vonnie had been studying Berry and Jaudon. She jotted Berry's cookie recipe on a scratch pad, peeking at MJ with a shy promise in her eyes.

After a while, MJ realized her hands were clinging to each other. She cleared her throat. "I'd like to invite you both to check out my auction property on Rooster Lake."

Berry hadn't changed from her scrubs, her curly hair was lank, and under her eyes were grayish circles. Jaudon's soiled Beverage Bay vest hung on the back of a chair.

"How about this weekend? I'm tuckered out tonight."

Berry nodded, fanning herself with a paper napkin. "I declare these cookies will be our entire dinner. Cooking in July heat after an awful day at work isn't on my agenda."

"I'll be overhauling my project this weekend. Let me write the address for you."

"Hand her that ink pen, Vonnie," said Jaudon, providing a paper napkin. "Where is this?"

"It's on the lake the city declared a conservation area. My property is grandfathered in."

Jaudon took the napkin. "I know where you mean—a bitty lake that is kind of rooster-shaped with those pointy coves at one end and the beak-shaped beach at the other. McBea's Cottages on Rooster Lake used to be a vacation spot."

"Thanks. I tried to make out what the faded sign used to say. McBea's. Huh." In truth, the faded, bullet-riddled ghost sign was what first beckoned her. The spot had history, though it was the little lake itself that sold her. The water was blue where it reflected the sky and became green and brown closer to shore. It was peaceful but not undisturbed—wavelets chased one another into the cattails to either side of the cove where she'd stood. The occasional mosquito landed on her, but her skin was sensitive enough and her reflexes fast enough that she was able to deter bites. A clearing in the cattails revealed two black and brown foraging moorhens, with their bright orange and yellow legs and beaks and their enormous feet. Anika strained at her leash, ready to go for a paddle, but there could be gators. She'd sat on a log, listening to the soothing, gentle landings of the small waves and the whistles, rattles, and muffled squeaks of the chatty moorhens.

Berry said, "The cottages were there before we were born, right, Jaudon?"

Jaudon nodded. "You bought one of those? Tin roofs? Virginia Creeper on the stilts?"

"I bought the one closest to the entrance—no stilts, and the roof has held up well. It's about eight hundred square feet. The Clerk of Courts office walked me through the auction process."

"The heirs tried taking those cottages condo a few years ago but shelved their plans and flew the coop. Remember the fires?" asked Berry.

"Do I ever. Two of them. Vandals."

"The best part of buying here is the Florida history that comes with the properties," said MJ. "Makes me want to invest in a run-down motel for the gaudy only-in-Florida neon sign alone."

"Not for our sinkholes and giant spiders?"

"Not hardly," she said with a laugh. "The clerk's office told me it sat there almost four years after they took it for tax delinquency. People don't want to buy where it's illegal to run their motorboats and Jet Skis. They could care less about the wildlife they disturb."

Berry fingered her left earring. "Where in the world did you get the money to buy property at your age?"

She dented her left cheek with her smile. "Let's say I'm a skinflint. Mrs. Lanamore knew my plans and told me to go to the county and search properties they wanted to get off their books. That's how she bought her property, and she'll develop it more one of these days. Seriously, mine was on the demolition list. Cost me fourteen hundred dollars, house and land. The years took their toll, but I'm up for it."

Jaudon told her, "All that section of the lake needs is tender loving care. Conservation lots are rare as hen's teeth. We took a ride out that way when Momma considered expanding. We saw someone went in there, and, without mawmucking everything up, built a couple of no-frills homes with exactly enough dock to tether a rowboat."

"I saw those A-frames."

Berry said, "Gran read in the paper that no trees were cut to build them. They salvaged wood from the fires."

"There's more of it lying around," she said. "I pulled all the usable boards and shingles I could find. There's scattered plumbing fixtures—it's like a construction supply swap meet."

"You're slicker than a boiled onion. That'll bring in a nice income when you're done."

"Thanks, Boss. Once I make the repairs, I'm calling it Serenity Cottage to get tourists who want the opposite of Miami Beach. Canoes and kayaks are allowed. People can swim in an alligator-free area. I'll do okay with it."

Berry said, "I know you went through hoops within hoops to accomplish this. We're trying to get Gran's land on Stinky Road registered as a conservation plot."

"Places next to them bring higher prices. Lucky MJ."

"Lucky? I kept my eyes open for this investment quite a while. I can't wait to show it to you."

"I can come with you today," said Vonnie.

She sat directly under the ceiling fan, yet a dangerous heat bloomed through her at the thought of Vonnie and herself alone in a cottage with the mattress she'd lugged from Mrs. Belda's—she'd left there for good now—to the station wagon, and into the fixer-upper.

Vonnie was categorically spectacular today in an apricot crisscross blouse, black shorts, sandals, and coral-colored nail and toenail polish.

She stuck her hands in the pockets of her cargo shorts to keep from twisting them.

"Unless you don't want me along." Vonnie's voice, normally low, suggestive, and confident, had gone tinny as a grade schooler's.

Her hands dove deeper into her pockets. "Well, sure, you can come," she said in a flat voice, trying to disguise both her longing and her misgivings.

Vonnie said, "I can leave my bike on your porch, can't I, Jaudon?"

Jaudon shrugged at MJ as if to ask, *How can I deny her?*

CHAPTER THIRTY-TWO

Anika, again displaced by Vonnie, paced the back seat as MJ drove across town in her yellow station wagon. She'd studied car ads for weeks to find a reliable, affordable, and roomy vehicle to get her back and forth to Rooster Lake. She knew how to drive from making her way around the survivalist property.

"I'd call this a boat," said Vonnie.

"My battleship," she half joked. "She's a 1961 model, two years my junior."

"The USS *MJ*?"

Her nervous excitement around Vonnie made her ramble. "She may be a boat, but she's a boat with a V8 engine, a four-door Ranch Wagon, and roof rails. I can haul anything I need to fix a house. Your seat reclines."

Vonnie's laugh was exuberantly playful. "That's handy."

She suppressed that visual and cleared her throat. "It was stored in the seller's garage, except for classic car meets. When he died, the daughter wanted the cash, not the car."

"Smells like lemon."

"He kept it detailed. It's definitely not a lemon of a car. Tad's mechanic friend went over it top to bottom."

"Did he warn you'll go broke on gas? What if we have a gas shortage like the one a couple of years ago."

"I'm not planning to take her to Alaska."

"Is that where you're from originally?"

Was Vonnie this curious about everyone she met? And this forward? Or did she sense the lightning between them too?

She drove the unpaved one-lane as it curved along the lakeside.

Anika whinnied for her temporary home. MJ would restore the cottage by Clearwater Beach next, but it hadn't closed yet.

Bulrushes grew thick around the lake, mostly obscuring a narrow public boat ramp. The rough remains of weathered gray pilings pocked the water. Lining the one-lane road were charred scrub oaks. She pulled in front of a narrow, neglected two-story house, which, from the day she bought it, filled her with pride. A roofed porch ran along the front of the house, shaded by a tall, green pecan tree. She liked to sit there, in a faded blue chair she'd found inside, watching the water ripple and the ducks dive. She planned to take the chair with her from project to project until she had a porch of her own.

Vonnie pointed at two lightning rods. "Maybe there's the reason it's still standing."

"Honestly? It doesn't look like much, but I can tell you right now it has good bones. Someone who knew what he was doing hand built the place, vacation by vacation. Come on, and watch for snakes."

Vonnie took her hand as they made their way along the side of the house, sidestepping the hood of a car, a pink plastic tricycle, a mound of metal plumbing elbows, and a tarp. Anika trotted ahead of them on a path someone had created with strips of flattened artificial grass.

A white ibis honked in annoyance, and they watched it take flight from a tree. From another tree, a dozen ibises lifted off. "With my last breath, I want to be watching birds like these."

"They'd be a sacred escort," said Vonnie.

They watched until the birds merged with the hazy sky. Vonnie looked at a wood barrel with a hand pump and disintegrating garden hose. "What's this?"

"Rainwater. The aquifer isn't deep." She sniffed. "I wouldn't drink this, but someone could water a garden."

"That's duckweed growing in it. There are kinds you can eat, if the water's safe."

"But you know what—there's not much safe water left in this whole county."

They entered the back of the house through a sprung door with bent hinges. Clawing away spiderwebs, they lunged over an exploded bag of kitty litter. Anika probed for edibles until MJ noticed and plunked the door's hook in its eyelet. She gave Anika a glowering look until the dog hung her head and moved away.

"I'll get to these messes. First, I replaced broken windows and mushy frames. I've hauled out the mildewed carpet and yards of smelly linoleum."

Vonnie revolved in the middle of the kitchen, arms outstretched. "Such a perfect room. We gravitate to the kitchen at home. Why not put a sofa in here since there's space?"

She hadn't asked for Vonnie's input. "Thanks. I'll consider it."

Vonnie raised her hands, palms up. "I'm sorry. You don't want me butting in."

"I need all the help I can get."

"Shush me if I babble. I'm having fun imagining a new house."

At one end of the empty sitting area a picture window framed comely little Rooster Lake. At the other end were exposed pipes, a filthy sink, and 220-volt outlets for appliances.

Vonnie observed, "Those pecans will be raining on your roof come fall."

"I'll gather and sell them, or save on food by eating them along with my duckweed soup. Come, there's a bedroom and bath through here."

She'd hung a dark green tablecloth across the lower three quarters of the window in the forlorn bedroom. A spreading sugar oak filtered the sun, but not the rains. Water stains spread under the window and along the floorboards.

Vonnie peeked in the closet and the bathroom. "You're keeping the porcelain tub, I hope."

"If I can figure out how to repair the flooring under it and scrub out the rust stains."

"My mother taught me about stains. Lemon juice, salt, and fine sandpaper. I can do it for you."

Vonnie's nature radiated a warmth that pulled at MJ. "You're...I don't know. Kind. That'd be a help. I was stumped."

"You'll come get me in your yellow submarine?"

"If you have to call it a boat, think yacht. I don't ever want to see that car underwater. Come on upstairs. It's in better shape. Honestly." She led Vonnie to a ladder.

"What happened to the stairs?"

"They were trashed. I used my mini crowbar and a jigsaw to pull them down. I might put in a steel spiral staircase—they come in kits."

"You took the steps apart by yourself, hotshot?"

"Sure. I learned the basics growing up. I loved reading *Popular Mechanics* at the library. Now I borrow books on do-it-yourself projects. There's a woman at the hardware store who's super friendly and knowledgeable."

"You're talking about Marge? At the hardware store? She's one of us, you know." Vonnie's eyes sparkled in this dim house. "She was a couple of years ahead of me in school. That big ol' tomboy."

Proud of her sharpening gaydar, she said, "I thought she might be in our club, but where I grew up, half the local farm mothers with husbands and eight kids dressed and acted like her."

Vonnie's smile stretched.

"Shoot," she said. "You and her—"

"She had trouble taking tests, and the teacher asked me to tutor her so she could graduate. We figured out a few other ways to pass the time."

"You're not with her—"

"We started hanging out at New York Pizza and met other girls. Marge and her girlfriend celebrated a year together right before I met you. You could say I was playing the field, maybe waiting for you."

MJ abruptly went to the ladder and climbed. Vonnie started up behind her, and Anika made disappointed sounds as she watched.

Vonnie's hands were soft and warm as MJ eased her from the ladder onto the upper flooring.

She pulled Vonnie to her feet and didn't let go. "You steady now?"

Vonnie faced her, nose to nose. Her breath smelled like a butterscotch candy. "I admire you," said Vonnie. "I can tell you never quit. You don't let stumbling blocks get in your way. You butchy little thing."

"Butchy?"

"You don't even know what that means, do you?"

"I don't go for those gay roles—I'll tell you that right now."

"Oh, you will, you surely will. Why fight what makes you who you are?"

"Maybe because I don't want to be pigeonholed. I get these panicked stares in public bathrooms."

Vonnie stepped back and inspected her, head to toe. "I don't know why. You're pretty as a pie supper."

"That's Berry and Jaudon talk."

"It's the talk I heard all my life. You best get used to it if you're settling here." Vonnie's expression grew plaintive. "I hope you're not the restless kind."

She assured Vonnie, saying, "I glory in the perpetual heat wave.

I miss my rowdy river, but you can't walk a quarter mile here without coming across a canal, a pond, a lake, aquifers, wetlands, fountains, springs. The air is so wet, I hardly need to drink water. The wildlife is preposterously gorgeous." She could have kicked herself. Was she being too enthusiastic? Did she come across as flirting?

To distract Vonnie from her surely reddening face, she used their linked hands to draw her along the hallway. She didn't want to let go, and Vonnie didn't seem to mind. "Notice the pristine claw-foot tub. Not a rust stain in sight."

"You'll keep the pink tiling? Grandma Brandon had the same in her bathroom."

"Are you kidding me? I'm becoming fanatic about vintage furnishings. Makes me want to find a turquoise toilet lid."

"That's a hoot and a half," said Vonnie. "I'm thinking pink and turquoise plaid shower curtains. A shag rug toilet seat cover. Love the bubblegum-pink color, but it's got to go."

"If I wanted to live at Rooster Lake long-term, I'd install pink flamingo wallpaper." She dropped Vonnie's hands, uneasy with their easy compatibility. Being in her presence was tantalizing when she wasn't scared half to death.

The two small-scale rooms under the eaves were both decorated in mildewed striped wallpaper, one pink, one blue.

"Perfect for a family vacation, but what about the grownups?"

She escorted Vonnie to the master bedroom.

"Who's this happy companion?" Vonnie cuddled Hop, clearly careful of his worn state. "You've had him for a while."

"Hop and I have been through thick and thin together. He was a present for my second birthday. I was told I took hold of him and made him hop."

"Strong handsome MJ has a wabbit?" Vonnie waggled its ears. "We'll go to a thrift store and get teeny-weeny infant clothes to stop him from wearing out."

"I never thought of that." She felt light-headed—Vonnie had used the word *we* for the first time.

Vonnie kissed Hop on the forehead and set him back on his pillow.

What a caring thing to do for the frayed bunny, she thought.

"You keep this room shipshape, don't you? A place for everything and everything in its place. My mother calls me the clutter queen."

"Shoot, Vonnie, I slept three to a tiny room. As the girls expanded, I learned to contract."

"Oh? You have siblings?" Vonnie's expression was expectant.

She admitted to siblings, but concealment was her default state of mind.

Vonnie bounced on the edge of the bed. "You and Hop must not be expecting company—one twin bed."

She didn't respond, embarrassed by the fantasies of Vonnie she'd entertained right in this room—Vonnie against cool, taut white sheets. Here Vonnie sat, patting the space beside her on the bed, and smiling that closed-mouth, knowing-eyed, womanly smile of hers, and MJ, with her few months of stolen touches, and despite the cool, black-clad image she tried to project, comprehended with horror that she was the least experienced lesbian in the world.

She made for the doorway, but bold Vonnie, long legged and swift, surged off the bed to stop her.

"Hoo boy." She remembered the Depot Landing railroad tank car she'd once seen implode after its vacuum safety valves were disabled and the air was sucked out. She kept herself from rearing back, but once again, her instinct urged her to shut Vonnie out.

"You know you're a looker, don't you?" asked Vonnie. "Those long eyelashes, that black hair."

In the tarnished mirror on the wall behind Vonnie, she saw her face, muscles tight with trepidation, eyes narrowed in resistance, and her parted, seeking lips. She saw Emma Jean Beaudry, perpetually too smart to accept what, to her, wasn't rational; Emma Beaudry, an enigma to her teen mother, who raised her with the threat of her soldier dad coming home and spanking her with a paddle; a misfit when the clone Beaudrys arrived, shiny and new and run-of-the-mill. In first grade, the teacher reprimanded Em Beaudry for helping the other pupils to read.

That isolation was good training. They never wanted her to start with, and she knew she didn't belong with them. Since her father pulled her from school, she needed no one other than herself and completely trusted no one but herself, with the exception of Christina.

But now: Vonnie Lowe. She'd never experienced desire like this before. It demolished her safety valves and was not the innocent play she'd had with Christina. Shouldn't she get to know Vonnie better than she did?

She leaned forward, arms at her sides, seriously shaking. Nothing aside from their lips touched, but that touch funneled fire into her nerves, muscles, blood. Her flesh softened, she tasted burnt butterscotch, she turned pliant from an abundance of love. With this boundless kiss, a corny scrap of song repeated in her head: her hard knocks were healed, her heart unsealed, her future revealed.

Vonnie's natural warmth was now heat and a luminescence behind MJ's closed eyes. MJ opened her arms. Vonnie moved her supple body against her. She moved with Vonnie, her hands at last touching her, their breasts pressed together, Vonnie's rounded hips an absolute fit for the palms of her hands. As their lower bodies met, Vonnie gave a yip and went limp. She moved her hands from Vonnie's hips to her tiny waist. They fell across the width of the bed, legs over the sides.

At their second kiss—or was it still their first—Vonnie's quicksilver hands grazed her. MJ made her caresses long and compelling, in a way she hadn't dared with Christina. Nor had she and Christina taken off their clothes. There never was an opportunity.

She sat up.

Vonnie's fleeting look of dismay changed to concern. She sat too and moved MJ's head to her chest where she held it, stroking the j-shaped forehead scar with a thumb. "What's up, Super Squirrel?"

Ineptitude paralyzed her. "I'm bummed to say it, Von, but I don't know what to do next."

"This can't be your first time, can it?"

"Pretty much."

"Are you saying I'm bringing you out?"

At this point, she wasn't sure if she trembled from nervousness, humiliation or…passion? "You could maybe say that."

Vonnie didn't waste a minute. She broke away and undressed beside the bed. MJ watched. Oh, the splendid womanliness, the dignity of her carriage. The generous golden brown-on-brown breasts. The soft, flat belly and the hair that hid—

"Come on, take your clothes off. Or do you want me to do it after I make Hop comfy?" Vonnie nested Hop in her denim vest, tossed beside the bed.

One touch after another, MJ found she knew her way after all. She let go of her stewing and said, "I want you to lie down." She shook off her black chukkas as she pulled her polo shirt over her head. Her shorts wasted more seconds.

Vonnie said, "You're sure you're new to this?"

"You inspire me."

Vonnie's voice deepened. "Oh, yeah, take over, take over."

She lowered herself to Vonnie. Their passion was without direction. The sole sounds were the sweep of their limbs along sheets and Vonnie's ahs and ums, and her own blood pounding. For a while they accomplished no more than to collide with each other, full body, in ravenous crushes.

"This is nice. Awfully nice," said Vonnie.

She wedged a thigh between Vonnie's legs, pressed, and moved slowly until Vonnie gripped MJ's bottom with both hands to quicken their pace.

Her eyes closed, Vonnie's face held an expression of euphoria, and her hands played MJ's back like a musical instrument until, with the growled word *lover*, those hands lowered to slap the bed, twice.

Soon after, at the touch of those hands, MJ was taken by a pleasure she'd never before experienced. Stunned, she panted into Vonnie's shoulder while Vonnie crooned and pushed her fingers through MJ's hair, sweat and all.

"Where did you get the scar?" Vonnie asked, finger tracing it.

She told Vonnie about her mother's rage that last night.

Vonnie embraced her and kissed the top of her head. "How awful. What an unhappy woman your mother must be. It's like she tried to brand you, but left out the *M*. You are mine to brand now—you hear, girl?"

True, she thought. When Vonnie left for college and encountered new women to call lover, she imagined herself suffering horribly, yet she'd hang on to her hat, see Vonnie at holidays, and make enough money for a home that Vonnie might consider sharing.

"Did I wipe you out?" asked Vonnie.

"Shoot, Ms. Florida, I'm just getting started."

She wanted to keep Vonnie close for all time, but Vonnie burrowed between her legs with one hand, while the other pulled MJ's hand to herself.

The thought of the amount of work she'd planned to do that day prompted her to ask, "Are you any good at following instructions?"

Moistening her lips with the tip of her tongue, eyes closed, Vonnie said, "Tell me what you want, lover."

She chortled, half from the pleasure of Vonnie's touch and half with amusement. "Seriously. I meant the written instructions that come with a spiral stair kit."

CHAPTER THIRTY-THREE

August 1982

On a stifling August evening a year later, Jaudon and Berry ducked into Rigo and Jimmy Neal's building without a moment to spare before the late afternoon downpour. To Jaudon, the apartment smelled like a hot pepper fest, mixed with a medley of Gran's spicier dishes.

Jaudon had been jawing on the phone with Rigo a week earlier when he said, "I want to have a party, Jaud. I've implored Jimmy Neal to make Mardi Gras food—I simply cannot wait until our Mardi Gras party next February."

Jaudon zipped to the half-size open kitchen, lifted a pot lid, and yelled, "Jambalaya. I love you, Jimmy Neal."

He batted her hand with a dripping wooden spoon. "You're letting the flavor out."

Jimmy Neal was red-faced from the kitchen heat. She remembered him reddening when he harassed her as a bullying grammar school boy. Now, she put her arms around him and scoped out the counter. "Are those sweet potato pies? And cornbread? No wonder Rigo fell for you."

"Git, cher. I'm trying to fix my braised greens."

Rigo served them icy bottles of Coke from Mexico and went to answer the doorbell. A big booming roll of thunder seemed to propel Cullie and Allison inside.

Right off her shift, rain dripped from the brim of Cullie's uniform cap. She said, "What's cooking? The smell is making me faint."

Rigo popped from another room. "I know we have nurses who can revive you, Cullie, but are there any doctors in the house?"

The guys from the Coconut Grove march, Gregory Kumar and

Larry Riyanto, raised their hands and rushed to put a chair under Cullie, who laughed and tried to wave them off. They made her lower her head and threatened smelling salts.

Into the laughter came Vonnie in wet denims and MJ in her waterlogged black shirt, shorts, and shoes, her hair flattened by the rain, her glasses—new, but not different—completely fogged over.

Cullie went closer to examine MJ, then backed away, hands raised as if to repel something fearsome. The partiers appeared puzzled until Cullie yelled, "ET, call home."

They'd all seen the film by then and held out their index fingers.

Vonnie announced, "As my aunts would say, It's pourin' bullfrogs out there."

Rigo whispered to Jaudon, Allison, and Cullie, "Has MJ grown taller or more solid or stronger? I'm seeing a change."

Cullie, eyes on Vonnie, was the one who said it. "MJ's standing tall because of her lushly cleavaged siren."

A flush zoomed from MJ's neck to her forehead.

Rigo tossed towels to them both and raised his voice. "I know you're dying for Jimmy Neal's feast." He reached for a box hidden behind a recliner. "But first things first. Come on out here for a minute, husband."

"Can't."

"For one second, my Manatee Man."

Jimmy Neal stepped into the doorway.

Rigo pulled a bouquet of flowers from the box. "Happy Anniversary, my one and only."

"Oh, Bub, man of my heart, you are a wonder." Jimmy Neal covered his tear-filled eyes and squeezed the much shorter Rigo, blossoms and all, to him before dashing back to the kitchen.

Rigo opened a low cabinet for a vase to fill with water. He deftly arranged the flowers.

Jaudon wiped her eyes with the sides of her index fingers and dried them on her shirt. "Can you believe it?" She took Berry's hand.

"And to think..." Berry, who dressed for the party in a flower-patterned skirt, a three-quarter sleeve top, and pink lipstick, clasped her hand tightly.

Jaudon, too, remembered what an awkward moose of a man Jimmy Neal was when she saw him at a gay bar the night he and Rigo met. Rigo, though they moved in together, strayed; Jimmy Neal detested

living that way. Drama was involved. To keep Rigo home, Jimmy Neal
improved his diet and established a workout regimen that reshaped him
from a pasty-faced galloot into a strapping, muscled adult. Rigo only
wanted Jimmy Neal after that.

Dinner was arrayed along the kitchen counters. They stood in a
line to serve themselves and, lacking a dining table in the modest flat,

Gregory stood, a bottle of beer raised high. "This striking couple,"
he announced, "deserves to have their union celebrated. They're
conscientiously available for their friends. They inspire us to make
lifelong commitments, and they're fabulously silly and fun. To Jimmy

After raising a flowered, throwback 1950s tumbler, Larry led
them in singing "When I'm Sixty-Four." Rigo provided the falsetto.
They applauded themselves. Excited conversations erupted, as if they
were coming together after years of absence. They raved about Jimmy

While too many volunteers crowded into the kitchen for cleanup,
Jaudon talked to Rigo. "How's your dad treating you these days?"

MJ and Vonnie were standing at her side, and Rigo included them
as he answered. "He wants my mother back as usual. She's done with
him, but he tries to get to her through me. Otherwise, he wouldn't give
me the time of day."

"Are you still disinherited?"

"He won't pay for grad school, unless I start dating women. He'll
sell his US business when he retires and live well. The property in Cuba
is long gone, and I won't inherit his royal residence when he dies. I
told him I'd turn it into the biggest shelter for underage queers in the

"That must be one massive house," said Vonnie.

"It's more than one person needs and right on Tampa Bay."

"Where on the Bay?" MJ asked.

"Only the best for Papi. It's practically a requirement in that
foot powerboat. Now he doesn't trust it to my sissy hands."

"If he ever changes his mind," said MJ. A few of the survivalists
were weekend sailors and she'd gone out fishing on a boat called

Phoebe, after a fish as elusive as the Loch Ness Monster. "I miss being on the water. The Columbia River is lively and downright dangerous at times, not a balmy gulf."

"He doesn't trust me with a key to his house, much less his fancy runabout."

"Watch what you say about that balmy Gulf," Jimmy Neal warned. "When it wakes up, it's lethal."

Rigo snapped his fingers. "I know exactly where he keeps the keys."

Allison folded the last tray and drifted into conversation with MJ.

"Watch out, MJ," Rigo warned. "You'll be a fanatic feminist before the night is out."

"What makes you so sure I'm not a fanatic feminist now?"

Rigo touched his mouth with his fingertips. "Oh dear, did I say something wrong?"

Allison laughed, head back and clearly happy after her own precarious years of rebellion. She'd cut her long hair shorter, and now her fashion taste veered toward hats, rimless tinted glasses, turtlenecks, and quirkiness.

Berry would have liked to listen in on the talk between Allison and MJ—she suspected it would be sparkling with wit and flirtation—but she went to help Larry wash dishes, both of them donning retro aprons from Rigo's collection. Berry's was black and white striped with a red patch pocket. Larry wore a green and white polka-dotted half apron with ruffled edges.

"Get a load of our little Susie Homemakers," called Rigo as he silently motioned Jaudon into his room, his gesture urgent.

❖

Rigo sat like a lead weight on the edge of the bed and held his head in his hands. He told Jaudon that his father was pestering him to help smuggle Cuban people into the US. "He says I owe him."

She sat on an uncomfortable antique wood frame chair. She was sure they set great store by it, and if she asked, Rigo would know the style and provenance. The room smelled of jasmine incense and pot. "I thought that happened a couple of years ago. Weren't they convicts and mentally ill people?"

"That was the Mariel Boatlift. Papi says most of the criminals were either political prisoners or retired from crime once they landed jobs and didn't have to break the law to eat. Mentally ill? I heard that too, but Cuba describes us that way. We're anti-revolutionary undesirables."

"Us? Gay people?"

The wind abated briefly but returned to splatter rain at the window.

"Castro has no qualms about getting rid of us. I know a straight man who claimed to be gay, in order to be part of the boatlift."

"But your father hates homosexuals."

"That's a piece of my problem with what he's doing. He'll only hire married, light-skinned guys for his business."

"What's the other piece?"

"You can't tell this to anybody, Jaud. Promise?"

She knew a promise invited more trouble, but she and Rigo had shared almost everything about their lives since the day they met as college freshmen. They remained friends after she lost patience with all the useless classes required for a degree and switched to business school.

A sharp clap of close thunder jolted them both and hushed the revelry in the other room. Rigo waited for the hubbub to resume.

"After Hurricane Alberto this June, the occasional boat coming over used the increased Cuban migration to camouflage drug imports, hard drugs. I'm ashamed to say, that's what Papi's doing here in Tampa."

"Your father? Seriously? And he wants to get his son involved?"

"The son he disinherited for preferring men. He's deported me from my own life."

"And you're conflicted about, what, enabling him?"

"Yes, and about ratting him out." He lobbed a crumpled tissue into the wastebasket. "Should I? I doubt I will."

"Lucky shot. I can tell you it didn't set well with me when my cousin pulled that trick, but he had ulterior motives."

"Maybe I do too. Maybe I want to punish him more than I want to be a concerned citizen."

From the rest of the apartment came talk punctuated by laughter, the scraping of a pan, Elton John singing "Honky Cat" on the stereo. The smell of Creole food seeped into the bedroom.

"Hey, do you know a guy named Milo? He wanted Cousin Roy Jack to let him use the Church Pond store as a warehouse. It sounded hinky, so I got nosy and asked Roy Jack what this Milo wanted to store. Roy Jack said a lot of things came in from Cuba on the hush-hush, and Milo knew a loaded Cuban guy with a boat."

They locked eyes.

Rigo said, "I have heard the name Milo." He frowned and raised a knuckle to his lips. "You're thinking my father's boat. Was Roy Jack game?"

"Of course—Roy Jack's never earned an honest dollar in his life." She cleared her throat. "As if I did when I sold moonshine. In the end, I'm no better than anyone else in the Batson family."

"You didn't let Roy Jack get away with it, did you?"

"Not on your life. I was wound tighter than a three-day clock the whole time I sold mash, but you know what? That money kept me clear of bankruptcy court." She clasped Rigo's hands. "You're not going to do it, are you, Rigo? Endanger what you've worked for?"

"What if I do owe my father, Jaud?"

"Hey, what the heck. Are you crying?" She patted Rigo's hand and offered the box of tissues from the night table.

He folded a tissue into a neat square, blotted his eyes, and dabbed at his nose.

"I'm not telling you to sic the police on him, but you do have to say no to getting involved. You have more to offer people as a shrink than as a jailbird."

He tilted his head back and laughed as if to fill the room, his red curls jiggling. "Oh, honey, who am I kidding? I don't need my father's help—I break the law by existing. You and I both do."

"I'm as aboveboard as I can be, but how does a person respect any law when we're born illegal? MJ says we're desperados." She shaped her hand into a pistol and blew smoke from its fingertip barrel.

"That's us—bandidos, banditas." When he stopped laughing, Rigo's face showed the battle of his choices, and she caught a hint of how he'd look as he aged.

"If I don't report my father, and I facilitate illegal entry of Cubans, they'll contribute as much as native-born Americans—more, compared with your momma's family." He grabbed his hair and rocked side to side. "I don't know right from wrong anymore, Jaud."

She stared at the rough straw mat at her feet and hung her folded hands between her knees. "Your Papi is the one in the wrong, putting his son on the line. He's as bad as Momma."

"He doesn't have the excuse of losing his mind."

"Sometimes I have my doubts about that. Did Momma lose it for real, or is she using dementia to worm out of responsibility for what she's done?"

"Good question. As an esteemed psychotherapist—"

"Hey, you're not there yet, Rigsy."

"Ahem…shall I go on, or are you competent in mental health diagnoses?" He didn't wait for an answer. "It's possible her dementia is a coping mechanism. Or," he said, with a toss of his curls, "she has properly diagnosed dementia."

"Thank you, Professor Patate. Doesn't your mother have a stone to fix your father?"

"I need to give him a rock for compassion, open-mindedness—a Golden Rule stone: treat your only child the way you want to be treated."

"You told me there's a stone for any need."

"I suppose I might sneak a piece of tourmaline under Papi's mattress. Tourmaline, for kindness and tolerance and his own good."

"And yours."

He raised his eyebrows. "I never said I wasn't a self-absorbed prima donna."

"How about a stone to keep trouble away?"

"We need to remove the millstones from around your neck, not add more weight, Ms. Jaudon Vicker."

"You'd have to amputate my whole head."

He pointed at her hand. "You stick to your onyx ring. It'll resist negative energy and keep you strong. Meditate on it occasionally to get full use of it."

"Listen to you. I thought you didn't believe in your mother's magic stones."

Rigo pouted. "Compared to my father, Mom makes sense."

"Your dad is willing to compromise you because you're not as valuable to him as a straight son, yet you're mollycoddling him."

"You are exactly right. I started as Ishmael, banned from the house. Now I'm Isaac."

Jaudon tried to remember what she'd read of the Bible.

"You know my mother is Jewish," Rigo said. "Papi won't acknowledge that part of us, but there's a classic story in the Hebrew Bible. God tells Abraham to sacrifice his son Isaac. A messenger from God breezes in to rescind the order. In some versions, the messenger is called an angel. Berry calls you—"

"Angel."

"I'm not letting Papi pull an Abraham. He may secretly want his fag son dead, but now you show up, an angel, to bring me a message."

She smiled at the thought that she'd helped and pressed one of her cowlicks flat. "I could use an angel myself."

Rigo laughed. "Don't ask me."

One of the physicians swung the door open. "Are you two hatching plans behind closed doors to defrock Anita Bryant?"

Rigo answered, "Isn't everyone?"

CHAPTER THIRTY-FOUR

September 1982

With Vonnie safely at college, MJ, irritable from menstrual cramping, trailed Rigo's father until he entered his specialty cigar factory and store amongst the pawnshops, Cuban sandwich parlors, and wrought-iron balconies of Ybor City. She stowed her too memorable wheels in the Tampa library parking lot, where she caught a bus. She exited a few blocks from Papi Patate's royal residence on Tampa Bay.

Rigo deserved more from his father. Mr. Patate deserved a lot less than he had. She bet the powerboat Roy Jack's freaky friend Milo piloted did, in actual fact, belong to Mr. Patate.

September was the muggiest month. With that in mind, she dressed for Mr. Patate's neighborhood. Rigo, if he saw her wearing these lightweight thrift store rompers, sunglasses, and wide-brimmed sun hat, would coin the phrase *housebreaking drag*. He'd flip at the white church lady gloves she'd bought for today. She'd be the first to admit she was a complete travesty.

The neighborhood was prestigious, historic, and filled with spacious, extravagant homes in pristine condition, many of them Mediterranean style or Craftsman bungalows, others brick or more generic, but with elegant and unique detailing. Trees shaded the streets, traffic noise was muffled, and a number of homes featured fountains. This Tampa neighborhood possessed an unexpected serenity.

Serenity was not what she needed right now.

At the Patate house, she moved her hand as if freshening lipstick, masking the dog whistle she blew, at Tad's recommendation, to test for barking. She went through the unlocked iron front gate and around to the back of the house, swinging her voluminous beach tote, stretching her lips into a smile only she knew was pure bile. She waved to the worker who mowed the grass next door, in case he was someone Mr. Patate transported from Cuba. As if expected, she called to the house, "Hello, I'm here."

She fiddled with the lanai lock, talking a blue streak to the empty room. These fancy screened porches with their colonnades were another Florida boon for burglars—they provided cover. She stood, kept talking, and spied two locks on the inner slider. Shoot, someone had installed the second lock with hex screws. She gritted her teeth and let out a hissing sound. Who carried hex screwdrivers? She didn't want to leave signs of her presence, but Mr. Patate asked for it. She slid a mini crowbar from her back pocket and jimmied the lock, careful not to let it snap and make a sound she couldn't muffle.

She was in. She slowed her breathing and transformed to her hypervigilant squirrel persona, scanning for cameras and wires, alive to sounds and movements. The air-conditioner's soft drone bolstered her.

She'd thought long, while working at Rooster Lake, about whether she'd be stealing Rigo's inheritance, but he'd lost it when he refused his father's demand to go straight.

She didn't count on escaping with spoils from Papi Patate's extensive Spanish Colonial, just satisfaction. He could be the kind who stored his valuables at his business. She didn't always walk away with spoils. At times she'd find a hidden alarm, or surprising signs that the residents lived lean. Other times, she came up dry, or someone she hadn't known about appeared. For each successful break-in, two didn't work out, and she learned another lesson.

A chill ran through her. These four walls made her jittery. What if smuggled men were hidden here, guarding shipments of drugs? Ghosts of spicy meals—tomato, oregano, garlic, onion—lingered on the air. A Cuban sandwich would be a treat after this job. The views of the sunny bay and high white clouds in the impossibly blue sky were captivating, but distracting.

The interior of the house was scantly furnished in aseptic grays and silvers with black accents and shocking spatters of indigo blue. The warm exterior was reflected solely in vibrant paintings of people dancing, harvesting, playing in the surf. She'd research the library for the name on the canvases: Oscar Garcia Rivera.

There might be a wall safe behind one of the artworks, but safes were too time-consuming for her. The closer she came to her financial goals, the less daring, but more creative, she became. Tad and Shady declared her a genius at finding not only easy-to-sell small electronics and heirloom brass candlesticks, but cash.

She entered a room appointed with wicker furniture and nothing else. She prodded the walls for a hidden panel. A large kitchen with a door to the garage was next. Its wall-to-wall stainless steel appliances gleamed. The counter in the middle of the room, also stainless, featured a second sink and more storage. She had a quick notion that someone who chose such chilly elements might associate them with the safety of bank vaults. She decided to concentrate on the kitchen.

She examined counters for hidden hinges, checked under and behind drawers, shook storage containers, rummaged through packages in the freezer drawer—tamales, arroz con pollo, loaves of Cuban bread, and a Morton chicken pot pie with a sell by date of 1975, seven years ago. Sure enough, the aluminum pie dish showed signs of tampering. Someone had swapped the frozen food for two tight rolls of bills and reassembled the whole package. Mr. Patate's escape cache. After landing in Rainbow Gap, she'd somehow accrued good cash karma, according to Shady.

She avoided greediness, and refused the arrogance to think rules applied to everyone but herself. But oh, how the loss of that frozen money would upset Mr. Patate's applecart, she thought right before her burglar drag caught on the edge of the refrigerator's snap-off grille. Damn, she wasn't used to women's clothes. She fell hard on her knees. The grille lay on the floor.

Why wasn't it plumb? On her sore knees, she switched on her mini Maglite. The space was clean—too clean. Either Mr. Patate had the most thorough housekeeper on earth, or cobwebs and dust bunnies weren't allowed to grow here.

Her watch warned that she'd entered the risky zone, but she seriously wanted to get to this man.

The light caught a metal box. Did rubber gloves prevent electrocution? She unhooked the clasp that held the box closed, and out tumbled two clear plastic bags. She examined them. Each held a rough dirty rock the size of a large ice cube. She'd seen precious gems in the rough in encyclopedia illustrations. Or maybe they were drugs, like the crack cocaine that set Richard Pryor on fire a couple of years ago. She dropped them in her tote with the bills and planned to ask Shady what they were. If drugs, she'd destroy the stuff.

As she fitted the damaged grille, she heard the garage door rise on its vertical tracks. She stopped breathing. The car door banged shut, keys clattered to the concrete. She secured the grille with the heel of her hand.

By the time Mr. Patate stepped into the kitchen, she'd reached the front door. She wanted to slam it behind her for Rigo's sake, but she was satisfied that her blow would eventually hit home. She locked the thumb turn on the doorknob and strolled, knees smarting, heart satisfied, through the oh-so-perfect neighborhood to the bus stop.

CHAPTER THIRTY-FIVE

October 1982

"Am I digging you correctly? I've been sticking my neck out for you, but it's fine to forget about your pal Shady?"

As part of her deal with Tad and Shady, MJ transported liquor to them from east county. Several suppliers, influenced by Roy Jack, objected to doing business with *those people*, but others were eager to make the money. Whenever she accumulated enough stolen articles to fence, she and Anika retrieved the alcohol from an auto body shop that served as a collection point. Over time, the arrangement made her nervous enough to want out. She also needed more time for rehabbing. She had a lot to learn, and that slowed her.

Two Housing Authority maintenance men carried a ladder, drop cloths, and the smell of paint from Shady's apartment. She sat with Tad and Shady to tell them her concerns.

Tad said, "You're pretty slick in your black threads these days. I bet you believe you don't need us anymore."

"I'll always need you—you're my friends." She ran a hand across the top of her short haircut; she couldn't get enough of its brushy texture. "But you know what I'm saying. I don't scare easily, and I have the survival instincts of sandspur. Carrying stolen goods in the same conspicuous car as gallons of rotgut is double jeopardy. If I'm stopped, they can try to pin an awful lot more on me."

Shady asked, "Not at all. Double jeopardy refers to multiple forms of prosecution for the same offense. For example—"

"Shady, we don't need to be schooled in the finer elements of the law right now. MJ made a good point."

Shady lifted his sunglasses to eye Tad while asking her, "What about making separate trips?"

"That's not cost effective, Shady. Shoot—it takes half a day as is."

"We're not seeing much of you lately. You've turned into a gremlin. Come mellow out with us more."

She no longer had time for visiting, and as she'd avoided telling the guys about her real estate ventures, they had no idea why. She wasn't going to steal forever and wanted to keep the building business legitimate.

She rolled the sleeves of her polo shirt until they were tight around her upper arms. Fall was supposed to drop the temperature, but it hadn't happened yet. She wasn't lying when she said, "I'm working in two of Jaudon's stores, legitimately. And you know my other occupation takes a lot of research and surveillance."

Tad grinned, teasing her. "Why are you doing break-ins if you have two jobs? Leave that to us poverty-stricken coloreds."

"Poverty stricken? Don't tell your industrious mom you said that." She locked her fingers together and could have bitten her tongue. What chance did Tad, a Southern Black man, have to buy real estate? His mother told MJ she'd entered the business world through the back door. When her boys were small, she opened an unlicensed restaurant in the sunroom of their single-story rental and saved enough from that to lease space for Pansy's Home Cooking. Saving dollar by dollar, she acquired title to the substantial yellow building that housed her restaurant and the lot where Tad washed cars.

What a long, slow, tough climb. She knew her white face made her own ventures easier.

Shady's grandniece came around the corner carrying a Scooby-Doo school bag. He stretched from the wheelchair to hug her, but she ran with her arms out to Anika. MJ had trained the dog to sit motionless and bear such friendly assaults.

"Those rocks you brought us were about enough to keep this one in pencils."

Once the girl left, MJ asked, "They were worthless?"

"You heard of bull thistle?"

"Come on. That bad?" Shady liked to needle her when he was annoyed. "Why did the owner bother to hide them?"

"Quit joshing her," said Tad. "You hit the jackpot this time. He knows a good East Coast trader. I can't wait to pocket a tidbit of that pretty payoff."

Shady hooted. "It's true. Little Michelle's college fund is filling as fast as yours did." The frown line in his forehead deepened. "Still and all, you agreed to move the joy juice, and you're leaving us in the lurch. We've made ourselves useful to you since day one, when you had nothing but your bag and a broken knife."

"What he's trying to say is if there's no quid pro quo, we need to renegotiate percentage-wise on what he fences."

Her pilot light flared. "I'm forgoing what I earn from the liquor sales, plus you're cutting my share of what I bring you. What is this, punishment?"

"Still better than you'd get anywhere else because it's us. We'll have to find a van to transport that crud now, pay for gas, not to mention grapple with those swamp crackers."

They tried to get her to stay on for an even split and bounced ideas around to make the drive safer. Shady threatened to stop fencing what she stole. Tad tried to negotiate.

"Go ahead," she snapped. "You do what you want and keep the rotgut and the money from what I brought you. It's time for me to ease away from the thieving business anyway. Any time I go out on a job, my chance of getting pinched swells."

Shady said, "Getting ticked off is never the answer. There's no need to quit altogether. We'll be paying your full cut on the diamonds."

"They were diamonds?"

"Not just diamonds. Round diamonds. They'll cut two stones from each because of the size and shape. I don't keep enough cash to pay you yet. I'll give you a call as soon as I see the green."

"Boy howdy," she said. She silently congratulated herself for going exclusively after people who needed a comeuppance. Rigo's father might have taken the diamonds as payment for smuggling. "Thank you, Shady. I'm still going to quit burglarizing once I get my feet solidly under me."

Shady said, "Don't stop on my account—you've got talent."

"Can you stop?" asked Tad. "Stealing is habit-forming."

"She can satisfy the habit legally. In the world according to Shady, there's business, and there's dirty business. There's not a lot of difference between the two, and sometimes they're the same."

Tad said, "Where did they hide the diamonds? Don't tell me. In a box of baking soda? A hole behind a baseboard?"

"Under the refrigerator. I literally stumbled across them."

"You are a cash magnet, Squirrel."

Anika yipped and pulled at her leash. The men's eyes were drawn past MJ's shoulders. She swiveled her head and was caught between an uproar of pleasure at seeing Vonnie and fear about how much she'd overheard. "Vonnie. You're here."

Vonnie pressed her lips together as if uncertain. "It's Columbus Day weekend."

"Not in Florida, it isn't."

"My roommate's Italian, from Rhode Island, and so's her fiancé, who's in med school here. He's a member of an Italian club in Ybor City, and she wanted to watch him play in their bocce ball tournament. What can I say? She needed to share the driving, and I hoped you'd want to see me."

Vonnie was standing on the colorful fallen leaves of a sweet gum tree.

The hug she gave Vonnie was chaste. "You know I'm not lying when I say I want to see you every minute of every day."

"You're not mad? Only, I don't want my parents to know I'm here to see you, not them. I went to Mrs. Lanamore's, and she told me you were headed this way."

Her hands seemed stuck to Vonnie, but she broke away. "You have made my day, week, month, Von."

She saw the men look from Vonnie to her, at each other, and back. They had their bargaining chip now: they'd threaten to reveal her thievery to Vonnie.

She hurried her last haggling with them while Vonnie stood by. Concessions made, Shady wheeled inside his apartment after cash for the moonshiners.

Vonnie's glowering face materialized, a mask of anger and suspicion. "What's going on?"

"Let me finish here. I'll clue you in right away." She'd spoken too sharply, irked and guilty because she wanted to keep Vonnie in the dark about breaking and entering.

Tad studied his shoes and whistled until Shady returned with the money.

As they drove away, she wrestled with her conflict, white-knuckling the steering wheel. She explained that she'd gone to town with her final delivery. "The envelope of cash is for the distillers."

"Oh?" Vonnie said, as if waiting for the rest of the story.

She decided she'd made it all worse. To top off this fiasco, she ground the clutch and nearly stalled. Whether or not Vonnie overheard what she and the guys said, she'd noticed MJ was shaken up.

Their silence dragged on through a long traffic light, and traffic fumes poured in through their open windows. She still missed the practically empty roads of rural Washington. The distances were greater, but you might not see another car for miles.

They started moving again, caught in a slow clump of traffic. Vonnie seemed to accept her explanation and chattered in praise of MJ's haircut. "Who did it?"

"A friend of Rigo and Jimmy Neal's. He owns a stand-alone barber shop with the original equipment and fixtures. He didn't know how to stop his antique windows from leaking. I fixed them in exchange for the cut. He's more of a stylist than a barber, and the little building is a classic. The decorative exterior tiling is extraordinary."

Vonnie ran the palm of her hand across the top of MJ's hair and, although not by nature the squealing type, squealed. "That silky shoe brush texture is yummy."

Vonnie's approval buoyed her mood.

"Tell me, what was going on with Shady and Tad? That was not business as usual."

She couldn't change the subject forever and didn't want to lie to Vonnie. Why not? she asked herself. *I lie to the whole world.* This hidden life nailed dread and dishonesty to her love. Vonnie in all likelihood would turn on her. Regardless, Vonnie needed to know what she was getting herself into, and MJ decided the time had come to tell her.

❖

MJ took Vonnie to the promenade, the weightiest site she could think of for her revelations.

The town of Four Lakes had grown around a good-sized pond. The water was ringed by a paved walk complete with fluted columns and low walls decorated in stucco relief. She'd stopped a few times to enjoy the tranquility and the relative coolness.

Today, swans glided past with slow grace. White ibises with long orange beaks, a stalking blue heron, spick and span white and black ducks flew and swam, dove, and conducted occasional honking disagreements. She was at the point where, if this came to nothing, she would have a hard time leaving the glories of Florida behind.

Anika walked at the farthest end of her leash but had learned not to pull. A man and woman strolled the promenade far ahead.

"Peaceful here, isn't it?" she said, loath to disturb this safe haven.

"If you don't tell me, I'm going to bust."

"You can't mention a word to anyone else. And I am serious as wildfire about that."

"Are you dealing drugs? Tell me it's not drugs."

"It's not that bad. Or else it's worse in your eyes."

"Nothing is worse. I lost two high school friends to drugs. One overdosed, and the other is at her grandparents' farm in Alabama."

A motorcycle made a racket on the street. The heron spread its wings and lifted off.

She took a deep breath. "I'm a burglar," she announced.

Vonnie grabbed her arm, then pushed it away. Two lines appeared in her forehead. "What? What are you saying—my dewy-eyed Romeo is a criminal?"

"A sneak thief, a housebreaker, a filcher, a rip-off artist, a criminal."

Vonnie shrank away.

"It's true, Vonnie, and now you know, I'll bow out if you want."

Or was she being too willing? She wouldn't put it past her evil child self to use the wickedness her mother saw in her as a barricade to the kind of emotional commitment Gregory talked about at the party.

Vonnie planted herself on a shaded bench built into the wall.

She followed, left hand gripping right, both pressed against her midsection as she prepared herself for rejection now that she'd exposed her evil, evil, twisted self. The shadows of the trees above them were a relief from the sun, but she was dripping anxious sweat.

Vonnie said nothing. MJ noticed she wore a college T-shirt underneath her sleeveless denim jacket. She must be thoroughly engaged in campus life by now. *Why aren't I walking away from this well-bred girl?*

A car door closed behind them. The other couple drove away, and the town went quiet but for a random quack. A duck on the grass tucked its bill under its feathers.

"You'd better take me back to school."

From the start, she'd feared a slow leak in the balloon of this dream. Today she'd punctured it once and for all. "C'mon."

They walked toward the park exit along the placid pond, waterfowl oblivious to their passage. Though her pace was slow and heavy with disappointment, she knew she should stand back and dispatch Vonnie from the sullied world she inhabited. Vonnie needed to find someone who deserved her.

At the car, she said, "I'm swinging by the house for Anika's food and water. I'll need gas before we head north."

"Beautiful Anika. What'll happen to her when you go to jail?"

She spoke over the white top of the station wagon. "I'm not going to jail—I'm too careful."

Vonnie scowled her way. "Dream on. Nobody's too careful."

"I'll quit before anyone can catch me. What I'm doing is a short-term solution."

"I'm not sure what's worse, your dumb confidence or your morals. It's not okay to steal."

"Yes, it's stealing, but for the good. Aren't I liberating these people from their materialism? It's practically a revolutionary act."

"Tell that to a jury. It's the dumbest rationalization I ever heard," Vonnie yelled over a passing utility truck. "How on earth does this fit in with your real estate plans? Are you going to swipe houses too?"

"I'm telling you right now, Vonnie, business itself is a thief—it steals whatever it can. I never do any major damage. I take a small amount of excess."

"What are you talking about? Are you a communist? A capitalist? A criminal?"

They didn't say a word as she drove to her new rehab. She and Vonnie were done, as they should be. She pulled onto the sandy driveway. Anika whined to get out, but neither of them budged.

"The more I studied finance," she said, "the more I saw the bottom line takes precedence over any other business factor. What's the difference between swiping a wealthy guy's fancy watch and raising the price on a carton of milk to make investors millionaires and mothers paupers?"

Vonnie bit her bottom lip the way she did when reasoning.

MJ added, "What's the difference between buying moonshine and putting a six-pack of beer in your shopping cart at Publix?"

"Don't play games with me, woman," Vonnie snapped. "One is legal and the other isn't. Needless to say."

Vonnie's tone stabbed her. "Same with investing in a stock and playing backroom poker. They're both gambling."

"So you're saying that businesswomen are as immoral as burglars?"

She held her arms wide. "Honestly? Yes. The difference is I can drop the threats that come with breaking and entering the day I have the means to steal like the Wall Street boys do."

"I get it. You're interning to climb a different dirty ladder of success."

Vonnie's outrage provoked her. "Listen, I know you're not from money, and your student loans will be colossal by the time you're through. You're under the impression you're paying back the government, which theoretically wants you to succeed and be a productive member of society. Right?"

"You don't know what I think."

"If you do, you'd be wrong. The government backs these loans, but the actual lenders are private and making money from the interest."

"Nothing improper with that."

"Nothing illegal, but don't you question why we have to, one, pay for higher education when education benefits society? Two, only educate those who can afford it, which is mostly white progeny. And three, say you borrow $10,000 to get your degree, and you pay, for example, three percent interest. Part of that interest goes to administer the loan, and part becomes pure profit."

"Which is capitalism."

"Perfectly legitimate system. So you're paying $300 to borrow that money."

"That's elementary."

She used her fingers to illustrate. "If half the interest goes into an investor's pocket, you basically gave away $150. And without lifting a finger or paying taxes if he can get away with it, he takes your money, adds it to nine hundred and ninety-nine other student loans, and he has $150,000 to pay for, what, country club dues? A yacht? To expand his business or send his brats through college, loan-free?"

While Vonnie remained silent, she said, "Meanwhile, you're eating Rice-A-Roni and canned spaghetti and trying to study between minimum wage shifts at Potted Palm Burgers. I mean, for real, education should not be a privilege available to families of means alone."

Vonnie pouted, tapping a foot, and twirled a ringlet of hair around and around her finger. Anika stood in the back seat and scratched at the car window with her claws.

"What I want to know is what makes it more ethical for someone to enrich himself with your $150 than it is for me to appropriate $150 of what he has?"

Vonnie, her voice subdued now, grimaced. "Your thinking is off. I believe you're as wrong as you can be."

She pounded one fist into the other. "Tell me it makes sense to you that Farmer Cornstalk is paid the lowest possible amount for his harvest and needs subsidies, consumers pay the highest possible amount, and the middleman is the only winner?"

"Don't get het up at me."

"Mad at you, Vonnie? Hell, no. I'm perpetually mad."

"That's not good for you."

"It propels me."

CHAPTER THIRTY-SIX

MJ's newest home was in a home owners' association neighborhood not far from Rainbow Gap. She leashed Anika before leaving the car. "Can't let her loose here," she said. "They have all sorts of rules." The dog sniffed the wide trunk of an oleander tree and pulled MJ toward the white stucco house.

"This house," she told Vonnie, "has been rented out and misused since the owner's husband died, and the wife is now in her eighties. She can't afford the upkeep. The flooring has so many broken tiles it's dangerous. I took the bus over here one day—"

"Casing the neighborhood? You didn't want them to see your car?"

Vonnie's sarcasm bit. "Look at the palatial residences along the street these little places back up to. Damn it, Vonnie, there are Americans without anyplace to live. I saw the *For Sale by Owner* sign and called her from a phone booth. She accepted my cash offer right away. Said her grandson put the sign out a month ago, and the sooner I took ownership, the sooner she could move in with him. Tell me it's not criminal that an old person can't stay in her own home."

The sinks throughout the home showed damage. "I'm checking secondhand dealers in the area for replacement sinks and exploring water softeners to keep the iron out."

A yellow and brown checked sofa filled the far wall of the living room. "I happened across this on a curb with a *free* sign. It's unbelievable, the good stuff people toss. I'm perfectly comfortable sleeping on it."

She'd made substantial progress, but Vonnie wouldn't look at her.

Cross-legged on the sofa, arms tightly hugging herself, Vonnie's lips were a straight, tight line. Anika lay at her feet, a toy between her paws, tail sweeping the floor.

"I'll just get my stuff and be right back."

Vonnie broke her silence. "You're no revolutionary. You're using economics to justify what you do."

"The guys in charge do the same. We read about trickle-down policies. In fact, Will Rogers concocted the trickle-down concept—as a joke. No one should settle for a trickle of income. It's justification for well-fixed guys to rake in the dollars while pretending that's the best way to provide income for us little people. That's what's improper."

Vonnie pulled Anika's brush from under a cushion and vigorously groomed the dog.

MJ crossed to a cabinet. For the drive north, she poured kibble into an empty bread bag. "Damn it. I don't need to defend myself to anyone."

Vonnie dropped the brush. She propped her elbows on her thighs and let her face fall into her upraised hands. Her words were muffled. "Why do I have to love you this much? I came to tell you I'm transferring to your college, Bone Valley in Four Lakes, next term. I'd lose my mind away from you for another three years and a half."

She parked herself next to Vonnie. The puppy, who had watched her pack dinner, sighed and rested against her leg. She petted her to soothe herself. And laid herself open to Vonnie with her story.

How she was an unwelcome disruption Dear Old Dad and his girlfriend created right before high school graduation. How because of her, he missed out on college, married her mother, and joined the army to support his wife and child, both the result of an evening's fun. That he served two tours in Vietnam before coming home an angry man and starting their legitimate family. She was a strange child, an estranged child.

Vonnie tilted her head the way she did when puzzled. "All of which convinced you that you're exempt from the laws most people respect?"

"It led me to question every rule in the book. I'm serious. If my ex-mother wanted me to stay in the kitchen and do the dishes, I went looking for Dear Old Dad to help him build shelves, repair a fence, cut firewood."

"Are you someday going to tell me where you were raised?"

Her inner workings went to their panic stations. She rubbed her fists against each other and crammed them into her pockets while she took deep breaths. Should she, if Vonnie was leaving her? What the hell, trusting Vonnie might be a last chance to keep her.

"I'm from the most negligible town in the universe," she started, interlacing her fingers and twisting her hands back and forth. "My grandfather was a railroad man originally from Montreal. He settled in Depot Landing, Washington, to work for a higher wage. The town is known for a rail yard and locomotive roundhouse next to the biggest river in the Northwest, the Columbia.

"My so-called family lived at the top of the barren bluffs, in a rental house at the end of the windiest gravel road in the county. The air was usually pure, and the prairie, that high up, was endless, parcels of it given over to farms and ranches. Summers, though, I breathed a lot of road dust, and in drier years, the smoke from forest fires and controlled burns. The quiet neighbors were fir trees, white oak, and pine, sometimes bear, deer, cougar, and always coyote. Spring wildflowers covered the meadows. Lots of gray basalt and volcanic rock. The north part of the county is Yakama Indian Reservation. The Tribe refused to leave their fishing grounds in the Columbia River."

"Way to go, Tribe. You weren't rural, you were backwoods. Did you have schools? A library?" Vonnie's voice had warmed, and she laid a gentle hand over MJ's, as if to say Vonnie knew how difficult this was for her.

"About a hundred of us, from preschoolers to high school seniors, all went to the same one-building school in town. It was a good school—you didn't not graduate from Depot Landing School. At times the school bus couldn't handle the grade of the hills in snow and ice, but I knew the trails and always went. Later, Dear Old Dad opted to homeschool his brood, but that's a story for another day."

"Is that why you came here, for the heat?"

"Partly. I also wanted to get as far away as I could imagine. To be honest, I loved that rough countryside, the clean river on its way to the Bonneville Dam, the toots and howls of the railroad engines, wild salmon off the grill, the smell of woodsmoke, but I was so eager to be elsewhere." She sat back on the sofa cushion, encouraged when Vonnie moved closer to keep her hand. "I wanted Key West. I read it's a good town for gay people. But my ride dropped me in front of Tad and Shady's car wash. I didn't starve on the streets or become a prostitute or get hooked on drugs because they protected me, and Mrs. Lanamore fed me, and Duval Lanamore showed me a job board at the college."

Vonnie took both her hands and massaged the tightness from them. "You were, what, sixteen?"

"Remember, nobody knows any of this but you, whether you want to stay with me or not."

Vonnie earnestly bobbed MJ's hands up and down. "I'll tuck your secrets far, far away and won't remember them myself."

She retrieved one hand and touched Vonnie's face with her fingertips.

Vonnie kissed the fingers. "No wonder you dress in black. You're a real bandit, a dreamy desperado."

She'd succumb to her hunger for Vonnie unless she kept talking. "I left at fifteen. Took a bus as far as my ticket took me."

"I'm surprised you didn't steal a car."

She backed away, palms raised in front of her. "Hoo boy, I'll tell you right now, I never stole until I came to Florida, the land of wasted housing. I was up for doing anything to stay."

Vonnie went silent, the back of her hand pressed to her lips, frowning in thought. Eventually she said, "I understand better now. You were up against it—a fifteen-year-old runaway in a region entirely strange to you. You're not the type to hide away and stagnate either. I'll bet you wanted to start your new life right then and there but couldn't. That made you mad and some kind of frantic. You're tough as a pine knot, MJ Beaudry, and I can't imagine a thing you can do to drive me away—on the condition that the end of your sneak-thieving is in sight."

She messed with her glasses to hide the hope from her eyes, but no one truly knew what drove another person. Romance, desire, and now the lure of the outlaw appeared to befuddle Vonnie, who didn't see what was right in front of her: this evil, evil, twisted child.

"Listen," she said, "we'd better get going if I'm taking you back to the dorm by curfew."

"Is this your idea of romance, rushing me from town—"

"You're right. I'm not good for you, Vonnie. You should run fast and far. Now."

Vonnie did her head tilt and raised a quizzical eyebrow. "Weren't you trying to lure me back a minute ago? Finish your story, my honey squirrel."

At times Vonnie demonstrated the authority, and wiles, of a full-grown woman.

"You want iced tea?"

"If you have sugar for me to add to that plain tea you like."

She went to the refrigerator—she'd bought it restored from an appliance repair shop—and set two jugs of tea on the counter. She pointed. "One for me and the other specifically for a certain Southern lady."

"MJ." Vonnie looked both pleased and tearful. "You weren't even expecting me."

"I'm always geared up for you. I'd make you a keg of the stuff to keep you around if I thought I was good for you." She added ice and brought the chilled glasses to the couch. At this point, she no longer knew if she waged war to keep Vonnie or send her away.

"I want to learn every nitty-gritty particular about you."

"Seriously?"

"And right now, while I've got you going. What happened once you were here?"

"What didn't tick me off when I hit Rainbow Gap—my parents, their brats, the woman I worked for, and the guy across the alley." She explained about Ike Keister living in the swank former resort next door, one of the many useless people who had the means to devote time and money to worthwhile pursuits but didn't.

Vonnie's eyes were anchored to hers.

"I couldn't stop my anger at the world and broke into Keister's condo. My relief was ridiculously freeing."

"Relief?"

"Anger clogged me up. By the time I escaped, it had gone whoosh, down the drain."

"You were never caught?"

"Twice. Keister walked in on me, but I broke away. And Cullie, before she became a sworn officer, caught me red-handed. I lucked out—she had more interest in saving me from jail than putting me in."

Vonnie put her long, slender arms tight around her. "You were a baby far from home. You were hitting back."

"I never lost the anger, Vonnie. Stealing from people who thrive on excess tempers the rage for a while. I became good at it. I used the proceeds from their excesses to educate myself and start a business. You'll see, when I get on solid ground, I have plans. I'm not wasting my money."

"I admit it's a little tantalizing to be with an honest-to-goodness almost retired bandit type."

"Keep your voice down."

"We're in your house," Vonnie whispered, pressing MJ's head against her shoulder and stroking it. "We're safe here."

"There is no safety."

"Aw, honey squirrel, you need me. I'm transferring."

She pulled away. "No, you're not. You told me you wanted to go to a status-heavy college and make a career in San Francisco. It's your dream."

"That was before you. Tampa is exactly my size if you're here."

"You wanted a gayer city."

"We'll make wherever we are gayer—San Francisco's doing pretty well without me. You're here, as is my family, Cousin Jaudon, Berry and their friends, the kids I know from New York Pizza—I have no reason to leave anymore."

"Do you honestly believe we're compatible? Can you live with a criminal? I'm putting you in danger."

"I'm not perfect either. I bend the truth and tell white lies too often. It's a bad habit. Lies come more easily to me than truth."

"Lying doesn't make you a criminal, Vonnie."

"It's like I have a spot of rot in me. You'll think I'm a total goofball, but I still recite the Girl Scout Law to myself: *I will do my best to be honest.* I've never lied to you."

She swept a hand over the lovely hills and valleys of Vonnie's spine. "It won't be forever, Vonnie, but you know what? I'm not letting go of my best source of income until I have what I need to support myself. You might want to put serious thought into not throwing your lot in with me before you make a final decision."

"You're not the singular reason I want to come home. They're football nuts at school. The girls are boy crazy and push, push, push me to date. The white boys are as bad as my aunt Floxie's husband, the lay minister, crowding me up against walls and telling me how they have a thing for half-breeds. It's one scary-ass institution."

"You never said a word. Have you reported them?"

"Nothing happens when I do."

"How integrated is it?"

"A lot more than Bone Valley, but people know me and my family around here, and I'd be coming home nights."

"No one's heard of Bone Valley. It suited my need to learn the ins and outs of business. I always planned to work for myself, and I didn't want to tear up my roots again by moving away. For you, though, it's important that state degrees open more doors."

Vonnie eyes were grave. "The change depends on you anyway. Since Bone Valley is a private college, it's going to cost more than the university. I can't afford the dorm, but I can pay some rent."

"You'd have to pay your parents rent?"

Vonnie adopted a coy look as she said, "Don't be a bozo. I want to enjoy every minute I can with you. Let's get started on our life together. Okay, you'll spirit away…whatever you spirit away. I'll be the silly wife who doesn't suspect a thing."

She didn't want to chance losing Vonnie by saying no. Worse, what if she said yes, and Vonnie got in trouble because of her? Vonnie might be a few years behind her, but her own confusion was like a child's. How did people make these complex decisions?

Together? Was that how they made them? She buried her face in the peppermint scent of Vonnie's hair, smiling to herself. For once, she didn't have to decide on her own.

Vonnie whispered, "I'd be adorable Anika's puppy mama."

She laughed, laughed harder, whether from relief or true mirth at Vonnie's words, she didn't know, but she lay back on the couch, laughing until her sides complained. "You're the adorable puppy," she said with a splutter.

Anika yipped and ran in excited circles.

Vonnie jumped on top of MJ, straddling her. "I am. I am. Whatever happens, I'm your adorable puppy."

Never would she drive this treasure away.

Vonnie lifted MJ's T-shirt and kissed every inch of her bare chest. The kisses tickled. MJ's mirthful complaints became ardor. Without a word, she stood, gave Anika dinner and a chew toy. She tossed cushions to the floor and opened the couch to an already made-up double bed. She gave a thumbs-up at Vonnie's cry of surprise.

CHAPTER THIRTY-SEVEN

"You're out of kilter, my angel. Take it easy—we haven't awarded ourselves a day off in weeks." Berry had persuaded Jaudon to steal a few hours from the stores and take some time for themselves. They were headed to Anna Maria Island south of St. Pete.

Jaudon spent the drive bawling out other drivers and bemoaning aloud the loss of her 1955 European motorbike, which had been stolen from the parking lot when she managed the Beverage Bay on Buffalo Street. She drove their aging but air-conditioned Buick onto the Manatee Bridge and came to another unanticipated stop. "I should have known the stupid drawbridge would lift the minute we got here."

Berry watched Jaudon's hands strangle the steering wheel. "You can't take it easy anymore, can you? I don't care if we're stuck in traffic till kingdom come—the Intracoastal Waterway is gorgeous. Smell the ocean. Admire that graceful sailboat."

"If we earned as much money as that sailboat cost, we'd be in clover." Jaudon pointed to the glove compartment. "Can you get me a couple of Tylenols? I've got a headache that won't quit."

"Tylenol? Didn't you take that off the store shelves when those eight people died? Here, I have aspirin in my purse."

Jaudon took the aspirin and swallowed them dry.

Berry put the Tylenol bottle in her purse, trying to think of a happier topic. "How's MJ doing at the store?"

"She's a hard worker, no doubt about that. Not real good with the customers, though. Sometimes acts like she has a grudge against them."

"What's that about, you think?"

"Beats me. There's an orneriness she's going to have to get over if she wants her grand plans to pan out."

"Maybe her upbringing was rough on her."

"Whose wasn't? The chip on her shoulder sticks out a mile."

Berry patted down Jaudon's cowlick. "I'd say it matches the five-hundred-year-old banyan tree perched on your shoulder."

As the bridge lowered, Jaudon studied her with one eye narrowed. Berry fluffed her curls, all innocence.

Jaudon signaled forgiveness with an exaggerated sigh. "One thing's for sure—MJ loves Florida. Every time I turn around, she's on about something new to her: a sunset, a surprise lake at the end of a street, the sight of a rocket taking off over in Canaveral. Yesterday she came into the store with a bag of blood oranges someone sold her from a backyard tree. The best I ever tasted."

"Turn right."

She'd wanted to visit Anna Maria Island since Gran told her she honeymooned there with Berry's grandfather. They'd crossed the long defunct wooden bridge and ate fish he caught in the surf, roasted over a cook fire on the sand.

Jaudon broke into her reverie. "You know a woman was murdered out here this summer."

"You're a barrel of laughs today."

"No, the papers said that Tampa pediatrician and his children were killed."

"I remember. Dr. Garza knew him."

"You never told me." Jaudon sounded affronted.

"Oh, honey, that's why I asked you to take today off. You haven't been around enough to tell anything. Let's take Magnolia Avenue and see if there's a manatee off Bay Boulevard."

"I don't know why you go bananas over those blobs."

"They're vegetarian—obviously I love them. They have such fun, rolling around in the water. They mother their cute mini-manatees for years, and they don't hunt other creatures."

"It's no surprise to me you don't mind bristly hairs and funny faces." Jaudon tooled along, sunglasses pushed to the top of her head, an elbow propped out the open window.

"Stop ridiculing yourself. You are positively debonair."

Jaudon pulled a face as she parked, but Berry knew she was trying to hide her pleasure.

Popcorn clouds hung high in the sky. It was hot but breezy by the Gulf. She remembered MJ telling her about her first day in Florida when she realized she would never be cold again.

"Let's go stick our feet in the water," she said.

Jaudon flashed her an ever-the-indulgent-lover smile. "And our heads in the sand?"

They left their shoes in the car. Jaudon slung a beach towel over her shoulder as they made their way through green goat's foot vine, knot grass, and pale sea oats, to the hot, pale, finely grained sand.

Three roseate spoonbills flew by, their splendid pink and white feathers always breathtaking to Berry. She walked, as ever, on the side of Jaudon's good ear. "Blue water, green water, blue-green water. Doesn't it make you peaceful? Let's plan to retire over here."

"Retire? That's not in the cards."

"Someday, maybe. When we're wizened-up ladies."

"They're not wizened up," Jaudon said of two white-haired, tanned, and fit women scattering sandpipers ahead of them. "I tell you what, my personal nurse is going to keep me in shape." She touched Berry's hand and at once let it go.

"Those women live pampered lives. Sarongs and hairdos like theirs don't come cheap."

The water cooled her. Jaudon splashed around, wetting Berry's thin-strapped sundress, and Berry said, "You haven't changed since you were eight."

"Do go on." Jaudon scooped water over her own head and shook off the drops. "I see you laughing."

A gang of pelicans skimmed the bay. Feral parakeets whistled, chattered, and squawked high in the trees. A lone bottlenose dolphin rose and dipped out on the blue-green water, moving with them for a while.

On the towel, they sat, hands almost touching. The sun burned the back of Berry's neck.

"Okay," said Jaudon, rubbing her onyx ring like a charm. "Now tell me what you brought me through all that traffic to talk about."

She briefly laid her head on Jaudon's shoulder. "Oh, honey, you know me too well. I love you more than Kajen loves tinned tuna."

"If you want to make me peaceful, out with it."

Berry waited while several skateboarders rumbled by on the road behind them.

"A national corporation in the Midwest wants to buy our practice. They're promising to give us more operating money and new equipment. We sorely need the upgrades, but they want to put in a fancy accounting system like they do in all the group practices they swallow. They take over, make the practice more profitable, and walk away with stuffed pockets, regardless of quality or staff."

Jaudon squinted as if trying to read her face. "You're not happy about this at all."

"I don't work to benefit a bunch of investors—I do it for the patients. It makes me cross. I suspect they're owned by an insurance company and get tricky with Medicare and Medicaid billing."

"How come?"

"Ask MJ. I can't follow these snake-oil operations, but they're legal."

"Why can't us little guys be left alone? Three convenience chains offered to buy the Beverage Bays rather than go head-to-head with us. We're not hardly making a dent in their profits."

"Insurance companies shouldn't be allowed to tell us what we can or can't do with our patients."

"You know I've said, as an employer, that insurers are getting too big for their britches. It's not just hustlers like Reverend Scully—it's these enormous corporations that flimflam us. Take your Gran. She's on Medicare now, but remember that procedure she went in the hospital for, and the insurance said the doctor wasn't on their list, and their doctor left her with an infection? Where's the ethics?"

"It's legal for them to get rich off sickness. Is nursing a healing profession or a production line?"

"And how come the insurance swindle is legal, when privately selling homemade liquor isn't? Does that make sense to you?" Jaudon bit her lip, then said, "Another year of what we made off shine and we'd be shut of debt."

"Oh, Angel. Were we that close to ending this siege?"

Jaudon nodded. "But I'll git 'er done, Georgia gal, I promise you that. And if your docs sell you out, you'll know it's time to open your counseling practice."

"I need you to promise me we'll have more time together like this, whatever happens."

"It's not that I don't want to spend more time together, Berr. You believe that, don't you?"

"Sometimes I might imagine I'm neglected, that's all. I didn't want to put more pressure on you by mentioning it."

Jaudon looked around. "The heck with what people think. Come over here." She pulled Berry close. "I never meant to neglect you, for heaven's sake." They watched the lapping water with their arms around each other. "Nothing is as important as what we have together. As you."

Her eyes moistened with gladness. She missed this tender connection with her Jaudon.

"I'll figure this out, Berr, I sincerely will."

Jaudon kissed her cheek. Berry knew the courage it took Jaudon to show affection in public.

"Now," Berry said, her sunburn stinging. "What if we forget about work and treat ourselves to dinner and a sunset at the Rod and Reel Pier? I want to see what Gran saw on her honeymoon."

They walked a long way on the beach to the restaurant. Sunburned and weary, Berry had a glass of white wine, and Jaudon ordered a Jax beer. The drinks made everything seem funny. They giggled till she thought they'd be asked to leave.

Dinner sobered them up. The sunset was extraordinary and seemed to go on and on. They ordered dessert to keep their view table. The sky tried on several shades of blue, each of them complementing the pinks, yellows, reds, and, finally, purples of the lowering sun.

She told Jaudon, "Your eyes are the colors of the sky."

"I never saw such a sunset as this before in my life. I want to make you see those colors next time we," she whispered, "snug up. You're right about taking time more often."

"I know."

CHAPTER THIRTY-EIGHT

November 1982

At Berry's weekly staff meeting, the five physicians talked about pros and cons of affiliating with the umbrella medical company. Dr. Garza opposed it, and so, bless him, did Larry Rinaldi, despite threats to leave the practice by the other two male physicians. She wouldn't miss either of the two—one was beyond arrogant, and she barely tolerated the way the other infantilized patients—but she knew many patients distrusted an all-female practice. On the other hand, male ob-gyns were a dime a dozen in Florida, and the clinic could hire substitutes for these men within the month.

Her heart quailed when the meeting ended. The physicians stayed. Patients were arriving, and the staff needed to get their bottoms in gear. From the flash of concern in Dr. Garza's eyes, Berry knew the docs were about to make a final decision.

She dreamed of her women's community clinic as a service, not a business. She prayed the Great Spirit would help her improve the lives of impoverished women, migrant women, old women.

In no time at all, Dr. Garza stood in the office door. Startled, Berry jabbed the pin of her name tag deep into her thumb. She pressed her lips together to keep from crying out and raised her eyes to the doctor.

"We're staying independent," Dr. Garza said, with a professional's subdued smile on her face.

Berry raised her arms in triumph.

Dr. Garza grimaced and reached for her bloodstained hand.

"I have this," said Berry. She went to the bathroom to wash the puncture, then dashed into an exam room to grab an antibiotic and a bandage. She rushed to take a file from Laura, the receptionist, and roomed the patient.

At her lunch break she crowed a bit.

Laura sat in the break room table eating her perennial egg salad sandwich. She swallowed and told Berry, "Praise be, that plan is deader than a doornail."

The two women had grown close over their years of employment. Laura Bathgate's sister was Olive Ponder, Jaudon's most trusted store manager. Laura jokingly took credit for Berry's hire because she'd told Olive about the RN opening, and Olive told Jaudon. Berry was hired right before she graduated college.

They spoke in low voices about the way the vote went.

"The women won against the men for a change. Imagine if we elected lady politicians, how powerful we'd be."

Berry sliced a banana and stirred it into her yogurt. "I'm not cut out for politics, but now that we're staying independent, why not have our free clinic once a month right here?"

Laura wiped her lips with a napkin. They'd talked about this before. "Hold it Saturday mornings? Persuade the doctors to donate their time? I know too many women who live packed in rooms with their kids at by-the-week motels, and gals past their prime in leaky shacks farmers once rented to field hands."

"Start it once a year for flu shots. Recruit volunteers for transportation."

Laura crunched her last potato chip and folded her paper lunch bag. "Pass out birth control information. There are too many humans on this earth."

The afternoon went quickly after lunch. Berry never nosed out a minute to speak with Dr. Garza about her conversation with Laura and couldn't stay late. Her Chevy LUV pickup was in the shop, and Jaudon, Allison, and Cullie were all working. Most often, she relied on Gran for a ride, but Gran was with her new gentleman friend, Benedict Lam. He was barely taller than her, his thin, gray hair neatly trimmed, his clothes pressed and starched. Never married, quick to show his boyish dimples, he called himself a retired playboy but was actually a retired attorney. Gran told the world, from Berry to the cashiers at the Winn-Dixie, how he treated her like a queen.

Lacking other options, Berry reached out to young MJ, who claimed to embrace the chance to give her a lift home. In her usual black outfit, MJ leaned on her car in the office lot, one leg propped behind her against the tire, reading a falling-apart paperback. Berry squinted at the cover—*The Affluent Society* by John Kenneth Galbraith. Anika was at her feet with the posture of a show dog. MJ straightened, assisted the pup into the back seat, and opened the passenger door for Berry.

Berry accepted MJ's hand to drop into the low seat, saying, "Our Northwest orphan has grown into one fine gentlewoman." Again, she noted the new confidence in her walk, almost a strut, which both amused and heartened her. Whatever she'd lost in her early years, MJ was finding again.

The ride to Rainbow Gap took twenty minutes most days, but not on a Friday evening right at rush hour. Rain spattered the windshield and accelerated to a downpour within seconds. The windshield wipers squeaked. The station wagon handled little better than a boat on a lake of glass. Roomy and comfortable as it was, she noticed the effort it took MJ to steer and the way she stood on the brakes to stop.

"How's that women's health project of yours shaping up?"

She went through her scaled-down plan.

MJ seemed to consider the information. "When I rake in enough money—and I do plan to be moderately well-off—I'm going to make sure you get that health center off the ground."

Difficult as it was, she made nary a peep at this gutsy talk. Maybe MJ wasn't as mature as she seemed to be. Her own thirty-one seemed a dog's age older and wiser than MJ's twenty-two. They were a whole lesbian generation apart. "How in heaven's name will you put away money when the Beverage Bay is your only income?"

"I'll invest in real estate."

"You don't have two nickels to rub together." She remembered Jaudon's story about chasing and restraining this runaway when the child broke into someone's home, scrounging for food. She chided herself for thinking it, but had MJ stopped stealing?

"That's all it'll take, a few nickels and lots of elbow grease."

"I hope Jaudon didn't lead you toward trouble by hiring you for that illegal operation."

"Jaudon didn't lead me any farther astray than I'm willing to go."

She wouldn't have asked, but for MJ's confounding secretiveness. "How far are you willing to go?"

MJ stopped for a red light, huffed on her glasses, and cleaned them with the hem of her shirt. She seemed eager to address the subject. "Vonnie and I talk about that. Sometimes it might be more ethical to break the law than not, to equal things out a tinch, and to send a message that some have way much more than they need."

"Oh, for pity's sake. Do you sincerely suppose that's okay? Civilization is built on laws."

The cement truck ahead of them lurched forward. MJ shifted but didn't give her car enough gas and stalled. Drivers hit their horns. MJ didn't rattle easily—she kept talking as she restarted the car.

"I honestly do believe it's okay. Laws for who? The law enshrines property. It needs to prioritize lives over property, and to stop the long, slow murders by deprivation. But who writes the laws? Usually the people with the most property. You know what? That's crazy."

"If that's the case, then let me out right now, so I can ransack these new houses we're passing."

MJ was driving at a good clip now, one hand on the steering wheel, the other gesticulating like a flag in a gale. "You mean these middle-class developments? People who buy them work hard, save their money, and pay usurious mortgages."

Her sarcasm had gone right over MJ's intent head. "You have to pay to borrow money."

"That's fair until the lenders get greedy. Consider Jaudon and the stores. She'd rather sell one than get a loan or remortgage your house."

"What can we do? Start a revolution?"

"Revolution brought us to this point. No, there'll be greed as long as there are humans. Your idea about ransacking houses—if they're over-the-top-fancy—is much better. Especially the houses that are empty half the year."

"When other people live in substandard housing."

"Exactly. With your concern for needy women, you're the quiet revolution."

"And you? Where do you fit in?"

With the palms of her hands, MJ struck the steering wheel. "I reassign wealth, one moneygrubbing person at a time."

Now they were behind a school bus unloading a sports team and its equipment.

"Tell me you're no bank robber."

"Not my style. But I'll tell you—and I'm serious about this now— once I get ahead enough so every penny's not tied up in the business, I'll be divvying what I have three ways. One third of my income will keep my larder stocked. I'll invest another third, and the last is earmarked for the good works you're planning. Maybe only yours."

"But how?" she asked, wary of the answer. Queasiness hit her; the car windows were shut tight to keep out the rain, and the sluggish air-conditioning blew lukewarm through the vents. She closed her eyes to settle her stomach.

At last the bus moved, and MJ shifted the gearstick more smoothly.

"The how doesn't matter. The way I see it, either an oil millionaire eats caviar, or a lesbian child gets the help she needs."

Berry thought of Jaudon back in elementary school, the way her androgynous appearance drove their classmates wild with meanness, and how pig-ignorant the do-nothing teachers were. And Lari, the mentally fragile college student from her women's group who almost died before Jaudon and Cullie took action.

"Or don't you plan to offer services to gay women?"

"I have to admit that's not been foremost on my mind for the clinic."

"But it will be now, won't you?" MJ idled outside the Vicker house. "Not all gay kids are born wily enough to get by on their own. Which may be good news for the world at large."

She thanked MJ with a kiss on the cheek, gratified to see the tips of her ears go red.

"You sure you won't stay for supper? We picked a passel of raging ripe tomatoes before work this morning."

"Imagine. Ripe tomatoes off the vine in November. Only in Florida, right? Sounds great, thanks, but I have to find materials for work before the stores close."

"It'll take but three seconds to run get you some."

"Thanks, but you enjoy them."

"You'll come for Thanksgiving, though."

"Vonnie's expected at her aunt Lessie's house, but we'll come as soon as we can get away."

"Do you get along with the Lowe family?"

"Good question."

CHAPTER THIRTY-NINE

Thanksgiving 1982

Two forty-five and the sun hadn't appeared all day. Nevertheless, the temperature was in the seventies, and MJ remembered how rainy and icy Depot Landing mainly was at Thanksgiving.

Benedict Lam opened the Vickers' door to the Lowes, each bearing a pie or covered bowl. Gran and Berry emerged from the kitchen, surprised looks on their faces. Jaudon, Cullie, Jimmy Neal, and Allison were gathered around a board game. Rigo had gone to Miami to be with his mother.

The house definitely smelled like Thanksgiving. She had developed an affinity for Southern cooking; the tastes, the rituals, the conviviality around it made her happy.

Cullie sang out, "Come play Aggravation with us."

"I am aggravated enough," Vonnie said as she led her family and MJ into the house, her voice strident. "You want to know how Uncle Roy Jack greeted MJ, on Thanksgiving of all days? *You're the cocky he-she who fronted my cousin's Church Pond operation.* And he wasn't smiling."

"Vonnie threw a hissy fit with a tail on it," said Vaughn, admiration in his tone. "The aunts and girl cousins didn't know whether to beat a retreat or lash out. The Batson men stared holes in unsuspecting MJ."

Vonnie said, "Jaudon, your pops, standing next to Momma in her wheelchair, he went to bat for us."

Jaudon cupped a hand behind her good ear.

Vonnie went on. "My mother grabbed Vaughn's and my hands and said to your pops, louder than I ever heard, *Thank you, Wayne Vicker.*

This family has never gone easy on Grady and our babies. We'll have our Thanksgiving dinner where we're wanted."

MJ drew Lollie Lowe farther into the room and lifted her arm in a prizefighter pose. "Lollie is my new champ." The household applauded.

Both of the Lowe parents carried the weight of middle years. Lollie's hair was a graying reddish brown that went well with a calf-length dress in an autumn leaf pattern. Her laugh lines were deep, and her pilgrim earrings jiggled when she burbled with merriment.

Vonnie continued in high dudgeon. "I'm damn downhearted we didn't say yes to you originally."

"Yvonne," said Lollie. "No cursing."

"Sorry," Vonnie said, lowering her eyes.

Anika and Puddin ran through the house, crazed with excitement at the company and the smell of the turkey. Kirby scrambled after them, her claws sliding on the floors.

"Make yourselves t'home," Gran told the Lowes and MJ. Gran now wore her old Helena Rubinstein makeup around Benedict. She'd had her hair permed and colored at Rustic Roots Styling Palace, a one-woman beauty parlor in a private home in downtown Rainbow Gap. She'd also gone on a shopping spree at Stein Mart and came home suffering sticker shock, accustomed as she was to buying her clothes at the Goodwill. "There's plenty for you folks. Be a good host, Jaudon, and hang their wraps. Berry, go take the grapefruit spoon to the second squash and scrape the hollow good."

Cullie contorted her face. "Ewww. She's making you touch the slimy seed glop."

Gran swatted the air in Cullie's direction. "And put the seeds aside with the others for roasting and growing next year."

Mrs. Lowe presented Gran with a pretty container of homemade divinity candy. "I made this for the girls to bring over, but I'm pleased to present it directly to you. Your house smells heavenly."

"Truth is," said Grady Lowe, a tall, balding Black man in wire-rimmed glasses, "you gave us yet another reason for gratitude today. What say you come to our family for the next holiday? That work for you, Lollie?"

Lollie nodded. "Grady and I formally invite you to come celebrate the December holidays with us."

Vaughn gave a thumbs-up. "Cool, Dad. We never get Christmas ribs at Aunt Lessie's."

"Or Mom's mac and cheese." Vonnie hopped in place, and with a child's glee said, "Much better than Aunt Floxie's. She uses canned peas and black olives cut too tiny to pick out. Can you imagine?"

MJ loved the way Vonnie's anger flared, then died out quickly.

Vaughn said, "The Batsons treat us like poor relations, but it's Dad and Mom who have the steady jobs." He wore a button depicting Martin Luther King Jr. and Robert and John Kennedy. "You know, this is nothing new. It used to be that African Americans weren't allowed to settle around here."

MJ shoved her fists deep in her pockets, fingering coins, her pocket knife, and keys. She hadn't known. Why did humans make one another suffer? Did her impulse to screen Vonnie from bigoted people do Vonnie any good? No, she admitted, it diminished her. Vonnie didn't need a white person to fight her battles—she had the power to keep herself safe, if safety was attainable for any woman, which she doubted. As much as Vonnie allowed it, she'd stand at her side.

Allison patted the couch. "I want to hear more, Vaughn. I won't claim we've made much progress against racism, because we haven't."

Gran said, "How about if I bring the cornbread to Christmas, Lollie?"

Lollie tied her holiday apron around her waist. They went out to the kitchen comparing recipes.

Jaudon and Cullie carried the kitchen table to the main room and supplemented it with a six-foot collapsible table. Allison and Vaughn covered it with pumpkin-colored vinyl tablecloths while Jimmy Neal, Benedict, and Grady consulted over the best way to carve the turkey.

Jaudon brought the turkey to the table. "Skedaddle, you men," she said as she bumped them aside and carved.

They all watched Jaudon.

"This is the best way to carve a turkey," said Benedict. "Get someone else to do it."

She sat between Lollie and Grady and politely evaded their personal questions. She could see Vonnie at the other end of the table, getting to know Benedict.

Grady pronounced the turkey perfect and lowered his voice to talk about Vonnie. "I don't care for our girl transferring to this local college. Who will hire her? Nobody's heard of the school."

"You'd think," said Lollie, "a girl wants to get out in the world, see new things, meet new people. Are you planning to stay in this area?"

"Try and drag me away," MJ answered, wiping gravy from her mouth. "I never felt at home till chance dropped me here."

"Our Vonnie maintains it was fate, so she could meet you."

She didn't know how to respond. Had Vonnie told them MJ was drawing her back? The day before, she'd told Vonnie the house she was working on wasn't ready for her to move into. True enough, but she knew deep down that was an excuse. The complications were unwieldy. If she ran into trouble with the law, she didn't want to put Vonnie in jeopardy. Now Vonnie's parents wanted her opinion. She was walking on eggs.

As she spooned Gran's crookneck squash and onions onto her plate, she asked herself, *What would Berry say?* Now she spoke what she guessed would be Berry's words. "Vonnie pretty much seems to know what she wants, and I'm not sure any of us can stand in her way. How can I help?"

"There is one thing," said Lollie.

Her body shrank from further entanglement.

"It might be a bitty bit too much to ask of you."

She waited attentively, saying nothing.

"We want her to live at home, but Vonnie won't if she changes schools. She said you bought a bungalow to rehab in Mango, and we haven't talked to her about it, but perhaps we can work something out? We'd pay for her expenses as a matter of course."

Grady said, "We know what you are to each other, and we bless your union if that's what Vonnie wants. Our children don't need to endure the family disapproval we've toughed out. Please don't hesitate to make household arrangements if that's your concern."

The Lowes completely floored her. No wonder Vonnie knew how to love.

She thought it might be about three years before she could support herself and Anika with her real estate investments alone. Breaking and entering held more potential for spectacular failure but would make her self-sufficient faster than any job a woman could find in her field. Finance was a fantasy game, money nothing more than board game pieces.

Kajen jumped into her lap and reached for the turkey on her plate. She captured the cat's paws. How to discourage these nice people from delivering their child into the hands of a woman who committed felonies? She remained silent, unable to find the words she wanted.

"You're not sure about living with Vonnie yet, are you?" said Mr.
Lowe.

Again, she channeled Berry's calm and forthrightness. "I hoped
to get on more solid footing before offering her a home, to tell you
the truth. I admire and respect your daughter beyond words and want
to give her the home and security she deserves. Honestly? My current
rehab is tiny and too close to its neighbors. It's in a bad section for two
women to share a home, or any mixed-race couple. I'll sell this one
when I can live in my next project, build it around me."

"Where will that be?" Mrs. Lowe asked.

"Thonotosassa, out near the Wilderness Park. It's tiny. There's
enough backyard to add a second bedroom and bath, but first, I need to
replace...pretty near everything."

Shy Vaughn's outburst startled them all. "That sounds cool. I
could give you a hand, if you wanted."

With an indulgent smile, his father said, "Don't be sticking your
nose into other people's business. The truth is, MJ, tackling projects
alongside someone like you is right up Vaughn's alley. He can't get
accepted into a carpentry apprenticeship program no matter his high
grades and aptitude. He's doing labor for a builder in my family who's
well past his prime."

Lollie didn't hide her proud smile. "Vaughn has built anything and
everything since he played with blocks. Once he chanced on LEGOs at
a little friend's house, there was no stopping him. You saw that child-
sized wood playhouse in our yard?"

Grady broke in. "He did that at age eleven. The other boys in his
middle school woodworking shop made memo holders. Vaughn made
his mother a cedar hope chest with a self-rising tray and a drawer in
the base."

Vaughn quietly drummed the edge of the table with his fingers,
his eyes averted.

Jimmy Neal came over to talk with the Lowes.

What made them trust her? She'd visited a handful of times, and
they seemed to have formed an undeserved respect for the evil, evil,
twisted child Emma Jean Beaudry. She wasn't exactly marrying into
the family. Or was she? What were the rules for loving someone's
daughter when you didn't have to sneak around? Was she obligated to
accept this ill-advised proposal?

She did need someone with Vaughn's smarts. He seemed to know at least as much as she did, for one thing, and he'd be a boon to tackling the spiral staircases and other tough projects.

It wasn't as if the Lowe twins were going to join her in banditry. She'd do her damnedest to insulate them from her other life, but why not face it? She wrung her hands at yet another reason to start backing off from breaking and entering. Her marathon run of luck could end tomorrow.

CHAPTER FORTY

Twilight stole all luster from the sky. The hush that arrived in the aftermath of holiday guests now filled the house, part wafting sadness, part satisfied fatigue. Everyone except MJ left in a procession of hugs, misplaced belongings, and planning for the December holidays.

Berry was finished but for the pots and pans soaking in the sink. Her hands, greasy and soapy, dipped a pink scrubby into the cooling water, and she smiled to think of moments with their burgeoning family. She heard Jaudon vacuuming the dining and living rooms. Gran had gone to bed in her pink plastic curlers to be all dolled up for work Black Friday.

MJ dried the pots with the flour sack towels Gran favored. More than once, she sensed that MJ was on the verge of asking a question. Under her fuzzy black hairstyle, someone who didn't know her might be confused about her gender. As if MJ wasn't good-looking enough, the haircut revealed strong facial features and, behind those prominent glasses, eyes of acute intensity.

Eventually, the kitchen was squeaky clean and smelled more like dish detergent than pumpkin pie. She invited MJ to sit and have a cup of peppermint tea. Puddin lay stretched upside down under the table. She bent to tickle the dog's belly, but Puddin was worn to a furry frazzle from the commotion. Anika's eyes watched MJ.

"That dog adores you."

"It's mutual," MJ replied.

Kajen stared at the turkey carcass until Berry lowered it into a pot of water for soup. She set a dish of scraps on the raised kitty kitchen.

"Ahh," she said as she sat. "I didn't realize how much my back aches. You'd think I didn't walk five miles a day at work."

MJ studied her steaming tea as if it held her fortune. "Did you ever have trouble figuring out where you belong in the world?"

She thought for a moment and said, "You're twenty-two, aren't you? I'm thirty-one, and yes, I do."

"You? You have it made. You have Jaudon, your grandmother, a home, a good job, you're about to get your master's degree. To top it off, you have a dream, your health center. Unless…you never talk about your parents. Are they still alive?"

"I don't know."

"Shoot, I'm sorry. I didn't mean to make you sad."

The ache spread from her back to her heart, and she fingered her lapis lazuli earrings, which, Rigo had assured her, boosted the intuitive powers she needed to counsel people. "It's okay. It happened ages ago."

"You know, I'm lucky. I left my parents—they didn't leave me. Not physically, anyway."

"Jaudon went through something akin to what you did. Ask her about being raised by Momma."

MJ studied her cup again. "I'm serious about this. Can you be part of somebody else's family? I mean, honestly part of?"

She smiled. "You're talking about the Lowes, right? I saw they were giving you a good grilling. Did you ask for their daughter's hand in marriage?"

"Well, no. I never thought—"

"I'm kidding. What put you off balance?"

"Shoot, I don't know how to act with the Lowes, what to say to them. They're awfully nice to me. Shouldn't they be put off that I'm sleeping with their daughter?" Hands off the cup, MJ pulled at her fingers.

Of necessity, MJ had become too adult, too fast. She went her way purposefully, and uncommonly self-possessed. Berry enjoyed seeing her questioning, youthful side. "Gran loved Jaudon because, young as she was, Jaudon treated me like royalty. The Lowes sense the same goodness about you."

"But you know what? They know nothing about me."

"Is there something they should know?"

MJ drained her tea and put her mug in the sink. "You must be pretty tired after cooking and cleaning, especially with the extra guests. I'd better let you rest, so you can work tomorrow."

Later, preparing for bed, Berry told Jaudon she was trying to guess what was bothering MJ.

"Rigo and Jimmy Neal are worried too. You saw that Larry and Gregory didn't make it today?"

"I wondered what happened to them."

"Gregory is sick."

She drew in a sharp breath. "Dr. Riyanto's lover? He never said a thing."

"Don't ask me to pronounce it, but he has a scary lung infection."

"What can we do to help?"

"The problem is, he's not an isolated case."

"Rigo? Jimmy Neal?"

"Neither. Larry told them it's a weird pneumonia that affects gay men."

"Just gay men? I don't believe it for a second. Did you ask what they need?"

"Hope and prayer is all Rigo told me."

"Larry hasn't come to work at all this week—I assumed they went away for the holiday. Let's make sure we don't bring home any bugs. Gran's age makes her more susceptible."

Jaudon opened a safety pin and started cleaning under her fingernails. "Speaking of bugs, you were saying something is bugging MJ?"

She used to turn away for fear of Jaudon puncturing herself, but Jaudon never did. She said, "MJ's spooked about Vonnie and her family."

"Did they warn her away?"

"Just the opposite, Angel." She fell back onto her cool pillow. "She doesn't know what to do with their acceptance. Not that she'd tell me any details. The girl is full of secrets—have you noticed that?"

"Sometimes it's like working with a young goat. The minute you get near, she scampers away. Or you make an innocent remark, and boom, she butts you with her little horns."

"Can you believe she's about to turn twenty-three? What age did she claim when Cullie dumped her on you?"

"Seventeen."

"And it's taken her all this time to reach age twenty-two?"

Jaudon's kiss was peppermint toothpasty. "Doesn't add up, does it?"

"I believe MJ has a slight problem with the truth."

"I don't know. I never caught her in a fib, but I was mystified that time we ran from the cops, and she happened to have a way to keep us under wraps nearby."

She rummaged through her memory. "Running from cops? When did that happen? Are you the one who's been fibbing?"

Jaudon winced.

"Jaudon? What are you keeping from me?"

"It's over now, and I didn't want to scare you when the changes at your work were heavy on your mind."

"Jaudon Vicker, you're a caution. You protected me again, you ninny. I don't want protection. I told you umpteen times I want to share your troubles."

Jaudon donned her shamed puppy face and worked at her cuticles with the butt end of the pin as she described the raid that came to nothing. "The police must have scratched their heads when they saw the building empty as a rain barrel in a drought."

"Did MJ explain how she knew where to hide?"

"She told me not to ask."

"I don't know whether I'm vexed that you hid this or impressed that MJ saved you both."

"Her smarts are staggering. She's handier than a pocket knife. Who would have thought she'd turn out this well and fit Florida like a native? I don't fault her for her quirks. She'll outgrow them."

"She makes me a smidgen uncomfortable. Be careful around her, okay? She has the best of intentions, but she doesn't understand that what she does impacts others. If nothing more, you're both free of the liquor business."

"Ah, Berry, about that?"

"Don't tell me—"

"Okay, I won't."

"Oh yes, you will."

"It's good, I swear. I sold my part of the operation. And I get a percentage from Shady and Tad until they pay me off in full."

"Oh, honey." She pulled their light sheet over herself and flounced onto her side, back to Jaudon, primed to cry.

She heard Jaudon change into her faded men's pj's, slip under the sheet, and not quite press her body to Berry's. Kajen burrowed between them. On the floor, Puddin scratched energetically at her bed, turned in a circle three times, and, with a doggy sigh, curled into sleep.

"You're not going to change your mind about me, are you, my

Georgia gal? I refused to sell them the family 'shine recipe. No one can connect me to the business anymore."

"Unless those men talk. I'm worn out thinking about it, talking about it, worrying about it. You do what you need to do, but don't tell me more." She moved another half inch away.

Jaudon rolled to the other edge of the bed.

Berry surprised herself by saying, "Your life is now, Angel, not after you fix everything first."

Sometimes, the Great Spirit gave her the words she needed.

CHAPTER FORTY-ONE

January 1983

In the cooler air of winter, MJ worked at the Mango house on her own. Anika watched and insisted periodically that MJ toss her dolly. Mango once was farmland, but this house was near the closed canning plant, where narrow lanes packed together crowded rental houses, too many cars, and a band of squirts who greeted her arrivals with singsong insults.

The downstairs toilet verged on falling through damp, rotted subflooring. She'd pulled the toilet out and now squirmed into the crawl space under the house.

As she put in a new piece of support lumber, she questioned whether she'd genuinely loved anyone. Sure, she'd loved Christina—with the passion of a fourteen-year-old. Real love was what Berry and Jaudon had, what Rigo and Jimmy Neal had. It was Allison and Cullie, Grady and Lollie. If she loved Vonnie, this evil, evil, twisted child should walk away.

The crawl space under the house was home to cobwebs, rodent leavings, fleeing bugs, snakeskins, and a rank, musty odor. She needed to bleach the foundation and seal the cracks. Rent a powerful dehumidifier.

And she needed to talk to somebody. She'd tried with Berry, but a quirk in her nature made her dress in suits of armor. Vonnie definitely sensed that; she boldly melted the layers of MJ's plates and shields. How had Vonnie figured her out when MJ was only now learning about herself? Vonnie's instincts were probably right. She'd be relieved to offload the armor; it weighed her down.

Damn, but it ticked her off, this inability to fathom what to do. The tests measured her as smart; she ought to be able make smart decisions.

Lying on her back, glasses filmed with who knew what, she brushed a spider off her face and sawed through the problem area. Anika peered at her from the hole in the bathroom floor. "Stay," she said, as she pulled a support beam to her and held it steady with her head and one aching arm while hammering nails through indentations she'd prepared. She needed Vonnie's brother, but gay slurs were bad enough—she didn't want Vaughn attacked for his beautiful color.

The Lowes were impressively trusting. They bore Lollie's family for years before losing their tolerance because of Vonnie and herself. Walking out on Thanksgiving—that must be hard. It had made her want to cry, but her armor prevented tears.

She envisioned normal families acting like the Lowes—sticking up for one another, working as a team. Did they generate such love that someone marrying in was loved by extension? Why rebuff such a gift?

Back in the house, she laid plywood, thanking the powers that be for how-to manuals. Now the toilet flange wasn't aligned. She forced the long bolts into their holes in preparation for installing the new wax ring seal.

For Vonnie's sake, that's why she ought to reject the gift of a new family, but she'd committed herself now, and she wasn't backing down. She took deep breaths to cool her hotheaded frustration and suffered a whiff of her now fusty clothing. She stomped around the first floor, Anika following, went back and tried hammering the mounting bolts where they fit. As a last resort, she focused on planning her next break-in while her hurting hands did their work.

She liked to find shortcuts on less-traveled county roads where she admired old bungalows quirkily decorated and their patches of gardens crowded with vegetables and bright flowers. It wasn't uncommon to see them next to bloated estates that flaunted period architecture and immense green lawns greedy for the shrinking water table.

On one of these roads a row of recently built homes lined the edge of an active celery farm. Celery was dying out as a Florida money crop. The farmers probably sold off these roomy plots separately, as there was an assortment of styles from ranch to Dutch Colonial to hacienda.

The plantings in the new communities were saplings. No hedges gave cover, a sure sign the owners were from away. The enchanting thing about Florida was that everything grew here. You stuck a fragment of green, an aloe, a coleus, a cactus, and it grew like Jack's beanstalk.

Everywhere—with the exception of these grassed-over, landscaped plots of land—plantings exploded, sending out huge leaves, air plants, countless weeds, heavyweight succulents. She doubted the sanity of anyone who eliminated the native exotic beauty to plant grass, but plenty of incomers did.

One of the houses had been shut up for some time. She'd have to go in unconcealed, and watching the house was not viable. Where were these owners during Florida's high season? She might skip the celery house.

Except, nothing else worked to chill her out, but this, her thief's joy. Someday she'd uncover what compelled her to steal her joy from others.

She walked the toilet back into place. Finished bolting it and reattached the water supply-line hose to the tank. When she flushed, it surprised her by working, not leaking, and not smelling. A good omen. She'd go into the celery field house the next moonless night.

At the new moon MJ was one day from finished at the Mango place. She'd accepted a cash offer from a local landlord and was painting the exterior to suit him. The neighbors had bored themselves with rude comments and berating her for doing men's work. Their repertoire was down to hard stares.

By the time she tidied and secured the work site and ate a late lunch, which included an entire basket of fresh from the farm stand strawberries, she was antsy—new moon was tonight.

The sun illuminated a cloud from behind, its rays an inverted golden crown spiking into the sky. The cloud moved on; the sun dropped closer to the horizon. A moonless dark approached. She painted faster as she thought of Rigo's father and his thirty-foot boat a hundred miles off Florida, of a grappling hook lowering a ton of marijuana from a mother ship, of lawlessness itself, this and her own.

Had burglary become a habit, as Tad predicted? Her agitation pushed her to tempt fortune, to rashness. She'd go into that celery farm house if it meant slithering in on her belly. She'd developed a cash antenna which sent a tingle through her body at the sight of these lifeless sealed mausoleums called homes, unblemished and professionally maintained.

Vonnie was at school and would never know.

She napped at the Mango house. When the night was pitch black, she left Anika to guard it for the hour she'd be gone. At an ungated development a quarter mile away from her target, she parked in a visitor space and snapped on the waist pack that held her tools, gloves, and nylon backpack. Dressed in running shoes and shorts, long-sleeved T-shirt, and headband, she jogged.

The solitude of her passage and the rhythm of her body soothed her as she slipped through the coolish Florida night past front yards rampant with violas, glowing alyssum, cheery gerbera daisies. Once in a while she caught a delicious flowery scent. Colorful plants, she thought, would be a surefire way to showcase a property, especially in this climate where she could do it year-round. Hadn't Berry once mentioned that certain greenery fed bees and birds? No matter what happened at the celery farm tonight, this jog was sublime.

She ran by to confirm no discernible threats had popped up. The house was the second to last before the road curved almost as sharply as a corner. On her next pass she dove to the ground, hugging the wall. Without delay she wormed her way to the rear porch where she imagined the well-off, absent owners sipping from thin monogrammed glasses and jingling ice cubes as they gazed across the celery field at dark-skinned men with harvest knives bending and straightening, bending and straightening, throughout the hot day. Were they the owners' entertainment?

She searched for tiny alarm lights, but knew, way out here, neighbors watched out for one another. By touch, she opened the lock. Her heart raced from recklessness.

She stayed below window level and switched on her penlight. She heard no sound—no air conditioning, no refrigerator, no ticking clocks, not one vehicle driving by. She sniffed for fresh smells, discerned a hint of insecticide. She visited the usual hiding spots, including the defrosted freezer.

She found audio equipment, multiple televisions, two Apple computers. This kitchen was more tricked-out than Mr. Patate's. A framed picture of Ronald Reagan as president hung in the living room. Did these people stay here at all? She steamed again about the wastefulness and unbelievable disregard for the needy.

The upstairs bathroom sprawled, even with a whirlpool bath built for a giant. She half-heartedly kicked the stupid thing. And jumped back. The surround dropped forward onto her feet. Skimpy materials. Stashed to the right side of the tub were rifles, a slew of them, with boxes and boxes of ammunition. Those would bring a pretty penny, but she'd learned her lesson: no guns.

To the left they'd bolted a safe to the floor. She didn't know how to crack a combination lock.

She used her flash to peer around the safe and came face to face with a wolf spider. She drew back fast. It, too, retreated. She probed with the flash. The light beam caught on an index card adhered to the back of the safe.

Oh, these foolish snowbirds—they'd left the safe's combination, written backward.

She moved the dial until she heard that beautiful click. Okay, but surely the dumbest of the well-off snowbirds weren't dumb enough to leave valuables worth stealing in a house so unlived in the spiders took out a mortgage on it.

Her penlight shone on bundles of bills. She hadn't known safes were made in such mini sizes—they'd compressed the money to within an inch of its life. She joked to herself that she'd better rescue every last bill before they suffocated. The cash, the rifles, the absent residents— all pointed to the house being a bolt-hole. The owners would never report this theft.

She'd almost filled her nylon backpack to the top when the bedroom phone rang. It stopped her, but she went back to work as she listened to the message.

"Sorry to call late, it's Herb from next door. I thought I saw a light in your house. Are you back from Macau?" Herb's manner was joking. "Did you lose your shirt? Okay, you and the little woman aren't answering. I'll call the sheriff in case. Call me back if you're there, okay?"

Mind your business, Herb, she thought. She could grab a rifle to wave around if needed, but she'd take her chances; the thought of violence, the chance of hurting someone, made her sick to her stomach. She pried loose the bills directly into her pack, reattached the index card, closed and locked the safe, shifted the surround into place, and looped the backpack straps over her arms. She took the dark stairs three at a time and locked the back door behind her.

She crouched behind the porch enclosure. The house next door was lit up, but the light didn't reach her. She stooped-ran the other way. Busybody Herb must have called over there too, because halfway across, spotlights came on at the front and back doors.

As if those lights could keep her from their damned stashes. Mr.

Gambler must consider the sticks of Florida safer than other options. Were the bills marked? Counterfeit? Shady taught her how to handle them.

Herb the busybody's backdoor floodlights aimed wide of his house. She made for the dense shrubbery in front. She crouched at the bush that smelled of peaches, of apricots, of the peace of never stealing again.

As she waited for her moment, she thought, where was the thrill in all this? Shocked at herself, she acknowledged an intoxication that usually came with the ritual of hunting, planning, executing each caper—until tonight.

One patrol car swerved into the driveway to Herb's house. She decided to move now, while the officer and Herb weren't looking. But at the road was a second cop, at his vehicle and watching. Oh, well, she who hesitated was lost.

I am MJ Beaudry, faster than a speeding bullet. I leap tall bushes in a single bound.

She heard the cop car door slam and a shout. She was a rocket at Canaveral as she launched across the road, entered the pitch-dark sandy woods, and headed north, away from vehicle access, far from the path she'd followed earlier. Flashlight off, she slid on soggy patches of soft dark mulch, expecting snakes, a black panther on a mission, a wild-bearded swamp dweller. Smothering elephant ear leaves flapped against her face, Spanish moss swept her neck, and philodendrons with split leaves as large as small humans tried to trap her as, once again, she tore through the magnificently tangled obstacle course of Florida woods.

The glow of streetlights far ahead distracted her. She tripped on one of the ropelike vines that stretched along the ground and pitched forward onto a fallen tree truck, nose first. Shoot, that hurt, she thought as she fought the shock and pain to stand upright. Pricks of light like distant stars swirled behind her tightly closed eyes. She willed them to squint open and saw the real lights of a police car prowl along the street. Coincidence? Had she left something behind? They couldn't know the cash was gone or that there was a safe.

She collapsed into the wet muck behind the tree trunk, waiting for the sound of the motor to fade, not sure she'd hear it over the roar of her hurt face. She saw the lights return, just enough to orient her.

When she reached her car and went to wipe the sand and mud

from herself, she discovered it was mixed with blood. That's when she touched her nose and smothered a shriek. Inside the car, she couldn't stanch the bleeding with tissues—the attempt hurt too much. Tears of anguish further clouded her vision as she drove, slowly, to Berry and Jaudon's house.

CHAPTER FORTY-TWO

February 1983

"Your life is now, not after you fix everything first."

Jaudon had chewed over Berry's words for a while and now agreed that saving the stores had become an obsession. She'd become just like Momma used to be, putting the stores first and everything and everyone else at fourth or fifth place. She'd assumed Berry was equally consumed by her nursing career, but no. It was people first with Berry.

The night MJ woke them, pounding the front door, Berry insisted on taking the kid to the emergency room. MJ refused, and Jaudon caught her when the kid tried to leave. Gran settled things with ice packs and a couple of Flexerils she'd been given for knee pain. The next morning, before hours, Dr. Garza realigned and taped MJ's nose and gave her a referral to a specialist. MJ's face was still bruised and swollen, but she claimed she was getting better on her own, though her nose would never be exactly the same.

Some of their time together she and Berry devoted to Gregory, spelling Larry, who was on a leave of absence, to give him time to decompress. Gregory used a nebulizer and had little energy. His doctors confirmed he was HIV-positive but said he didn't have full blown AIDS. Yet.

This wasn't a Gregory day. Jaudon drove to the attorney's office again, determined to settle both Momma's debts and her hearing loss suit against the county. She zipped over to Laughney Road and, like always, ran into a jam at the multiway traffic lights crossing Laudre Flats Boulevard.

She nodded in time to Annie Lennox singing "Sweet Dreams," the radio volume high. She closed the windows and ran the air-conditioner to block the street noise of buses, trucks, revving motorcycles, an occasional horn or siren. As she watched each lane proceed except hers, she regretted the years it took her to swallow her pride and bring suit. It had taken her more time to get it through her head that the suit might cancel out the business failure. Once she got the picture, she called the attorney's office weekly, then daily, for progress reports. The county kept offering less than she needed to cover her debts and rebuild the business, but Berry's happiness counted more. She'd decided to end the dithering and accept an amount that would enable her to pay off her debts and improve the stores she had left slowly, from store profits.

The lawyer had an office across from the small Beverage Bay on Margaret Street. She parked at her store and waved at a clerk as she walked through.

Rouie Waver was in Attorney Brass's hushed waiting room. A vase of spicy-smelling carnations sat on the secretary's desk. Rouie patted her on the back.

"I'm plain over the moon you're willing to hammer out a deal," he said. "This has been hanging over your head beyond a month of Sundays. Worry and overwork like yours shorten a person's life."

"I thought I bore the entire burden, but I made Berry and Gran suffer alongside me."

Through the window she watched Pops park the Caddy Momma bought when times were good. He'd grown heavier since Christmas and walked with a worrisome shuffle. She'd carefully shepherded the income her parents earned from the stores and made sure they didn't skimp on medical needs.

The receptionist showed them into a conference room. Pops shook Rouie's hand and squashed Jaudon to him. "We haven't seen you since Christmastime, Daughter. I miss you."

"Same here, Pops. Let's sit and jaw before the lawyer comes in."

"I'm pleased to sit. I dropped Momma's power recliner on my foot, trying to move the dang thing."

"It hurts bad?"

"Like a son of a gun."

"Have you seen the doctor?" asked Rouie.

"Life is too busy. Momma and me are moving."

"What? Don't joke with me, Pops." She was thrown for a loop. Was Momma behind the move, and how many scarce dollars was she throwing away this time?

"It's a good thing. One of your mother's chamber of commerce buddies came visiting. He's buying properties on our street to put in a strip mall. I tell you, I can't handle the amount of work Momma's fancy house takes anymore, but I held out until he offered enough that interest from the sale will keep us comfortable. You can put what you pay us back into the stores."

She didn't hide her relief and didn't mind Pops noticing it on her face.

He nodded and smiled. "Your Pops may not be the smartest nickel in the roll, but even a busted clock is right twice a day. I hope to take some of the burden off you. We're fixing to downsize over to Sun City."

"Sun City? You?"

"Yep. We visit there with people I met in that group the doc has me going to, so I don't go crazy taking care of Momma day in and day out. Momma's docs are in Sun City. She enjoys when we stop by to see our friends and ventures a word or two. Though"—he scratched his head as a hangdog grin took over his face—"it might not exactly fit into the conversation."

"And Momma's okay with this?"

"Your momma is the happiest I've seen her since we courted. Yes, there's bad days, real bad. Even so, I swear, a whole mind was a hindrance to her. She giggles like a three-year-old and takes life easy where before, she'd be determined to squeeze a hundred and one pennies from every dollar. She's forgot about her rough childhood. The doc says she's living in the moment now."

"But it's killing her, Pops."

"So far she's somewhere between stage four and stage five. That's moderate to moderate severe. She might stay there for a few years. Or not. I want her to have a good time while she can."

"Sun City will make you a damn Yankee," said Rouie.

Pops looked to split his sides laughing, which delighted her no end.

"Not much chance of that, Rouie. You come over and you'll see other locals who—"

The conference room door opened and a slight, short-haired man in his late thirties strode in, a legal-sized folder under his arm.

"Rich Slumkey here," he said, leading them to his office and giving each a brisk handshake, asking their names. "Mr. Brass said you want to arrange a settlement with the county. I don't blame you. They tend to postpone and postpone in hopes that people in your shoes, Ms. Vicker, will fold and take a pittance. I admire your persistence."

"I'm going to need hearing equipment and specialist appointments the rest of my life, Mr. Slumkey."

"We'll get you everything you need. Are you willing to settle for less cash to sew this up?"

"I'm listening," she said.

Slumkey flipped through her file, a large one from the years of fighting the county. "There are actuarial charts that put values on body parts, whether a lost arm or brain damage. Hearing loss in one ear is, quite reasonably, rated lower than total deafness, and your latest medical report reads…" He wet his fingertips and rifled through several sheets of paper. "Here. Recent advances in electro-acoustic amplifying devices for both ears are appropriate for you. I have Mr. Waver's report on lost income. There are other factors to bear in mind, such as false arrest and lifelong pain and suffering. Those deputies, by the way, were let go by the county and both got jobs out of state."

"Your momma made sure of that," said Pops.

"You never told me. I've been looking over my shoulder all these years." For a moment, she thought her mother had taken that step to benefit her. Reality kicked in. Momma's steps were for the business. She bit her lip. Like mother like daughter—lately she hadn't bestowed much in the way of benefits on Berry and Gran.

The attorney jotted figures with a stick pen as they spoke. He closed the file and slid the paper of calculations over to Jaudon. A figure was circled. "I can go to the county right now and get them to agree to this."

Pops and Rouie leaned in to look.

Rouie said, "They'll come back with a lower figure, won't they?"

He knew, thought Jaudon, this would just about pay off everything and take care of her hearing, with nothing to spare for replacing the lost stores.

Pops said, "We need a few minutes now, son."

Once the three of them were alone, Jaudon said, "I'll take it if the figure is firm."

"This fella is either sharper or hungrier than Mr. Brass."

"A no-nonsense guy," Rouie said, "from what I hear." He regarded Jaudon. "You wanted enough to expand, though."

"Jiminy, maybe I don't need an empire. Five stores are enough now that Pops doesn't need his portion anymore. I never wanted to be made of money like Momma did." And, she thought, there's the payments coming in from Tad and Shady.

Rouie said, "You have nice safe investments too, both of you."

"You've made us good money, Rouie, with the mutual funds. Daughter, if you're not expanding, talk to Rouie about putting more by for your later years."

"Rich is giving us the quick and dirty amount," said Rouie. "I'd recommend asking a third more. He'll bring in the difference."

Slumkey agreed to push the county lawyers hard. Laws dictated their deadlines too. If they tried putting her off again, he'd demand more money plus interest.

The relief of finishing off Momma's debt was a sight closer. Jaudon wanted to dance. The five remaining Beverage Bays were good earners. She'd eventually update them to compete better with the mushrooming convenience franchises and gas station minishops. She'd go slowly and ask MJ and Vaughn if they wanted to get experience doing commercial construction. Spending time with Berry was more important than rolling in clover.

CHAPTER FORTY-THREE

June 1983

MJ's recovery had been long after doing that runner from the celery farm house back in January. In addition to the broken nose, she'd been peppered with bug bites, scratched by branches, torn by thorns, warned away by a grunting wild hog, and speared by stinging nettles. Despite the tens of thousands of compressed dollars, she'd lost interest in stealing. She poured her spates of anger into renovations with wrenches, pipe shears, and the claw ends of hammers.

She had healed, or she wouldn't be driving north to bring Vonnie home for the summer after her sophomore year without serious explaining to do. They'd compromised: Vonnie would earn her degree from the more prestigious university and attend transferable classes at the local college during the summers. She'd live with MJ during those months and school breaks.

Vonnie's college pals, a mix of foreign students and Americans white and Black, poked fun at her the previous summer. Someone's boyfriend called MJ's station wagon the yellow bomber, but they teased no more when she effortlessly piled Vonnie's belongings in the rear and on the back seat with room left over, while the dormmates were overstuffing Bugs, Colts, and Gremlins. She and Vonnie went from car to car, offering to push and squeeze pillows and suitcases in with compact refrigerators and bicycles.

MJ relaxed on a shaded bench, basking in the lusty smell of native azaleas, stealthily fingering her nose, hoping Vonnie wouldn't notice it was slightly bent, hoping that getting physical together wouldn't hurt it much. Behind her, Vonnie shared farewell hugs complete with yelps and squeals. She smiled at the happy sadness of parting for a couple of months. Sprinklers soaked keenly green, uniformly cropped lawns. An ancient southern live oak spread regally in the distance. Magnolias dotted the campus.

Someday she'd buy a car with adequate air-conditioning—the black denim shorts and polo shirt she'd bought new for this trip were damp from her sweat. Her style hadn't changed, but Vonnie's had—she wore straight-leg black slacks and a silky indigo T-shirt under a wheat-colored cotton blazer, sleeves rolled back from her slender wrists. It was plain the woman was beginning to have some inkling of her personal power and potential. Damn, she looked terrific.

After a surprise stop, she and Vonnie would drive home to a cottage on Treasure Island, part of a small, defunct resort along motel row. Vaughn worked with her full-time now and was staying there with Anika until they returned.

Without Anika, the car was lifeless. The traces of marks she left from leaning on the passenger door made MJ smile. Poor Anika might fear she'd been abandoned again.

She and Vaughn had recently finished a cinder block house in Thonotosassa backed by a small wooded area on a small loop of a road, but quiet, convenient, and astoundingly cheap. Like the Mango house, this property held no appeal as a vacation rental. She sold it at three times what she paid, which covered the work they put into it with a gratifying profit for them both. She had learned more skills from Vaughn, from DIY library books, from Marge the hardware store clerk, and on her own by trial and error.

Her repeat tenant at Rooster Lake accepted a teaching job in Idaho, reducing that rental to a capricious and seasonal income. She learned what a hassle cleanup could be after short-term guests. Nevertheless, when another cottage at Rooster Lake verged on foreclosure, she jumped and turned it around with light work.

Shady thought the bills from the bathtub safe were clean, but she took her time, and when no red flags appeared as she used them, she bought two economy condos in move-in condition. Their rental income gave her enough to make the Treasure Island beach cottage larger, sturdier, and classier. She and Vaughn had finished glassing in the front porch and adding hurricane shutters to the windows.

Vaughn—someone ought to canonize that man—took on more of the remodeling work while she handled the business end of buying, selling, and renting. A natural designer, he painted Treasure Island's exterior pink and light blue with a golden yellow trim, which fit right into the strip. Very South Beach, and she expected it to rent well year-round because the beach, and lower lodging rates, never stopped beckoning.

She left her bench and got behind the wheel.

"I'm home with you for the summer at last," Vonnie said as she climbed into the wagon, smelling like another tantalizing flower.

She gestured with her glasses. "Put your seat belt on, lady."

"Say what? You installed seat belts in this primordial bucket?"

"That or listen to you beg for them forever."

Vonnie slid across the bench seat to MJ and tongued her ear. "That's not all I'll be begging for—I'll tell you that right now."

She concentrated on the sluggish traffic as they left town, attuned to the pleasant inside quaver Vonnie's moves evoked.

"I know you're smiling behind those aviator sunglasses. Where's Anika?"

"With Vaughn. It's you and me today."

"Is everything okay? You're not running from the law, are you? Because if you are, you can let me off right here. Vaughn told me about the broken nose. I am not even going to ask."

No wonder Vonnie sounded increasingly worried when they spoke by phone—Vaughn tattled on her, probably concerned too. Frankly, after the last harebrained risk she took, she worried about herself. Her luck held, but when she didn't steal, her anger seeped out at the wrong times at the wrong people.

She fumed. "Didn't I promise to shield you if I ran into trouble?"

Vonnie visibly started at her tone.

"I'd never go anywhere near you if I was on the run."

"You don't need to bite my head off for asking."

"I apologize. I'm edgy. Seeing you is the cure."

Vonnie stayed where she was, and MJ realized she was failing at warm and convincing mode. She was working her way to asking Berry Garland why she blew her top so easily. Berry might not be a licensed counselor yet, but if she needed a guinea pig, MJ would volunteer.

She reached for Vonnie's hand.

Vonnie squeezed her hand back, loosened her seat belt, and moved closer. "That's a relief, because I'm on top of the world."

MJ's half smile broke out as she drove. Vonnie fidgeted in her eagerness.

"Oh, honey squirrel, I never thought I'd see the day," Vonnie said. "The university added two Black history courses for fall semester and approved them as electives for me."

"I'm walking on air, Von. I know you were pushing for this."

Vonnie bit her lower lip. "We're forced to push for scraps."

"Isn't Black history taught as part of history?"

"What did you learn about us? That Abe Lincoln freed the slaves?"

She nodded. "You're right, that's about all. What a ridiculous omission."

"That's what bigotry and oppression do—deliberate erasure."

Vonnie had taken a while to find a major that suited her. She told MJ she cared about people, but social work wasn't her thing. Writing came easily for her, and she was attracted to researching injustice, but she didn't see herself as a journalist; she wasn't interested in promoting businesses or politicians. She wanted to work for a worthy nonprofit, writing grants and raising funds. She chose Nonprofit Management with a focus on fundraising and a minor in public relations.

"Because that's the key. Funding is what makes those programs work. My friends at school are going into direct services. I'm going to make sure there are services."

"You're starry-eyed, Vonnie, and I love you for it."

One-handed, elbow out the window, MJ steered west instead of taking their usual route south on 75.

"Where are you heading?"

"To your congratulations-on-Black-history-courses gift."

Vonnie squealed—she was such a girl child at times.

"Where? What? Give me a hint." Vonnie covered her mouth. "Sorry, I know I'm not a ten-year-old."

She glanced at Vonnie, speculating. Sometimes Vonnie did act like a ten-year-old. Should she have more experience with love before settling down? They were mostly good together. Neither strayed. She thought of one of Cullie Culpepper's favorite phrases: *If it ain't broke, amigo, leave it be.*

She let go of Vonnie's hand to slow for a large farm tractor trundling along in front of them. They passed fields and fields of forage land, pecan orchards, and grazing cattle. A sign announced one small town as the watermelon capitol of the world.

Once MJ overtook the tractor, Vonnie asked, "How's Gregory?"

"They've traced his HIV. A needle stick got him. The patient came in, and both she and her husband are positive."

"How about Larry?"

"No symptoms."

"I don't believe prayer works, but it won't hurt to send good thoughts their way." Vonnie went on to talk about school and the dangers of the health professions, and described in detail her roommates' plans. She listened to the outpouring of Vonnie's words. She didn't have a whole lot of conversation herself, though she duly reported the latest on Anika's newest cute behavior, her work, and their friends. She ran into few cars on the road over to Cedar Key, so, content, she took her time as Vonnie pointed out long-legged stilts, heads bent to the shallow waters. She shouted when she saw a little green heron with a frog in its beak.

Vonnie wiggled around to lean her back on the passenger door and rested the soles of her now bare feet against MJ's thigh. MJ caressed her ankles and calves with one hand.

"Don't you go any higher, or you'll have to find a secluded pull-out along the way to wherever you're taking me."

She hadn't seen a car or a structure in several minutes of driving. "Miss Queer Sunshine. You know that's what they call you, right?"

"Who?"

"Rigo heard it at New York Pizza."

"I'm not sure I deserve the title, but I'm glad they see me that way."

"Come on over here."

Vonnie didn't hesitate to unbuckle her seat belt entirely and crawl across the bench seat. When their legs touched, MJ kept her left hand on the steering wheel and nimbly undid Vonnie's tie-waist pants with her right.

"Is this my present?" asked Vonnie, opening her legs to allow MJ access.

"One of them," she said. Her hand moved under the loose fabric and shifted Vonnie's panties aside. Her thumb circled.

"You are one crazy"—Vonnie leaned her head back and orgasmed, just like that. After a deep breath, she finished her sentence—"lover. It's been a while."

"I missed you, Miss Sunshine."

"I missed that hand and the rest of you, my honey squirrel." Vonnie pressed MJ's hand to herself and wriggled. "That was sensational. You're going to have to do it again."

"Okay…if we have to."

Vonnie gave her a good smack. "A whole summer with you."

The rest of the drive seemed to rush by, and they were over the bridge. Pelicans perched on wooden pilings. Fishing boats motored inland.

"Cedar Key?" Vonnie asked. "I know it's not on your way, and you have to get home to work, but can we stop and poke around for a few minutes? I've never been, and I want to sample real Cedar Key clams."

"Sounds appetizing to me. Why not stay a few days?"

She watched as Vonnie's face went from incredulity to the extraordinary luminescence that rose from her like a sunrise. MJ had put aside a little money from each house sale in order to give them this time together.

"Oh my God, MJ. You're too good to be true."

She saw teardrops on Vonnie's eyelashes. "You're sunshine, Vonnie. I mean, in my life. I mean, you perk me up like sunshine. You're the best thing about Florida, and that's saying something."

"Better than strawberry shortcake? Than your addiction to Cuban sandwiches?" Vonnie knitted her brow. "You aren't paying for it with ill-gotten gains, are you?"

"I'm sorry you have to worry about that. No, Von, it's legit. Part of the sale of that cinder block cottage in Mulberry is paying for the room."

Vonnie sounded pouty. "You never showed me the Mulberry house."

She teased Vonnie. "We can skip the vacation and go to Mulberry right now if that's your preference."

"Watch yourself or I'll tweak that cute new kink in your nose."

❖

MJ drew in front of the Island Hotel, a modest square block of white constructed over a hundred years ago. Plastered with french doors and windows, aged cedar dominated the restaurant and bar. The parlor near the registration desk was furnished with dark antique pieces like Shady sold—perhaps had sold them. Ceiling fans spun at low speed, stirring the ocean air and the flourishing flowers in half-barrel planters. A second-floor balcony with white rocking chairs overlooked the street.

The hotel proprietor followed them to get their license plate number. "I wanted to see this beaut closer," he said.

She was used to men reliving their youths at the sight of the Ranch Wagon and lounged against it, arms folded, knowing what came next.

"Want to sell it?"

"Not on your life."

"Must be expensive, finding parts for this classic."

"I have a good mechanic. He machines what he can't source." Tad's mechanic friend had recently established himself in the derelict garage at the back of the car wash lot in exchange for loaning Tad his tools and equipment to keep the Lanamore vehicles—and Shady's—in good shape.

"I'd give you five thousand."

She smirked.

Vonnie watched this with her mouth slightly open, nodding yes to the offer.

"Ten? No? Twelve thousand and a free room? That's as high as I can go."

Vonnie's eyes went wide.

She smiled and slowly shook her head in refusal. "I'm glad to find a fellow admirer, but honestly? I'll be riding this jalopy into the sunset."

"If that Sally Ride gal can put a satellite into orbit, a woman can come to grips with this primo baby. You know where to find me if you change your mind."

Upstairs, their room featured a four-poster bed with a large ceiling fan right over it.

She took Vonnie's hand and led her to the bed. "Let's try it out," she said and took off her glasses.

"I wish you wore contacts," Vonnie said. "You have the warmest eyes, milk chocolate pudding eyes. Except when you're up to no good. Then you look like a little kid about to get herself in trouble."

Lying naked together later, Vonnie said, "Thank you for indulging me in this outrageous luxury."

She had never stayed in a hotel before, nor slept in a luxurious bed. They were lodging in an antique, the manager explained, and this room could not be plumbed for sink and toilet. They marveled at their quirky private bathroom across the hall with its curtained, freestanding tub and shower, claw-footed of course. Vonnie swore she'd name her first cat Clawfoot. From their window they saw shops and relished a breeze off the Gulf of Mexico. Other than one stippling of tiny clouds all in a line, the sky was solid blue.

She squired Vonnie along the narrow streets of the sun- and wind-worn fishing village that afternoon. Pleasure boats were scattered, moored in the downtown channel; dinghies were pulled onto sandy spots and upended against the daily afternoon deluges. They explored the docks and Gulf birds with a pair of binoculars and a Leica camera she'd lifted from a disgustingly oversized, overdecorated, overstuffed house near Limona Park, an affluent area west of Rainbow Gap.

Appalled to find herself measuring her life by thefts, she shrank away from that memory.

They browsed the Cedar Key Historical Society Museum, reading about the abundance of red cedar that once covered the island and the decline of wildlife since the trees were used up for lumber. The land was originally opened to white settlers in order to drive the Seminoles away. Whites looted the oyster beds to extinction.

"I have a low opinion of most white people."

"I see why. We are greedy racist vermin and thieves. We converted nature into the cash used to buy the high-roller yachts moored out there."

"Look around this museum. How many images of Black people do you see? How many tourists?"

She was thrown to admit she hadn't noticed. "It's not tourist season."

"You don't understand. We are not represented. Oh, a few pictures of slaves at work. Maybe a handful of us come here for winter vacations. If that. If we're welcome. You don't see them advertising in Black publications. It's only my skin, people, not my brains."

That night she spent thinking about the indisputable truth of what Vonnie said. How inconceivable and unconscionable it was for white people—any people—to think buying and selling other human beings was by any measure acceptable. How whites continued to strip Blacks of their dignity and safety, all the while stripping the planet itself for profit. How unequipped she was to change any of it.

Sleep wouldn't come, only inadequacy and anger. She dared chance Vonnie's ire, dressed in the separate bathroom, and made her way along the silent streets to a house they'd passed twice while walking, an architectural eyesore that clashed with its established neighbors. Large angled windows sprawled three stories up, blocking the views of surrounding homes. MJ Beaudry, she told herself, was not one to bypass the opportunity to strike a blow at such a fortress of arrogance.

Though the house was of recent vintage, it was no stronghold. She entered seconds after she reached the steel front door. A roaring came into her ears, the sound of blood pulsing through her body. She stood in one spot, breathing and listening, breathing and listening, until she detected no sign of life. A part of her loved walking around the homes she targeted, made her want to rebuild, renovate, build a thousand houses for a thousand families.

The ground floor, entirely open, held but a few sticks of metal industrial chic furniture. The owner had painted the exposed ducting bright yellow; electrical raceways were black. The kitchen area featured a scaled-down multiuser wash fountain like the one at the quarry where she'd worked. Two sets of red metal steps spiraled to the second level at either end of a narrow, thin-railed balcony that ran from the south wall of the house to the north.

She quick-stepped to the usual stash sites.

Two master bedrooms opened off the balcony, and a short hallway between them led to a bathroom. Revamped lockers served as closets, shelving, and dressers. A stark white ladder accessed the third-floor loft.

She'd left her break-in tools in the trunk of her car. The black bandanna from her back pocket served as a glove as she scouted for cash. Opening and closing the innovative crannies and cubbies became noisy, slow work, and she soon gave up. This breach was more about protest than theft. Aside from the Bang & Olufsen sound system, the owner's flamboyance seemed to end with the home itself.

She let herself out, empty-handed, into a concrete slabbed backyard. It faced a commercial fisherman's dwelling, nets drying on a fence, a peeling white dory upside down on sawhorses, crab pots lining the covered back porch. At almost four a.m., a light went on in the cottage—fisherman's hours. She didn't move, didn't breathe, half obscured by thorny bougainvillea and oleander shrubs with their faint apricot scent. The door opened. From it spilled light and a large dog. Would it smell her fear over the fishiness of its yard?

The door opened again and a thin, white-haired wrist and hand set a bowl on the top step, drawing the dog. She made it to the sandy street and strolled to the hotel, satisfied with her outing.

Anger doused, she twisted the handle on the hotel room door with infinitesimal slowness.

She stopped short in the doorway when she saw Vonnie sitting up in bed with her arms folded.

MJ cowered inside when Vonnie said, "You bonehead. You're going to get arrested one of these days, and they'll take you away from me."

"How long have you been awake?"

"I heard you leave." The aggrieved steeliness in Vonnie's voice frightened her more than the closest of close calls.

"Busted," she said, holding open her empty hands, trying to hide her contentedness. "I toured the house and didn't take a thing."

"Damn it, you assume you're not a criminal unless they catch you. You know what you'll be when they do? You'll be powerless. Believe me, I watched my cousin go through it."

"Jaudon?"

"No way. Jaudon's so upright you could climb her, not to mention she's white as white can be. I know she was up against the wall to let herself be drawn into bootlegging. No, he's a cousin on my dad's side. One day he was an eighth-grade honor student, the next day he was in jail for talking to a friend who was a watcher for drug dealers. Age thirteen. You do not want to go through that."

She sat on the bed and took Vonnie's hand. "I mean, honest to goodness, I didn't know you were awake, worrying."

Vonnie withdrew her hand. MJ apologized, wringing her own hands as if they were dirty wet rags.

"You drive me mad. You don't give a hoot about how what you do affects others."

"Yes, I do, Vonnie—down the line I want to have money to donate where it's needed."

"Oh, hail the conquering hero. Don't you see how selfish you are?"

"Selfish? What the hell? How?"

Vonnie sat up, holding the sheet against her shoulders, voice grown croaky. "It's only about you, you, you. What you want to do. How you'll be the glorified savior with your money. We're separate enough with me in college. I don't want you locked away for ten years."

"But I—"

"But you, but you." Vonnie cried. "What about *but Vonnie*? Vonnie who's lying in bed waiting for the sirens, waiting for the phone call, waiting for the shots. What if you were killed?"

"I never thought—"

"That's exactly right. You never thought. Honey, I know your folks didn't treat you right. I know you were expected to handle whatever came your way before you had the means and lived in a loveless home.

But I do love you, and you don't trust me any more than you did your parents."

"Yes, I do. I never shared this with anyone."

"Which I understand and appreciate greatly. It's day to day that you're not up-front with me, your lover. You don't get how love and trust go hand in hand."

She stared at the floor between her feet, hands gripping her thighs. Vonnie spoke an alarming truth: falling in love was a breeze, but it was a whole other deal to trust someone. She tried to imagine herself standing at an altar making vows. She wasn't right in the heart. It must be the evil child in her.

She ached to cry with Vonnie; after holding back tears for years, they were not a reflex action. When she fell or skinned her knee as a child, she'd taken care of it herself to avoid an outsized scolding. She stood and said, "I'll take you home."

Vonnie moved to her and kissed her face with quick, moist kisses like a kitten's nose tapping on her cheek. "No. No. No. You are my home, MJ—that's what I'm trying to say."

"How can you care for someone as horrible as me?"

"You're not horrible. I'm telling you this because you're exactly who I want. You're as exciting as you are worrisome."

"I warned you I'm not good for you, Vonnie. You deserve more than I can give you."

"Not so fast. Do you want to live your life alone? Because if you don't, you're going to have to deal with this eventually. I'm not above begging you to do it now."

"Do what? And how?" she asked, pointing her finger at Vonnie. "You're telling me what's wrong—tell me how I can fix me."

She'd put off talking to Berry because she knew her own resistance to change, but she needed help—these last months she was at the mercy of unpredictable rages that were as dangerous as getting caught with her hands in a stranger's safe. She must, must, must, make an appointment with Berry and promised herself to call when they got home.

The next day they were less spirited, not touching as they dawdled through Cedar Key and the Lower Suwannee Wildlife Refuges. A hiker they met on a boardwalk trail through the marsh pointed out nesting colonies of brown pelican, heron, ibis, and egrets. Sharp-edged saw grass and cruel sandspur grew everywhere. Low tide bared tiny islands with darting necklaces of foraging seabirds. Near slick mud flats, dingy water lay stagnant and foul smelling.

She walked tall, but she was scared silly about trying to change. What if she never put out what raged in her? Could she handle prison? What if Berry didn't want to help a thief?

They made their way by car and foot to the Shell Mound, five acres that lay twenty-eight feet above sea level, now overrun with trees and brush. Until about AD 650, local Native Americans discarded their clam and oyster shells on this site.

History this close reminded her how miniscule she was in the immense design of the universe. Her troubles, like her, were insignificant.

"Up there. A great horned owl." Vonnie pointed to a high branch in a lordly oak. It appeared to be sleeping, striped brown feathers lifting with the breezes.

Around a bend, they followed the progress of a small dark-colored crab scuttling over the heap of broken shells. She wanted always to be the owl, not the crab.

Watching the Suwanee River churn under the late afternoon wind, bringing with it the tonic of salty air, they concocted a story about meeting on a steamboat they'd seen in a photograph at the museum.

"You were MJ Beaudry, a gambler, in your dove-colored gambler hat, with your fancy derringer."

"And I rescued you from rough laborers on their way to raid the Shell Mound for roadway materials. You wore a shimmery ankle-length dress."

"My last living relative, Lord Viscount of Shellmund, known for his indeterminate shooting, perished in a duel and left me his hotel on Cedar Key."

"The very hotel we're staying at. Hey, how come I'm paying for our room if it's your hotel?"

Several warning drops of chilly rain splattered on their bare arms.

Playful Vonnie leaped away, running back along the path. "I'm a secret heiress. Try and catch me, gambler."

Her Queer Sunshine was back. She set off with a burst of get-up-and-go toward a cut across the midden and raced along it, springing onto the trail as Vonnie rounded a bend. This place, this place, it reminded her of the meadow high above Depot Landing, so open about its deep life force. Vonnie was radiant with it.

The afternoon deluge arrived. Rain splashed into puddles of itself like a tot in yellow rubber boots.

Slippery wet, in high spirits, they collided into each other's arms, and she understood at that moment how she was simply happy and pledged again to protect, from herself, this nearly corporeal force that they gave rise to together.

An extended loud burp of thunder sounded. Didn't love overcome all obstacles?

Chapter Forty-four

Early December 1983

"Berry. Berry, you out here?"

Berry left her built-in desk and went to the door of Gran's repurposed travel trailer to call back through the twilight. She couldn't tell if Jaudon heard her.

Jaudon crested the hammock that sloped toward the back of the Vicker property. Puddin ran behind her, tail wagging, stopping to study strange doggy scents.

"Yow."

Berry winced. Jaudon must have run into that pesky saw palmetto yet again and ripped her shorts. She saw Jaudon press her hand on the damage as she jackknifed through the stand of slash pine that screened the camper.

The first thing Jaudon said was, "I'm not sure I can handle this much good news in one day."

Berry opened her arms at the sight of Jaudon's ebullience. "What's happened? Did the county give in and settle?"

"Not yet, but I bet that's next." Jaudon hugged Berry to her. "The store has a buyer."

"Church Pond Road? That's sensational." She clamped herself to Jaudon and rocked her with happiness.

"So many new homes are going up, the postal service plans to expand its inadequate office next door, and they want to do it on our site."

"But the poor peahens." With a lighthearted laugh, Berry put her arms around Jaudon. "They won't dare pester the customers anymore."

Jaudon lifted her clear off the floor in her excitement.

"And, Georgia gal, remember me telling you about the orange grower who sold Momma that plot of land and his corrugated metal shed for the original store on Mobley Road?"

"Natch. That's the man who refused her offer to buy more land to expand."

"We still own the plot. MJ spotted in the obituaries that Mr. Mobley died."

"What's MJ doing reading obituaries?"

"She watches for properties that might come on the market, Berry. No matter, she came right over to Buffalo Street and covered the store while I went to find the son and heir. He's clearing the land for a thumping mammoth subdivision, naming it like the rest of them for what they took away. This one's Grove Trails."

"Oh," she said, her abdomen clenching at the loss of yet another piece of nature.

"I know, I know. That's the sad news." She held Berry, patting her on the back now.

"I'm sorry. I don't intend to ruin your glad tidings."

"You didn't. You can't. The patch, as it happens, is exactly where the county's requiring Mobley Jr. to build the gated entryway."

Jaudon spoke quickly, clearly invigorated by her tidings. Berry pulled her into Gran's revamped trailer to get away from the bugs.

"Jiminy, it's comfortable with the window air-conditioner running. Another of Vaughn's good ideas."

"My clients claim it's why they keep their appointments faithfully."

They sat thigh to thigh, arm to arm on the textured double sofa. Her radio softly played "Every Breath You Take." A few weekends in a row, MJ, Vaughn Lowe, and Benedict Lam had come over to make a comely office of the trailer for Berry to meet with clients. Benedict brought a retired electrician friend who rewired the whole trailer, connected it to the house power, and installed the AC.

Next weekend she and Jaudon, MJ, Cullie, and the guys would add a covered deck. Back when Gran lived in the trailer, Jaudon's brother Bat and his friend John, both on leave from the army, hacked out a driveway. Berry's clients drove right to the door.

Berry's work friend Laura Bathgate wood-burned a sign Jaudon read aloud each time she saw it: "Garland Counseling, LMHC, ARNP."

"There's more. MJ said to take advantage of the son's haste and be stubborn. Beats me why he doesn't know the zoning laws changed.

We were grandfathered in. Once we shut the store, the property was no longer zoned commercial—I have no use for it."

"You held out."

"He's desperate to clear this snag. You know I despise those developments as much as you do. I said no to his offers. It's clear as day his father never told Junior Mobley that Momma paid two hundred dollars for it at the time. In those days someone like Mr. Mobley didn't want to bother going to the courthouse to fill out paperwork. That left Momma in sole possession of the bill of sale signed by both of them and notarized."

"The suspense is getting to me."

"He thinks I'm giving him a break at ninety thousand dollars cash. I want the money in hand before Junior finds out about the zoning."

"Ninety thousand dollars?"

"I'd never think to ask anywhere near that amount without MJ's money savvy. She's quick as a squirrel and twice as handy to have around."

If Jaudon refused to sell, thought Berry, she'd save that land, those trees, the animal homes—but Berry said nothing. What's done was done. The sale lifted Jaudon's debt worries and eventually would decrease pesticide use. Overpopulation was to blame for this crazy amount of housing construction in Florida. She wasn't waiting for her clinic. Any chance she got, she handed out birth control literature, pills, and doodads. Too many humans thought their genes took precedence over wildlife.

Before thanking the Great Spirit, she asked, "Between the two sales, will you have enough for everything owed?"

"I just about will. The stores will be on more solid ground. What do you think?"

Yes is what she thought, her arms going around Jaudon's neck, her cheek brushing the soft stubble along her jaw. Yes, she'd cut back her hours at the clinic soon, grow her private practice, and give her energy to hounded, self-doubting women and gay people. Yes, she'd start saving again toward her dream. Yes, she'd have her Jaudon, a whole Jaudon, back.

Life was funny, though. You thought you turned a corner until you found a locked gate and your keys dropped into a street grate.

❖

When MJ asked to be her inaugural client, Berry only just managed to hide her jubilation and relief. From the little MJ had thus far revealed about her childhood, she needed to talk to someone. Berry might be a novice at her job, but she knew the lesbian heart. She was aware, also, that gay people by necessity devised some unsafe coping mechanisms—from drugs and alcohol to overwork to general instability, reckless rebellion, and suicide.

She was so used to scrubs, she hardly knew what professional clothes to wear. She decided on a light pink pullover blouse and loose black slacks, and changed her mind twice before she accepted that, friend or not, she was nervous about the appointment.

MJ chose to sit on the couch. They chit-chatted, both excited by news that the cause of the AIDS virus had been identified.

When MJ started talking about herself, though, she went directly to the crux of her problems.

"Vonnie says I act like I don't have emotions. I know one thing is true: crying hasn't come easily to me since I was, I don't know, an infant."

"And that troubles you."

MJ's eyes took on the shine of gathering tears. She choked them back and answered, "Well, yeah. That's not normal, is it?"

"It's okay, you're safe here," she said, wanting to embrace her as a friend, but, as her counselor, refraining. She rubbed her thumb over the malachite necklace Jaudon had made her from one of Rigo's fortifying stones. Berry offered her the box of tissues—one of the tools of her new trade.

Dry-eyed, MJ waved off the tissues. "You must be a virtuoso therapist. What a fast cure."

"You needed somewhere to put your guard down."

"I suppose."

"You carry yourself like you bumped into a great big Florida black bear and are perennially trying to present as more substantial and less afraid than you are."

"The world is a great big Florida black bear. You have to rage back or surrender, the same as h—"

"Home?"

"Florida is home." MJ's eyes narrowed as if Berry might challenge her.

"Was your family that bad?"

"Aside from the fact that they didn't want me?"

"Your parents? Did they reject you so blatantly?"

"Did they beat me? Only once. Then I left." MJ held her hands over her heart. "I lived with a constant unease, a certainty that if I blew it in the slightest way, I'd be in serious peril."

"You were living in a personal state of siege."

"I'll tell you right now." MJ's whole body folded in on itself, as if the cushions were swallowing her. "I hated them."

"Do you think that may be where your little problem with authority came from?"

"I don't have a problem with legitimate authority."

Berry came close to letting a sigh slip out and reminding MJ that she didn't get to decide which authority was legitimate. For a smart woman, her first client didn't know much about the workings of her mind, or perhaps anyone's. "Why don't you tell me how you rage back."

MJ spoke bleakly about an anger that came abruptly and for no reason, her arms by turn outstretched, withdrawn, supplicating as she talked, as if imploring Berry for a solution.

"I can't stop it, can't restrain it. It's going to get me in trouble."

"You're lucky that reservoir of anger never led you to crime."

"Ah…" MJ's fingers traced whorls in the textured design of the couch.

Berry waited.

"What we say is word for word confidential, right?"

Berry learned in her practicum that trust must be earned. "To a point, yes. Are you planning to harm anyone or yourself?"

"Oh, shoot no. It's the other way around. The way I plan, nobody gets hurt."

The precious woman's ears, not just the tips, were red enough to burn her.

"Hurt by you?"

MJ unhooked her glasses from her ears and rubbed the stem between her nose and upper lip, watching Berry's face. "When I get hopping mad, I burglarize houses."

One careful fact at a time, MJ again earnestly told the story of Ike Keister and how that break-in purged her of wrath for a while afterward, how she chose targets, and how reckless she'd become lately.

MJ endlessly twisted her hands, as if to tie her fingers into knots.

She took few notes, cautious not to scare MJ into silence. She asked some questions, trying to decide if MJ had chosen the right counselor. Berry did not want to refer her to another professional who might interpret state standards differently than she did. Ethics obligated her to examine the whole picture and weigh possible harm with confidentiality.

Legally, she had no duty to report past crimes, and MJ had a right to refuse disclosure. If a client told her she planned to harm herself or others, Berry had no choice. In this case, MJ was seeking help to stop her criminal acts, so there was no stated intent to break the law.

After they set another appointment and said good-bye, she thought about their friendship. Confidentiality prevented her from revealing information to Jaudon, which was awkward. She questioned both treating a friend and protecting a criminal. She'd love to discuss both with Jaudon.

MJ said she didn't pilfer, shoplift, or rob. Just these fury-fueled break-ins. Very simple on the surface. To survive, MJ muted her emotions growing up. She broke out of the family home and now broke back into home after home, always with the wrong emotion at the wrong house.

CHAPTER FORTY-FIVE

Spring 1984

Berry had given her one assignment: stop three times a day and check in with herself.

MJ set aside her hammer, took the nails from between her lips, and, squatting, rocked onto her heels. *Let your hands*, Berry had instructed, *hang loose and relaxed.*

Over the weekend, she and Vaughn worked on a bank-owned half-acre lot in Four Lakes that Cullie told them about. Vaughn's credit union had approved his loan, and he wanted to finish the install yesterday. With a borrowed heavy truck, they smoothly maneuvered a good-as-new single-wide manufactured home between two lines of crape myrtles and their spreading branches.

She marveled at Vaughn, unremittingly polite, fair, and hard working. His clean and sharpened tools were organized to be convenient to both of them. They found the same things funny, and he taught her loads of trade secrets about keeping material waste to a minimum, the best way to use a hand saw, and simple tricks. He said, if she didn't have a tape measure handy, a dollar bill measured a consistent six inches. From her back pocket, she pulled the list of emotions Berry supplied and spied the right one: grateful.

Gratitude, especially when she expressed it aloud, was an extraordinary sensation of relief—relief verging on happiness.

She couldn't recall sincerely thanking much of anyone as she grew up, except in politeness, never from the bottom of her heart. Today she was grateful to have Lady Luck on her side, keeping her free of jail for the time being.

"My mother," she'd told Berry, hearing the derisive bitterness in her voice, "turned thank-yous into criticisms so I'd get her point: *Thanks for finally doing one little thing for me. I know you don't have much time to help out.*"

Berry had answered, "As a result, the whole concept of showing appreciation was lost on you."

What kind of freak was she, that she needed to teach herself the many ways of demonstrating real gratitude? She vowed to start trying Monday, but it was Thursday before she found a way.

"Hey, Vaughn?" she shouted over their mess of junked cabinet doors, crumpled wallboard, shelving, discolored hardware, empty mousetraps, and stained rugs. "I'm going to get us a pizza. What do you want on it?"

Taller than Vonnie, Vaughn wore his hair short and kept his deep voice modulated, a pleasure to listen to, but he continued to act tentatively around her. Employer or not, she was his sister's lover.

"What's the occasion?" he asked, wiping the sweat of demanding labor from his freckled face with a shop towel that without fail hung from his toolbelt.

This morning she'd read in the news about the drug overdose death of a twenty-eight-year-old Kennedy son. White, never lacked for anything, and held the keys to the kingdom. Then there was Vaughn, so mature, responsible and sober.

She pushed out the words. "To thank you for your reliability and your skills and your problem solving. That's the occasion."

Her praise appeared to knock him back a couple of steps. "Oh. Okay. Thanks. Or, I mean, you're welcome. You're great to work for. With. Thank you for giving this new guy a chance."

Neither met the other's eyes more than a second at a time.

"So, pizza?" she asked, adjusting her glasses, embarrassed.

"Yeah, yes. Uh—sausage and onions, please. Thanks."

"We'll do it more often."

"I'll treat next." He stepped over Anika and went back to work.

They commuted to Plant City for this rebuild, a two-bedroom cabin with a kitchen in a deteriorated auto court that was condo-izing its units. It was another FSBO. The sellers sweetened the pot when she wavered. She and Vaughn were putting in new floors, windows, roof, and adding a miniature screened back porch with a view of a wooded area—across railroad tracks that served Amtrak and long Seaboard System freight trains.

As she anticipated beaucoup vacation rental income from other properties, she increased Vaughn's share of the profits. He applied for a general contractor's license, which was required for window installation and drywall work, among other specific tasks. Now they'd receive contractor discounts on materials and appliances.

She drove along Route 92, past the legendary Parkesdale Farm Market, her pizzas steaming under a wool blanket in the back seat because Anika claimed the front. She'd run to Parkesdale another day for milkshakes. People traveled by the busload to imbibe everything strawberry. She experienced a flood of well-being. Life was darned good at the moment; she lived in the land of opportunity and was making something of herself.

That's when she saw the sheriff's car blocking Vaughn's truck. Shocked, she lost her cool and drove past.

She'd stay away until the police were gone. Had someone seen her breaking into a house? Had Shady or Tad or Berry talked? Never. And Jaudon didn't know. Vaughn loved Anika enough to take care of her.

She gunned the car and went back to the pizzeria, where she'd seen a pay phone. This time of day, Jaudon worked in the back room at the Buffalo Street store, which served as her office.

Jaudon answered on the first ring. "I didn't know how to get ahold of you. They gave me a summons. Roy Jack is suing for employment discrimination, claiming he asked for a transfer to an open store when I closed Church Pond. He's going after you too, but that's just harassment on his part."

"What can they do to us?"

"Roy Jack has no grounds for employment discrimination. It's a sneaky way to get back at me. He'll try to bring attention to the liquor operation. Possession of moonshine is a third-degree felony, and then there's tax evasion. Jumping Jehoshaphat, Pops never got in this much trouble. My hard-done-by Berry would be better off without me."

Once more, she stopped herself from saying anything about the price of doing business. "If he manages to expose the Schoolhouse operation, they can get me for selling. Let me tell you, and I am serious as a heart attack about this—I need to stay clear of their system."

"I should have known Roy Jack wasn't letting it go. He conspired on this with his deputy buddies."

"I'm honestly going to lie my head off if they catch up with me. I need to warn Tad and Shady now. I'll stop by your house after Vaughn and I finish later, okay?"

"And don't forget Sunday. You and Vonnie's family are coming to Pineapple Trail for Easter. Stay away from those good-for-nothing Batsons, you hear?"

Vonnie might not want to come home for spring break once she told her about the police visit.

She grabbed two bottles of orange Crush from the cooler, paid, and stared at a guy now hogging the pay phone. She jumped at it when he hung up, and she rang Tad at the café to fill him in. Back in the car, her heart sounded like a gong at the mercy of a high-speed padded mallet. Her hands tightened on the searing steering wheel. What if Roy Jack got his way, brought her to the attention of the sheriff, and some smart deputy connected her to the burglaries? A minute ago, she wanted Jaudon to face facts. Now she understood that she might take some flak too.

She wasn't a minor anymore. Far from it—she'd be twenty-five this year and a successful businesswoman. She needed to apply for official permits, pay fees and taxes, and get her own license, so Vaughn didn't have to be her front man. How could she if this exploded in her face, and she found herself with a criminal record? They'd better not ask for her fingerprints, just in case she'd gotten sloppy and left one at a victim's home. Her paranoia had become a habit by now.

She parked at the work site. Anika watched everything she did with the pizza boxes.

"Vaughn, I sure hope you don't mind cold pizza."

"I'm so hungry I'd eat it frozen."

"Sorry about the delay. You understood why, right?"

"You wanted to avoid that deputy. I don't know about you, but it's better for me to stay away from them."

"Oh, damn me. I was scared as hell when I saw that cruiser. It never occurred to me that a cop might take it out on you."

There was that word again: scared. She'd check it on Berry's emotions list.

Vaughn was about to take a bite of pizza but gave the narrow slice to Anika and lifted another. "She didn't hassle me. It gave me a shock to find a lady in uniform at the door. She needs to give you papers, that's all. I told her you were at lunch."

"Thanks for handling it. I talked to Jaudon. It has nothing to do with our work here."

She passed him his Crush. "Here you go, Vaughn. Warm soda and cold pizza."

"Glad you weren't around to hear my stomach growling."

Vaughn donned work gloves, safety goggles, and a dust mask to hang drywall and apply joint compound. She kneeled to pull out the tarnished box wall heater and inserted a shiny new one.

As she worked, she tried to imagine a safer life without breaking and entering, without compulsively following the obits, profiles of politicians, and society pages to find people who'd made it to easy street on the backs of the poor, and to learn when they were traveling. Enough income came in to get by for now. But ripping off the moneyed had proven supremely satisfying.

❖

MJ charged into the Vicker home, eager to talk about the papers Jaudon had been served, or maybe eager to forget her own problems.

Gran, smelling like a perfumery, gave her one of her priceless hugs. She relaxed into it for once, until Gran let her go. Benedict was taking Gran to the fancy Don CeSar restaurant in St. Pete, a first for Gran. She was dressed to the nines.

Jaudon sat at the broad kitchen table, an iced tea in front of her. "Benedict had the bright idea of calling my lawyer."

"Merely because I am a lawyer," Benedict said, arms outstretched, palms up, humble. "Retired nine years now."

"Well, heck," Jaudon said. She had Kajen on her lap, the cat suffering a vigorous belly rub. "If I hadn't been shaking in my sneakers, I might have thought to do that. I wanted to come home and hide for the rest of my days."

"I'm with you there, Boss. I left defenseless Vaughn to deal with the police. What a drip I am. He's a young Black man—completely vulnerable."

She ran a finger over her forehead scar. She thought about the time she fled with Jaudon, hiding in that garage, exposing Jaudon to further charges if they'd been caught. What a coward she was. Her fear and doom-filled thoughts were demolishing her ability to think, to act rationally or responsibly.

The compulsion to burgle hadn't revisited her since Cedar Key. Until today—and the letter in her post office box from Vonnie.

What, on Berry's list, described a heart withering? She dreaded telling her what Vonnie wrote and how she comforted herself by holding good, patient Anika and stroking her clean, soothing fur. Vonnie wanted to give their relationship a rest until MJ stopped stealing. She couldn't blame Vonnie for this knockout punch. Vonnie, who brought her nothing but good, was well within her rights to safeguard herself against such an evil, evil, twisted child.

Aloud, she asked, "What did the lawyer say?"

"His secretary is going to squeeze me in tomorrow. I begged her."

"We can be halfway to Canada by tomorrow."

"Then you'd be desperados for certain," Gran said.

Benedict, in his soft voice, said, "Better to face the music than run."

Berry gestured to the gathering. "Especially when you'd be leaving the whole orchestra behind."

Benedict said, "You have no reason to flee, MJ."

She exchanged looks with Berry. "To be honest, I don't want one iota of police attention, and I'm not leaving my hot, buggy adoptive state."

Jaudon offered the document to Benedict. "You know I'll toss and turn about this. Would you be willing to go over it?"

The living room went silent as Benedict changed his glasses and perused the papers. Gran methodically sliced her birthday cake and passed it around. Kajen jumped on the table, trying to nose her way under the papers. Berry scooped her up and nuzzled her.

Benedict read and reread, wetting his index finger and thumb as he finished each crisp page. The room stayed hushed, waiting. He changed his glasses again and said, "I primarily dealt with legal issues concerning public utilities and other regulated industries. Commercial law isn't my field, but I advise you to take this seriously."

She clutched at her hands until she remembered Berry's instruction to breathe. Serious meant too many questions, too much suspicion, a chancy investigation.

Benedict said, "Nonetheless, I believe a lawyer can make it go away. Particularly if, as you say, there's an ulterior motive on the county's part, namely, your pending suit." He passed the papers to Jaudon, shaking his head. "What do they have except the accuser's statement? With his record, he's not a reliable witness."

"Nothing, as far as I know, unless he took pictures from the woods behind us. You know we put the whiskey jars in plain brown pokes. Cousin Roy Jack can swear to the heavens, but he saw nothing other than paper bags change hands. Could just as well be kettle corn."

"How did they find your hidden cache?" asked Benedict.

"My cousin helped build it into Momma's store."

"So the whistleblower once used the same property for the same purpose?"

"Yes, but Momma owned the store and knew they were doing it."

"Did they pay her?"

"Cash under the table. No receipts or checks. Based on what you and your friends pulled in, Roy Jack held back far more than his family's share."

"Give that information to your attorney too. It might come in handy."

Berry was brushing the cat. "What a complicated mess."

"I did what I had to do to save the stores."

Gran said, "It's the way of the world for us common folk to pay in the end."

Into the silence that followed Gran's conclusion, a mockingbird sang its repertoire.

MJ couldn't stop a fleeting smile, though her hands continued grappling with each other, and she cracked a knuckle. "So preposterously many people with money break laws without a second thought. It's how they do business. Fines don't wipe them out, and they never go to jail. Seriously, sometimes I think we should all become desperados, and not by any accident of circumstance."

"The Gran Clan," suggested Benedict with the sharp laugh he used as punctuation.

Gran laughed with him. "You'd better start learning some criminal law."

Berry raised a warning eyebrow at Jaudon, who continued collecting payments from Shady and Tad, but MJ knew Berry meant her as well.

"You're not in actual fact going to jail, either of you," Berry said, "but what about the business you've fought for, the people you'd impact if you did: your employees, your family and friends."

"I wish you didn't make such sense," Jaudon said. "At the time, I thought it was worth going out on that limb."

Berry said, "I may not be super smart like MJ, but—"

"You have native wit," Gran said, "and a college education, thanks to the life insurance your grandfather left." She pointed a scolding finger at the group. "You wiseacre desperados listen to my granddaughter. You'll never see her run from trouble."

MJ smiled at Gran's attempt to shame Jaudon and herself into submission.

The Vicker living room faded into the background as she squirmed. Vonnie's letter solved one problem. She didn't need to tell her about the trouble Roy Jack was stirring up. In the back of her mind, she surmised Vonnie wasn't being up-front with her. Had she met someone else? Fears bombarded her, and she tried to sort through them. Her priority was taking care of business if she wanted to win Vonnie back. She needed cash if it came to paying a fine for selling liquor. She also had her eye on a neat two-story in Causeway and was looking to sell the Plant City rehab.

Right now, all her money was spoken for, pending the closings on two properties. She needed working capital from a last lucky break-in, however many tries it took, and had settled on a likely prospect. She'd stick to her former precautions and stop the impulsiveness she yielded to in Cedar Key.

Then she'd quit the desperado business for good. Vonnie envisioned her as a gambler. Well, she'd kick ass on stocks and bonds. No Wall Street millionaire sucking the country dry had a brain keener than hers. And the same principle applied in the market—honesty got you nowhere.

She pictured herself in a green Robin Hood hat: MJ Beaudry investing a large slice of her earnings in a trust for Berry's Health Center. The Nature Conservancy would get a chunk too, to help save Florida from overdevelopment. Yeah, she thought, crunching a white Jordan almond from Gran's candy dish, one last score, and she'd walk the straight and narrow.

CHAPTER FORTY-SIX

MJ returned to Ike Keister's duded-up building for what she swore to herself was her last unlawful act. She'd never stopped fuming at the hoity-toity owners like him. No rentals were allowed. The part- and full-time residents lived high off the hog with money to spare. She'd studied more than Keister when she lived in its shabbier neighbor.

One part-time couple in their forties stood out back then. Their first-floor patio door faced the pool where they spent their visits tanning, playing in the water, smoking, and drinking. For a while, they'd driven a Jaguar XJ to restaurants that evidently required formal attire. Then it was a Lincoln Town Car convertible.

Sleaze and Floozie, she'd called them, and a second man, wide and bald, always accompanied them. A brother? A bodyguard? A disgusting love triangle? She confirmed they were again in town when she saw them driving a brand-new BMW with the license plate frame of a local dealer. A new car annually. Must be nice. On the day she went in, she waited until they settled on chaise lounges at the pool, fresh drinks in hand, backs to the condo.

She entered a plush two-bedroom that stank of carpet cleaning chemicals, cigarette smoke, and a powerful perfume. She passed a locked glass cabinet full of Hummel figurines, but neatness stopped there. Wine, liquor bottles, and glasses, full and empty, cluttered surfaces. Belongings were strewn about. On the bed lay a black minister's shirt, clerical collar, and stole. His slacks were draped across a chair and held a thin wallet with credit cards and a Massachusetts driver's license. She started to put the wallet back when the name Scully caught her eye. She tried to place it, but an initialed full money clip in another pocket distracted her. Who carried that much cash? It went into her cargo shorts. Tad called her luck finding money bizarre. Shady accused her of left coast wizardry.

On the kitchen table the woman's handbag stood open, exuding the flagrant smell of new fine leather. A fat french purse lay inside. It unsnapped with a crack loud as a starter pistol, to reveal twenties, fifties. Underneath the purse, she saw an actual pistol lying atop an envelope thick with green.

"What do we have here? A palm rat?"

She went stiff at the sound of a male voice behind her. Oh, boy, she thought, the wizard just lost her magic. *Take the gold clip and go, go, go*, she commanded herself, but no, the lava of her discontent erupted and goaded her on.

"Stay where you are, fellow, and take your hands off that bag." Sonorous, formidable, his voice could be a minister's. His accent matched the address on his driver's license. He almost didn't have to say his next words: "I have a gun."

With her gloved hand, her back to the man, she eased the envelope from the pocketbook and under her tucked-in shirt. She gave a split second's thought to seizing the pistol but drew her hands away. She wasn't faster than a bullet. She tensed to flee.

The front door crashed open. The wide, bald man stormed in, swim trunks dripping. He most definitely held a gun.

Now a woman spoke behind her, followed by the sound of two beeps from a touch-tone phone: 9, 1—

"What're you, bonkers? No boys in blue," croaked the minister, whacking the phone from her hand. "We'll see to him ourselves."

She was in a fix, and it was no fun. She hurt from remorse. *Vonnie*, she thought, *I'm sorry.*

For a frozen period of time, the four of them stood without moving. She pictured the now silent tableau as if watching from a theater balcony. The couple behind her, lethal danger in front, herself and a weapon within reach.

Regret put its arms around her and squeezed. She gasped for breath once, twice. Burning fluid rose in her throat. She'd broken from her parents; she'd survived the dangers of the road; she'd made her way. She wanted to live long enough to make good on her promise to Berry and all the women a clinic could've helped.

Vaughn would care for her faithful Anika. Who would take care of Vonnie, about to lose a lover and a home? She heard Berry blaming herself as a novice counselor. And the boss, poor honest-to-the-penny Jaudon, what a disappointment to her.

Berry had guided her until MJ understood the need she tried to fill in herself, the enormous amount of nurturing withheld from her that now compelled her to steal back anything to satisfy needs once burned to ashes within her.

Stupid thoughts pinballed in her head: cement shoes, garroting, a shot in the back of the head, a slit throat. Scully seemed vicious enough to put conditions on her to keep her in his thrall the rest of her life, married to crime. She'd have to distance herself from Vonnie if she lived through this.

What a jerk she was, returning love with loss. Fear bolted through her. *Another new emotion from your list, Berry.* She trembled with its unfamiliar magnitude.

That's when it clicked. The name Scully, the piles of cash, the Yankee voice. The man behind her was the sham clergyman who ripped off Jaudon's mother. This might be Jaudon's money. How dare this charlatan squander it on posh cars, and how dare he show his face around here. She might be a thief, but…but what? Did she think she was higher on some morality scale?

"Just kick the rip-off artist to the curb," said Scully. "We cowed the living bejesus out of him."

"Naw. Listen, Rev." The man in the doorway spoke in a Northern snarl. "I bet you dollars to doughnuts they sent him to snoop."

She stopped breathing. They? Who was they? The mob? The police? Was he on the FBI's radar? She sank deeper into the hot water of her own making.

"Is that who you are, a goddam buttinsky?" asked Scully. He took her by the shoulders and forced her toward him. "What are you sniveling about? Jesus Christ—it's a girl."

The tears rose from a deep salty sump almost as old as she was. It was one thing to cry in Berry's office, but this was an explosion of long-denied fear and long-sustained control. She couldn't clever herself through this one.

"Did they send you?"

He went to give her a brutal push. She skipped away from it. Then he shook her, the way her father shook her. The last time Dear Old Dad did it, she bashed him in the shin with as much ferocity as she could muster. Today, taller, stronger, she kicked this guy's shin with the potency of her unaccustomed fear.

Evil, evil, twisted child? No. *I am MJ Beaudry.*

He tottered on one foot, then fell on her. The counter hit her midback. The sharp and sudden pain made her lose her footing. She and the woman's handbag dropped in a jumble. She saw the french purse drop from the handbag as she scrambled to rise. She grabbed it. *I'm MJ Beaudry*, she thought and launched it at Scully with a bombardment of outrage.

She clipped him in the eye. He cried out and covered the eye. She rushed him and used the heavy purse as a second cudgel to his face. Unprepared, his head snapped sideways, his body following. The woman shrieked, leaped for MJ, who whirled around her and barreled toward the thug with the gun who blocked the doorway.

Voice hoarse, Scully called, "Let her go. We don't want the cops. She didn't have time to see anything."

"Who's talking about cops? I'll kill her myself," said Floozie. "That's an expensive pocketbook."

Before they discovered their losses, MJ broke away and ran for her life into the familiar sand lots and side streets, shoving her gloves, with the last flickers of her rage, deep into a full, sun-stewed dumpster.

Unarmed and incredibly, she'd prevailed over three people with guns. She wanted badly to speed over to tell Jaudon about Scully, get him arrested, but to do so, she'd eventually have to explain how she rooted him out. Jaudon didn't know she was a burglar. As of this moment, a former burglar.

She drew in the hot air and realized she was shivering. Once on a main street, she made herself walk sedately away under the cloudless blue sky, through Florida's cotton-candy world of blossoming trees and flower-filled yards.

CHAPTER FORTY-SEVEN

When the city ultimately paid out, Jaudon and Rouie Waver finished settling Momma's debts. For the considerable amount that remained in her bank account, Jaudon had a lengthy shopping list of new equipment for the stores.

Then Berry put her foot down. "Be sensible. We're putting that money aside to pay for a new roof."

Jaudon stomped down their porch steps and out to her rickety tree house. She was counting on that capital to compete with nearby flashy new convenience stores. Now Berry wanted to wreck her plans. Berry knew she worked too hard to forfeit the business in the end.

She reached for the tree house ladder. The rung, mossy and rotted, came off in her hand. She tipped her head against the tree and wept. Her once hallowed sanctuary was falling apart. Darn Berry—she'd object to buying lumber to make a new ladder. This had been where they became closer and closer to each other, where they pronounced themselves married. She kicked the broken rung away and tore off the others within her reach, heaving toward the pond with the strength of embitterment.

Yes, she was throwing a childish tantrum. No, she didn't care. The stores were her life. Berry had her counseling office—shouldn't she use the settlement money for the Beverage Bays?

At least Rich Slumkey, the attorney, convinced the county that the Church Pond store investigation wasted time and public monies.

She walked to the bench by the pond of brown water where they'd spent a great deal of their childhoods. Puddin plowed through the Kissimmee grass, bulrush, and cattail into the water, careful to wet nothing above her belly. Jaudon kept an eye out for Ollie, the menace of her childhood, or any other alligator and flattened the mosquitos on her skin.

Like the ladder, the bench would collapse under her if she tried to sit on it. She supposed Berry had a point. They could use some of the money on the house. She didn't want to boil down to fanatical Momma. Those stores were Momma's life. For Jaudon, Berry came first, second, and third. How much time had she been taking her Berry for granted? And today she stooped to bad-mouthing her.

She and Puddin ran flat-out from the pond and barged back into the house.

"I'm sorry, I'm sorry, I'm sorry," she cried.

Berry came to her bedroom doorway, alarm in her eyes.

She crashed against Berry and held her close. "I'm sorry. You're right about everything. Please forgive me. I'll never be mad at you again."

Puddin flopped at their feet, soaking the floor beneath her and panting.

"Berry, you're too good for me."

Berry soothed her, patting and caressing her back.

Jaudon moved around Berry and pulled her to the bed. "I'm sorry, let me show you how sorry. Gran's at Benedict's tonight, isn't she?"

Berry went limp at the knees as Jaudon kissed her face, her earlobes with their tiny citrine stud earrings, her neck, as she opened the buttons on Berry's uniform and kissed her shoulder and the tops of her breasts in their practical white bra.

Jaudon kept kissing as she undressed her. "I'm lower than a snake's belly in a wagon rut. I've neglected to give you and your pretty doodads enough attention."

Berry helped wrestle off her clothes. "You have reason to be preoccupied about your business."

She dropped Berry's underwear to the floor.

Just before she touched her tongue to Berry, she said, "Not as much reason as I have to focus on you, Georgia gal."

Considerably later, Jaudon went to the kitchen for a bag of pretzel sticks and a Coke to share.

"Now, what exactly is it I'm right about, Jaudon Vicker?"

"Our house, for one thing. The peeling porch paint, the wisteria vines taking over the sides, and the moss on the roof. It needs tending."

Berry fed her a pretzel.

"You're right about putting part of that money into savings. If I get killed in a store robbery, I want you taken care of. We need a will too. I don't want my brother to claim everything we accomplished once he musters out of the service. He'll sell it to the highest bidder."

"Oh, you take care of me all right, Angel."

Was there anyone on earth sexier than her Berry? Jaudon stretched full length, savoring the sensual pleasure that coursed along her nerves. "How did I get this lucky?"

"I'm the lucky one. If you'll take it easy for a minute, I want to show you what came in the mail today."

Berry left the bed and hustled from the room without a stitch on. She returned, offering a fat brown envelope.

"Uh-oh. Who do we owe money to now?"

But Berry thrust it at her. "There's no postage. No return address, just the name."

"What the heck?"

"I opened it to make sure it wasn't bad news."

Jaudon removed a second envelope. In it, wrapped in newspaper, were stacks of green bills.

"Jumping Jehoshaphat. Is this fake? Somebody's idea of a joke?"

"Count it. I guesstimate about twelve thousand dollars."

"I don't get it."

"I'm tickled pink. That'll cover the roof and more."

"But who? We don't know a soul with money, much less a philanthropist."

"Scully found religion and is giving away his worldly goods?"

"I'd say Pops, but this isn't his style. He'd want to see how happy he made us."

"Gran wouldn't sell Stinky Lane without telling me."

"Then her ex, that Eddie Dill loser, is back from the dead and making amends."

"Eddie Dill? He's not a sharing kind of ghoul."

"Benedict Lam throws money around."

"He only spends on Gran. She said his kind of lawyering never brought in bushels."

"It occurs to me we do know someone with financial training," she declared, lining the bed with rubber-banded stacks of cash. "MJ Beaudry majored in finance, and she's got a lot of pots on the stove."

"I wonder," Berry said. "Some people are good at conjuring up riches. But if it's her, she wants to make a secret of it. I don't think she'd appreciate us asking."

"I think it's her, but she can be secretive. I'll let you know if I can get her to fess up, so we can at least thank her. Meantime, we have a laundry list of ways to spend it, whoever supplied it."

They returned to their plans for the settlement money and came to terms. Jaudon ordered spanking new curved glass bakery cases for each surviving store. They were essential to meet the growing demand for Pansy's Pastries. At present the goodies were showcased in outmoded, scratched-up, yellowing Plexiglas countertop cases that did nothing for the appearance of the baked goods, or the stores.

"Let's share this windfall, Angel, and ask MJ and Vaughn Lowe if we can hire them to do our roof."

"You want me to ask MJ for an estimate?"

"Why don't you. After we celebrate more." Berry ran her palm across Jaudon's slight breasts. "MJ told me Vaughn has the start of a crew of workers now, none accepted into the apprenticeship programs."

"That makes me madder than a wet hen, the unions throwing away good talent."

"He hired a nineteen-year-old man who completed construction training in the Job Corps. Now he's asking around for a woman to add to the crew."

"One of my part-timers started training in that federal program, CETA, but it ended, and she's trying to get on with the city or the county in maintenance. She aged out of foster care. She makes it as far as interviews and has never once heard a yea or nay. Of course, she wears her pants so tight I can see her religion."

Berry grinned. "The first time her slacks rip while she's roofing, she'll get over tight clothes. She must be ambitious."

"Like we were until we came back from our honeymoon and were hit with the news about the stores. My whole life, except for you, seemed to come to nothing."

"That tornado, it picked us up, twirled us around, and slammed us down." Berry grew quiet for a moment. "Practically ten years ago."

"And now money is falling into our laps."

"Thank you, Great Spirit. Pull the shades now, Angel—it's dark."

"Do you want to move to the kitchen and have supper?"

Berry beckoned her back to the bed. "How about dessert first."

Chapter Forty-eight

Summer 1984

One sunshiny Sunday, MJ and Vaughn met at Berry and Jaudon's house to assess their leaky roof before hurricane season seriously started.

Allison and Cullie were already there, celebrating the Democratic nomination of Congresswoman Geraldine Ferraro for Vice President.

"I hate to rain on your parade," MJ told them. "There isn't a hope for a Mondale/Ferraro ticket—we're going to have to suffer through another four years with a stinking rich celebrity president who can't handle the job and wears so much makeup he looks embalmed."

Allison tore into her, and the rousing discussion only ended when MJ secured her glasses on her face and ventured, with Vaughn and their powerful flashlights, to inspect the Vicker house's rafters and the underside of the roof sheathing. The three of them carried an extension ladder and climbed. Cullie tagged along, her dog Kirby barking at them as Cullie tossed Cheetos to her from the peak of the hipped roof.

"I'm telling you, Cullie, that dog of yours is a bad influence on Anika," MJ said. Anika was chewing the last Cheetos before Kirby reached them.

"Sheesh, you're just filled with envy you don't have Kirby's pedigree. When you start this roof, count me and my doggolette in when I'm not working."

"Kirby will bark the livelong day."

Cullie said, "I'll let Allison mind Kirby for a while after rigorous retraining—of Allison, not my princess."

Jaudon nodded toward the roof. "What do you think, Vaughn?"

Vaughn laughed into the stifling air, shooing no-see-ums away from his face with a slender hand. "You're past needing a new roof, is what I think. These cedar shakes have seen better days, and the flat tin sheathing? You want to keep it?"

"I'd like to, but you're the expert. I was hoping you'd tell me what I need if you take on the job."

"Owners at the last senior trailer park we worked in were waiting to ambush a sucker like me to play weekend discount handyman. I'll see if I can reschedule."

Cullie held out two thumbs. "Good man."

MJ lifted the edge of a shingle. It fell apart to mush and splinters.

Jaudon grimaced. "I don't need any convincing about the shakes, but the tin is supposed to last forever. I recall Pops and my grandfather putting it on. I was about five. I whined and cried as bad as Kirby, pleading to climb up. Once they finished, Pops piggybacked me to the top. He showed me a mockingbird nest."

She saw the delight from long ago in Jaudon's eyes. As they descended the ladder, she announced, "We need to go out sometime, Boss. I want to know what birds I'm seeing. Which one is singing now, that *tow-wheet* song?"

"Don't ask me," Cullie said. "I can tell a crow from a sparrow, but that's about it."

"That's a cardinal. Lots of them around." Jaudon laid an arm across her shoulders and gave her a squeeze. "Berry knows them all. Give us a jingle when you want to go birdwatching, buckaroo."

She patted Jaudon's hand, a little choked up over the gang's companionship and kindness. It helped lessen the sting from this period of uncertainty about Vonnie.

She'd stuck to her vow to Vonnie so far and followed Berry's advice about dealing with her anger and kicking the burglary habit. She was still scared spitless after her last score. She'd find other ways to kick the overrich in their overstuffed wallets, but Berry was right. She'd essentially said MJ's parents had a few screws loose. In blaming baby Emma Jean for disrupting their plans, her parents had taught her to sabotage herself—from recklessly coasting Depot Landing's long steep hill on her bike, to recklessly ignoring Vonnie's appeals that she stop stealing.

In any case, she and Vaughn were too crazy busy for her to find break-in targets and study them.

Vaughn passed the exams for a residential contractor's license, with one holdup. Since traditional companies had stiff-armed him for training, he couldn't verify his years of experience. The man he used to work for had let his license lapse—mostly retired, he didn't earn enough to cover the state mandated insurance and fees, but he'd spent his life in the industry and built enough respect that a crony agreed to vouch for Vaughn.

Vaughn's crew had become a mixed bag of women and men. Benedict's electrician friend agreed to occasionally subcontract. When it came to plumbing, Vaughn had been his handyman granddad's right hand and knew it well.

With more cash coming in from rentals, she bought an eyesore double-wide in a fifty-five-plus park. The manufactured home was slated to be pulled out, but she and Vaughn transformed it. Whenever possible, they repaired instead of replacing, sourced supplies locally, and developed relationships with mom-and-pop shops. She loved scavenging teardowns and pullouts. She refused jobs that might disturb wetlands, riparian zones, and forests; she wanted no part of covering Florida with concrete. Word got around that they rehabbed manufactured homes for less than builders who didn't recycle materials.

Doing real estate ethically proved to be thorny work. Everywhere she turned, someone tried to swindle or take advantage of her. Substandard materials, overcharging, and sexual come-ons from renters and suppliers of every gender got her dander way up. She'd smirk in her lopsided way, getting some distance from wherever she was and making herself take a time-out.

"I'm ready to tackle this roof," she said.

Vaughn concurred with a dip of his head. "I'll ask my crew to be available."

Cullie said, "Let me know when."

"It'll be good to have a cop along. You can fend off the hordes of girls we'll attract."

Vaughn's grin was endearingly bashful.

She and Vaughn went to the porch to discuss the roof work, a feeble citronella candle between them.

"I never used tin on a roof before," Vaughn said.

"The Vicker homestead started out as a cracker house. Tin was common when they could get it."

"If I was Jaudon? I'd for sure want to put in a rubber water shield. You can see the seepage at the eaves."

"We can install fans and vents high enough to blow hot air out while we're at it."

"And I'd like to encourage Jaudon to replace the tin and shingles with corrugated galvanized steel."

They worked on a list of options and materials they'd need. Vaughn went off to price them. The job wasn't going to be cheap.

Cullie climbed the porch steps from exercising Kirby and walked inside with MJ. Berry never had to ask—she poured Cullie a glass of sweet tea.

Allison was laughing with Gran.

"Jujube, I can tell you're listening to Gran's tall tales without me."

Allison put her hands over her heart and caught her breath. "Who was it that insisted on seeing the roof, Officer Culpepper?"

Cullie sank into a chair, pouting, and hoisted Kirby onto her lap.

Gran continued talking about an encounter at the produce stand. With Jaudon's money troubles on the mend, Gran had cut her job back to two mornings a week. "Those are the days my crowd comes in. It's more fun than playing pinochle at the Senior Center."

The package of cash MJ had anonymously delivered to Jaudon hadn't contained the entire bounty she wrested from Scully. Jaudon would call it another trick up her sleeve but had told her enough about her dreams that MJ predicted she'd use the money to get loans for a new Beverage Bay and become overleveraged. She advised Jaudon to go after fresh markets for the existing stores. With the rest of Scully's cash, she invested in three stocks and would share the earnings.

She was confident the stocks were destined to rise. A couple were tried and true blue-chip corporations, and the others were the future. The new microcomputer industry fascinated her. Rigo, who had withstood his father's pressure to assist in smuggling people or anything else, convinced her to buy a Commodore computer like his, not the Macintosh Allison used at work. She invested in both companies, swearing to ignore market fluctuations until she retired.

Childhood behind her, she, MJ Beaudry, determined her life, picking her way between boulders of a different order, toward a current as powerful as the Columbia River.

CHAPTER FORTY-NINE

MJ needed PVC pipe from an outlet near Shady's address and decided to visit. Tad wasn't there, but Shady lounged beneath the apartment overhang, a portable typewriter on his lap.

"Ah," he said. "The prodigal sapphist returns."

"Cut it out." She fist-bumped his shoulder.

"We missed you." He called out, "Michelle, honey, bring a chair for Auntie MJ, please."

"Wow. You're shooting up fast, Michelle." She took the kitchen chair from the child, who struggled to drag it through the door. "What are you doing these days?"

Michelle, as shy as ever at age eleven, edged back into the apartment. "School. I have homework."

"I'm impressed," MJ told Shady. "You and your sister are raising her right."

"Living in the projects doesn't automatically limit residents. I'm preparing a small group of teens and another of parents for their high school diplomas. Please join us to celebrate graduation."

"I'd love to."

A teenage African American boy sauntered by in wet swim trunks and flip-flops, a towel around his neck.

"Hey, Teach," he said to Shady as he passed.

"That," Shady said, "is an Olympic swimmer in the making. I had the honor of getting his reading skills up past grade level to keep him in school."

The teen skipped backward. "I'll give you my trophy when I win the gold." He jogged away.

"That young jock swims two hours, twice a day. His dad found a coach for him, and he's won every meet he's entered. Guaranteed, the colleges will be begging for him."

"It's funny, Shady, but you know what? A lot of people look at public housing and see hopelessness. You see solutions and act on them."

"We all have a gift to give the world, including me. I have an education to share and time to pass it on."

"I don't know what would have happened to me if I hadn't met you and Tad the minute I left that truck."

"Same here—it's what we all needed. I was stuck in a bad space, drinking too much on top of the weed, accomplishing little. You extricated me."

"Me? How?"

"I saw this tuned-in girl about to tank her life. When you appeared again with goods to sell and bread in your pocket, I saw someone who used her smarts, both to survive and to give herself a future. The university threw me to the wolves, but you and Tad are beautiful people who made me hip to the idea that I don't need a state-sanctioned classroom to do good in my circumscribed realm."

Had her life gone terribly wrong anyway? She never stopped scanning behind herself for the Boston thugs, yet her fury wasn't tamed; the temptation to relapse into burglary crept back too often. All the same, she didn't miss or want the thrill at all.

She resisted, not wholly to win Vonnie back again, but for herself, for the resolute, successful MJ Beaudry she'd determined to create. If her luck ran out, she'd lose the rentals and her investments in order to pay for an attorney and restitution. Living in a prison or in her car far from here, she couldn't put aside money for the woman's clinic she was mapping out with Berry. She'd have no choice but to make up for her loss by stealing in order to start over.

What had Vonnie said, lying next to each other in the dark? *Never gamble being taken from me. Never.*

"Thanks, Shady. Thanks for telling me. Thanks for teaching me."

"Come on. Let's go see Tad and get his news."

Shady wheeled into the apartment to talk to Michelle. She heard Michelle lock the door behind him as he rejoined MJ.

Pansy's Home Cooking smelled of scorched grease. Tad was sweaty from scraping the grill. "Hey, Whitebread," Tad called over his shoulder to Shady. Neither customers nor Mrs. Lanamore were in sight.

"Haven't seen you for a while."

Shady said, "She's too busy for us, Tad."

"Doing what?" He came out wiping his hands on a towel and sat at a table with them. "Running north to keep your girl happy?"

Shady sniggered.

Her self-confidence had risen high enough to mention her investments and stave off any wheeler-dealer schemes of Shady's. He seemed to have enough on his hands to keep him busy.

"No, I'm playing with real estate," she told them. "Buying, fixing up, renting out."

"You saved enough money to buy property?" Tad asked, bumping his forehead with the heel of his hand.

"I saved enough money to buy one dirt-cheap property the county needed to unload, put in a slew of sweat equity, and went on from there."

"That's our girl," Shady said. "Smart as a whip. Tell her, Tad."

"Duval, Shady, and me, we're investing our cash in the bakery end of my mother's business. We're savers too. Come see."

Tad led her to the back of the cooking area and lifted aside a door-sized piece of plywood to reveal a space she'd never seen before. "Step right in to the new and improved Pansy's Pastries."

"You and Duval did this?"

"Used to be offices in here. A door sat exactly where you're standing. We knocked out walls to give us space. Under your feet is thick nonskid flooring that ought to last a while. Muma wanted these white tile splashguards around the room." He pointed with his feet. "They'll be barrels of fun to clean."

Everywhere in the huge room she saw shining steel. She patted a table.

"That's food grade stainless, brand new, sanitary. A bitch to find it secondhand with drawers." He pulled a drawer out to reveal dough scrapers, spatulas, spoons, whisks, and oddments. "And these were at a government repossessed property sale, hardly used—a heavy-duty food processor and a floor mixer."

He offered her a warm tart. "We call this a pinch-me-round."

She bit through a crunchy shell into a gooey coconut, nutmeg, and vanilla mixture. "That is super sweet. You never said you were making a full bakery happen."

"It's my mother's dream. Her friend Laura is designing a logo for our packaging, hats, and staff T-shirts."

"Laura? Not Laura Bathgate."

"Muma used to babysit Laura."

"She did the sign for Berry's office. They're friends at work."

"Laura sometimes helps out here on Saturdays. But notice these ovens. We went clear to Orlando for this nine-pan floor oven. The second is wall-mounted—Muma won't have to bend as much. The baker retired. The white dude practically gave us the freestanding warming drawers. Do you have any idea what these cost new? I can smell the plantain tarts, gizzadas, and sweet potato pies."

Their mother's dream. She envied them their devotion to Mrs. Lanamore. "You can make a lot of pastries here, Tad. Can Jaudon sell them all?"

"Didn't Jaudon tell you? She's changing the name to Beverage Bay and Bakery. She reinvested the money we owed her by forgiving our debt in exchange for being our sole retailer. We have the rights to supply wholesale. Muma and Duval are out there right now, trying to make deals with restaurants and the county for schools, the jail. Duval will keep the books, do payroll."

They were back at the table with Shady, who, as usual, had his nose in a thick library book. "Mind-blowing, isn't it?"

"Shady wanted in," said Tad.

"I invested cash as a partner, and I'll be taking over marketing and promotion. I decided depending on luck to stay out of prison is not my bag, especially not the way they treat disabled prisoners."

"And I'm clear of the stealing business," she said.

Tad high-fived her, his hand dwarfing hers. "We're making smarter money."

"That's a state-of-the-art operation Tad showed me."

Shady seemed to study her as he slid a bookmark in his book. "You're on the ball as usual, Squirrel. You want to know how a small-time fence like me collected enough funding to pull off a kosher deal."

"You might say that," she replied, disposed not to believe a word he said.

Shady took off his granny sunglasses and rubbed his eyes. Tad stayed silent.

"We sold the hooch business," Shady said. "We're now invested in Pansy's Pastries, Inc."

"Sold it?"

"And put it into that kitchen, aboveboard and legal."

"Who wanted to buy the liquor business?"

"Remember Jaudon's older cousin who badly wanted it back?"

"You sold it to Roy Jack Batson, a bigot who won't do business with African Americans? What were you thinking?"

"Don't guilt-trip him," Tad said. "They roughed Shady up. His sister came to his defense."

"They tipped me off my chair. I couldn't reach my gun. Michelle let out a shrill howl for help. Sis rushed them with the baseball bat she keeps at the door. She smashed Jaudon's cousin's knee to bits. His pal—that Milo guy—latched onto Michelle, started dragging her away. Tad came just in time."

"I left Muma's to get some supplies, when I heard Michelle give her battle cry. Milo saw me come running and let go of the girl. When I saw the dude on the ground holding his knee, I told Milo to lead me to their wheels and took the dude to the truck in a fireman's carry. Shady was down, yelling for his gun." Tad shrugged. "Was it worth fighting their dirty tactics to keep the business? Not when they had cash in hand to buy us out. We have what we owe Jaudon right here, but we're all concerned she'll freak out on us when we give it to her."

She checked outrage on the emotions list.

"Don't look at me that way," Shady said. "I have a sister getting her master's and a grandniece to put through school. Tad and I needed bread to invest in an honest business."

Tad said, "When Roy Jack returned in a wheelchair of his own, he acted civil. I showed him the numbers. He gave me the cash. Don't fret. The last laugh will be on Roy Jack. Rotgut is dying out—drugs are where the money is now."

"You're not—"

"Didn't I just tell you I don't plan to go to jail? No dealing, no moonshine, no more fencing."

Tad said, "He has his grow closet, locked from Michelle. Just enough to keep himself high."

"I share with a certain friend of mine." Shady laughed. "Not naming any names. You amaze me, Squirrel." He slapped the arms of his chair. "You can make a mint with fixer-uppers. Are you rehabbing houses to sell?"

"Some. I make more on the ones I rent to vacationers."

"How's that going?"

"It started slow. I was keyed up for weeks that my venture was a mistake. Then a retired couple rented the first do-over for an entire month. After that, a family used it for two weeks to commute to Disneyworld. When I posted it on college bulletin boards, a botany teacher at Bone Valley College called to reserve it summers to study plants, and for research classes."

"You made enough to buy another."

"Honestly? I'm dizzy from the long hours and with how well I'm doing. I signed with a vacation rental company. Once I learn their methods, I'll take over or hire family to do it."

Tad asked, "Are the rebuilds designed for wheelchairs?"

"ADA all the way."

"Did you buy something to crash in yourself?" Shady asked.

She explained that she made a habit of living in the newest purchase, revamping it around herself.

Tad gripped his chin. "Like where?"

"Don't worry, I'm not buying nineteenth century tenements. The current one's in Causeway. It's so fine, if I didn't need the money for the next purchase, I wouldn't rent it to vacationers."

Causeway was home to about eighteen hundred people in winter. Quiet, a bit run-down, the original sidewalks around City Hall were made entirely of oyster shells, but sand eventually covered them. It reminded her of Depot Landing, an odd town with lots of quirky history.

"Who are you teamed with?"

"You remember Vonnie? Her brother Vaughn."

Shady asked, "What's happening with that girl of yours?"

"Not much. She decided to stay at college this summer in order to graduate sooner."

"Don't give me that," said Tad. "She's left you high and dry."

She wrung her hands until she saw Tad watching them. "Vonnie's just an adolescent, basically."

"So are you," said Shady with a sad pursing of his lips.

"I had to find my way faster. You know what I'm saying. I told her from the start I want her to enjoy her college years."

"And now she's enjoying them too much?" Tad asked. "Will she come back?"

She tipped her head back, afraid to cry again.

"Will you wait for her?" asked Shady. "I'd hate to see you kiss off your youth."

"I'm trying not to delude myself with expectations. She says she'll be back if I stop stealing, and meantime, like I said, I'm pretty busy."

CHAPTER FIFTY

September 1984

On a blowy Saturday, Berry drove Jaudon to her final hearing aid fitting.

Jaudon said her whole body relaxed the minute she stopped straining to make out what people were saying. Which, she grumped, was the lone benefit of living with a clump in her bad ear. But as Berry hurried behind MJ's yellow bomber and Vaughn's pickup for a tour of their current building projects, Jaudon reverted to her kid self, falling out laughing, eager and attentive. Berry had feared she'd never see that part of her again, but her high-spirited gremlin hadn't disappeared.

They all wanted to reach the last of the work sites—a cottage on a canal in Causeway—before the weather worsened.

"The weatherman said it's a cat three, headed toward Cape Coral, too far south to totally mangle us."

"As Gran says, *It's comin' a cloud.*"

Near the Gulf, as they were, the air before a storm had a fresh scent, with a whiff of chlorine in it. Benedict had once explained that storms drew ozone, with its metallic scent, from the stratosphere. The smell told her they weren't in for a little bitty storm passing through.

MJ had been her baby goat self at every work site, leaping from one accomplishment to another, demonstrating, explaining, not quite showing off, but close. The Causeway house had real potential, MJ said, detailing their plans like the pro she'd become. Vaughn took Jaudon out in back of the two-story bungalow to talk about replacing the rotting dock.

"Careful of the loose planks," MJ warned.

Berry and MJ settled in lawn chairs on the open front porch.

Puddin flopped on a rag rug, thumping her bump of a tail and panting. Anika paced. A number of birds worked the undergrowth, feeding fast. Wind blew palm fronds upside down. Gran always said rain was coming when the leaves showed their bellies.

"How've you been, Dr. Berry?"

"Life is good." Berry lifted both arms in exaltation and enjoyed the moist wind that stirred her curls. "We're running ourselves ragged, no doubt, but that's who we are. I'm trying to enjoy this peaceful plateau while it lasts."

"You and Jaudon deserve to mellow out."

MJ didn't seem to expect an answer. Berry waited, thinking about the mystery cash and if that was MJ's way of helping them to mellow out. Jaudon never did succeed in getting MJ to open up.

"Do you believe in retribution?" asked MJ.

Her question brought to mind Gran's churlish former boyfriend and his horrible death by sinkhole. Of Gregory's suffering from what the news called the gay disease. Of her own faded, irrational, but lingering suspicion that she, as a tiny girl, made a mistake bad enough for her mother and father to leave her with Gran and drive away forever.

"Believe in it? No. Do I suspect I've witnessed it? Yes. It's human nature to want to attribute misfortunes to vengeful supernatural forces."

"Shady asked if I thought Vonnie will come back. I'm anguished she won't, that I'm paying for my crimes by losing her." MJ reached for a twig and snapped it in two, tossing it off the porch. "She has untold prospects out there. I'm small potatoes—why choose me?"

She ticked off MJ's attributes on her fingers. "Cute as a bug's ear. Smart as a tack. You work hard, use your money well. You're loyal and trustworthy and fun—"

"Okay, enough, stop." MJ put a hand up, face and neck flushed.

"Vonnie's not going to have an easy time matching you no matter where she is—you have to know that."

"Thanks." Her hands dove into her pockets, her shoulders hunched, and she stared at the floor. "Why is it nobody my age thinks twice about splitting and switching partners?"

"It's not just couples your age. That's the way it is for most gay people, and we learn that behavior from one another. It's what sneaking around and constant disapproval do to a relationship. Jaudon and I were isolated enough to skip that lesson. Or maybe we're old-fashioned and traditional to our cores."

MJ's wide eyes took on a shiny glaze. "Is Vonnie traditional?

Otherwise, why bother curing myself from stealing, from my emotional deep freeze? Losing her is a heck of a payback."

"Think about Jaudon. Why did my beloved Honest Abe almost lose her life's work? Why did she lose her hearing? Why did bullies go after her in school? She never stole, never harmed anyone."

"In other words, keeping your hands clean gets you pretty much nothing and nowhere."

"Oh, honey."

Puddin watched MJ's hands wriggling around each other. Anika's nose worked overtime, sniffing at the wind.

MJ rubbed behind Anika's ears. "I'm serious. That's how it is in the business world. You have no idea how badly the public is ripped off. Vaughn and I learned more than we wanted to know when we priced your roof. And the more extensive the company, the more they get away with. Seems to me, with Reagan getting a second term, there's less oversight. Overcharging for materials, careless flashing that dries the tar out fast, rushing, switching out inferior materials. You name it, too many businesses do it. You can be a thief without breaking and entering."

Berry didn't respond. She worked with three clients, two referred from the practice where she worked. Neither of the new clients frightened her as much as MJ. Not because she feared her, but because MJ intensely believed what she told Berry, while Berry saw it for the deluded, self-destructive thinking it sometimes was. How could a smart person be this in the dark about herself?

Anika was too large to be a lap dog but put her paws on MJ's knees. "This little dog knows there's a tempest coming in."

The soggy heat and increasing barometric pressure were oppressive. MJ stretched her shirt and blew through the neck.

Berry stretched to pat the dog too. "It's okay, girl. MJ and I will take care of you."

MJ sniggered. "Who'll take care of us? Vaughn tells me stories he's heard. Respectable-seeming businesspeople steal from the government, from the earth, from one another—"

"Stop manufacturing nightmares." Metal scraped against the house before rolling away. Gulls flew in circles over the water, cawing. "Is this rage of yours seeping past your new defenses?"

"Every time I blink, I see more unfairness and cruelty in the world. What dumbass abandons a puppy like Anika? Defrauds employees? Manufactures toxic products? Stints on inspecting food people eat?"

The picture window behind them rattled hard in a gust of wind.

Berry clutched her throat in fright. "I near jumped out of my skin." She didn't yet trust MJ and Vaughn's workmanship. They were tender sprouts.

"We'll be recaulking the windows. I'm surprised that one has stayed in one piece," MJ said, rising and jogging to the side of the house. Anika and Puddin went after her, barking. MJ shouted, "Come away from the water, Vaughn, Jaudon."

Rain soared down seconds later, making a terrible racket. Berry hastened inside. MJ backed in behind her and plonked buckets under instantaneous leaks. The dogs skidded in the door too.

"I suppose we should have seen to this roof."

"Your crew did our roof in Rainbow Gap before you took care of your own investment? We're not as vulnerable inland."

"That's your home. And Gran's."

"Isn't this your home?"

"I'm a vagabond."

"I don't know why you haven't caught pneumonia, sleeping in some of the drafty shambles you renovate."

By the time Vaughn and Jaudon blew in, they were slick as river otters. It took the two of them to shut the door against another terrific gust of wind.

"You sure this weather is just a lickspittle outer band," asked Jaudon, "and not a cat five that changed its mind to head our way?"

"Darn," MJ said. "I don't have much plywood. These windows won't hold."

Vaughn held a portable radio to his ear.

"Not cool," he said, tinkering with the knobs and antennae. He tuned in NOAA as they bunched around him. Between eruptions of static, they confirmed the storm had veered north and east and amped to a category three.

"But the weatherman called it a two this morning, not even headed our way."

Vaughn patted MJ on the back. "They called it a two, then a three, then a two. Be on standby, this may be a frog-strangler."

Jaudon covered her ears. "From the pressure in my ears, it's going to take out a lot of frogs. Poor little things."

"Oh, honey." Berry kissed her bad ear. "Your inner ears are oversensitive now. We've weathered a cat three and worse."

"If we're not close to a three right now, I'll swim across Rainbow

Lake, alligators or not," said Jaudon. "What about Larry and Gregory? Are they safe in that new beachfront high-rise? I swear the thing sways in a breeze."

Berry apologized for not updating her. "Dr. Riyanto extended his leave of absence. He and Gregory flew to New York yesterday for an HIV research program Allison tracked down." She crossed her fingers. "Rigo and Jimmy Neal are taking care of the doctors' seven cats."

"Seven?" said Vaughn. "Those are brave men."

Berry laughed. "Rigo's sending out embossed invitations to an afternoon tea party so we can meet the Royal Monsters."

Jaudon's new worry lines deepened. "Don't tell me Rigo and Jimmy Neal are moving in with the cats."

"They brought the cats home. Their apartment building is solid brick and lower to the ground. It's been through much worse."

Something large hit the roof, and they all looked up.

Vaughn said, "This bungalow isn't safe at all."

"Maybe," MJ admitted, "we should have done the roof first."

They were practically reconstructing it from scratch. Positioned on low-lying land between a narrow, dead-end canal and a heavily treed dirt road, it was no more than a tenth of a mile from the bay itself. Most of Causeway reminded Berry of the classic Florida she and Jaudon loved. The town had never taken a direct hit in her lifetime. She shivered, thinking, *What if?*

"We'd better get home to Gran," she said. "Come with us, Vaughn, MJ."

Vaughn said, "Thank you, but I better head home too, or my mother will worry herself sick. I'm relieved Vonnie's up north. You're welcome at our house, MJ." Out the window, nature's power wash was strengthening. "I have a good truck."

Jaudon stopped biting her lip. "I hope it floats. Our Buick too."

MJ's eyes were on the fierce outdoors, her hands folded together so tightly the knuckles paled. "I'm staying here."

Berry grasped her arm. "You'll get blown clear out west if the eye comes closer."

"I'll keep busy hammering these bits of plywood to the windows. Boss, take your lady home and keep her safe."

"We'll help with that, so you can come home with us or go to the Lowes, but we're not leaving you. You combine this rain with a surge, and you'll be afloat if a tree doesn't pin you beforehand."

"Don't be a sap, Boss. I can take care of myself. It's fine."

"No, it's not. My stores are stripped of the basics, and I told my crew to go home if it started to look like we'd be taking a direct hit."

Berry asked, "You have another place in the works, don't you? Where you can camp?"

"I always have another place in the works, but everything I need is right here. But I tell you what. You go, all of you. Vaughn, take our tools, just in case."

Vaughn and MJ gathered the tools into their carryall. As he opened the door, a light blue Volvo station wagon, speckled with leaves and sandy mud, windshield wipers going at full speed, slid to a stop in front of the house. The passenger door opened, and a figure in an orange-red belted trench coat, its skirt whipping around in the wind, backed out, pulling a canvas boat bag.

"Who the heck's that?" Jaudon asked.

"It's my dumb sister," said Vaughn. "Dad's going to kill her."

Jaudon opened the house door and shouted over the wind, "Do you have more luggage, Vonnie?"

Berry watched MJ's blush spread from her neck to her ears. None of the others knew about the impasse between the two girls. She didn't blame Vonnie for backing away. There was no getting around the fact that MJ's criminal activities put them both in danger.

A while ago, MJ told her the business was barely supporting her and Vaughn, and she needed more working capital to purchase properties and diversify her investments. Given the way she carried on about missing Vonnie, Berry prayed MJ would from now on shun the wild side, but where else would she get money? She wouldn't rule out the young squirrel working herself to the bone to increase her cash flow.

Vonnie ran to the porch and flung her bag at Jaudon, then returned to the car and put her arms around two overflowing grocery sacks. Vaughn hurried to take them from her while Vonnie shouted good-bye to the driver and bumped the car door shut with her hip. The Volvo splashed off before they closed the bungalow door.

Anika danced around Vonnie, who stripped off her coat to stonewashed jeans and a V-striped pullover. Her high cheekbones were brushed with color. Vonnie was casual elegant to beat the band despite walking into a half-dismantled house in a storm. She would draw eyes wherever she was, big city, small town, backwater bay.

She hugged Vonnie, held her just far enough away to examine her. "You lost too much weight this semester."

"She didn't have that much to lose," said Vaughn.

"Speak for yourself, brother string bean."

MJ spoke sternly. "I thought you were safe at school."

"I knew you'd be mad."

"I'm not mad, but riding into the storm is one crazy thing to do."

"Okay, it is, but Yolanda's mother is disabled and lives alone near here—nothing could stop her coming home. Traffic was headed in the opposite direction, so the drive took no time at all. I arrived safe and sound, all right?" Vonnie's chin was up, her voice challenging.

MJ removed her glasses, put them back on again for no apparent reason, and said, "You landed with no time to spare."

The young lovers faced each other with do-or-die expressions. Berry sensed everyone in the room holding their breath.

Vonnie's hands were folded as if in prayer. "What if you were swept away?"

"What if a tree blew over on you?" MJ retorted, retreating away from Vonnie.

"This is a fine how-do-you-do," Berry observed. "The two of you greeting each other by batting disasters back and forth like Ping-Pong balls."

Vonnie lowered her eyes. She held a hand open toward the groceries. "Before we left the city, we bought two buggies full at the Food Fair. I knew there'd be nothing left on store shelves here, and you're a novice at hurricanes. One of these bags is for Mom and Dad. The other is for us. If you were trapped, you weren't going down without me."

MJ seemed to drop her evolving tough-nut-to-crack business persona, plainly rattled by Vonnie's mixed signals.

Vaughn said, "I'm cool, Von. Mom and Dad have emergency stashes enough for nuclear war. Leave the supplies here. My truck will power me home. Unless you'll ride with me."

"I'm not budging. You better get going while the going's still good. Let Mom and Dad know I'm safe at college."

Vaughn grouched at her. "I'm not lying to them, Von."

"They'll have your head on a platter if you let on that you left me here."

Berry saw Vaughn's conflict. Another man might have insisted she go with him, or agree to lie, but in the power dynamic between these twins, Vonnie led.

MJ got a can of common nails and a claw hammer and followed Vaughn to the door.

Vaughn told her, "I'll check the other properties when the weather calms down. Take good care of my sister, okay, partner?"

"You bet. Be safe out there." MJ tilted upright a piece of plywood. "If you're staying, come grab the other end of this, and let's get our little shelter buttoned tight before I lose my investment."

Jaudon raised her eyebrows at Berry, who nodded and called Puddin. They'd head inland and race the storm home to Rainbow Gap.

CHAPTER FIFTY-ONE

After sealing the house, MJ filled the bathtubs and sinks with water.
Vonnie packed perishables and bagged ice cubes from the freezer into
MJ's prehistoric red metal chest cooler, then washed her hands at the
kitchen sink. The wind smacked wetly at the bungalow.

"I never thought to save water," she told Vonnie. "My family
always lived on a well or a spring."

"Here, you never know how many days, weeks—or if—you'll be
cut off."

"Did you lose weight on purpose, Von?"

Without answering, Vonnie tossed her two packets of D batteries.
"Where's your steel police flashlight?"

She puffed out her cheeks and expelled her breath with an
exasperated hiss. "It's under the house, I think. It went dead, and I
forgot it. But I do have plenty of batteries in the car once I put my
hands on the flashlight."

"Your car is as well-supplied as a warship. Remember naming it
the USS *MJ*? Listen. There's a lull in the wind. Find the flashlight, and
bring in your batteries. We'll need everything you have if this whirlwind
hits us hard. You did take Benedict's advice and buy insurance?"

She laughed at herself. She'd never thought of insuring those
cheap early purchases. She'd be out more than a trifle if she hadn't
insured this house. The water and nice neighborhood made it her best
location yet.

"I did." She went out into a landscape of grays, Anika following.
She emerged from the soaked ground under the bungalow with the
flashlight, dripping muck. Anika sniffed around and made outdoor
commodes of several spots.

Dark clouds rushed along like last-minute shoppers. Vonnie said they needed water to flush the toilets in case the city water was shut off, so MJ grabbed two buckets from the car and jogged to fill them from the canal. Water sloshed across docks and over the bank, swamping her steel-toed work shoes. Someone had left their State of Florida flag up; it flapped in the wind while its berserk halyard clanged the pole.

She lugged the full buckets to the porch. Anika stood guard over them. The rain increased and with it the wind, coming toward her insanely hard. Only its yellow and white colors made the car stand out.

She kept a canvas post office tote behind the back seat and tossed everything she thought they might need into it: first aid kit, the batteries, another flashlight. On top, she piled her extra sleeping bag and a couple of garage sale army blankets.

The clouds were now iron gray and swifter, overtaking one another in a mad dash toward chaos. The wind pushed her from behind. Vonnie opened the door, stepping almost behind it to give her room. Anika shook the rain off her coat and onto everything else in range. "Shoot." She dropped her supplies to push the door closed alongside Vonnie.

Clucking, Vonnie pretended to ring out MJ's soaked shirttail. "Don't you have dry clothes to change into?"

She hesitated, trying to read Vonnie's face. In place of her usual sexy friskiness, Vonnie avoided her eyes. "Well, sure. I live here."

Vonnie headed from the room.

"Vonnie. What is it? Did you come back to announce you're breaking it off with me?"

Halting, Vonnie said, "That makes no sense at all."

"You slept with someone else, didn't you?"

Vonnie's lips pursed, and she cast her eyes down. "Just a friend."

"You did it with—"

"Him. It just happened, my faulty science experiment, so I could see what it was about."

MJ bent as if from a physical blow. She blocked tears one minute and thought she'd vomit the next. She was ready to never touch Vonnie again, and to beg for reassurance that Vonnie chose her. One unnamed emotion canceled the next and the next until, dragon-like, she breathed out anger. She hissed. "What's the matter with you, coming here after what you did?"

Vaughn had left the portable radio and Prince was singing "When Doves Cry." She twisted the power knob off so hard it came loose in her hand.

"We were movie friends. He knows I'm gay. I decided I should know more about life, and from what you said, you wanted me to get these experiences over with. Which is exactly what I did."

Vonnie was right, which stung more deeply. Vonnie gave herself to—it made her stomach churn. She'd wanted Vonnie to get what she could from college, yes, but a man touching her… She shuddered and turned away.

"No wonder you cut me off. If I had a phone, I swear I'd call you a cab. I can't look at your face right now. Take your bag and get in the car—I'll drive you to your family. You can tell them good-bye from me."

Vonnie spoke to her back. "Is this your way of about-facing? You know damn well you've fought me off as much as you let me in. You have no idea how many nights I cry myself to sleep, not sure of you, but lonely for you and your touch. Not that you'll believe me, but it was one of the stupidest stunts I pulled at college. The experience baffled me. Why do women want men?"

"Stop. I don't want to know any more. Get your stuff."

"No. Listen to me. I didn't come all this way here to force either of us into the storm. I didn't do this to hurt you."

She did stop. Berry's list flashed in front of her. Hurt. She was hurt. And angry, a different kind of angry. She wanted to die on the spot even as she longed, ached to hold Vonnie to her. A cascade of open wounds and squelched anger made their way through her.

Turning back to Vonnie, she explained this. "I apologize. You just lit a fuse stretching all the way back to Depot Landing. Give me a minute, okay?"

She collapsed on a step stool to think. The retreat of adrenaline was giving her the shakes. Vonnie dropped a blanket on her shoulders, and she drew it around herself. A gust of wind forced the front door open. Vonnie leaped to push it closed and stood with her back against it.

She hurt. It was her anger, of course, fighting its way out by accusing Vonnie of betrayal. Fear, at the same time, that the evil child would succeed in driving love away.

After a few minutes she looked up and saw Vonnie watching her from the door. It occurred to her that the world hadn't ended. Vonnie was still with her. "Lock it. Lock us in."

Vonnie did and came to stand beside her, a tentative hand on MJ's shoulder.

"Just tell me you're not…You can't be…You didn't take any chances?"

"Not in a million years. I do not want to make the world more crowded. Him neither. He's gone, moved to Michigan for grad school. And I got sick."

"Not morning sickness?"

"My period is regular. The symptoms are fluish but won't go away. I get nauseous and dizzy. My head's foggy, and drowsiness takes me over."

"Mononucleosis?"

"I saw a nurse at the campus infirmary. She checked me over, did blood tests, said everything looked fine, and asked if I'd like to talk with someone."

"Like a therapist?"

Vonnie nodded. "What would I tell a therapist? First of all, Rigo once told me that most therapists would hear the word *gay* and diagnose it as the root of every problem. Instead, I asked myself what was going on with me. Had I cheated on you? I know we made no promises, and I'm supposed to be living the college life, but even my gay body told me I'd cheated on myself as much as on you. I might as well have experimented with heroin. Or strychnine."

"And that's why you didn't want to communicate with me?"

"Partly. I was also having long, involved nightmares of visiting you in prison for decades. In others, I went to pick you up on your release, but they'd found evidence of more break-ins and extended your sentence."

She spun to Vonnie, nearly overturning the stepladder. "You don't have to worry about that anymore. I stopped. So did Tad and Shady. No more housebreaking—if it's a choice between riches and you, there's no contest."

"I thought coming home, seeing you, would fix me up. Sure enough, the physical symptoms eased once we started south today. My mind is clearer."

MJ stopped herself from knotting her fingers together, but they were again contorted seconds later.

Vonnie said, "You took it harder than I anticipated. I regret telling you."

"It's better that you did. Secrets fester." But she'd always have a lurking fear that Vonnie might be tempted again and for good. Vonnie was attractive enough for men to chase her, no question.

"I don't know. We promised no secrets, but you're tense as a hunted animal. Better to have spared you the pain."

Through her internal conflagration, she managed to ask, "The hurricane was the impetus?"

Vonnie's smile was sad. "You may be the brightest person I know, but when it comes to taking care of yourself—"

She hated herself for lashing out. "You're doing a fine job of that, aren't you?"

Vonnie backed away. "MJ, MJ, I was curious, okay? It was selfish of me and made me ill."

"What if you get curious about doing it with another woman ten years from now?"

"You're not hearing me. I don't want to leave your side. Ever again."

She wanted to believe that, but white-hot whetted blades sliced her insides. She searched for the methods Berry had given her to keep herself together.

She closed her eyes and drew in a breath, made herself aware of her feet solidly on the floor, of Anika watching her, of her hands furling and unfurling at her sides. As the noise in her head quieted, she heard Berry's calm reasoning in her mind. *Name the emotion.*

Vonnie watched her, hair in disarray, the freckles on her face as conspicuous as they became while making love. It was wrong to expect Vonnie to know the ease with which bygone bruises became sore again. Selfishly, she asked, "Other girls?"

Vonnie's voice was scratchy, close to tears. "Are you asking if I slept with women at school? No. Never. Why are you acting like I assassinated Martin Luther King all over again?"

"Because, because—" Yes, she was distraught, and now she knew better than to believe her upset came only from Vonnie's disclosure. The new disturbance in her must be on Berry's list. When she found it, the words came out in a husky whisper. "Because I'm jealous."

The storm thumped and whistled around them. What right did she have to object? There were no canons, no holy commandments to hold gay couples together.

"It's here," whispered Vonnie.

"What do you mean?"

"When a hurricane hits land, it slows and stays."

Accelerating drops of water plunked into her wastebaskets and buckets. Rain dripped through a light fixture at the front of the house. The electricity quit. The roof creaked. By happy chance, Vaughn hadn't installed the upstairs deck or sliding glass doors.

"Forget cooking. The weather out there is crazed."

"You're enjoying it."

"Except for Anika—poor doggy, what have I done to you—yes. The storm is magnificently ferocious."

"Will it hold, do you think?" asked Vonnie.

"The house? Or us?"

❖

Without a word, they prepared the upstairs walk-in closet as a safe room. They gathered lanterns, blankets, and pillows.

"Shoot. Am I grateful to be on land."

Vonnie joined her at the upstairs window as a storm surge washed into the canal and the boats, overflowing the banks.

They went back for the canvas bin from the car. She told Vonnie to leave the candles lit—it could be hours before the storm drove them to the confined space upstairs, if it did at all. She didn't want to think about what she'd do if the roof went and water invaded.

The slicing of her heart continued. Had he been Vonnie's age? Black? Handsome? She didn't want to picture them together, but blurred images plagued her. Vonnie amused by his jokes, letting him touch her. Her touching—

She set about sealing the doorsills with duct tape. The best thing was to keep busy while her brain rehabbed her reality.

Behind her, Vonnie was at the kitchen counter slicing the store-roasted chicken she'd brought and making sandwiches with lettuce and MJ's favorite barbecue sauce. The next time she went by, she saw Vonnie had sealed enough sandwiches in plastic bags to feed them for days. That was Vonnie: practical, vital, enterprising, smart.

Sweat dripped from her face and fogged her glasses.

Vonnie hadn't set out to hurt her. She needed to accept Vonnie's rites of passage. It came down to whether she wanted an ideal Vonnie or the real woman.

Slowly, water crept under the front door and loosened the tape. The back door window splintered and spewed glass into the hall. She cursed herself for not thinking to cover it. Their feet were soon covered by chilly rising water.

"I should have made you go with Vaughn. I mean, seriously, I should have insisted. Come on, let's douse the candles. We need to get upstairs."

Vonnie made room in the cooler for the sandwiches. "I'm genuinely sorry. It was a moment—granted, a bad one. Don't let it ruin our life together."

She leashed Anika. "I believed whatever college life brought you, I could come to grips with."

"You're softer than you let on to yourself."

"You're my soft spot, but I'm not going to lie to you. How can I trust this love business ever again?"

"Oh God, honey squirrel, look what I went and did."

A great rending sound came from above.

"The roof. We're losing your roof."

This, then, was real, honest-to-goodness fear searing through her. The scare that loss of Vonnie's love put into her paled in comparison to the terror of losing Vonnie to this hurricane. If they lived through this, she'd find a way to be the softer person Vonnie saw, to stop living rigid with fear.

She kneeled to comfort a quaking Anika. "Florida's gone haywire on us. What in hell do we do now?"

She saw the horror in Vonnie's eyes. "Run for the car."

They coaxed Anika through the door into the pelting, oddly cold rain. In the yard a frond from a bending palm cut across MJ's face, and blood came away when she touched her cheek. Next door, sparks scattered from an electrical box. Vonnie stopped beside her with the food.

The car wasn't there.

If it had been any color but yellow, they might not have spotted it at all, ass over teakettle, half submerged in the canal.

Along the bay, longleaf pines swayed with the winds, their whistling branches bending low, almost to the point of snapping.

If a tree bent that low without breaking, couldn't she?

CHAPTER FIFTY-TWO

The squawk of a pesky monk parakeet woke Jaudon. Birdsong? A good sign.

She rolled over to find Berry smiling, eyes still closed.

"It's over." She gave Berry a full-body hug, scratched Kajen's head, and swung off the bed to let Puddin out. She turned the switch on the beside lamp. "Uh-oh."

"Still no power?"

Gran met them in the kitchen. "Once the rain stops, you need to get out your chainsaw," she told Jaudon. "There are enough fallen branches to build a bridge across the Gulf to Texas."

Berry lit the gas burner for the stove-top percolator. "Good old gas stove." They made bread and jam to avoid opening the refrigerator.

The sulfur smell of the match was familiar and calming. "I need to do the rounds of the stores. Make sure they're staffed and keeping the perishables refrigerated."

Berry said, "Before you do that, let's bring jam sandwiches and fill a thermos for MJ and Vonnie. Between the storm outside and the storm between them, they might need it."

"Jiminy, you took the words right out of my mouth. Seemed to me, MJ wasn't thrilled to see Vonnie."

Gran said, "They're so gone on each other—I thought they were as stuck together as you two."

"Speaking of which, you'll be okay here without the electric or phone?"

"Pet, our family didn't live near enough to the road to have electricity until I was twelve."

Berry laughed. "I know, I know. You're still getting used to indoor toilets."

The rain was a steady drizzle. Jaudon and Berry started off full of the elation of survivors. They swung by Mrs. Lanamore's restaurant and saw she was open for business. The worst of the storm hadn't come far enough inland to do more than break branches. No one was directing traffic, and there was little enough to direct, which allowed them to take their time. Except for buzz saws cutting downed trees, the post-disaster hush deepened.

Nevertheless, they'd gone through this before, and Jaudon was careful as she drove along roads partially covered with wet sand. The farther west they drove, the more blue tarps they saw on roofs, and the more concerned they became. Had this weather bomb, relatively minor in Rainbow Gap, made landfall in Causeway?

She said, "It looks like this little storm took a swipe at everything near the bay."

Jaudon drove around a wide new pothole. "Radio said it was only a three, but I would not have wanted to be near the winds at high tide and hit with a storm surge."

Leaves and fronds lay helter-skelter. A tree had crashed through a furniture showroom window. Displaced, disoriented locals stood in line at a makeshift aid station in the drizzle, a few pointing at the particulars of mauled homes and businesses. Through the open doors of a high school gymnasium, they saw dozens upon dozens of emergency shelter cots. The smell of dead fish leached into the car.

"People are shaking their heads at the damage, as if that'll undo the storm."

"I noticed that. To a person, they're saying, no, no, no."

Fast-moving water floated a dumpster into the street. She barely evaded it. They saw half a roof lying in a driveway and a gas station canopy flipped on its top. A clothes dryer tilted on a fire hydrant.

Portable power saws whined on blocked side streets. The smell of newly cut wood made a slight dent in the fishy air. A colossal oak tree with four trunks and broad, bulky branches lay across MJ's street. On its way it had crashed into two houses, a car, a garage, and a wooden fence. Debris-filled water covered the pavement. Homeless snakes and lifeless fish lay all over. A white lineman in a yellow hat and olive bib waders checked for downed wires. Clearly, they had no business sloshing into the mess. What wasn't clear, wasn't in sight, was MJ's bungalow.

Speechless, motionless, they stood on tiptoe and craned their necks. No bungalow and no yellow station wagon.

Berry tugged at her earring. "Did they escape in time? The car's not there."

Jaudon boosted herself onto a slick stone post. "The car is there. It blew or floated itself nose down into the canal."

"Oh, Jaudon, no. Can you tell if anyone's in it?"

Jaudon lowered herself and took Berry's hand. "There's a strip of dry land over there. We'll go in that way and find them."

They shouted for Vonnie and MJ as they made their way across the sodden ground, weaving between fallen branches, clumps of wet palm fronds, shredded lumber, an overturned dining room table, and an upright bed frame without a mattress.

Berry pointed at the ground. "That's MJ's cooler against that tree stump."

Jaudon knew now that her friend was not safe.

Boats from the docks lay in backyards or had smashed into each other at the splintered docks.

They called and called, their shoes and socks wet from the ground, their clothing soaked from the persistent spritzing rain. Berry stopped and grabbed Jaudon. "I hear barking. Where's it coming from?"

"How about if I raise the volume on my ear trumpets?" She pivoted in place. "That way," she yelped, pointing and breaking into a run.

She'd jeered at the odd round house on stilts across the street from the bungalow. Sissy snowbirds, she'd called the owners. The structure resembled a puny water tower, but by gosh, with the shape and that pitched roof, the house pretty much deflected the wind. She bet the builder used top-notch lumber, metal strapping, and tough windows. The pilings were reinforced concrete.

MJ, Vonnie, and Anika peered from a porthole-style window on the upper level.

"Are we ever glad to see you two," Vonnie called.

MJ said, "I presume we can emerge?"

"Come down—we'll take you on home."

MJ did something Jaudon never saw her do before. She stretched over a bedraggled Anika and nuzzled Vonnie's neck. At once, Vonnie moved to give her an ample kiss.

"Aww," said Berry.

Jaudon whispered, "We can reassure Gran now."

"Nothing better than unruly weather to make it clear what's important."

Anika pulled MJ out the door. MJ's black outfit was brown with dried mud. She and Vonnie ran behind brush and trees to do what Anika did in the open.

When they returned, Jaudon and Vonnie walked toward the spillover from the canal, lifting planters and plastic yard art upright. Berry stood by as MJ cast her eyes over her demolished home, her sunken car.

"Vonnie called it right," said MJ. "It's a yellow submarine."

The only part left standing was the porch, of all things. MJ's blue good luck chair, the one she'd kept from her first project up at Rooster Lake, was intact. She disentangled it from where it had fallen, on its back, legs woven with the porch rails.

MJ smelled almost as foul as the rest of Causeway. Two tears slid past her fogged glasses, and she said, under her breath, "For all I have stolen."

"That's over now, isn't it?" asked Berry.

MJ nodded brusquely. Jaudon and Vonnie came back, and the four wandered through standing water to the lower deck of the neighbor's house.

"How did you ever get Anika over here in one piece?" Berry asked.

"The wind rose and rose until it sounded like a runaway freight train. When the roof flipped, I was—ah—familiar with this mostly uninhabited round house."

Vonnie's glare could have reduced anyone to a pile of cinders.

"We put Anika in that tarp." MJ pointed to a canvas cover. "We used the grommets to rope it closed and each held an end."

MJ's voice was weary, but not as devastated as Berry expected.

Vonnie added, "We also clipped one leash to her harness, the other to her collar for good measure. Both leashes were wrapped around our wrists. Tender trusting doggy didn't fight us at all. We were afraid she'd get swept out to sea if we walked her over or if either of us tried to carry her this far."

"All three of you were in danger of drowning," Jaudon said.

Vonnie said, "No kidding. I was petrified the whole time."

Jaudon asked, "But how did you get in?"

Berry saw Vonnie's lips twitch down again. She wished she could remove Jaudon's foot from her mouth.

"The neighbor said he built his home to withstand a hurricane." She looked straight at Vonnie. "Next time I save our lives, you'd better check my methods beforehand, in case they don't meet your standards."

Jaudon adjusted her hearing aid to try to make sense of their exchange.

Vonnie stepped hip to hip with MJ, pressing their clasped hands to her heart. "Nothing but survival occupied my mind last night—by any possible means. Thank you for knowing where to shelter."

Pummeled and exhausted, MJ nodded at Vonnie, straightened her back, and raised a corner of her lips almost into a smile. "I can't wait to tell Vaughn we're rebuilding—a round house on pier blocks."

"We're going to live in it," announced Vonnie.

"This area is starting to remind me of Depot Landing. The storm brought on the wild and woolies. All the power of nature rushed us."

Vonnie said, "We waded through water to our knees, against the wind, with Anika high between us. We pushed through an endless sideways waterfall. Who knows what things bumped against us? We heard wind and water tearing at the bungalow behind us."

MJ stretched, dislodging caked mud from her jacket. Vonnie walked around her in an affectionate, proprietorial inspection, brushing off more mud.

"The round house is bone dry, as far as I can tell. We fell asleep around dawn, the three of us bundled together and hanging on tight." MJ's face softened. "I'm sorry I put you through this, Von."

"I'm glad I came instead of worrying myself sick." Vonnie's hands were on her hips now, scolding.

MJ took off with a bound, sprinted to a half-submerged privet bush, and delicately freed a soppy lump from its branches.

"It's Hop." Vonnie cheered, arms in the air. "Hop's her childhood bunny rabbit."

MJ loped back, grinning. "I thought Hop washed away. I put him in my jacket pocket, and he wasn't there when we got inside. All night I had visions of him crashing into things and dropping to the bottom of the bay."

"You've lost too much," Berry said. Hop was dressed in a denim romper with the arms and legs folded to fit.

Jaudon said, "Look at you all happy. I'd be cussing and kicking things about now."

"Choosing my battles, Boss, I'm just choosing my battles. I remember wishing the next storm would lash at mansions, not our waterside shack. That house, it doesn't matter. My other belongings don't matter either. It's Vonnie that matters. And you and Jaudon, Cullie and Allison, Vonnie's family, Anika. Haven't you told me that, over and over, Berry?" Her eyes were fixed on the collapsed bungalow site. "It's gone, no two ways about it." She scrunched her chin. "We'll build a better one."

At that moment, Berry saw in MJ's eyes the last pieces fall into place. She'd failed to steal from strangers what she needed, and she could build a thousand houses without having a home of her own. A home wasn't made of plumbing parts, window sashes, but of the attachments that had grown to enclose her when she lacked any shelter at all.

Once the waterlogged, amorous, somewhat smelly couple and dog were in their back seat, Jaudon started the car. "What's next?"

Without hesitation, Vonnie, a few leaves and a twig embedded in her hair, declared, "After I come home for good, I'm never letting this woman get away again."

Berry believed her.

MJ declared, "Vaughn and I are going to learn how to build a round house from the ground up. We can do it weekends. Vaughn, if he's willing, me, and, weekends after graduation, Vonnie. She's yearning to learn construction to prepare for running HUD someday. We'll put our round house on stilts, give it impact-resistant windows." She smiled. "There's a locomotive maintenance shed back in Depot Landing where the trains are turned. It's called the roundhouse."

"Oh, honey, you miss living there," said Berry.

MJ laid a fist against her chest. "I carry it here. I loved those trains and the wide river, the power, the strength, the forward movement. Didn't appreciate most of the locals or Confederate flags on porches."

"Out west?" Jaudon slowed the car through a stretch of water pooled on the street. "You had to submit to that hatefulness at the other end of the country?"

"There's no escaping prejudice. Vonnie lives it full-time."

"From my own Batson family. I'm sorrier than heck. When we were little, I had fistfights with my boy cousins over the way they treated classmates who didn't look like us. Talked myself blue in the face trying to make them see reason. They didn't want reason."

Vonnie kindly broke the somber mood. "That must be a sight, a blue Jaudon," she teased. "MJ goes pink."

MJ pushed her glasses higher on her nose. "We'll paint the round house tan and pink, like you and me."

"That sounds hideous," Vonnie said. "You'd better let me be your design consultant."

"Sorry, your brother has that position. I'll talk to this owner about disaster-proofing. We can add it to our portfolio of services."

"Lowe and Beaudry, Affordable Housing Builders," suggested Vonnie. "Or Beaudry and Lowe."

MJ quietly and definitively said, "VONCO."

Vonnie's eyes opened wider. "I would prize it, but—"

"No buts."

"I'm honored, and it's a good business name. I told MJ last night that the Plant City Housing Authority accepted me as an intern. We decided I'll say yes. It's a brand-new organization. I'll be helping them create their donor relations job, which I plan to apply for. When I have to be up north on campus, I'll take the bus."

"Maybe I can find a way to buy a company car you can use. I'll bring a rental trailer in here until the house has walls and a roof. It'll be VONCO's inaugural project."

Berry looked from one to the other.

Vonnie told her, "MJ gave me her word that she'll color inside the lines from now on."

"I thought Vonnie ditched me."

"I almost did, you hardheaded fool. I only came back for that pink flamingo wallpaper you promised to put in our bathroom." Vonnie kissed MJ on the cheek. MJ put an arm around her.

Berry swiveled to watch their captivation with each other. Anika's head lay on MJ's thigh. "You know what Gran's favorite saying is? *Life is fragile, handle with care.* The same advice goes for what you have."

"We'll be together the rest of our lives now."

Vonnie bounced on the seat. "Just like you two."

MJ lifted that corner of her mouth again and revealed emerging laugh lines around her eyes.

A dark-skinned flagger in a yellow hat held a red stop sign. They were stuck while a white man operated a derrick to remove a snapped utility pole.

As they waited, the sun appeared, and the dripping palm fronds sparkled, shadows returning to frame the jagged angles of residences and stores. The shining peace of everyday life restored, Berry stretched her arms to embrace it. Jaudon's hand curled around the back of her neck. The back seat lovers, who might never have known light again, applauded.

"I made some promises too," Vonnie said, squirming closer to MJ.

Berry saw her thoughts reflected in Jaudon's pensive face. The storm, their survival, helped resolve a number of concerns for this foundling squirrel and her heartthrob. They were holding on to each other for dear life. She hoped they always kept hold; she really did.

The flagger rotated his sign from stop to slow. Jaudon withdrew her hand from Berry to steer with care through the newly opened lane.

About the Author

Lee Lynch (http://www.leelynchwriter.com) wrote the classic novels *The Swashbuckler* and *Toothpick House*. Her most recent award-winning books are *Rainbow Gap* and *An American Queer: The Amazon Trail*. She is the namesake and first recipient of the Lee Lynch Classic Award from the Golden Crown Literary Society, the recipient of the James Duggins Mid-Career Prize, the Alice B Reader Award, and an inductee to the Saints and Sinners Hall of Fame.

Lee wanted to be a lesbian writer since she read *The Well of Loneliness* and the mid-century pulp novels at age fifteen. She supported herself managing grocery stores, providing vocational counseling, driving a cab, as a Girl Scout professional, etc. Now she writes full time and shares her life on the Pacific Northwest coast with her beloved wife, Lainie Lynch, King the cat, and Betty the dog.

Books Available From Bold Strokes Books

A Fae Tale by Genevieve McCluer. Dovana comes to terms with her changing feelings for her lifelong best friend and fae, Roze. (978-1-63555-918-7)

Accidental Desperados by Lee Lynch. Life is clobbering Berry, Jaudon, and their long romance. The arrival of directionless baby dyke MJ doesn't help. Can they find their passion again—and keep it? (978-1-63555-482-3)

Always Believe by Aimée. Greyson Waldsen is pursuing ordination as an Anglican priest. Angela Arlingham doesn't believe in God. Do they follow their vocation or their hearts? (978-1-63555-912-5)

Courage by Jesse J. Thoma. No matter how often Natasha Parsons and Tommy Finch clash on the job, an undeniable attraction simmers just beneath the surface. Can they find the courage to change so love has room to grow? (978-1-63555-802-9)

I Am Chris by R Kent. There's one saving grace to losing everything and moving away. Nobody knows her as Chrissy Taylor. Now Chris can live who he truly is. (978-1-63555-904-0)

The Princess and the Odium by Sam Ledel. Jastyn and Princess Aurelia return to Venostes and join their families in a battle against the dark force to take back their homeland for a chance at a better tomorrow. (978-1-63555-894-4)

The Queen Has a Cold by Jane Kolven. What happens when the heir to the throne isn't a prince or a princess? (978-1-63555-878-4)

The Secret Poet by Georgia Beers. Agreeing to help her brother woo Zoe Blake seemed like a good idea to Morgan Thompson at first…until she realizes she's actually wooing Zoe for herself… (978-1-63555-858-6)

You Again by Aurora Rey. For high school sweethearts Kate Cormier and Sutton Guidry, the second chance might be the only one that matters. (978-1-63555-791-6)

Fleur d'Lies by MJ Williamz. For rookie cop DJ Sander, being true to what you believe is the only way to live…and one way to die. (978-1-63555-854-8)

Love's Falling Star by B.D. Grayson. For country music megastar Lochlan Paige, can love conquer her fear of losing the one thing she's worked so hard to protect? (978-1-63555-873-9)

Love's Truth by C.A. Popovich. Can Lynette and Barb make love work when unhealed wounds of betrayed trust and a secret could change everything? (978-1-63555-755-8)

Next Exit Home by Dena Blake. Home may be where the heart is, but for Harper Sims and Addison Foster, is the journey back worth the pain? (978-1-63555-727-5)

Not Broken by Lyn Hemphill. Falling in love is hard enough—even more so for Rose, who's carrying her ex's baby. (978-1-63555-869-2)

The Noble and the Nightingale by Barbara Ann Wright. Two women on opposite sides of empires at war risk all for a chance at love. (978-1-63555-812-8)

What a Tangled Web by Melissa Brayden. Clementine Monroe has the chance to buy the café she's managed for years, but Madison LeGrange swoops in and buys it first. Now Clementine is forced to work for the enemy and ignore her former crush. (978-1-63555-749-7)

A Far Better Thing by JD Wilburn. When needs of her family and wants of her heart clash, Cass Halliburton is faced with the ultimate sacrifice. (978-1-63555-834-0)

Body Language by Renee Roman. When Mika offers to provide Jen erotic tutoring, will sex drive them into a deeper relationship or tear them apart? (978-1-63555-800-5)

Carrie and Hope by Joy Argento. For Carrie and Hope, loss brings them together but secrets and fear may tear them apart. (978-1-63555-827-2)

Detour to Love by Amanda Radley. Celia Scott and Lily Andersen are seatmates on a flight to Tokyo and by turns annoy and fascinate each other. But they're about to realize there's more than one path to love. (978-1-63555-958-3)

Ice Queen by Gun Brooke. School counselor Aislin Kennedy wants to help standoffish CEO Susanna Durr and her troubled teenage daughter become closer—even if it means risking her own heart in the process. (978-1-63555-721-3)

Masquerade by Anne Shade. In 1925 Harlem, New York, a notorious gangster sets her sights on seducing Celine, and new lovers Dinah and Celine are forced to risk their hearts, and lives, for love. (978-1-63555-831-9)

Royal Family by Jenny Frame. Loss has defined both Clay's and Katya's lives, but guarding their hearts may prove to be the biggest heartbreak of all. (978-1-63555-745-9)

Share the Moon by Toni Logan. Three best friends, an inherited vineyard, and a resident ghost come together for fun, romance, and a touch of magic. (978-1-63555-844-9)

Spirit of the Law by Carsen Taite. Attorney Owen Lassiter will do almost anything to put a murderer behind bars, but can she get past her reluctance to rely on unconventional help from the alluring Summer Byrne and keep from falling in love in the process? (978-1-63555-766-4)

The Devil Incarnate by Ali Vali. Cain Casey has so much to live for, but enemies who lurk in the shadows threaten to unravel it all. (978-1-63555-534-9)

CPSIA information can be obtained
at www.ICGtesting.com
Printed in the USA
BVHW030924170321
602757BV00005B/14

9 781635 554823